Wade of Aquitaine

Blueberry Lane Books
New York

Copyright © 2008 Ben Parris
All rights reserved.
ISBN: 1-4196-9139-2
ISBN-13: 978-1419691393
Library of Congress Control Number: 2008902420

BEN PARRIS

WADE OF AQUITAINE

BLUEBERRY LANE BOOKS
NEW YORK
2008

Wade of Aquitaine

CONTENTS

For My Family
Who Taught Me The Value Of Creativity
And For Rozzie Fliegelman
First President Of My Fan Club

PART I
Dark Age Traveler

"Space and time are not conditions in which we live; they are simply modes in which we think."

—Albert Einstein

CHAPTER 1
The Synesthete

WADE LINWOOD WAS a synesthete, his mind's eye larger than any. With senses keener than all the animals that ever lived, shapes had colors for him, words took physical form, and feelings had greater consequences than anyone could imagine. Yet when he heard the call that crossed the centuries, would he recognize it? Would he want to know?

~ *W* ~

WADE drove under the Long Island Railroad overpass and joined Woodbury Road at just over the speed limit of forty miles per hour as he did every day on his way to work. His throat seized up when he saw the baby carriage enter the intersection against the light, only three car lengths away. The woman pushing it chatted on a cell phone, enjoying a good laugh, fall breezes tossing her hair. She didn't see him.

As an automobile insurance salesman, Wade was keenly aware of how much room he needed to stop. With his heart punching out of his chest, he knew he might not make it. The woman in front of him, and the car behind him, had to be warned. He lifted his left hand to hit the horn as his foot moved to the brake. When his hand made contact, pain like a knife edge started from his wrist and carved along his arm straight to his shoulder. Wade drew on forgotten lung capacity like a man trying primal scream therapy as a subway train comes roaring into the station. The pain enveloped him, drawing a shade across his perception.

He had dim impressions of slamming a pedal and cranking the wheel hard. It looked as if he were now driving toward the stores on his right, and skipping past them too. Chul Huk's Take Out went by, Rachel's Real Estate, and the Laundromat with no name, before his eyes refused to track. The last thing that registered was a viscous fountain of dark red muck. Linked with that image, he smelled burned motor oil as vividly as if he were drinking it. Wheels locked, the car rocked like an old Chevy with a tricked out suspension. Though he never felt the thump, he thought he must have crashed and maybe even killed someone.

His eyelids trembled as they rose and his vision cleared. The woman with the auburn hair stood dead in the middle of his lane with only her top-half visible until a low curtain of smoke passed. Then he saw her gripping her baby tight. With her cell phone forgotten on the ground, she stared at Wade as though he were a monster.

Skid marks with the shimmer of misty heat all around suggested Wade's car had turned full circle. The street was a still life of witnesses waiting to see if the danger had passed, if the monster were done. Forcing his straining right foot to relax on the brake, Wade turned the car around again, and headed straight for Dr. Nesky's office.

~ W ~

"YOU look like hell," said Dr. Nesky. His penetrating gaze claimed he already had a good idea what brought his patient running. Wade could barely hear the Russian accent anymore.

"It's just a pain," said Wade, rubbing his left wrist.

If a look could yank the DNA from your bones, Dr. Nesky had it, and did not hesitate to use it.

"I got in a little trouble this morning," Wade allowed. There was no use holding anything back from an acupuncture specialist who saw pain every day. "This thing almost got someone killed."

Dr. Nesky looked surprised, alarmed and bit intrigued all at once. "I'll fit you in and you'll tell me about it when I finish with my patient," he said. "Make yourself at home." He turned to his receptionist with a quirky smile. "Please give Mr. Linwood anything he requires. Thank you."

"Oh, I'll be fine," said Wade, on his way to the magazine rack, looking for something that wasn't too battered.

Dr. Nesky paused before going through the door. He said, "You should never have neglected your carpal tunnel syndrome."

Wade looked away like a dog that peed on the rug. He had learned from his neurologist that the median nerve travels from the forearm into your hand through a tunnel in your wrist. Wrist bones form the bottom and sides of this tunnel. Wade's problem first came on when he applauded at a conference, possibly jarring the bones together, pinching the nerve. While he could skip the acupuncture for his carpel tunnel syndrome, the alternative was surgery. That meant cutting the ligament roof of the carpel tunnel in hopes of relieving pressure on the nerve. For a procedure that might not work, he risked bleeding, infection and nerve injury, as well as a slow recovery that would keep him off the job.

Wade trusted Dr. Nesky, and had friends who told him acupuncture worked on them. Why not go for the least invasive option first? His apprehension and delay in coming made no sense, unless of course he factored in the far more unusual condition he walked around with, and buried in even deeper denial.

When he broke discipline, otherworldly—impossible—perceptions intruded on him. A glance at the office's African Violets tricked his salivary glands into watering over a taste of buttered toast. *No*, he told himself, *you thought you tasted something, but you didn't. People see a bottle cap on the ground and think it's a coin, but it isn't. Normal, normal, like everyone else.*

Wade tried to make his life as ordinary and routine as possible amidst all the strangeness. Like any other patient, he sifted through the table's old magazines one by one without seeing them. The seventh jumped out at him, headlined, "Modern Acupuncture: Twenty-First Century Meets Ancient Marvels." The article called it "the pre-scientific product of ancient China employing concepts with an unknown basis with the aim of restoring health." At the same time, the article went on to say that, "neuroimaging research indicates that known acupuncture points, when stimulated by needles, have distinct effects on cerebral activity in specific areas that are not otherwise predictable anatomically." Wade found the information both comforting and disturbing.

Dr. Nesky pronounced it "needuhl." Wade shuddered, his discipline shattered again so soon. The combined consonants and vowels unfolded as a tangy grapefruit in his mouth while the air was thick with charcoal residue tinted forest green.

He didn't think in terms of the average patient's fears or concerns; didn't wonder if the sharp instruments came fresh out of a sterilized package; didn't wonder if he would jump like a startled rabbit or cry like a baby; didn't wonder if the doctor knew his craft, or if the whole concept of a needle cure made any sense in the modern world. No, he pondered how the word made him feel, and why it was the strangest word he ever experienced. His condition, the flare and flash of his senses, made his awe and unease inseparable from the color and flavor of the word. And it was not the apprehension of a treatment that was novel to him; somehow he sensed his trouble stemmed from something about to happen that no one had ever encountered. Or at least, no one normal.

The clinic door knocked open from the bump of a wheelchair. A rather severe looking couple that may have been a father and mother parked a young helpless woman in the doorway. As they said their lengthy goodbyes to the doctor, Wade felt a pang of regret for the girl. She suffered nearly complete paralysis from the neck down, and even her neck appeared to lack some of its muscles as her head lolled to the side, barely controlled. She communicated by motions of her index finger when she was not using it to control the motorized chair. She wore a vague smile like a mask. Only her eyes were fully alive, a quick, dancing intelligence hiding inside her fixed form. She commanded, too, a moaning imitation of laughter to show that she followed the conversation. Every once in a while, her father wiped drool from the lower tilted corner of her mouth, and clucked as if she should know better.

As the doctor pulled away and turned his back, her eyes came to rest on Wade, and he witnessed her expression change from one of sedated amusement to a soft, fine blue dust on a cold, smooth surface. If he had to describe the sensation to a non-synesthete, he would call it powder on ice.

To surface perceptions, she presented a look of surprise with raised brows, and a burgeoning smile almost of recognition.

And then the look faded, replaced with her previous vague dreaminess with eyes that tracked everything. *Like always*, came a thought behind his mind, a voice that sounded like wisdom itself.

But Wade felt certain that they had never met. His extraordinary memory boosted by the synesthesia would not allow him to forget her even if they met before she became paralyzed, at a time when she would have looked very different. What was it she recognized in him? Could it be the kinship of one handicapped person to another? Not likely because he never thought of himself as handicapped. Or was synesthesia what they had in common, just one of her conditions, and she was somehow able to recognize it in him?

It almost pleased him to have carpel tunnel syndrome in that it made him somewhat common. One out of ten people suffered from it. The estimates of how many synesthetes existed in the world varied from one out of every twenty five thousand to one out of every hundred thousand. Each one usually had multiple traits coupled with the condition, sometimes including an impairment of cortical motor skills like the wheelchair girl suffered. Still, that combination was rare.

As her father pressed the down arrow for the elevator, he shifted his attention to Wade in a dark and potent motion that belied his size. Obviously, the father had seen the look that passed between his daughter and the stranger. It seemed as though she were drugged giddy, and temporarily broke free of the narcotic when she saw Wade.

When he heard a bell and saw number three light up, her father commanded, "Kreindel, go to the elevator."

When she headed off in a trajectory that would bump her against the door, he barked, "Kreindel, what's the matter with you? Get your damn chair moving right."

Wade felt his anger rise at the father's mistreatment of his daughter.

She corrected her course toward the elevator, rolling into the empty space with a level dose of serenity.

The man said to his wife, "Helen, go ahead with Kreindel. I'll catch up with you." When he spoke to his wife, it was neither kind nor unkind, but matter of fact.

When the elevator doors closed, he turned on Wade. As badly as he behaved with his family, Wade saw a flash of something worse in him, something akin to the way an iguana conveys danger. "Alright, what the hell did you do?"

Wade squinted. "What are you talking about?"

"How did you do that—make my daughter's face change? What kind of poisoned, voodoo magic is in you?"

Far be it for Wade to find other people unusual, but this one struck him so in every way from his strange choice of words to his close, fetid demand for answers. "I-I don't know. We just looked at each other."

"She doesn't have the muscle control to do that. Her face never changes."

"Well maybe it does now."

With a snarl of displeasure, the father turned again and charged down the steps, presumably to question the girl.

As Wade started after the man, the doctor reappeared and motioned for Wade to come inside. Wade frowned over his shoulder and decided that angry words with her father might make the girl's situation worse. He put her out of mind, but he couldn't forget.

~ W ~

Doctor Nesky's every movement revealed an eagerness to heal, calm, and impart his wisdom. Wade, at an inch over six feet, had to look up to meet the thin man's brown eyes. The two of them had a longstanding ritual to shake hands in greeting as though congratulating each other on unspoken victories. Since Wade's job involved sales, he appreciated a solid, dry handshake. For Nesky's part, he appeared to be continually assessing what Wade was made of.

Wade allowed the doctor to lead him to a sparse room holding a padded table-bed with a fresh roll of paper snaking down the middle. At a gesture, Wade sat. Dr. Nesky's level gaze never left Wade's eyes, and yet Wade felt as if he were being separated into his component parts, and reassembled like a monkey puzzle. Wade shifted around and heard the paper crinkle beneath him. At this point the doctor didn't even have to utter "needuhl" for Wade to feel charcoal, forest, tang, wonder, and apprehension.

Wade cleared his throat, and attempted to reset his mental template to the mundane and the practical. "Are you happy with your auto insurance, Dr. Nesky?"

"Yes, yes, you did a very good job in getting me the right coverage, although it's not something I think about every day." Nesky flashed the kind of smile that begged to be shared, and Wade promptly returned it. The doctor had actually said "sink" instead of "think," which Wade attributed more to a slight lisp than his accent. Nesky looked at Wade's wrist and frowned with concern. "Does it affect your sleep?"

"Is the pain that strong, you mean? Yes. It hurts whenever I move, and that wakes me up." He wanted to add that the pain-induced smell of burned motor oil emanating from a churning fountain wakes him up too, but as usual he kept the crazy-sounding aspects to himself. He acquired the self-editing habit as a child on the day he told his teacher that the smell of carrots scared him because it was shaped like a wire cutter. In the cafeteria, he could see one floating out in front of him. She whisked him to the nearest psychiatric help. The school psychologist, who had no knowledge of his rare disorder, and little knowledge of anything else, told him to stop lying or he would be locked in a mental hospital for the rest of his life. No one agreed with him that smells had shapes, let alone dangerous ones. Most of the time he enjoyed his visions, so he hid the knowledge like an air bubble cupped in a bathtub, always trying to rise to the surface, but easily secreted away.

"What kind of music do you like?" asked Nesky. "I'll put it on for you."

"Beethoven's Ninth, please."

"The Ninth, really? You know he was completely deaf by the time he composed that one?"

"Yes, I know. It soothes me." What Wade wanted to explain was that he wondered if Beethoven might have seen, touched and tasted each note from vibrations alone. Perhaps, like Wade, the First Movement in D minor felt to Beethoven like beams of sunlight reflecting upwards off a calm ocean. Or perhaps the composer, if he were a synesthete, felt something else entirely. Synesthesia did not produce the same experience from one person to another, except to some extent between relatives with the same condition.

"You're in luck, my friend, I have that one. Lie down, if you please."

Nesky set the music going as Wade shifted to his own cacophony of crinkles.

Nesky placed a hand on Wade's shoulder and no doubt felt the trembling. "There is no need to be nervous, Wade. I assure you the needuhlss I use are not your ordinary sewing needuhlss."

Wade laughed. "I'm sure they're not."

"You will not feel the sensations you would expect."

"I never do." Wade got a glimpse of the special needles before he closed his eyes. They were uniformly narrow, so thin they were hard to see but for their colored tags at the ends. "Filiform," the article had called them. While he couldn't tell where the first one went in, he knew precisely when. The sensation was purple and fuzzy like a king's robe, and he knew that acupuncture would always be that shade and texture to him. The association of his crossed senses shaped his recall.

Then something astonishing happened, something that never happened before in his life: The color changed. Now it was the color of honey.

Wade gasped. "What are you doing?"

"I'm working the needuhl in deeper. It hurts?"

"No. No, in fact the pain is weaker than before."

"How about now?" Wade felt purple again. A different spot or had he pulled back? Wade watched him. Deeper again, the honey color returned, and at last, rust. When it turned rust, the pain shut off along with all the unpleasant sensations that belonged to it. Wade, who worked with computers all day, sensed that the needle had reached a synesthetic port in his brain that had never before been opened. Every muscle relaxed at once.

Between the sights, sounds, and feelings of Beethoven's Ninth, the word association, and now the unexpected layered colors, Wade moaned as blood retreated from his head, and he grayed out.

When he woke up, the first thing he noticed were the needles going into the trash, the doctor slamming them in there as though frustrated. "What are you doing?" asked Wade.

"You passed out. That never happened before. I stopped the treatment."

"No, no, no, absolutely not. That's typical for me."

"Typical?" asked the doctor.

"Yes, the sudden relief."

"I don't want to do anything dangerous."

"I get very...emotional about sensations."

"I would say so."

"I need that treatment, Dr. Nesky. You shut off the pain, and now it's returning." *Along with the sluggish fountain and the motor oil.*

"It would. I wasn't finished."

"Then continue. Please. I'm feeling fine."

"Okay, but I will stop if you pass out again. And then we will find a different sort of treatment."

"It's a deal. I won't pass out again now that I'm used to it. You'll see."

"I hope so."

Wade lay back again and forced himself to relax. He kept his eyes open this time and glanced over at the doctor opening a new package of needles. He kept watching as Nesky approached. One needle went into his left wrist yielding purple, honey and rust. A second one went where his ankle met his right foot, somewhere between his fibula and heel. At the third layer of depth, rust, the constant pain in his wrists shut off again, and Wade breathed a sigh of relief.

"Good," said Nesky. "You're awake, but you must lie still for a while."

Wade wanted to let go of his confusion. He had so many questions he couldn't ask, and only one that he could. "I'm good now, Dr. Nesky, but how do you keep the pain from coming back to me once the needles are out?"

"I will leave you to rest, and I will return in twenty minutes. Then I will push the needuhlss in further. The relief will linger after that. Over the next few weeks, a few more treatments, and…we'll see. Eventually, it has a lasting effect. So far you are responding to the acupuncture as well as anyone ever has. I think we will see a good result."

Then Wade was alone with Beethoven and the sunbeams soaring high above the ocean, and a steady rust, rust, rust from needles pushed deep. He felt pleasant and content. He lay so still for what appeared to be so long that he shifted just to see if he was capable of movement. And while he waited for the doctor's return, another sensation crept in.

The feeling was as certain as it was indefinable. Portentousness came in undulating, queasy waves. It came as a constant, usurping the calm. Within the space of his twenty minutes, he lived a lifetime of bewilderment. He tried to concentrate, to lift the veil. His efforts yielded nothing but complete, undeniable foreshadowing. He felt this way on rare occasions, when something unusual was about to happen. But the feeling never came anywhere near this strong. And that in itself was wrong; when feelings arose from his condition they didn't have changing strengths. Each always had a one-to-one correspondence with a set of sensations. This portentous feeling was unique, like colors coming in layers when there should have been a single color for a given sensation: His second discovery of the day. This time, in fleeting strikes to his delicate subconscious, he sensed something far worse on its way, as unsettling as it was inevitable.

Wade was unaware of Nesky entering the room until

the man was leaning over him. "Do you feel well enough to continue?"

"Yes," said Wade, "please." *Anything to move on to feeling something else.*

Without another word, the doctor began to work the ankle needle deeper. Fighting a twinge, Wade felt it continue within the rust boundary layer. Nesky twirled the needle like he was fiddling with the tuner on an old radio. While he did so, he backed up into the honey layer, then rust again, and finally he twisted it a level deeper.

In that motion, the room around Wade vanished, and the balance of his life would never be the same.

CHAPTER 2
The Man With The Axe

WADE LINWOOD SMELLED a horse. He could smell its sweat and breath and leatherwork. He could even smell traces of dung and hay. He heard it too, that unmistakable equine snort. Wade looked around to see what caused the association, and saw that it was not a synesthetic artifact but an actual horse tethered to a post. The walls of the doctor's office were gone to reveal open sky and trees. The table was gone, and Wade lay on dirt, leaves, and weeds nodding in the wind. Then an odd-looking man drew beside the horse. When he saw Wade on the ground, the man's eyes widened in surprise.

A chill of fear shot through Wade. There was no way he could be experiencing all of this. He never sensed an experience as a person, or a horse, or any coherent object for that matter. An individual sight, sound, smell, taste, or feeling led to other combinations of sights, sounds, smells, tastes or feelings in the form of generalized sensory perceptions, not fully realized ones. Even when he perceived the smell of carrots as wire cutters, he didn't see the actual object with handle and all; the tag he reached for was a shorthand way of describing the closest concept—two short, sharp edges. It was what Wade called visualizing an objectoid. Some synesthetes called the null space the object occupied the astral plane. And while he was the most complex synesthete he ever heard of, these full-fledged multi-sense, multi-object experiences of a horse and a man with scenery wrapping all around him were far beyond anything he was capable of. What's more, the things he sensed never sensed him back. Until now.

The apparition of a man hefted an axe, choking his hand up toward the metal head to reveal a saddle of wear on the handle. The vision edged towards him, opened its mouth and pulled breath to speak. Wade drew in his shoulders and covered his face with his hands, regressing to when he was six years old and his teacher, Mrs. Cobletz, threatened to slap him awake. The last thing he wanted was for one of his perceptions to speak.

The vision said, "What's the matter?" in a bit of a Russian accent. Wade lowered his hands to find walls with diplomas hanging on them, and the platform with the crinkly paper beneath him. No axe man or horse shared the room. Beethoven continued unabated in D minor, now in his playful second movement, a *sherzo*, which Wade remembered meant "joke" in Italian.

Just as the timpani solo began, Dr. Nesky turned off the music. "Why did you have your hands over your face?" he asked.

The obvious word for what Wade experienced was hallucination. Up until now he had pretty much thought of his synesthesia as a gift, a trait adding the kind of texture and context to everyday experience that very few people could enjoy. The key to its practical benefits was that everything was a constant. If you saw the number nine as fire engine red, it would always be fire engine red. The mixed associations gave you additional ways to remember things. Your favorite plumber's telephone number digits might be red, blue, red, green, gray, gray, gray. Together it made a single indescribable, but unique, color. First you recalled the right color, then the numbers that matched, then you dialed. But if your ability were to morph into something else, where things were not constant and simplified, where nine was no longer red, but a dragon, the result would be a nightmare.

"Did—" *How do you ask someone if the room just vanished and returned?* "Everything is fine. You removed the needles and I feel very little pain." *The motor oil smelled faint, something he could ignore.*

The doctor paused before answering as though he were at a deli trying to decide whether he wanted the brand name or the house variety. "That's...a good sign. However, the pain is likely to return, and it may happen before your next appointment."

"I don't like the sound of that. I spend the whole day working on the computer, flexing my wrist."

"You sell the auto insurance over the Internet?"

"No, these days I take calls at a call-in center. I look up and input information, sell them a policy and then underwrite it, which is a fancy word for following my company's instructions to complete the electronic paperwork. It keeps my hands on the keyboard throughout the day."

"Can you slip your shoes off at work?"

"I could get away with it for a few minutes at a time."

Nesky nodded with tentative satisfaction. "Can you recall with precision if I show you a precise spot to press?"

"Yes, recall is what I'm best at."

"Good. It's right here." The doctor pressed a spot above Wade's heel, eliciting a startled yelp from his patient. Wade flashed through purple, honey, rust, and then, unaccountably, an even briefer scrap of sky blue. During that second, the pain disappeared and took all its manifestations with it. The sky blue had to be his imagination, an echo of his hallucination.

Since when did I start second-guessing my synesthesia? What is happening to me?

"What did you do to me just now?" said Wade.

"It's called acupressure instead of acupuncture. It substitutes when you don't have a needle."

"Why not use that all the time?"

"The long-term benefit is far less potent. Acupressure, done correctly, might work for hours. With a few sessions of acupuncture, we may cure you for many years."

"That sounds good to me."

"Terrific. Now maybe next time, or one of these days, you will trust me enough to tell me what is actually happening to you."

Wade gave Nesky a surprised, measuring look, and then recovered. "Doctor, if I figure out how to explain it to myself, maybe I'll let you know."

~ *W* ~

WADE signed on to his workstation, his usual rapid-fire touch feeling pain-free at the outset. He sniffed the air for errant motor oil. If his brain generated any whiff of the phantom fumes it was hidden by the smell of fresh carpet, bagged lunches and perfume from across the aisle. Wade felt grateful for every moment of relief he could get. Although synesthetes led an unusual life, acupuncture was the closest thing Wade had ever seen to magic. It worked, or at least it worked on him. What frightened him was his peculiar side effect, the bending of reality. Could an ancient treatment turn his so-called disability into a kind of ability? Or was it a dangerous illusion that threatened to topple the mainstream life he craved?

He tapped away at his keyboard, worked his mouse, and tried harder and harder to focus on the electronic paperwork leftover from the day before, anything that took him further from thinking about himself. The pain built up again, dragging an oily residue in its wake. The doctor had told him to change the height of his chair to lessen the strain on his wrists and get a different mouse pad. Having arrived late, he had done neither.

He put on his head set to sign into the call system, and then thought better of it. If the pain spiked, he didn't want to scream into a customer's ear. He could get away with doing paperwork a while longer. He dipped into his drawer of completed sales for things he wrote by hand when away from the keyboard.

As he entered his third vehicle identification number, the pain and stench ratcheted past any threshold he could ignore. Bile rose in the back of his throat. He clamped his mouth shut and swallowed hard, hoping he would not vomit in the middle of the office. He checked around to see if anyone was looking, then slipped off his right shoe and pulled down the sock past his heel. A gentle stroke revealed the tender spot. As he plunged his thumbnail into it, he got the rapid but distinct sensation of purple, honey, and rust. And no relief. He held the pressure while the stink and the pain clouded every natural sight and sound. So inspired, he pressed harder. Rust gave way to blue sky with the odor of a horse. No vision came with it. No vague objectoids either. The pain left him.

Then something new happened. The wind shifted, and he smelled fresh air; fresh, unbelievable air beyond his imagination. It seemed to reach past his lungs to infuse his every organ with vigor.

Although he was accustomed to strange sensory mixtures, the air evoked a bizarre emotional slush of fear and joy. He pulled a deep breath until his lungs hurt, then he cleared that breath to suck down another. This gulp came in foul, making him cough until he thought he would see a lung on the floor.

"Hey, what are you doing? Hey, stop that." His boss, Maria, came on the run.

"What? What did I do?" Wade wanted to know.

Maria waved her arms, exasperated. "You were clutching your bare foot and hyperventilating."

"That wasn't hyperventilating. That was—"

"What?"

"Excitement over making a sale."

"Yeah, right."

"I'm fine now."

"No, you're not," she frowned. "Your shirt is soaked in sweat."

"It's hot in here."

"No, it isn't. I'm sending you for drug testing."

"There's nothing wrong with me!"

"It's company policy. If you have a problem you should get help."

Wade eased back in his chair to find the comfort of its lumbar support. Since his first visit to Dr. Nesky, he had done some new research on his condition. The ladder of changing sensations from an acupuncture needle sliding deep had been reported by other synesthetes. Vision-dreams in sleep had been recorded as well, but not the wide-awake bending of reality that Wade had experienced on the holistic center's table. Even if it were somehow a window on another world, something Wade didn't quite believe, real abilities had value. This job stealer did not.

Wade said, "Well...yes, Maria, maybe I should get help."

His boss gave him the strangest look. He raised his eyebrows, wondering what it meant.

"Drug testing means you're suspended," she clarified, "until Health and Safety clears you."

Wade tossed away his head set in surrender, and watched Maria stalk away. He thought that maybe Doctor Nesky gave him a drug on the needle. That would give a better explanation for how acupuncture worked, some dirty little secret of the industry. How else could a needle to the ankle relieve wrist pain? Why else would he hallucinate? *The simplest answer had to be the real one, right?*

~ W ~

WADE padded around his apartment barefoot, tempted to try the experiment again, this time alone where no one could judge him.

On the downside, that also meant no one could help him. Why, he wondered, did pressing the spot without a needle bring on any part of the hallucination? Some kind of lingering drug residue? Why couldn't he think this through? A job suspension wasn't supposed to be a mental suspension. Some of the things he had seen, felt and heard since the acupuncture were impossible. Being a synesthete redefined normal in the first place. On top of that, he seemed unusual among synesthetes in the degree of his synesthesia—how many senses were mixed. Then he found out that layered sensations were possible. Now he had gone through an experience that had never been recorded by anyone.

Wade soon found himself in the company nurse's office, waiting for a verdict. At least the suspension kept him from reinjuring his hand, and that kept the pain from getting worse. He hated waiting.

He became engrossed first with the choking hazard sign, and then with the double-beam balance scale. He stepped on and took it for a ride. The bar tipped over with a thunk before he began his adjustments. One large weight and one small, considered the most accurate device for human weight. That is until the springs got old. The human body and mechanical devices were not so different. Animate or inanimate, nature broke things down without remorse like the great composer turned deaf as a block of granite.

When she did appear, the company nurse, Ms. Emiliancheck, barreled in double time, knocking a jar of cotton swabs across the near counter. Wade hopped off the scale, a little embarrassed.

"You're supposed to be up on the table," she snarled. This same woman who took her time with friends on the telephone, proved very brisk when it came to moving people out of her office.

"I was…before," he said, sounding lame even to himself.

"Linwood, right? The drug test was negative," said Ms. E. "You can go back to work."

"That's it?" Wade asked her.

"Yeah. You got no more excuses. You want a medal or something? Take a walk."

The drug test was negative. A new thought to echo in his mind. If the drug test was negative, where did that leave him?

The insanity test was positive?

CHAPTER 3
Glass Portal

WADE STOPPED HIS car at the large Canadian goose in the road, eventually backing up the single line of vehicles for several blocks. Like a traffic cop, the mother made sure everyone knew whose turn it was. A long train of downy little ones executed a blue-blooded imitation of their parent's measured pace, followed by more adults. The goslings bobbed their yellow heads while the mature ones sported dark heads and necks with big white chinstrap markings. If anyone honked them, the fowl honked back.

Wade wasn't among the impatient. He looked forward to the morning show as a great way to start a workday. With Wade's physical failure to separate his senses, the full-grown birds conjured the flavor of dark chocolate while the juveniles brought the delicate scent of day lilies. He soaked it up with pleasure.

When all the Canadian geese had migrated to the south campus, Wade parked, and entered the low-slung Wheelwright Insurance Group building with a delighted spring in his step. Wade did not have to lose any time checking in with his boss, Maria. She would "see" him on her workstation when he signed onto the system. Avoidance worked best. Who knew what good mood spoilers she had up her sleeve?

Back at his desk, Wade spread out the policies he'd sold that week, like he was arranging trophies on a mantle. He felt relieved that his suspension and threat of losing his job hadn't gone on too long. He wasn't enamored with the profession but he loved the company he worked for, and enjoyed the thrill of convincing people to take a good deal. Once he got everything in order, he fed the keyboard his password, and let the incoming calls flow to him.

The first caller wanted her son Matty to have a Dodge Viper as a reward for doing his drinking at home these days. "A red one," she clarified, as though the color choice might have an impact on the insurance quote. "He's going to turn seventeen soon."

Wade couldn't prevent a low whistle from escaping his lips. The sticker on that beauty was over eighty grand. He asked her to wait a moment.

While his first customer rested on hold, Wade checked motor vehicle records to clarify Matty's history. It seemed the DMV had some police reports for Wade to read. As he scrolled, the obedient letters on the screen displayed multi-colors that Wade had seen many times before. He felt relieved that they did not jump out at him, and turn into something else. It was back in Wade's high school shop class in basic household electricity that he first realized that somewhere in his brain was a set of crossed wires.

Wade entered the code that told his computer Matty rear-ended someone at the tender age of sixteen. Some clever algorithm would decide what that meant in insurance dollars. In the cubicle across from him, beautiful Tammy tried to get his attention just for the sake of attention, while Maria from her supervisor's station kept spying over at him as though he might fly away. Maria waxed a bit high strung to begin with. Middle age hadn't tempered her ambition. And Tammy's beauty was tempered by a face and nose that were a bit too long, which somehow made her even more interesting.

Through it all, Wade got his work done. The seriousness of any condition depended on whether or not it made you dysfunctional in the tasks a human being has to perform every day. That remained true for problems as mundane as drinking too much, or as exotic as synesthesia. His synesthesia, up until now, tended to make him more functional, not less. Seeing objects that saw him freaked him out. Yet if his pain receded daily from the acupuncture treatments, it seemed he wouldn't have to. No more pain meant no more needles and no more hallucinations, if he were lucky. Unfortunately, some part of him wanted to know more about the odd man and his horse in the place with impossibly clean air.

As Wade expected, the computer kicked out a stratospherically high quote to discourage sixteen-year-old alcoholic Matty with the red Dodge Viper from doing business with the Wheelwright Insurance Group. After breaking the news to the boy's mother, Wade wanted to find out why this girl in front of him, Tammy, was jumping up and down, but he had to wait until the end of the day.

His next call came from a doctor's wife who had enlarged her driveway to fit ten cars. She was up to number seven, a hummer.

"I have to do it for the sake of numerology," she said as Wade managed not to laugh. "My husband was born on the first of October. The digits of ten add back to one, but we can't live with just one car, so we have no choice but to get nine more." She wanted to know if getting up to the number ten would cause the insurance price per car to soar.

"Not unless you intend to drive all ten cars at the same time," Wade told her.

The day went like any other. There were the usual calls from students whose semi-annual insurance premiums would cost more than the used car itself. A few always said they would go without coverage. Then came one very unusual call from a father who wanted to know if he had to insure his daughter's wheelchair. It put Wade in mind of the young woman at the clinic.

"Why would you think that?" Wade asked.

"It's a motor vehicle."

"Does she plan to take it for a spin on the highway?"

"I have no way of knowing what she plans."

"Well, if not, then no, she doesn't need insurance."

"It can go faster than walking speed," the voice on the phone insisted, sounding a little more familiar. "I would have to run if the damned thing got loose."

"Does the chair have a spot to attach license plates?" asked Wade.

"I haven't checked."

"You would have noticed that."

"Will you sell me something that protects me from bodily injury?"

"Sir, if your daughter needed insurance, I would be happy to sell it to you. She doesn't, so I can't."

The man gave an oddly dissatisfied grunt, and for some reason Wade flashed on an image of an iguana. He fought off an urge to ask if the daughter's name was Kreindel. That would be too much of a coincidence and too intrusive to ask. If it turned out to be the man from the clinic, the question might piss him off to the point where he would complain to the insurance company. Wade said goodbye.

The bulk of the afternoon brought more routine calls from nice people who were happy to save some money. They wanted to be convinced, and get on with enjoying their new cars, so Wade helped them "pull the trigger," as they say.

Wade's coworker, Tammy, was doing a hot foot dance for his attention, as she had been doing more or less throughout the day. If she meant it to be distracting, she succeeded. Her body language said she was angry at being ignored. Wade imagined the moves to be not too different from the ones a female praying mantis does before it kills and eats its mate. The nature channel said that it was the only insect capable of moving its head from side to side like humans. On the bright side, they did copulate for six hours.

Finally, Wade said, "What, Tammy? What? What?"

"I sold three policies today!"

"That's very good." He lent his voice all the encouragement he could muster.

"How many did you sell, Wade?"

"Seven."

"I hate you."

"You'll get better."

"At hating you?"

"That too."

Maria, already busy keeping an eye on Wade anyway, shot over. "What is the problem, Tammy? What is it this time?"

"No problem," said Tammy.

"Well then what's with the talking when you should be working?"

"I can talk once in a while. It's my right."

"Your right? Anyone who sells three policies a day doesn't have any rights."

Tammy looked stricken and bewildered. "Three is good for me."

"That's because you're not very bright."

The next thing Tammy said probably had something to do with the fact that everyone began watching to see what she would do.

She glanced around and said, "All right you sorry ass bitch. Now I'm taking the rest of the day off."

"Take every day off," said Maria. "You're fired."

Wade said, "Maria, it's five minutes to five anyway." Maria planted her hands on her hips and stared at Tammy as though Wade hadn't said anything. They were two women locked in on each other.

Wade didn't have to be a synesthete to see smoke coming out of Tammy's ears as she grabbed her purse and took a fast walk toward the double doors. She looked daggers at a rival or two along the way. This was not how Wade expected the day to end.

"Wade," said Maria, sighing, "You're the closest thing that ditz has to a friend. Hurry up and go after her. Make sure she doesn't do something stupid." Maria finished the thought under her breath, "At least until after she leaves the premises."

For the rest of his life, Wade would wonder why he listened to Maria and moved so quickly to catch up with Tammy. He knew he had been something of a jerk with women in college, and he overcompensated for it now—his age of chivalry.

Wade just about caught up with her as she went through the doors into the main hall. He reached out and called her name to get her attention. Too late. He thrust his hand ahead of him into the doorway. Without looking, she used all her strength to slam the door, catching him in his injured wrist. The glass in the doors revealed its inherent liquid nature by shattering into thousands of splashing shards.

Waves of shimmering pain rippled through him in every direction. Severe trauma can sometimes cause an ordinary person to have a sense barrier breakdown, visualizing the pain as a sheet of red or a cascade of star-shaped flashes. The impact on his wrist and the many cuts treated Wade to a grand fireworks display. At the same time, he felt like someone had jammed a funnel into his mouth and poured the noxious motor oil in directly. He saw neither Tammy's condition, nor the circle of gawkers. In a coughing fit, he curled into a fetal position.

The pain would not relent. In the midst of his nausea, he experienced brief flashes of despair like a hopeless animal that wanted to die. He reached toward the floor without consciously knowing what he would do.

Someone said, "Stop him. He picked up a shard of glass!"

Before anyone could stop him, he gripped the long glass triangle with his less injured, right hand, and stabbed it into a spot between his anklebone and his heel.

Even without the purple, honey, and rust transition—he stabbed too quickly to experience every nuance—all pain ceased. The entire office ceased to exist with it. The space above him turned blue with sunlight, his lungs filled with pristine clarity, and a horse exhaled loudly through its sputtering lips.

And then the man with the axe he had seen in the first vision did a double take, came toward him, and pressed the blade to his throat.

CHAPTER 4
Are You a Lunatic?

THE AXE MAY have spent the afternoon hacking large blocks of firewood, but the man's familiarly with the tool made him as dexterous as if he were wielding a knife. Wade didn't know where the jugular vein could be found. He was comfortably certain the attacker had it figured out.

"What are you doing here?" the man demanded.

Wade tried to look harmless even as he stared. The man wore a leather apron over a loose fitting top and wooly leggings. He had his smooth shoes tied at the ankles with leather string, and his apron splattered with multi-colored paint. When he turned slightly, Wade could see some kind of kilt under the apron as well. On his head he wore a form-fitting cap that covered most of his hair. Wade had never seen anyone dressed like that.

The words themselves were a synesthetic experience. Wade heard two sets of words, a strange language, almost intelligible, overlaid by somewhat modern English. As with all of his doubled experiences, he was adept in picking the one he wanted to pay attention to. Yet, nothing else about this situation could be related to his condition as he knew it.

Something about the immediacy of a blade to your throat remedies all indecision and doubt, Wade realized. Without ever having had the experience before, you glean in that moment that something has come down to you through the generations, a kind of instruction book on survival that tells you not to act rashly. You live on that cold edge pressed up under your chin with no other sensation to trouble you. Even breathing becomes unimportant because from there a tiny shift would make all the difference in the world. Refusing to accept what was happening was not an option.

"I'm lost," Wade pleaded.

The stranger withdrew the edge a fraction, allowing Wade to breathe fitfully, and looked him up and down. "You're hurt, too. Why did I not notice that before?" He slid his tool's handle into a loop at his side.

Wade himself hadn't noticed his glass door injuries until the man with the axe pointed it out. His face and right hand stung badly. His leg bled where a long sliver of glass protruded. And only socks protected his feet. He remembered why he had no shoes, having slipped them off in the office.

"Come, get up." He gave Wade a hand. While Wade was distracted, the man pulled the glass sliver out in one quick motion, and tossed it aside.

"Ah," Wade gasped, and instinctively clamped his hand on his thigh to pinch the wound closed.

"It's not a vital spot," the other observed. "The bleeding will stop on its own."

From Wade's motion, something else captured the man's attention.

"What manner of wode is this?" he said with some intensity.

"My name is Wade. How did you know?"

"Some say wade, yes. It is obvious from your breeches. I am Olich the Dyer. Whose man are you?"

Wade could not be sure he heard correctly. *Olich the Dire?* He concentrated harder on ignoring the odd words to focus on the simultaneous English words.

"I like to think of myself as my own man," said Wade.

Olich narrowed his eyes. "You don a curious disguise for someone of wealth."

"Oh that's what you meant. No, I work for a company."

"A company of what? Surely not of soldiers. You're too weak."

"Thank you. I'm with a group that sells auto insurance."

"I know nothing of auto ensurance, and I see that you are not from around here. Is this how a man of auto ensurance dresses? I ask again—What manner of wode is this?" He indicated Wade's pants.

"You did say 'wode.' I don't know the word."

"Wade, then. Very well, if it is a trade secret, keep your own counsel. Don't you find it confusing to be named after a dyer's plant?"

"I didn't know that I was."

"Wade is not wode where you come from? Very strange."

"Where am I?"

"You're in the Frankish Kingdom, the region called Swabia. Were you not in the Frankish Kingdom before?"

"No," said Wade.

"West then?"

"I don't know."

"Are you a lunatic? You don't appear to have a head injury." He reached out to check, but Wade flinched away from the contact.

"Ow, it's nearly healed, but...tender."

"Your hair is dark, your skin medium, and you are tall. By your coloring, I would guess you hail from Aquitaine."

The unfamiliar names and strange clothing made Wade cautious. He knew he visited some other place. Perhaps some other time. As a synesthete, you learn to trust your instincts. "How far is Aquitaine?"

"Distant by my sights and means. I've not seen it."

Wade paused. "I think that's where I'm from."

Olich stared and then laughed. "So we'll say, for now. I have some ale to dab on those cuts if you like. I was just about to eat anyway. You should join me."

"Thank you for the hospitality. I should be moving on soon."

"Nonsense. As a stranger, you're my guest. I'm a thegn, or soon to be. As such, I have...responsibilities."

Wade did not know what thegn meant. He chose not to advertise his ignorance any further, or at least not all at once, if he could help it. If it became necessary, he would learn as a child would. "I really have to get back to Aquitaine, Mr. Olich."

"I might add that as a trespasser, you're in my charge. I would find out what you are doing here. You'll go nowhere until I do."

The gleaming edge of Olich's axe backed up his wishes. Wade did not see any way out of it. He followed his host to his home, eager to look for more clues as to his circumstances. He needed something to hold onto.

Wade's eyes went to the largest object first, the house itself. He saw a dwelling of sound construction if not standard dimensions. The style wasn't a ranch, a hi-ranch, a cape or a split. And not a log cabin either, although the shingle siding appeared to be real wood rather than aluminum trying to look like wood. No lawn, garden, or landscaping were evident. Stranger than that, no pavement ran to the door, no garage or driveway broke the untamed vicinity, and the surrounding weeds looked like no car had ever disturbed them. He might have dubbed it a Mad Bomber hermit shack if it weren't so large and well suited to utility. Although the door creaked a long greeting when they entered, its owner didn't seem to care. No bomber would have advertised his presence like that.

Inside, Olich handed him the ale and Wade used it as suggested, grunting as it stung. Then he examined his hands. The right one had two slashes from the glass shard he used to stab his foot. He flashed on the idea that this was all Tammy's fault, but he wasn't sure why. Wade found it exceedingly difficult to think of the world he knew, temporarily suspended, and process all the new information at the same time.

Olich said, "Where are my manners? Here is a cloth to wipe the blood from your hands."

"I was thinking of washing them."

"Maybe I was mistaken about your origin," Olich snorted. "You may be a Northman of mixed blood. They have this habit of washing hands for no reason. That might also explain why you're missing your tunic. Perhaps you don't get cold easily. Very well, there's a bowl of water I was saving for later. Be so kind as to empty it out the window when you're done."

Again, Wade did as he was told while Olich brought out the food. He examined the table and chairs with great interest. They were not the product of commercial manufacture, and not flawed either.

"You gawk at everything as if you've never seen it before. Do they not have chairs where you come from? Does everyone sit on the floor?"

Wade laughed. "No, they don't sit on the floor."

"Eat your portion then."

Wade put the food in his mouth as if he were facing a firing squad. When he tasted it, he smiled.

"This is good." Wade's voice came out laden with surprise.

Olich reddened. "Why shouldn't it be good? Do you think I would poison you? That's fresh curlew."

Wade swallowed. "No, I meant exceptionally good." He took a quick sip of ale, and found it heavy.

"Ah. It seems my skills with mixing dye give me a flair for cooking as well."

"Oh, I see, you said 'Dyer.' Olich the Dyer. That's what you do for a living."

Olich got sore again. "If you are getting ready to tell me that where you come from, each person does his own dyeing, then I don't want to hear any more. In the morning we'll see the Saxon. He's a man of letters and law. He'll sort you out for what you are."

In the morning? Wade wondered. *Will I be here in the morning, and the morning after that?*

CHAPTER 5
Opinion of The Saxon

WADE WATCHED THE candle burning and dancing on the dinner table as it gave off the distinct odor of meat. For a second he thought it a synesthetic smell, but he recalled dimly that old candles were made of tallow. The word sounded quaint at the time. Now he realized that tallow must be animal fat. Revolting.

Olich watched Wade as intensely as Wade watched the fire. "Your shirt is wool," said Olich between bites. "But the tiny stone buttons are exquisitely crafted. They must have cost dearly."

"I bought it when I was better off," said Wade defensively, hoping Olich would not actually touch the buttons and wonder at the oily surface of plastic. Olich nodded, accepting the answer for now.

If Wade were going to face the Saxon, as Olich called the impending visitor, he needed as much information as possible, and he urgently wanted a change of subject. "Olich, what year is it?"

"Relative to what? Crop rotation? Are you a part-time farmer now?" he laughed at his joke.

"No," Wade experimented, "a year in your...long measure."

"In Swabia we celebrate seven and forty, and four hundred years of Frankish Kings, and the first to wear the crown of the

Old Western Empire. I don't know what standard of years you use in your land."

"We measure the year of...Our Lord?" said Wade.

"Ah, you're not complete barbarians in Aquitaine, then. Why didn't you say so? The Year of Our Lord is 813."

Long after the fall of Rome and hundreds of years before the Renaissance. Wade shuddered. *This must be the Dark Ages, then.* He didn't know his history well enough to know what barbarian king ruled the Dark Ages at any given time, and he was afraid to sound foolish, especially if the answer wouldn't help him.

Olich stared at him. "How long have you been out of contact with cities that you forget the Year of Our Lord?"

"Long enough, I suppose."

"If you live in the forest, are those good quality clothes that you wear stolen?"

"No, I traded for them."

As casual as ever, and without interruption in eating, Olich said, "Those who live off the land tend to steal from landowners like myself. In your case, I suspect you trespassed in order to sleep with my daughter."

Wade spit ale in surprise. "What? I don't know your daughter."

While Olich did not rush to wipe the spill, he did stop eating. "Everyone knows my daughter. Well, I don't mean that as it came out. She's a virgin, after all. Here, I'll bring her around." He clapped his hands. "Rotrud, come in here, my dear."

Rotrud filled the doorway and just barely cleared it, coming in sideways. Wade stared at her with his mouth open. Her most noticeable feature was her eyes and the surrounding area. She had a single eyebrow, four times the thickness of a usual eyebrow, and brown orbs that met near the bridge of her nose. Her mouth was crooked and her face lumpy with large, longhaired warts. She smiled to reveal a train wreck of teeth.

"I see you're quite taken with her, young man. You stare as many do," Olich said proudly. Rotrud flailed her hands about in the shy negative deference of one too modest for frequent compliments.

"Ahhh," said Wade.

"And isn't Rotrud the most beautiful name you ever heard? I named her after the daughter of Charles the Great."

"It's a very special name."

"To befit a very special woman. But however grand you think you are, Wade of Aquitaine, you will not lie with my daughter in shame."

"No," Wade recovered enough to say. "I would never do that."

"No," agreed Olich. "Then the two of you will wed."

Wade coughed violently. "Oh, that's not possible." *How could he put this politely?* "I am meant for another."

"Betrothed?" sputtered Olich. "And yet you would hide on my land to bed with my Rotrud? That's despicable! Yes, you shall see the Saxon when he arrives. He's coming here on other business, but we can add yours. He will sort you out." His last words were the same as when he was puzzling over Wade's identity, only this time more tightly spoken.

~ *W* ~

THE bedroom with its square posts, lanterns, and lack of décor, looked to Wade like an indoor stable without the horse. It obviously doubled as a workshop for the manufacture of small goods. The air had a pervasive sawdust tinge. No telling what some people would do if they built their own house.

"I like to craft household items before I fall asleep," said Olich motioning him closer to the bench like a man who didn't get much company.

The only household items Wade could recognize were a rolling pin and some bowls. The largest article looked like a giant letter "I" with extended, droopy serifs. Without the context of some yarn stretched over it, or maybe shoes on the ends, he had no clue about its use. The woodworking tools were easier. Wade's grandfather used to work in wood. Olich had a sanding block, saws, hammers, drills, whittling knives, miter box, guide blocks, and several vices. Nothing electric of course. Then Wade saw the freestanding saw horse with guide grooves, clamps, cranks, and cutters.

"Beautiful lathe," he said.

Olich brightened. "Go ahead, try it."

"I can't. My grandfather used one, but I never cared to learn." *I would introduce you to my grandfather, but he's not been born yet.*

Olich grunted. "A unqualified suitor and useless too. I would have taught you my trade," he said sounding wistful as he trailed off.

Unlike Wade's grandfather, Olich made no toys or sculpture in his woodshop, not a spark of fun. Maybe Olich was actually the caretaker of an old restoration house, Wade thought fleetingly. *Maybe I haven't gone into the past.* The problem with that theory was that Olich's place didn't look like some little house on the prairie or a colonial village. It defied style, a wooden wonder so old it could never have survived to be the centerpiece of a tourist trap. If not for the tools, there would be nothing to recognize at all.

Wade looked over at the corner to imagine what it would be like sleeping there, assuming he could sleep at all.

"That's fresh hay," Olich boasted, pointing to a wooden platform at bed height. "You'll not lay with my Rotrud tonight. You'll stay right behind me on the guest bed in this room. And if you cannot do honest work, you may as well sleep now."

Apparently, Benjamin Franklin hadn't been the first to invent early to rise and early to bed. There was no recreation for someone like Wade in a rural corner of Swabia when the sun went down.

Wade tried sitting on the hay platform. He found it softer than he expected, and the planks beneath had some give. When he lay down, his feet stuck off the edge over a hard lip built to contain the cushioning. He had a choice of bending his knees off the end, or curling up.

Olich turned. "You'll find some night clothes and a covering on the hook."

"Thank you," Wade said automatically.

Wade stuck with his own clothes and took the blanket. That felt like it had been stolen from a horse too. When Wade spread it out in all its glory he decided the horse must have traded it in for something better.

"Was this sack too tattered to hold potatoes anymore?" Wade muttered.

"They are out of season," said Olich.

Wade reminded himself that it could have been worse. He remembered the time he had to sleep sitting up in his car on a camping trip gone bad. There was a storm that night and the rental car's windows would not close.

This situation with the dyer had a good-enough-for-one-night feel to it. Hallucinations didn't go on forever and neither did synesthetic experiences.

Wade lay with his knees bent, remarkably tired. Whatever he had done, wherever he had gone, a veil had been drawn over his mind so complete that he couldn't think straight. Poised at the edge of sleep, Wade's mind nearly floated free of his current situation even as it tangled with confusion. He saw himself tumbling through a void, braced for a crash through a wall of green glass, and landed in a soft dune of blue powder as a red Dodge Viper drove by. His last thought was one he didn't understand at all: Could Tammy really copulate for six hours?

~ W ~

OLICH roused Wade early and practically dragged him outside, long grasses beating wetly against his feet. Two people had arrived on horseback, drawing a cart behind them. The arrangement appeared crude but well built.

"Here is The Saxon, Grimketil Forkbeard, and his assistant, Snorri," said Olich.

Wade saw a forbiddingly large man distinguished by a vest of mail, a short cape and a long beard that split in half. For a man of "letters and law," thought Wade, it wasn't much of a business suit.

Snorri, a wasted creep of a man, circled Wade, and sniffed. He was not lent a nickname.

Grimketil addressed the Dyer sharply. "You need not refer to me as Saxon. I prefer to be called Grimketil of Lowestoft."

"Yes, of course you do, Forkbeard. You've come a long way from your pagan origins. I just find it pretentious when you wear the Roman chalmys around your shoulders." Olich indicated the short cape.

"I'm a respectable Christian—born a Christian!—and a Frankish scholar," Grimketil bristled. "Do you want my help or not?"

"Why not? I've paid your fee."

"Then stick to your basic wode, vermillion, and madder, and let me do my job."

"Very well. While you are here, I would like you to meet Wade, The Seller of Auto Ensurance, trespasser, and would-be adulterer."

Grimketil furrowed his brow. "You think everyone is after your daughter, Olich. Although I admit he does look indecent with his tunic off. From where does he hail?"

"He claims to be from the Duchy of Aquitaine."

"Claims to be?"

"He claims a head injury as well."

"Perhaps he is a dullard, not to know his duchy."

"I'm not a dullard," Wade protested. "It's Aquitaine all right. You can speak directly to me, Grimketil of Lowestoft." He felt ludicrous just speaking the name.

The examiner said, "Very well, Aquitainian. I know my Latin. You say you perform acts of ensurance. What kind of ensurance?"

"Car insurance." Something he admitted to before he thought better of it.

Grimketil turned to his companion. "Car is another word for cart."

To Wade, he said, "Is it your business to ensure that wheeled conveyances do not break?" He laughed at the absurdity.

Wade had a sinking feeling. "That's part of it, yes. I sell and underwrite, but I'm part of a corporation. A guild, rather. They insure it, not me."

"Do you understand this?" Olich asked Grimketil.

"Yes, Olich. Ensurance is not really a profession. It's a speculation game that gets tried once in a while. Never works. He takes a fee as a wager that the cart will not come apart within a certain time. If it crashes with another cart or breaks, he must buy the owner a repair, or provide the purchase price of a new one for the owner. If the cart does not come apart in the agreed upon period, he keeps the entire fee, thus winning his wager. We've tried it in Swabia. There's too much bickering involved, and no one wants to pay a fee to someone who has done nothing but make a bet."

"He takes the fee in advance though?"

"Yes, yes, but it can lead to bloodshed on the one hand when the fee is kept, or on the other hand if the ensurer loses the bet, and tries to flee. It's a thoroughly disreputable occupation associated with gypsies and the like."

As they went on in their indictments of him, the restless Snorri continued his circling investigation, making Wade doubly nervous.

"I'm not a gypsy," Wade blurted. "I stay put."

"Then how do you come to be here?"

"I mean, I stay put when I'm in Aquitaine practicing my profession. I'm honest too."

"That's what they all say," replied the man from Lowestoft. "Professing honesty is practically a declaration of guilt. Snorri, if you please—"

Snorri moved more quickly than Wade would have imagined. He produced a hinged wooden block with metal latches. Grimketil held Wade from behind while Snorri maneuvered Wade's hands into the wrist holes, closed it up, and applied a lock.

"What is this?" Wade exclaimed through a growing panic.

Forkbeard leaned in close for the charge. "You are to be tried for trespass."

"And seduction," added Olich.

"Please go back to work, dyer," the Saxon advised. "I will take it up from here. Our other business can wait."

The craftsman shrugged and went back to his house.

Wade's mind worked furiously. He realized that when Olich said he would be sorted out he should have realized it might be connected with serious consequences. At the present juncture, he saw the greatest safety in appearing calm and talking it through.

"What will happen?" Wade asked Grimketil as Snorri settled him in roughly the cart. It smelled like someone had used it to carry away horse manure. Some of the hay clung to him.

"You will have a fair trial under all the rules of the Folkright," the Saxon said as if astonished someone would doubt it.

"Yes, but I'm not familiar with the rules."

"I know they have the Folkright in Aquitaine, backward as it is. We are all in the same kingdom."

"Of course they do." Wade was gaining confidence in the language, and getting more elaborate at lying. "I've seen my share of thrilling executions for the most dangerous criminals. I applaud that. It's just that I've never run afoul of the legal system personally. I don't know how it works for very small crimes like mine, and...I'm mostly illiterate."

"And I suppose this also has to do with the head injury you claim."

"Right."

"I was joking," he glared. "Hm, well, smaller and larger crimes are not distinguished from each other. You will be given an opportunity for compurgation first." He paused to assess Wade's comprehension and found none. "You must have heard about Trial by God and Country."

"I'm hazy on the details," said Wade, meaning he had no idea.

"If you make an oath that you are innocent, you will need at least six commoners or one count to vouch that they believe you from knowledge of your past character."

"I don't know anyone around here," Wade remonstrated. All this time, Snorri said not a word. At Wade's exclamation, Snorri lifted his nose as if to say the answer was just as inadequate as he expected.

"That's not a problem," Grimketil continued, "In that case, without Trial by God and Country, there is always Trial by God alone. I think that's even more fair to keep the county out of it. You may undergo an ordeal."

Wade didn't like the sound of that. "Before you ask your next question," said the Saxon, "whether you face trial by fire or by water, and all the particulars of such, is up to the scabini."

Wade took shallow breaths. He tried as best he could to conceal his distress while getting more information. "Ah, yes, the scabini. That would be some good church men from Rome."

"Not always from Rome. They can be local bishops and a count, but generally under the Pope's direction, yes. I see that your brains are not entirely scrambled."

"No, some things are coming back to me."

Grimketil raised his eyebrows as he closed up the cart. "You are a lucky that the scabini are in town, ready for a case to try. I advise you to plead guilty and save yourself a lot of trouble."

~ W ~

IN the lower depths of the court, Wade wore shackles of heavy chain link. His guards hauled him into a damp chamber, shoeless on the wet stone, to stand before the scabini. Grimketil stood by his right with Snorri sort of hanging around, looking as though nothing could moisten his parched flesh. Olich shifted uneasily in what Wade took to be the accuser's box. His multi-colored apron was gone.

The younger of the scabini spoke in a sonorous voice. He wore robes, had a well-trimmed goatee and the longish hair of a middle nobleman. "Wade of Aquitaine, I am Count Gerardus of Ravenna. With me is the Bishop Egidio." The old Bishop, in identical robes, nodded almost imperceptibly. His eyes pulled shut in a slow blink as though he were going to sleep. Then both lapsed into expectant silence.

Wade thought furiously for something appropriate to say. Gerardus' eyes widened with anger when Wade did not respond. Wade said, "I am humble before you."

Gerardus seemed mollified. "You stand accused of trespass on the land of Olich the Dyer, and...no other charge." He looked crossly at Olich, who flinched and glanced elsewhere.

Egidio drew a strenuous breath. "Wade of Aquitaine, how do you plead?"

"Innocent."

The count gave a small shrug and lifted his quill to make a long, looping notation. "Let it be recorded then. Olich has given testimony and you have denied it. I understand you are not capable of compurgation. I think you will find we are a fair court. Bishop Egidio and I have discussed this matter at the proper length, consulting the Folkright for the appropriate measures, etcetera. You are to undergo the ordeal of the stone and the boiling water. Do you wish to change your plea?"

"What happens if I plead guilty?" Wade asked.

"Then you shall be forgiven, and your hand shall be severed. You will suffer no confinement."

Wade swallowed. "I will stick with innocent."

Snorri led Wade to another part of the chamber where the group that now reconvened included two large men with swords. Wade took his place between with leaden feet. He looked around at the only people he knew in this world: Olich, Snorri, and Grimketil Forkbeard. The grotesque Rotrud had joined as a spectator as well. She showed her wrecked teeth. He couldn't tell if she were angry or still hopeful of his change of heart and their eventual union.

Count Gerardus spoke with growing enthusiasm. "Wade of Aquitaine, the cauldron before you contains boiling water, into which you shall plunge your—have we determined that he is right handed?" Gerardus dropped his voice for the aside. The Bishop nodded carefully as though he were not sure if his head would be able to rise again.

Gerardus turned back to Wade, cleared his throat, and continued. "You are to plunge your left arm into the water. Somewhere in the vessel, you shall find a stone and several slots. You are to insert the stone into the slot that fits it. And I would advise you to find the slot quickly. The fire under the cauldron will be maintained throughout your ordeal. If you fail, we shall start over—with boiling oil."

CHAPTER 6
Trial By Water

OLD BISHOP EGIDIO rose. The assembly could hear his bones crackle.

The guards adjusted Wade to ensure that he faced the cauldron squarely. He could see the water boiling with enormous bubbles, the steam rising furiously, while flames licked the vessel's base. Wade couldn't believe the ordeal was grinding mercilessly forward. The guards looked eager to strike him down if he attempted to flee.

"Aid, O Lord, those who seek thy mercy," the Bishop addressed Heaven, "and pardon those who confess their sins." He looked pointedly at Wade to await the accused's belated confession. Hearing nothing, he continued. "Let us pray."

The guard's tore away Wade's shirt. The heat shimmered everything in front of him.

"I adjure you, Wade of Aquitaine, by the Father, Son, and Holy Spirit, by your Christianity, by the only begotten Son of God, whom we believe to be the Redeemer of the world, by the Holy Trinity, by the holy gospel, and by the relics of the saints which are kept in the church above us, if thou hast done this offence or consented to it, confess now, and accept the penalty and forgiveness."

Hushed silence followed as a black robed assistant stirred the coals, and fanned the flames. A pain throbbed in Wade's wrist where it would be severed to remove his hand if he were to change his plea. Wade did not stop the proceedings for his confession. No alternative was a good one.

This cannot be happening. This is just horrible. I want to go back to my life, back to where I'm Wade Linwood again.

Relentless, Egidio summoned from inside himself a strong, rising voice of finality: "The ordeal begins. Free now the innocent and make known the guilty."

Timed with the word "guilty," guards on either side of Wade pulled the pins on his manacles so that they fell to the floor with an echoing clang. Wade coughed violently. Feigning a retching fit, he bent to reach for the place between his ankle and heel. Finding the spot, he jabbed his thumbnail in. Wade closed his eyes and gave himself over to the experience of royal purple, honey, and painless rust, rust, rust.

A sharp pain in his ribs opened his eyes.

"You have more important things to worry about than an itchy foot," admonished the guard with the sword. "Do as you're bid, or die where you stand."

The sequence had ended at rust. No blue sky. No disappearing act. Gone was the entire extent of Wade's plan. He had to put aside hope of escape and take up hope of short-term survival.

Quickly, he sucked a deep breath, and plunged his left arm deep into the boiling cauldron. Instinctively, he pulled his hand halfway back with a scream, and then had to plunge it in again. Every split second in that water equaled an eternity. Moving his hand around in scalding water and steam railed against every ounce of common sense he owned. No light came back from inside that hole; he worked blind. Only one thought kept him on the insane task: *Boiling oil in the next round, if there must be one, is far hotter than boiling water.*

At the bottom, he found a small pebble, discarded it with trembling regret, and then found a large, flat stone suitable for a narrow space. Now he had to find a slot as he struggled to ignore the excruciating pain. *Cold, cold, cold,* he kept telling himself. His red eyes were streaming tears. He found the first slot in the center. The rock would not go into it. Giving in to fear, thinking of this trial as the destruction of his arm, would have been easy. *It's cold,* he swore, *I'm on a frozen mountaintop. Keep moving to stay warm.*

Wade panted through gritted teeth like an Olympic weightlifter going for a world record. He held the rock between thumb and forefinger, and splayed the rest of his fingers, which he used to sweep the entire bottom in ever widening circles. His entire body shook. He found the metal hotter by far than the water itself. With palpable despair, he completed the circuit of the outer edge, and discovered there was no other slot there.

He let out an inhuman cry that tore his throat, began to draw out his hand in defeat, and miraculously found another slot in the side of the cauldron. It was almost as though another presence took over and acted through him. He rammed the stone home with inhuman speed and fury.

Wade took back his arm, cradled it tight, and issued a moan that resounded on every wall of the chamber.

Snorri was engaged to work the lever that tipped the cauldron so that the water put out the fire beneath. When the steam cleared, Count Gerardus held a candle to the cauldron's interior, and announced impartially, "He has done it."

No cheers resounded. No heralds raised trumpets to their lips. It sounded more like grumbling.

The guards wrenched Wade's arm away from him while Grimketil unfurled the bandages. His entire arm and hand were bound up and held a distance from his body by means of a fastened stick and a leather belt that encircled his torso. They shackled his right arm to a chain that connected to two large cuffs around his ankles, and a second chain that ran between them. The team held him tightly again while the Count approached with a branding iron. With the aid of the heated iron and some gum, he applied his official seal to the point where the last of the bandage windings lapped.

At last, court functionaries thrust Wade prostrate before the Count.

Gerardus intoned, "Now begins the three day waiting period, after which God will manifest the guilt or innocence of the defendant by controlling the outcome of the physical test to which the defendant was subjected. If I inspect the seal and find it broken, I will know there has been intervention by man, and shall find guilt. The additional crime of tampering with the Count's seal will result in further penalties. This court remands the defendant to the custody of Grimketil of Lowestoft, and from him thence to be imprisoned until Judgment Day."

Grimketil and Snorri hauled him to his feet. He drifted off into numbness.

~ W ~

WADE awoke on his back inside a urine soaked stone cell. His bandaged arm on the stick stood up on its own as though raised against an attack. The cell came without a door; scant consolation as Wade's chains were affixed to a stout ring set into the wall. He groaned in pain and recognition of his plight. Grimketil had not left yet. Snorri was absent.

"You performed bravely and did well, Wade. Very few succeed at that task. Perhaps you are not burned too badly."

"Do you care?"

Grimketil straightened his small tunic. "I've done my duty. Still, I think the stone in the slot test is a bit harsh for plain trespass."

"If you think it's harsh, why the hell did you put me in here?"

The other squinted one eye at him. "Since I am your only visitor, you might want to keep a civil tongue."

Wade sighed. "All right then. Why did you bring me before Gerardus and Egidio?"

"A respectable citizen accused you. In truth, I thought they would simply give you a dunking and make you wear a fool's mask."

"A fool's mask?"

"Sure, you would walk around town with a comical iron mask locked on your head—they're great fun. As it happens I suppose you paid the price of not being from around here."

"Why aren't I free, Grimketil? What will happen to me?"

"In three days, the Count will inspect his seal, and then cut open the bandages. The Bishop will say a prayer and examine the wound. If it is found to have festered, you are guilty. In that instance, the appropriate parts of your hand and arm will be cut away, and you will be incarcerated for some years. Thus the sentence is carried out. The cutting is a favor to you at that point; those parts would be useless and your suffering could be fatal if you kept them."

"What are my chances?'

"By choosing this route, I take it you believe in divine intervention. Barring that instance, mostly, an untreated burn does fester. That's why I advised you to plead guilty. You are guilty."

"Why must it fester?" Wade pressed.

"Because you cannot open the bandages. If you were a free man, you would drink water, allow the wounds to drain, exercise the arm, and, most importantly, coat the wounds with a special preparation of silver. I've learned the technique, and it works. I suppose you can drink, but you're not allowed to do any of the rest."

"Do you have access to silver?"

Grimketil shook his head, his beard wagging a beat behind. "Perhaps you were too insensate to hear. If the count's seal is broken, you are found guilty regardless. Then your hand is chopped off, plus whatever other punishments Gerardus finds proportionate to his ego."

"Maybe not. If I were home, there's a device with a hollow needle, a pipe and a plunger. The pipe is filled with whatever fluid is needed, and then injected into the skin by means of the plunger pushing through the pipe and the needle."

"Injected? Like the venomous bite of a viper?"

"Very much like it. I could inject the silver past the bandages."

"Clever. I knew you couldn't be illiterate. How would you write your ensurance contracts?"

"Can you obtain a viper's poison fang, and the other materials to make the device?'

"Easily. I have the ingredients."

"And smuggle it in here?"

"That's the least of it. It will be difficult to fashion." Grimketil stood to leave.

"But you will do it?"

Hearing the footfalls of a guard, they both fell silent. The unhurried gait grew louder in a series of interminable steps, and finally trailed softer as he passed on.

Before the echoes died away, Wade repeated his question in a whisper tight with urgency. "Will you do it?"

"I will try," said Grimketil.

"Why are you helping me?"

"I'm not sure that I am. It's naught but an experiment."

"But why are you trying?"

He winked. "Because there is more to you than I can yet explain. The kingdom needs learned men, and you never call me the Saxon or Forkbeard. Besides, in case you have not noticed, I am for hire."

CHAPTER 7
Needuhl By Another Name

WITH HIS INJURIES and the stress of events, Wade's exhaustion took him cleanly the very moment Grimketil passed out of sight.

In his dreams he relived the terrible ordeal of boiling water, only this time Tammy joined them in the chamber as well, jumping up and down and trying to get his attention as he fought to find the stone and the slot. Then she turned into Maria, demanding that he stop wasting time and get back to work. His dream self concentrated on convincing arguments that the immense heat was actually cool and powdery. Irrelevant to the task, he conjured an unbidden image of a boxy object with spoked wheels. As he struggled mightily in the savage heat, Maria came up and nibbled on his ear. He turned to see that it was not Maria, but the frightful Rotrud, stinking of motor oil. Upon meeting his fear, her laugh shattered her into a thousand stinging pieces. The shards passed through him harmlessly but for his left arm, where the pain flared intense.

Wade awoke stiff and shaky, in a cold sweat. His midday bowl sat nearby. They didn't trust him with utensils, so he had to tip the gruel to his mouth with the one limb he had free. In his groggy state, he thought the bowl trembled with a fear of its own, and found that it was only his hand. He felt so hungry he didn't notice how awful the lumpy mess was until halfway through. The smell of the dungeon's stale urine pervaded everything. Setting aside the bowl, he flexed his left arm, hand, and fingers against the stiff bandages, discovering that he tired quickly. Many of his nerves were burned away, but the whole arm throbbed fiercely. When he moved too much, he hit the limits of his chain pulled taut from the ring in the wall. To quell his rising panic, he concentrated on taking deep, steady breaths, listening to the sound of air. If he had a paper bag, he would have used it to ward off hyperventilation. No luxuries like that around. Deep breaths were all he had.

A drop of water ran down the wall, changing speed as the surface grew more or less porous, changing direction, taking the path of least resistance. He found himself rooting for the tiny bead to make it the bottom, not wanting it to be absorbed along the way. *Where is Grimketil? Will he really return? Why should he? What is in it for him?*

Without any task to go off to, his nightmare lingered. Details of the dream came back to him, demanding attention. Something in the middle of all the imagery struck him more forcefully then the rest because it manifested as a synesthetic experience: blue powder on a cool surface. The wheeled object was a wheelchair. The image coupled with a feeling of portentousness. Or did he just imagine so now? Back in his comfortable world, he used to wonder if dreams had meaning. *Were they things to hope for or fear? Or were they only the sparkling detritus of a mind sorting the day's events?* Today, all those questions seemed more urgent.

"Do you yet live?" It was Grimketil in the doorway, looking altogether too hale and hearty.

"Have you brought the device?" Wade whispered.

"First, you will answer a question for me."

"I knew there was a catch."

Grimketil moved close to Wade's face either to talk low, or to look for the tiniest reaction. "When your shirt was torn off, a curious thing happened. Olich claimed the discarded cloth, and immediately stuffed it in his pouch."

"I didn't see that"

"I'm sure you cannot claim you do not know why he did it. A torn shirt couldn't have been much compensation for his trouble."

Wade swallowed. "I think I know. He admired the buttons."

"Why?"

"He called them exquisite fine stone work. Do you have the silver solution?"

Grimketil nodded slowly. "Silver is a precious imported metal."

"What of it?"

"Olich also discovered a finely blown section of glass on you. That too was imported, from the lands of Islam, I adjudge."

"What are you getting at?"

"My assessment of you has changed, Wade. It is obvious to me now that you led a soft life as a servant in a rich man's house. You ran away, and found out how hard life could be for the common man. Such an origin is the only thing that can explain you, and your secrecy. Am I right?"

Wade hung his head.

"I take your reaction as admission enough. When you are a relatively free man again, I will expect a hefty fee."

"Done."

Grimketil reached under his imperial cloak. He brought out the product of his handiwork with pride. "I could not fashion this piece nearly as well as I would have liked. Your time is short."

"I understand. Thank you. I promise you'll be properly compensated just as soon as I can."

"I'll leave you to it then. I cannot be here when you commit your crime." He laughed, turned, and faded back into the shadows.

Wade paused, daunted. He expected the homemade hypodermic to appear crude. He should have anticipated its immense weight and unwieldy disposition. Somehow he'd hoped it wouldn't be quite what it was: a viper's fang, a short lead pipe, and a screw protruding from a cork.

A couple of painful experiments proved the pipe too thick to put between his fingers like a hypodermic. Instead, he grasped it like a knife hilt as if he were preparing for a clumsy overhand stab. Wade bent the bandage at his wrist to spread it out as much as possible. With one last look to see that no one interfered, he slipped the viper's fang between the top layer of windings, wormed it in as far as it would pass, and finally relied on its point to find the rest of the way down. When the tooth bit his skin, he felt a small thrill of victory immediately followed by a frightening thought: *Did Grimketil make sure there was no venom left in the fang?*

Wade decided he couldn't afford to worry. He reached his thumb to the top of the screw head and pressed. After just a quarter of an inch, he felt resistance against the liquid. On the other end of the screw, the cork took the lead, sopping up any silver solution that wanted to go the wrong way. He could feel the thick fluid pushing under the bandages. Wade felt tension ease from his muscles.

Then he felt the resistance go out of the plunger. Wide-eyed, he watched the silver escape where pipe met fang, a second before the tooth snapped off entirely. Grimketil's solder had failed to hold the incompatible materials together. Wade could hear the footsteps of his jailer, making rounds. He had just a minute to swallow his panic, and salvage the fiasco.

Wade tipped up the pipe to preserve what he could. He put the open end up against the back of his knee and held it there by doubling back his lower leg. That brought his heel into reach. The guard loomed in sight. The man had to interrupt his gait to pull his sword.

Quickly wiping off the tip of the fang, Wade put the snake's old dental work to good use at his ankle. A feeling of royal purple confirmed that he had found the acupuncturist's spot once again. He took a breath, and pushed into honey, and then rust. He took a deeper breath, and pushed again. This time he experienced sky blue with a mix of fresh and stale air in alternating drafts. At the same time, he heard, "Hey, what have you there?" together with quick footsteps. A weak fragment of thought or memory teased at the corner of Wade's subdued mind. One phrase: *traveling on the astral plane.*

He pushed still more, and the footsteps disappeared along with the stone cell.

CHAPTER 8
Horse Thief

ONCE AGAIN, THE first breaths of fresh air overwhelmed him, even more so without the immediate threat of a man with an axe. His body responded with a surge of energy, and if not optimism, then a lessening of his pessimism.

Wade sat on the ground outdoors, again near a horse, a familiar dark brown mare. Olich was not standing next to it this time, but Wade sighed when he recognized the homemade saddle and the hitch post. *Why couldn't I have gone home instead of here? What is tying me to this place?* As if in answer, Wade felt a nagging recollection, or near-recollection of his fading dream from the dungeon. A cool powder, a boxy object with wheels, and Rotrud. The more he tried to recall, the more the fragments fled away from him, compelling him to give up.

Wade assessed his situation. He still had his bandages, and part of the stick that went from his bandages to his torso. The middle of the stick, the section most distant from any body part, had vanished. The chains had not gone with him. However, he had an iron circlet around his right wrist, and each ankle likewise had an iron cuff. In the sunlight, he could see that they were well rusted, which should help in removing them. He could feel the heavy pipe tucked warmly in the crook of his right leg despite the cold outdoor air. Wade still had no shoes, and by native standards, he had no tunic. By his own preference, he would have liked anything that served as a jacket.

Wade unbent his leg and removed the pipe carefully to avoid losing any more silver. Whether anyone sat in judgment of him or not, he needed the silver solution to prevent infection. How far behind in space and time would his pursuers be? Although he had not been blindfolded on the journey into town, the circumstances were so startling that he wasn't really sure of the distance. As for time, without Olich's presence at the site, it was obvious that Wade hadn't gone back to the moment of his first arrival. With leaves crunching underneath him, it appeared to be the same season. He couldn't tell much beyond that. Wade knew that even if Olich found him on his property, and was not overwrought by his presence, he could not again ask him what year it was.

Wade left the clearing for a stand of trees that allowed him cover from both sides. If he leaned slightly, he could spy back on the clearing without exposing himself too much. In relative quiet and safety for the first time, it occurred to him that his synesthetic senses had been largely suppressed ever since he came to Swabia. Everything was just so bizarre, he hadn't noticed. What it all meant, he couldn't guess.

His first order of business was to treat the wound. He broke Count Gerardus' seal to find the edge of the bandages, and carefully unwound them. The burn looked mottled, but not infected. It wouldn't be if he could help it. He tipped the heavy pipe so that the silver liquid distributed slowly on both sides of his hand and forearm. He saw immediately that there wouldn't be enough for more than one treatment, so he rewrapped the bandages to protect the wounded area, keeping his thumb independent from the rest. Lastly, he removed the broken seal.

He turned his attention to the iron circlets chafing his limbs. For that operation, he dug his right hand into the dirt beneath a small log. With his throbbing left hand, he scooped up a heavy rock and slammed it down on the rusted metal band. The clang came out much louder than he imagined possible. In the clearing, he could see the horse react, yanking on its tether.

The rock had produced a gap in his wristband large enough to scrape free. He shoved the pieces into the hole under the log, together with the spent pipe, and Count Gerardus' seal, and pushed the dirt back. Although he wore two more circlets, he wouldn't try the noisy trick again just yet.

He gazed around the empty clearing, and then back at the horse. He felt the need to move a great distance quickly. It was here that Wade reached his first moral dilemma. *Should I steal that horse? Is it even possible for a novice to steal a horse?* Wade had tried a bit of horseback riding before, though he was no expert. Mounting and steering without an active left arm were no problem. Would the horse cooperate?

He was relieved to see that stirrups existed, albeit long ones, which meant he would really have to stretch to get his leg over. He let the horse sniff, and then lick his hand. He stroked the horse and spoke soothingly for as long as he dared delay. Luckily, he was not a complete stranger to begin with. The equine disposition, at least among those who were accustomed to people, had not changed in the thousand plus years between Wade's time and this. Even so, it occurred to him that familiarity was more difficult without being able to call the horse by name. For now, he dubbed it Eo, after eohippus, the ancestor of horses. That reference made him smile, probably for the first time in this benighted land.

He had to undo the tether knot with his right hand alone, which took some time, and spoke of an incompetence that made the animal restless. Holding the lead in his right hand, he put his left foot in the stirrup on Eo's left side, then swung himself across, landing heavily, occasioning several skittish adjustments from the mare. The stirrups were tied up high, causing less trouble than he thought. Naturally, these people, and this horse's owner in particular were shorter than he.

Astride the horse, he wondered, *Am I changing history?* Wade gave it a little thought, and quickly dismissed the question. After everything that had happened, leaving Eo alone wouldn't save history.

Just then, Eo started moving without any conscious volition on Wade's part. He let the horse have its head because he didn't know where to go anyway. In a few yards, he saw that they were atop a commanding view where the ground fell off steeply enough to make Wade whistle through his teeth. There are at least two things, Wade knew, that could get an inexpert horseman in a great deal of trouble: speed, and steep hills. He wanted neither.

The sound of a river drew his attention, and the sight took his breath away. Down by the river was Olich with his unmistakable multi-colored dyer's apron. Beside him, Rotrud with her unmistakable…everything. Olich was either teaching her his trade, or he needed an assistant. Their attention was clearly engaged on each other.

The sound of rapids had covered Wade's approach, so the two did not spot him yet. A bit too frantically, he urged his mount away from the scene. Wade would have accepted any direction. His lack of decisiveness contributed to his problem as the horse rotated a full turn back to the position he started in. With rising panic, Wade faced the pair again, certain that they would see him now, that the motion at least, would attract them. They were engaged in animated conversation. Wade had no spurs, and both legs pointed straight out due to the length of the stirrups. He had to pull one leg up to nudge Eo with his heel, surrendering the stirrup in the process. Eo ran to the thickest tree he could find, and turned broadside to slam his inept burden into the heavy trunk. The impact drew a surprised grunt from Wade as the air went out of his lungs. He knew he couldn't take another one of those.

Eo stepped away to try again. Whatever trouble he got, Wade was grateful that he and his mount were no longer visible from the base of the hill. This time he held tight, and lifted his leg up and across, almost sidesaddle, so that the horse only hit itself into the tree. This blow was heavier than the first, almost knocking Wade off. It had to hurt the horse's ribs. This time when he urged and cajoled Eo away, he got more cooperation. The horse took off.

Although the breeze made him even colder, his newfound ability to exert a modicum of control gave Wade a charge. Eo followed a well worn trail at no more than a fast trot, so Wade concentrated on finding the stirrups again, starting with the left, which he would need for dismount. Even with his feet back in their proper place, he had less control than he thought. Eo went straight home to Olich's house.

Wade looked around, confirming his recollection that this was a forested area with no visible neighbors. Now that he was there, Wade felt desperately hungry and cold. He knew for sure that Olich was not home, and hopefully would not return home, or look for his horse in the middle of a working day. Wade carefully dismounted, hitched the horse, and ran inside.

In a kitchen window box he found dried meat and fruits, the latter of which he began to chew immediately while he looked for a large sack. He found one with a drawstring, and checked that it was not made to hold dye, before putting his bounty inside. Two gourds of ale went to join it. In another room, he was surprised to find a closet where clothing was neatly hung through the armholes on thick wooden rods that extended out and slightly upward from the wall. He slipped on a heavy tunic and a pair of shoes wider than his feet, tying them roughly at the ankle with the aid of his teeth and right hand. The closet also held leather so pungent he thought he might pass out. He avoided those. Wade tucked some lighter clothes under his bandaged arm, and fled for the front door. Maybe now Olich would understand that Wade was not after his daughter.

Wade paused at the doorway, slightly alarmed. Eo had moved around, possibly to get a better view of the road, should his master return. Seeing and hearing nothing, Wade made his break. He put the clothes in a saddlebag, and mounted up. For the sake of a quick getaway, he took the only other clear path, the one that led back to the city. He could always turn to another route later.

Wade saw nothing but trees along the rutted road, and heard nothing but birds. He had the vague idea that he was in Western Europe, and realized he did not know where. He wished he had studied birdcalls. The varieties might have given him a clue. The place names he heard so far did not mean anything to him. What's more, he had failed to ask what direction one place was from another. So even if he had a better idea where he was, he still would not know where to go, or what places to avoid. *If I end up in Aquitaine, do I then call myself Wade of Swabia?*

After what he guessed to be several miles, he found a clearing and turned off. Wade dismounted by the edge of the woods, retrieving the saddlebag, and all of his gathered food.

He said his goodbyes, and sent Eo back to Olich with a swat on her flank, knowing she would find her own way home. Which was more than he could say for himself. Recalling the words of the blocky man in his doctor's office, he thought *Wade, what kind of poisoned voodoo magic is in you?*

CHAPTER 9
Sanctuary at Sintlas Ow

WADE VENTURED INTO the woods, marking his trail by noting landmarks, and penetrating as far as he dared for fear of being lost. Although the idea of being lost on top of lost was something he couldn't explain. In one of those moments where he looked back to memorize the path he'd taken, he snagged his foot under a tree root, and his trip turned into a tumble as the ground fell away. Though his saddlebag and food sack scattered, the loss soon became the least of his worries.

Wade landed in water flowing strongly enough to begin pulling him along. He thought he could swim, but the river disagreed. His strokes kept him above water and barely allowed him to fend off protruding stones rather than push him nearer to his starting point. The distant far bank looked even less promising. An abundance of small leafy branches borne on the river bespoke a recent flood and a strengthening while the water sought equilibrium. He spied a rock where he hoped to rest, get his bearings, and maybe launch himself out. But slippery moss below the waterline made him spend even more energy trying to stay in place. Despite his shock at going from hiking to swimming for his life, he still had the capacity to be surprised when a foot appeared on the rock, and two strong arms lifted him out of the current, setting him face down on the muddy shore. Beyond his nose, a disturbed worm dived for cover.

Wade scrabbled up and faced a stranger in brown robes. The man appeared middle aged but not much softened by time.

"Thank you. I thought I was far away from the water," Wade said sheepishly.

The stranger laughed. "The Bodensee is one of the largest bodies of water in the world. You would enter another country before you would pass it in this direction. Here it is the thinnest point where it runs like a river. That may explain your confusion. But I nearly forgot my manners. I am Tankred, an oblate of the Abbey of Sintlas Ow." He bowed.

"I am Wade...of...Aquitaine." While he adopted the high-sounding name, Wade shed what was left of his dignity by shivering and sneezing.

"I was on the road coming back from Konstanz when I saw your horse run out of the clearing without its rider. With my loaded cart I had no chance of chasing it. Moreover, I knew that somewhere a thrown rider was in need of help. And here you are."

"And here I am," agreed Wade, who never expected to run into anyone so quickly.

"I will not ask you your business in Konstanz, however, I see that your arm is bandaged, and—." Wade followed Tankred's gaze down to his ankles where the iron cuffs were still in place. Wade explained things to people every day on his job. He knew that in this case, anything that didn't approximate the truth was going to sound even more outlandish than what he was about to say.

"In my travels, I wandered onto someone's land. The dispute is settled now, but my jailers lost the keys to these leg irons."

"Perhaps I can assist you with that. Meanwhile, I am headed back to the abbey. Have you a place to stay?"

Wade thought about it. His best option was to hide and stay out of trouble until he could figure out a way home. "No," he said.

"Staying outdoors in your condition is a gamble. Would you wish to stay with the monks for a few days?"

"I can do some work to pay for it," he sneezed.

"That will not necessary. We can afford to host the occasional guest in need."

Tankred made room for Wade and his belongings, or what he could find of them, on the cart's bench. With a flick of the reins, they were off on a bumpy ride in the direction of Olich's house. Wade considered jumping off. Before Wade could think of an objection, they turned off onto a road Wade had not noticed before.

After about three times the distance he had yet traveled, they arrived at a true lake, toward the westernmost part of the Bodensee, as Tankred explained. In the center sat a lush island that Tankred referred to as Reichenau. A causeway connected it to the mainland, allowing their cart to cross.

Wade did not know what to expect of a Dark Ages abbey. He tried to picture something between Olich's house and the wood walls and earthworks of Konstanz where he had been taken for trial. What he found was a cluster of buildings with brick arches and fine Roman columns arranged in patterns more elegant than anything he could have guessed.

"This is Sintlas Ow," said the oblate with a grand sweeping gesture.

"It's beautiful," Wade said in awe, not realizing he was speaking aloud.

"We take great pride."

Inside, Wade marveled at the carpeting, the plastered walls, and the art.

"To the left is a mosaic of our founder, St. Pirmin, to the right a depiction of our first great patron, Charles Martell. In the center, you see St. Benedict," Tankred beamed.

Benedictine monks, that's what they were here! Even without knowing their customs, Wade felt wonderful hearing anything that sounded remotely familiar.

Tankred led Wade on a tour of the great, dedicated spaces, allowing him to soak up the ambiance, which he knew was better than anything his guest would encounter in the surrounding country. They began in the dormitory where Tankred asked a lay brother to run ahead and announce that they had company. From there they went to the church, the chapels, the cloister, the gardens, the fraterhaus, bakehaus, brewhaus, the piggery—where Wade felt glad of his stuffy nose—and the buttery, where ale and wine were stored. Tankred lingered fondly in the buttery. Wade was to stay in the infirmary, which he would see later.

Lastly, they arrived at the Locutory, where it was proper to receive outside guests. Wade could see movement in the shadows.

"There are of course many monks here," said Tankred. "Our leader, the most humble of all, is one whom we simply call the Monk of Sintlas Ow. Before you meet him,"—and here he whispered—"Brace yourself"—before continuing. "Protocol dictates that you first meet our most prominent citizen." Wade thought this tour was attracting entirely too much attention, but could think of no reason to demur the honor if he wanted a place to stay.

After hearing a few coughs in the darkness, Wade saw a rough shape drag itself into the candlelight at Tankred's urging.

"Wade of Aquitaine," said Tankred, "here be Pepin of Aachen." The scant introduction ill prepared Wade for what he saw. The oblate indicated a man so badly stooped that his back nearly formed a second head behind his own. The way he moved, his legs must have been equally bad. This Pepin appeared to be aging with every tick of the clock. Wade noticed that Pepin snorted at the word "prominent" in Tankred's description of him.

"I'm honored," said Wade, wondering if poor Pepin were prepared for visitors, or would ever be capable of being prepared.

"Yes," said the sorry figure, flashing red-rimmed eyes, "behold Pepin the Hunchback, bastard son of Charlemagne. Pepin, disinherited at the Diet of Thionville. Pepin, disregarded in the Diviso regnorum. Are you pleased to meet me? Are you really?" Pepin was more animated and forceful in his anguish than Wade would have thought possible.

"Pepin is out of sorts at the moment," the oblate explained. "We just received news that Louis the Pious was crowned this very day to establish the line of succession. As the first born son of Charles the Great, Pepin had certain...expectations."

In case anyone didn't hear him the first time, Pepin added, "First *bastard* son. The kingdom was mine to inherit before father changed the rules. Now I'm shut up in a besotted monastery. No offence, Tankred."

"None taken," said the oblate. To Wade, he said, "You see, as an oblate I really come and go as I—"

"We were talking about me here. Not you."

"Forgive me, Pepin."

Pepin sat down resignedly, which gave his guests license to sit as well. Tankred allowed Wade to sit first. The beautifully contoured bench almost made the wood feel soft. If the monks built and sanded it themselves they must have had a lot of time.

Tankred said, "May I interest you in some fruit?' Without waiting for an answer, the oblate handed Wade a small ivory casket with high-relief carvings of biblical scenes all along the outside.

Wade was struck by a synesthetic reaction, all the more potent because he hadn't felt one in what seemed a long time. In addition to the object he held in his hands, he experienced a smooth, cold surface before his eyes, fading away in all directions, tinged with a hint of color and texture that eluded him. He shuddered.

"What is the...origin of this piece?" Wade asked.

"That was a gift to the abbey by Kreindia of Byzantium."

That name, so familiar.

"Kreindia the Strange," amended Pepin energetically. Wade felt a shiver of foreboding to discover that someone called hunchback could be prejudiced against someone else.

"Please ignore his bad mood," said Tankred.

"Fah, my bad mood. She's a heretic. It's a crime against God. You should know that."

"What makes her so strange and heretical?" asked Wade, almost afraid to hear the answer.

"She says," Pepin spit the words in disgust, "that she can taste shapes."

CHAPTER 10
Decline of Charlemagne

K REINDIA IS UNDER The Monk's protection," said the oblate. "Even you must respect that, Pepin."

Pepin shot Tankred a glance that was part defiance and part wounded pride. As Pepin knew, the feeble support he got from his father enforced local respect for him. Outside the walls of the monastery, he would be reviled even on the bottom rung of society.

"What do you mean 'she can taste shapes'?" asked Wade in the most controlled voice he could muster. He put a finger under his nose to prevent his sneezing from blotting out the answer.

Pepin warmed to the topic. "I mean that her mind reaches into another realm where natural folk never trespass. Her observations come not from our world. Such powers as that could be unbounded, dangerous to the rest of us. They are not of the Lord."

Wade listened, entranced at the Hunchback's Dark Age perspective on the condition he apparently shared with the Kreindia the Strange. It somehow provided a clearer window and nearer fit than the clinical views and descriptions he learned from modern science. He listened, too, with fear of discovery for himself. Who would protect him from accusations of heresy if his talents became known?

Pepin leaned in and continued, "One sense crosses to another sense unaccountably, wherein she dips into a pool of visions unimaginable to you or I." Maybe to *you*, thought Wade. *He is definitely talking about a synesthete. I don't want to hear anymore.*

"I think the lady is naught but a poet," offered Tankred, lightening the mood, perhaps picking up on Wade's unease. "The only thing on her tongue are the descriptive words of an eccentric."

Pepin was undeterred. "It is said that Kreindia can flavor her soup however she pleases simply by choosing a different shape or sized spoon. What does that tell you?"

"Perhaps her spoons just need to be washed," said Wade, joining in on Tankred's dismissal of the subject. Pepin smirked, and then smiled broadly, and finally released a well-bottled mirth.

The laugh temporarily transformed Pepin so that Wade could see he was probably no more than fifty. "I know I have not been very good company, and I am still restless from the day's foul news. Not a surprise to me, but even so. I will go get The Monk for you." Without waiting for farewells, Pepin the Hunchback did them the favor of leaving the room. Wade sagged in relief.

When Pepin was out of earshot, Tankred said, "The king regards all of his illegitimate sons with fondness. Oh, don't look so surprised, Wade. I know you were too polite to ask why Pepin is entitled to special courtesy. The king is the one who installed Pepin in this monastery. Pepin of Aachen enjoys a status similar to that of any deposed monarch."

"Are there many of those?"

"Yes, Desiderius, the former king of the Longobards, for example, defeated by Charles the Great, also resides in a monastery. Then, too, there is the Longobard bastard Raginpert, who fled the monastery when Desiderius was deposed. Pepin views his birthright as far more significant than that of any Longobard. The pension he receives is small consolation for his lack of inheritance. His father did change the rules, you know. In accordance with Christian values, he felt he had no choice."

Someone cleared his throat. Wade turned to the door, grateful to be saved from any expectations of comment by the appearance of a newcomer.

The oblate got to his feet quickly, so Wade copied him. He wondered how anyone recognized anyone else in the perpetual candlelit darkness.

"Wade of Aquitaine, I give you The Monk of Sintlas Ow." The Monk had black robes, a kind face, and a penetrating intelligence, evident at once.

Wade sneezed his greeting.

The Monk gestured to Wade's nose and handed him a cloth. "It is cold for the calends of September."

"Yes, it is," said Wade. Even he knew that much.

"Abnormal weather. A bad omen, if you believe in such."

Wade opened his mouth and closed it. A few days earlier, when he lived in his own time and place, Wade would have said he did not believe in omens. Today, he was not prepared to discount anything.

"Louis is crowned, though Charlemagne is not yet dead. You have traveled far to come here. What changes happen abroad? From whence you came, I know the least."

Thus far, Wade had seen very little of the middle world; his knowledge of modern America was worthless here. "Well, you know how Aquitaine is," he equivocated. "One never knows."

"It is a frontier, yes. I'm sure that with the Moorish incursions, life can be uncertain even in the best of times, let alone the current situation."

"You're concerned about the transition from one king to another," Wade probed.

The Monk appraised him with eyes that took in more than candlelight. "With the weakening of Charlemagne and his impending loss, we are in crisis. I predict that a kind of dark ages will befall the Western Empire. All manner of savage Northmen cunningly await the day."

Wade responded with the appropriate surprise; he thought he was already in the Dark Ages. He hazarded a guess. "You mean to say that things will return to the way they were before Charlemagne?"

"Yes," said the Monk with enthusiasm. "You are learned. Have you lived in a monastery before?"

"I've not had the honor. Would I be allowed to study here?"

"Our guests have full access to all but sacred relics. The need for enlightenment is a great and urgent matter."

Wade gazed at the ivory casket on the table, remembering the impact it had on him. He stretched out a trembling hand, but dared not touch it again. "What can you tell me about Kreindia?"

"Kreindia of Byzantium?" Rather than being put off, The Monk was intrigued by the change of subject. Wade could see that The Monk understood people above all else. "She is one of the finest scribes and scholars that I know."

"She's a writer?"

The Monk thought about that one for a bit. "If you mean a storyteller like Ovid or Aesop?" He shuddered. "No, no such frivolous nonsense. She works in a scriptorium. She knows her Latin and Greek, a most exceptional woman."

"What do you make of these powers she has?"

"Powers? You've been talking to Pepin. One would think he could be respectful of his neighbor's peculiarities. If Kreindia were a man, with her many valuable talents, she likely would be at the king's court beside Alcuin, if not in the royal scriptorium. In my selfishness, I would prefer to have her right here." Clearly, The Monk had hashed through these arguments before.

"But instead?"

"Instead, she is not here or in the king's court. Under my direction, she pursues her trade as best she can from a convent."

"Is her memory extraordinary?" Wade guessed.

The Monk picked up the ivory casket that so obviously interested Wade. "Yes, our Kreindia is very special. She says that her crossed senses help her to remember." The Monk appeared to look right through him. "She reminds me of you."

At that, Wade began coughing, and continued in great, powerful heaves. The coughing would not let up. When the cloth in his hand turned red, The Monk summoned a group of lay brothers to carry him away to the infirmary.

CHAPTER 11
You're Like Me

WADE COULD NOT have said whether his bed was made of hay, or sawdust, or the finest goose down. Such was the extent that he was robbed of his senses. For Wade in his turmoil, day and night rolled over each other in undistinguished fury. His earlier injuries were forgotten as they paled in comparison. Wade spent waking hours twitching, and insensate hours convulsing.

Early on, when his thoughts rose to the surface, he struggled to pass the time without losing his mind. In relatively stable moments, he demanded maps, and absorbed their contents, using his synesthetic ability to cross-reference the areas by color. Somewhere squirreled in his addled brain, he finally knew where Aquitaine was.

Forced oblivion warred with an ache to give meaning to his drastically changed, and now diminishing life. With a short attention span, he tackled books of mysterious text without conscious memory of ever opening them. The abbot, who was known as The Monk, allowed the indulgence in order to honor the extraordinary requests of a man in serious decline. However, Wade had no say when it came to dispensing meals and medicine; he ate and drank whatever his caretakers fed him, or, when fever came, nothing at all. The periods of nothing to eat grew longer and longer. He was dimly aware of fervent prayers at his bedside in the worst throes of his suffering.

All the while, his synesthesia provided him with thunder in the absence of a storm, a unique experience that belonged only to this illness. Whatever these germs of the past were, Wade had no defense against them. Though he was certain at one point or another that he saw The Monk, the oblate, and The Hunchback in turns trying to communicate with him, and arguing passionately with each other, he held his hands over his ears as if to block the titanic sounds that no one else could hear. Since the thunder was synesthetic, no amount of plugging his ears could lessen it. The wet coughing spasms returned, more intense than before. His fever became a constant heat. In his endless cycle of better and worse, worse was clearly winning.

When Wade's hopes faded, and he could no longer hold a book or a map, Pepin ushered in a priest clad in a simple black robe partially obscured by a white cloth that covered his uppermost body down almost to his elbows. Wade's vision had narrowed to a tunnel, so that he could just see a stubby German cross in red gracing the cloth's center. The priest stood over Wade administering last rites in elaborate ceremony. Wade's last view shrank to a mote, and he closed his eyes in a world of thunder with nothing left to see.

~ W ~

AMIDST the rumbling susurrations, Wade was shocked by the sudden appearance of an impossibly smooth, cold surface identical to what he had experienced when he held the ivory casket, only this time the surface boundaries stretched far into the distance. Just when the cold smoothness applied an instant balm to temper his suffering, making him think his end might be bearable, the thunder redoubled, threatening to crack the surface.

Now he saw the icy horizon pushing the darkness, racing out to infinity, even behind him, even through him, damping the sound as it went. A bizarre synesthetic battle raged, one source tearing from within, and another repairing from without.

As he struggled to see how far he could perceive, a feeling of vertigo shook his weakened frame. The thunder peeled and rumbled like a cornered beast. The finest blue powder danced in the air, shaped by the sound waves, scattered, torn, and reformed despite all manner of turbulence. The smooth relentless plain grew to engage the ragged blasts head on while the powder simply endured, its particles too small to be affected.

The enemy that robbed his health gave way. The fever, to which he had grown oblivious, began to subside, and then broke, precipitously falling back to a safe range. The thunder carried off harmlessly into the distance. His convulsions went with it.

She appeared at his bedside in charcoal grey robes with a long stole of deep forest green. Embroidered gold crosses at each end of the stole formed the only ornamentation. A white garment swaddled her neck and forehead, and a dark grey cover went on top. When his eyes cleared, she smiled, his heart leapt, and he knew he beheld Kreindia of Byzantium. Her brilliant smile was indelibly etched into his memory—powder on ice, and blue like her sparkling eyes. She was Kreindel, without the wheelchair—not someone who looked like her—someone who *was* her; his synesthetic associations did not duplicate or lie. Only this incarnation of Kreindel or Kreindia had a shining countenance that did not return to a slack cage of bodily limitation. And somehow he felt he had a connection to her that overarched his life.

She bade him sip a preparation that tasted like grapefruit, and spoke her first words, "This will help you the rest of the way."

"Do you know me," he said as a statement. In his weakened state, he tried to sit up. Her gentle fingertips were all it took to hold him back. Instead of restraint, he felt a nurturing strength. His eyes posed the question again.

"Yes, you're like me. I never knew your whole name before, Wade Linwood of Aquitaine, but somehow I knew you."

Those words: *You're like me*, in her soft musical voice, rippled through him in a visible wave. He was certain that somewhere in all his delirium, his secret must have come out.

"Quiet and rest," she admonished to his silent next question.

He parted his lips to ask more, when a metal clad man strode boldly into the room. The startling sight in the middle of a monastery—not quite like anything Wade had ever seen in pictures—was difficult to take in all at once. He looked like a half-dressed Roman soldier with the helmet of a conquistador. His chain mail shirt was short-sleeved with a long-sleeved linen emerging beneath. His midsection appeared to be without armor, but sort of a high rise set of breeches held up by suspenders. He had a short metal skirt over a longer cloth one. His knees were protected, again, only by cloth, and his open toed shoes featured leather bindings that climbed high on his ankles.

Tankred trailed close behind the soldier, apparently trying to slow him down, and not succeeding. The Monk entered the infirmary immediately after, in the unwelcome company of a second soldier that took up a post and stood silently by. He differed from his companion only by a fine pair of boots.

"Kreindia of Byzantium?" said the first soldier. "You have been summoned to Aachen by the *Abbas Palatinus*."

"The Abbot of the Palace," whispered the oblate in awe.

"What is this about?" said Kreindia.

The soldier glanced at Wade, but spoke to Kreindia. "It is fortunate that your work here is completed, as I would have been compelled to take you north regardless. The fact that you were successful in your ministrations at Sintlas Ow confirms what we already heard about your special abilities."

"What abilities?" said The Monk, trying to protect her.

The emissary from Aachen ignored the ploy, but nodded his willingness to provide the abbot with a courteous response. "After Charles the Great crowned his son, Louis the Pious, he rode out on his traditional autumn hunt in the Ardennes Forest. The game proved uncommonly elusive. In the unusual cold weather, he was felled by a cramp in his chest."

"There have been terrible rumors," said The Monk heavily.

"Like this one here," the soldier continued, indicating Wade, "the king has long been abed with fever. He is a septuagenarian. Fasting has not cured him, and we fear the worst."

"No matter who summons me, I must help one at a time," said Kreindia, crossing her arms. "I need to stay one more day to ensure that Wade does not relapse."

"The king has no time for that."

The silent soldier moved quickly to get behind Kreindia. Wade summoned every ounce of strength that he had, and managed to fall out of bed. A solid boot to his skull led him back to oblivion.

CHAPTER 12
Longobard's Revenge

B EING UNABLE TO run, Pepin caught up with all the excitement only after the soldiers had gone. His suffering eyes blinked slowly at the bedside, the first thing Wade saw.

"It's impossible for you to yet live," said The Hunchback. "Your fever went on too long, and you nearly shook your bones apart."

"Think how surprised I am," said Wade, coming fully awake.

"We gave you last rites!" Pepin yelled indignantly as if the process could not be taken back. "At the end of it all, I hear you were kicked in the head."

Gazing down, Wade noticed that a woolen blanket was drawn up to his chin as if to secure him in place. Throwing it aside, Wade rasped, "Where is she?"

"Gone to Aachen," said Tankred, as he set a tray of food and water at the bedside table.

Still irrational, Wade said, "I have to go with her."

"You're not well enough," Tankred informed him.

"Whatever it is she had me drink, I'm feeling entirely better," said Wade, gaining his feet. "Except for a headache."

"I doubt that."

As if to confirm the oblate's doubt, Wade tottered a few dizzy steps forward, and backward, tracing the wall for support.

Tankred's hand on his shoulder sat him back on the bed. Wade took a bowl of water from beside the bed, drank deeply, and splashed the rest in his face. Then he reached for whatever food was at hand, and began to chew ravenously.

"How far ahead is she?" said Wade around mouthfuls.

"Not too far to catch up if you were well. She delayed them some, saying there were essential items to gather, and preparations to make. Then she insisted she could not ride a horse, at least not for any great distance, so they took our best cart."

Wade inexplicably felt he would never see Kreindia again if he did not pursue her now. She had done too much for him, and there were too many mysteries and connections for him not to be at her side. When he finished eating to build his strength, Wade turned to Tankred. "Find me clothes, get me a blade, and strap me to a horse. I'm going after them." Wade was on his feet again, steady with determination.

"To Aachen? You have no invitation to the palace," protested Pepin.

"No, but I know exactly how to get one."

"Perhaps the cure was the kick in the head," Pepin muttered to himself.

~ W ~

WADE dressed suitably, and Tankred went with him, both of them armed, yet not much of a fighting force. He did strap Wade to the horse, with cord that could easily be untied if Wade had to dismount in a hurry.

At Wade's request, the monastery's stables lent him a spirited horse for the task, younger and far less broken in than Eo. He didn't stop to check personally if it were a mare or a stallion. He did get its name, which was Sabine, so he supposed it was again a mare. Although the stable hand had no problem saddling her, Wade had difficulty holding Sabine's attention. With a little help from Tankred, they were on their way.

They crossed the causeway and took the road to the left, traveling north. When they were past the local traffic, Wade pushed his horse with all the anxiety pent up inside him. However, when Sabine took the turns and he was forced to change speed, jolting him up and slamming him down, it quickly proved too much for Wade. Being tied in kept him from being thrown on his head, but he imagined that if he slipped down, her hoofs might make short work of him, or worse he might trip her up to fall on him.

Tankred, who was a good horseman, managed to slow him down before he fell over, saying, "This pace you attempt is sure to overtax the horses. Since we cannot be sure to obtain fresh mounts, I suggest we moderate our haste."

Wade had to agree. They settled on a pace where Wade would still gather bruises, but would keep him from rolling to Sabine's underside.

To give Wade something else to think about, Tankred said, "It's a long way to Aachen, my friend. Perhaps we can take this time to get to know each other better."

Wade smiled and nodded amiably. That kind of talk was the last thing he wanted.

"I am a wine and ale merchant," Tankred offered. "What is your trade?" It would have been a harmless question where Wade came from. In his circumstances, he'd learned, answering wrong could be fraught with danger. He tried to put together an acceptable answer that would not raise too many more questions. The silence made Tankred stare at him.

Finally, Wade said, "I lived an easy life as a servant in the house of a rich man. My master died. His sons preferred their own servants. I decided to see more of the Christian world, maybe find a center of learning. Along the way, I tried my hand at a few things." To explain his delay in answering he added, "I've been told that some of them may have been considered disreputable."

"Never mind. You found your way in search of admirable goals. Had it not been for the Abbey of Sintlas Ow, and The Monk, I too would have been wandering."

The forest grew thick. That, combined with bends in the road prevented them from seeing ahead. After what must have been two hours, the ground rose ahead of them, making Sabine and her partner breathe hard.

Tankred said, "We're making good time. At the top of the hill, the horses will need water and rest."

The pair came to the end of the rise and looked down on the valley beyond, where the trees gave way to an open plain. Well ahead, they could see a trio on a cart, two of them helmeted soldiers with a smaller, darkly robed figure between them. A stripe of green showed around her neck. Wade felt a giddy surge of joy beyond what might be explained by his having ridden well, or might have been relief that she was not out of reach.

Wade and Tankred were preparing to dismount when they saw that Kreindia and her escorts on the plain were facing a dozen colorful and well-armed men on horseback coming from the opposite direction. The large party bid the king's men halt. The new group quickly surrounded and disarmed them, except for Kreindia, who had no weapon.

One among the raider's number had long hair, the sign of royalty.

"They ride under the banner of the Count of Pavia," said Tankred incredulously. "That's Raginpert and his men."

"The deposed Longobard?" said Wade, repeating what he'd heard. "What gives him the authority to accost the king's men?"

Before Tankred could answer, both of Kreindia's escorts were simultaneously put to the sword. Horrified, she watched them fall. The bloody swords were next pointed at her, but not used. They were for compulsion, to transfer her to their custody.

Raginpert's triumphant shout carried to the hill. "You'll aid no Frankish kings today, Byzantine witch! I'm placing you under arrest for heresy!"

Wade lifted and snapped the reins. Tankred moved too, catching up and grabbing the reins out of Wade's hands to bring his horse to heel. "Come to your senses, man! You and I alone cannot stop Raginpert by force. You couldn't even fight one soldier. You're no help to her if you are dead."

Wade had no illusions that he was immortal. "Then what am I supposed to do?"

"Raginpert must try her here in the local country. Come back to the Abbey with me," he frowned thoughtfully. "The Monk will know what to do."

CHAPTER 13
Hope Lies to The East

WADE MADE SURE Pepin was not around when he told his tale about Kreindia being arrested for heresy. The embittered king's son might have seen it as vindication of his own theories about her, and Wade didn't want to see the hunchback's victory dance.

When Wade revealed what little he knew, The Monk breathed a heavy sigh. "My worst fears are coming true. Back in 4726 *Anno Mundi,* or you might say, 774 *Anno Domini*—well before you were born, I should think…?"

Wade readily acknowledged that it was before he was born whatever system was used to measure it.

"Well," The Monk continued, "I believe I know what is behind all this. Back when Charlemagne took the great walled city of Pavia, he declared himself King of the Longobards, a kingdom within his empire, just as Aquitaine is a lesser kingdom as well. In doing so, he made new enemies both in Pavia and Constantinople."

"Raginpert can't be old enough to remember it either."

"Raginpert The Insolent, they call him, and, no he would not remember it first-hand. In addition to him, there are other rebellious factions that may join his uprising. Forty odd years is nothing in the memory of a lost country."

Wade rubbed his sore arm through the bandages. "How

did Charlemagne make enemies all the way to the east in Constantinople by fighting the Longobards near here?"

"The Byzantine king Justin II wanted to be the one to defeat the Longobards. And then Tiberius II after him, the entire Heraclian Dynasty after that, and so on for two centuries. It was never going to happen. But even so…"

Wade gulped hard. He had learned a few things about The Monk on his ride with Tankred. The reputation of the monastery and this abbot's power had gained steadily over the years. Rome first named him a Deacon, and then a Bishop. Wade had no choice but to bring what was bothering him out into the open. "Sir, as a Bishop in the Catholic Church, where do you stand on Kreindia's…skills?"

"As a Bishop in the church, her abilities are heresy, plain and simple. As a thinking man…there are things on Earth that you and I do not understand. I am dedicated to learning all of His works for the greater understanding of Creation."

Wade let that sink in. Then he said, "How do we gain control over the situation with Kreindia?"

"By recognizing that this crisis is not only about Kreindia. Any plan we formulate must take the full picture into account. Enemies from without will ravage every border of the empire. Even in the interior, in the most secure of lands, old scores will be settled. Unless and until Louis can demonstrate the extent to which he is in control, the strongest local influences will press their luck. For us, that means Pavia."

The Monk paced to stimulate his thinking. "Just as Charlemagne was protector of the Papal State, this place shall require a protector now."

"How did Charlemagne build strength for this abbey in the first place?" asked Wade.

"His grandfather, Charles The Hammer, became our first patron. When Charlemagne wiped out the barbarian Avars, he gained the city of Annau, and with it, the greatest treasure of gold ever known. The Avars were not so much a people, but a confederation of heathen bands that engaged in no livelihood save plunder, so they were rich beyond imagining. Even after every triumphant prince, duke, and count tallied their personal rewards from that victory, the royal coffers overflowed with unprecedented wealth. One portion Charles generously conferred to us."

"Does the abbey retain power in our current circumstances?"

"We will be sorely challenged, though I promise you, we will take action. I need to gather our resources. There is time for you to rest. You will need every ounce of strength for your mission."

His audience over, Wade was settled in the dormitory. With his initial burst of adrenalin subsided, he felt every bit like someone who had been cut, burned, starved, and kicked. Nothing he could do prevented him from falling into a long, almost comatose sleep. That didn't stop the dreams from coming, more like a series of images, disjointed like shadowed premonitions.

Sunset on the blades of double headed axe. Manacles chafing his hands. A vertical wall of water reaching up to the clouds, ending in mist.

Just as Wade began to awaken, in the half-dream state, he experienced a flash of blue powder. Even though he had an enormous task ahead of him, he struggled to hold on to the delicate balance of conscious and unconscious, hoping to learn the powder's significance, but it was gone.

~ *W* ~

THE oblate had a hot meal rich in meat prepared for Wade, who proved to have a strong appetite. Without further ado, he ushered him in to see The Monk. Wade found the master of Sintlas Ow very busily securing a large batch of scrolls spread out on his desk.

"Tankred tells me that you have a plan," said Wade.

"I do," said The Monk. "For the time being, we will legally transfer most of the Avar gold from the name of the abbey into your name. Here is some to take with you." The Monk produced a heavy pouch.

Wade's mouth dropped open. "What would I do with it?"

"In this manner, we will solve two problems at one stroke. First, we will prevent Raginpert from immediately seizing our gold as an asset of the kingdom in dispute. And second, you will finance your mission. Much of the gold is still in the form of Avar coins. You will travel to the south and east, as a thegn, and my agent to appeal to Leo The Armenian for protection of the monastic properties and its people, including Kreindia. Since Kreindia is a Byzantine, that will give you the opening you need. I, in the meantime, will travel west to appeal to Louis the Pious, and the Duke of Frijuli, who is Raginpert's rival."

"I've studied the maps," said Wade. "I have to choose between several routes to Constantinople."

"Yes, and every one of them will be exceedingly dangerous now. Many tribes have already tried to take advantage during the past few years of Charlemagne's decline. When word of his eventual fate spreads, every pagan tribe in Europe, Asia, and Africa will be at arms."

"From what direction will they come?"

The question brought a sardonic smile to The Monk's lips. "If you fancy a short answer you should ask from whence they will not come. Murderous Danes will rush in from the north after their fashion of hit and run attacks. If you instead choose a coastal route, you will meet with Aghlabid pirates from the south. In a middle route through the Balkans, you must engage Bulgars, and possibly Slavs, who spread from the east with a vengeance. And that is at the least of what I foresee."

Surrounded. "Why don't I go west with you? Surely the king's own son would be our best ally."

The Monk shook his head. "Louis continues his seat of government from Aquitaine. There they would know you as low born, and pay you no respect. Besides, I know Louis. He is not his father. He is not one-tenth of his father. The only real hope for civilization...is Byzantium."

"I don't suppose there is any hope of raising an army?"

"No army we could raise would overcome the disadvantage of attracting the attention of the inevitable larger armies abroad. Your only chance of slipping through the countryside is to go with a single experienced hand, and gain allies as you can. You will require the services of someone who is at once a fierce warrior and at the same time a man of letters who may guide you in matters low and high. Therefore I have hired you a most qualified traveling companion known to me from Lowestoft, to ensure your safekeeping. And here, I see he arrives."

A man of letters? Wade looked in the direction The Monk had turned. His hair stood on end at the sight.

In the doorway stood a very large, dangerous looking man burdened with chain mail and weaponry, with a disproportionately short Roman chalmys about his shoulders. His other distinguishing characteristics were a great red and white forked beard, and his scowling, withered assistant, whom The Monk did not bother mentioning.

"Now Wade, I give you over to the care of The Saxon," said The Monk. "Godspeed."

CHAPTER 14
Disaster at Aachen

"I DO NOT LIKE to be called The Saxon," Grimketil shouted to The Monk's retreating back. "And not Forkbeard either."

The Saxon. Wade wondered if it would be safer to stand his ground or to run while the old warrior had his attention divided. Wade could just imagine the kind of pandemonium his strange disappearance caused at the prison. How much would the bounty hunter suffer the consequences?

When Snorri came near, Wade ducked away, only to be grabbed firmly by Grimketil. "Let me see that arm." Not waiting for an objection, he rapidly uncoiled Wade's bandages. Carefully appraising the distinctive ripples, whorls, and ridges of scarred tissue, he snorted his approval. "You won't be needing these wrappings any longer. My silver solution did a fine job."

"And I thank you for it," said Wade, grateful for the neutral subject.

Then Grimketil pulled Wade all the way up close. "When Count Gerardus and Bishop Egidio heard you were missing, they pardoned you," Grimketil said in disbelief.

Wade said, "I wouldn't have guessed that was an option."

"Cowards!" the Saxon barked. "They are trying to curry favor with the king-to-be, and protect their interests in Ravenna at the same time. Admission of incompetence would not recommend them well."

"It ended happily," said Wade. Snorri sniffed his disagreement.

The Saxon narrowed his eyes at Wade. "I thought you might have bribed the guard with the silver to get away. Apparently you did not. So how did you escape?"

Grimketil never let go of Wade's burned arm as he spoke, giving Wade the impression he might break it if he didn't get the answers he wanted. The parched Snorri raised his nose up, equally interested in the answer.

"The chains were rusty," said Wade. "And the guards weren't very attentive." That was the truth, as far as it went. Sticking to some of the facts helped the bluff along.

"Hmm. Not a very satisfying answer."

"Oh, I'm sorry. I'll try to have a more entertaining story for you the next time my hand is boiled!"

"You are a bit more bold then the first time we met," Grimketil commented approvingly. "Now you owe me a fee for my services plus the fine I had to pay for losing you." He let go of Wade's arm.

Wade counted five gold Avar coins into Grimketil's palm, which was outstretched as soon as he saw Wade reach into his pocket. "Will this be enough?" Snorri's eyes over his shoulder were wide.

"Just about. Try one more...there we go. You pay in Avar gold like the monastery," said the discerning Grimketil. "If you have more of that, it will come in handy on our journey."

~ W ~

WHILE Snorri laid in provisions for the trip, Grimketil and Wade retired to the Locutory. Wade considered the possible life and death decisions of their route, based on his study of the maps and what he learned from The Monk. As best he could, he found it helped to overlay a mental map of modern Europe onto the map in front of him, which he based on the shape of the coast. They were starting out on the Bodensee, which he now knew wrapped around them and the city of Konstanz in what would one day be known as southwestern Germany. The lake would probably straddle the meeting point of the future Germany, Switzerland and Austria. The Monk, on his way to Aquitaine, would be venturing to the Southwest of France, via the top of Italy. For Wade, more of Germany, then Austria, Yugoslavia, Bulgaria, and finally Greece lay ahead to the east and south on the way to Constantinople. Even in this world, his memory remained sharp.

"Grimketil," said Wade, "we have to decide on a route. I take it you've been to the southeast and know what to expect."

The Saxon pulled at the two icicle points of his beard for reassurance. "That I have been, Wade of Aquitaine, but the idea of knowing what to expect in distant lands is not exactly possible in these times. Since I have never encountered Aghlabid pirates, it is best we do not encounter them now, so that keeps us from sailing or hugging the beaches of the southern coast. Since I know the Danes all too well, we would not want to skirt around to the north to meet them either. As for the middle path, the Bulgars are abroad because their old oppressors, the Avars, have been put down. Their anger extends to the gates of Constantinople as well. Just recently, they killed the emperor Nicephorus, and made his skull into a drinking cup. Our best chance is to pass among them where they run thinnest."

Those sobering comments about enemies in all directions shook Wade out of the fantasy that he would stroll through quaint old Europe, and possibly even enjoy the scenery.

The Monk entered, out of breath and disheveled. He had his hood, which he wore down when indoors, askew, and one sandal half laced. "Our time to rest has come and gone. We must do any further planning on the run."

"What happened?" asked Wade.

"I have word that Charlemagne has died."

"Who knows about it?" Grimketil seethed.

"The news will not spread from anyone at Sintlas Ow, but nonetheless it will be common knowledge soon, impossible to keep. The roads will clog with refugees in the initial panic. We must leave now."

"Without the king's illness as an excuse, Raginpert will no longer have a reason to hold Kreindia," Wade said hopefully.

"Raginpert will no longer have his *first* reason," The Monk corrected. "His hand will actually be strengthened by a trial that demonstrates the corruption of the Carolinian line."

"Charles' line," Wade offered, "with Louis in succession."

"Yes." The Monk didn't have to articulate that evidence of corruption might include bringing in a Byzantine witch.

Wade would not leave just yet. An awful feeling caressed his spine. "What will keep Raginpert from quickly trying and executing her while I'm gone?"

"The *missi dominici*," said the Monk, "part of a system put in place under Charlemagne that will not easily fade away. Until Raginpert gets a greater following, he can only go so far. The *missi dominici* will travel to Konstanz to try to ensure fair treatment. Representatives of the empire will no longer have absolute say in these matters, but fear of Byzantium will do the rest for him. Raginpert dares not take any action that cannot be undone while Leo's resolve is unknown to him. You must get to Leo's court before Raginpert's men do."

And find a foolproof way to convince him, thought Wade.

CHAPTER 15
Skirmish at Bodensee

EVEN THOUGH WADE may not have been equal to the horse before, he still requested Sabine. A good horse was a good horse. He needed no strapping in this time, although he found it considerably more difficult to mount, failing at the first effort, outfitted as he was with chain mail, helmet, long sword, short sword, boots, and spurs. Despite the dearth of mirrors, Wade thought he must look much like one of the king's soldiers, or even better. The monastery, it seemed, was well prepared for war.

A stable hand offered him a stool, probably thinking his attempts to mount looked pathetic. Wade waved him off. There wouldn't be any stools where he was going. On his second attempt at mounting, he pushed hard against the ground with his right foot, and put more strength to stiffen his left leg in the stirrup. He hit the saddle very nearly upright. In his triumph he didn't worry that the muscles in his left thigh were bunched and sore. The secret lay in being consistent from the start rather than trying a belated increase in effort halfway through the motion.

Sabine started slightly from the impact and whinnied as he struggled for balance. When he felt settled, Wade made that wet clicking sound that gently urges a horse to begin walking. Or at least, that was what he thought it did.

As he left the stable, Wade was surprised to meet Tankred, dressed in the same manner as he, the fit more exact. "Are you coming with us?"

"Proudly," said the oblate, sounding less sure than his choice of words.

"I assumed you had your business to tend to in the buttery."

"I am pledged to aid monastery and king. I have no doubt that someone in the court of Louis is drawing up a capitulary this very moment to draft such as me into service. If nothing else, I can supply the wine and ale." He looked resigned, if not enthusiastic. His outfit, where it crossed to metal, had little shine as if he had tucked it away somewhere from a previous campaign, or perhaps had never seriously provided for its use.

The group, now four, mustered in the damp courtyard as the sun rose. Wade examined his small company in turn. Grimketil, his eyes on fire, never more alive; Snorri, as unreadable as a sheaf of sandpaper; and Tankred, heavy with obligation. As they trotted the length of Reichenau Island, and the long causeway to the mainland, Wade felt charged up and uneasy at the same time.

An eerie quiet had settled on the road to Sintlas Ow as though the country around them were sheathed in a wet cloth. No sound could be heard save that of the company; every hoof landing, twig snap, and cold breath were magnified to echo off the dense forest on either side. Wade had never seen woods like this. Even in the strongest daylight, and the broadest path, the sun never completely held sway. *How much of this will be swept away in my time?* he wondered.

Their first decision involved crossing or otherwise getting around the Bodensee, which was forked, and longer than it was wide. Since they were near the crux of the fork, going around meant half a day's hard riding in the wrong direction, north and west, and another half a day's journey in reverse. Going through the body of water meant fording the narrowest point, where the bridge had washed out. No matter how skittish the horses might be at that juncture, Grimketil would not allow a day wasted. Their future, through hostile territory—which all the empire might be by now—promised sufficient delays of its own.

Beyond his knowledge of the maps, Wade had been this way before when Tankred first plucked him out of the water's wash. And previous to that he'd seen a portion of it on the road near Olich's house. This thin local neck of the Bodensee included the town of Konstanz where Raginpert had likely taken Kreindia. Wade longed to clash with her captors in a head-on assault.

"We shall not enter into Konstanz," said Grimketil firmly, as if reading Wade's thoughts, or his transparent expression.

"But how will we—"

"I've already had a rider confirm for us that Kreindia is inside."

Now Wade wanted to enter the city walls more than ever.

"That detour will accomplish nothing," said Grimketil, "and will only slow us down. Do you understand? In these matters, I am in charge."

Wade looked at the formidable Saxon for a long moment before replying. "Yes, I understand."

They rode in the company of their own thoughts until Wade said, "Grimketil, what will the *missi dominici* do when they get here? How will they enforce their will to protect Kreindia?"

Tankred shook himself awake at that. "Lèse-majesté," he said emphatically.

"I don't understand."

"One authority will travel to Konstanz with a small force to oversee the courtroom. Another will go to Pavia and install himself and his retinue in the count's house at the count's expense. His word is law. Any resistance is treason. Any attack on the person of a *missus* is considered the same as an attack on the royal person, and is punishable by immediate death without trial."

"Will it work that way even now? Even during the transition to a lesser king?"

Tankred's silence and troubled face were answer enough. Grimketil didn't look his way at all.

None of them had to be clouded with dark thoughts for long as they all heard the clear ringing of sword on sword. The city walls were just in sight. The sound, however, came from the direction of a path that turned off the main road, and led to the water crossing they sought. Grimketil charged ahead first, closely followed by Snorri, well attuned to his master. Wade drew in his heels. The spurs, which he didn't have before, did more than he expected. Sabine leaped after the others, and Tankred brought up the rear.

The trees gave way to the busy neck of the Bodensee where a confusing mass of horses and men roiled the waters in a bitter clash. At the center, Wade saw a wagon with two able men attempting to fend off four.

"They've been ambushed," Grimketil shouted, charging into the fray.

Too late, they witnessed a defender run through to the hilt. The other lost a finger, but managed to hold onto his sword.

Grimketil took on two by himself, hacking them to bits by turns, his arm describing two loops in the air like the sign of infinity. Wade got the impression he might have taken on two more opponents if they were nearby.

Snorri moved toward the other side of the wagon, striking with speed and accuracy. Wade mentally filed that fact while he chose the same side of the wagon to fight on. Wade accidentally drew his short sword when he meant to draw the long one. Before he could do anything about it, an attacker's horse reared up when Snorri finished off its rider. The horse fell against Sabine and Wade, panicking Sabine, and knocking Wade into the water.

Tankred, just arriving, hauled him out of the drink once again, and helped him remount. Neither of them saw anyone within reach to fight. While all of them were occupied, a small man with a face like a hatchet had broken off, and now rode for the trees. They just about discerned him disappear into the forest in the direction of Konstanz.

Wade turned in time to see Grimketil's foes drop like butchered meat. He couldn't believe how quickly the violence began, and how quickly men were dead; how swiftly the rapids carried off their blood. Wade's hands trembled at what he witnessed.

The survivor on the wagon had his left armpit clamped hard over his wounded right hand to stop the blood. "I recognized the one who got away," he said bitterly. "With the hatchet face, it's Ratpald. He works for a Longobard dog named Raginpert, one of the last Longobards to retain a position of power in their precious Pavia."

"Then we made a grave mistake in letting him live," pronounced Grimketil.

"He got one of my caskets, too. Half of the taxes that were going to Aachen!"

"This Ratpald is the one we're racing to Constantinople?" asked Wade as he produced bandages for the wounded man. He had them at the ready, thinking that by past experience he would need them sooner than anyone.

"Probably," said Grimketil. "My guess is that Ratpald is trying to gather gifts for Byzantium, things he cannot, or would not finance from his own pocket. Byzantium, as we too will find, is not easily impressed."

CHAPTER 16
Intruder in Camp

"THANK YOU ALL FOR saving my hide, and what is left of the imperial property. I am Odalman," said the wounded tax collector, still applying pressure to his hand. He indicated his deceased partner with a tilt of his head, "His name was Karl." The party introduced themselves.

Wade could see that Odalman was probably chosen for his profession due to his simple and inconspicuous nature. His average face and plain attire in brown and beige gave nothing away. Wade found it difficult to spot the chain mail hidden underneath his tunic. Someone would have to have known about him and his route to intercept him carefully picking his way through the shallows of the Bodensee. Wade frowned in the direction that Odalman and Karl had come; the way he himself had to go.

When Odalman saw Wade anxiously eyeing the south bank, he said, "I have to get to Aachen to swear a complaint against our attackers, and, well, paperwork for Karl. Will some of you come with me into Konstanz? I can pay you for the detour."

Grimketil said, "That is a foolish idea. If you recognized Ratpald, and he, you, then a search party will soon return. He cannot afford to let you live."

"Not let me live? I work for the royal treasury. Ratpald

will find his eye cut out for his offense! If we find a witness to another day's thievery, the court will have his nose as well."

Wade noticed that thievery in these parts seemed to be the greater crime than manslaughter, which went unmentioned. In this way, he also learned some of the other punishments available for things worse than trespassing. It brought a whole new meaning to the whimsical phrase *I got your nose.*

The Saxon was shaking his head. "I don't think so. Charles the Great is dead," Grimketil said to Odalman's widening eyes. "The law will not be reliable now. Ratpald will guess that you may have the news, so he will probably split his party to try to intercept you either on the road to Aachen, or routes toward the new seat of government in Aquitaine."

"If there is no longer any punishment for killing a tax collector, I might as well drown myself right here," Odalman lamented.

"You have another choice,' said Grimketil. "You may ride south and east with us to the end of the Bodensee, and then turn north, rounding the far side of the lake, and confounding your pursuers."

"Where will I go from there?"

"It's Louis who holds the empire's treasury, so you may wish to turn west."

"It is a good plan for me. Are you certain I will not get in your way?"

"Anyone who can hold onto his sword while losing a finger is more than welcome among us."

"What is your errand?"

"We're on a mission from the Abbey at Sintlas Ow to Constantinople to seek protection for Christian lands against a breakdown of order within the empire, and heathen incursions from all sides," Tankred answered.

"And to seek protection for one of our own threatened by Raginpert," added Wade to make sure no one forgot Kreindia.

Odalman said simply, "Your authority is as strong as mine. We have to bury Karl first. The five of us can do it quickly."

They buried him with his possessions, and the oblate said a few words. Then they unhitched Odalman's horses from the wagon so that he could ride one directly, and use the other as a packhorse for the second tax casket and extra supplies from Karl. They had to hurry to put some distance between themselves and the scene. Although Ratpald needed to gather men and materials to cover north and west bound routes, he would also be back to the same spot to clean up what evidence he could of his crimes. If Ratpald found his victim again, he would insure the odds were much more in his favor.

~ W ~

A DAY of hard riding followed by two days at a sustainable pace brought them nearly to the far end of the lake, where they planned to part with Odalman. Well-supplied, they avoided the tiny villages along the way. The five were encamped for the night on Wade's guard duty watch when the attackers struck.

Deep in his solitary forced wakefulness, Wade watched the fall leaves constantly detaching and swirling to the ground. He could have been observing nature's venerable cycle in any century at all. When he looked away from camp to watch the firelight dance on the trees, he could imagine he was on an innocent camping trip. A very extended camping trip, with life and death choices to be made. *Wade Linwood of Aquitaine*, he mused, *halfway between what I am and what I was, borrowing the name of a place I may never see.*

The signal, a birdcall, inconspicuously joined the other sounds of night. Then came twin movements in the underbrush, too large for any bird.

Wade made the same mistake of reaching for his short sword when he really wanted to keep his attackers at the greatest distance possible. Only now the short sword was gone, and he wasted precious time grasping at empty space where the hilt should have been. He never understood what use a short weapon could be anyway. At the same time, he cried out to raise the alarm.

Fortunately for Wade, the intruders had well-defined roles. One, moved not to engage, but to block him, while the other stabbed through the center of the sleeping form on the ground. None others came. When Wade drew his long sword, the first melted back into the woods, while the second took on the next opponent. Unfortunately for the second, the next opponent was Grimketil, who had positioned himself near the decoy. Only half up, Grimketil impaled the man from below in a ghastly moonlit thrust. As bad as it looked, Grimketil knew how to be mercifully fatal.

By now the whole camp was up. Odalman was armed. Even Tankred held a weapon. Snorri did them one better, and stalked the perimeter, sniffing at every noise.

The Saxon lifted the limp man by a clasp on his tunic so that Tankred could see it. "Yes," Tankred agreed, "he wears Longobard ornaments. No doubt he was pledged to the house of Raginpert." Odalman stared at the carnage and the ripped decoy that could have been him.

Once again, Wade found the violent episode and the

cessation of violence startling in its rapidity. A few impulsive decisions made with deadly weapons, and everyone's fortune changed.

"They were mere scouts," said Grimketil. "One tried his luck with Ratpald's prey while the other saved himself to report back." He looked at Wade. "Don't worry. He gave you no chance to engage."

"Even so, I might have been quicker. And I should have gone after him."

"Never leave the camp at night. There could have been many more, and he could have drawn you out of the fight while the rest attacked. No, you did your sentry duty well."

Odalman stirred their campfire, looking grim. "Knowing where I am now, Ratpald will guess the plan for me to take the road on the far side of the lake. He probably won't chase us. By the time that scout finds him and tells him where I am, he might be as much as eight days behind. But if he waits for me to go back north, he can take me at the fork. Only if I stay with you, can I be safe for a time and choose another way back."

"Stay with us," Grimketil confirmed as he meticulously wiped his sword on the clothes of the dead man, first one side, then the other. "But understand that we are now on the edge of Bavaria. You might not find a safe way back. None of us might."

CHAPTER 17
Incident Near Pavia

ALTHOUGH WADE'S WATCH had not ended, and no one from Ratpald's group was likely to attack again, Grimketil prudently took over, resetting the decoy, and stoking the fire in preparation for defense. Ordinary bandits would always be a threat.

Wade sat at his bedroll. How many times had Grimketil saved his life now? How many more times on this journey would his presence make all the difference in the world? Wade's trepidation about the Saxon leading the expedition had evaporated entirely. The Monk had chosen well. It struck Wade that he was beginning to think of Grimketil as a kind of father figure. What a bizarre thought that a fork-bearded ninth century barbarian-turned-Christian-scholar could bring out these kinds of feelings. Somehow, human relationships endured in similar fashion across cultures and over the millennia.

Grimketil, thankfully, was entirely unlike his real father. His father had always been distracted, erratic, and unpredictable. The worst part was the deception. Allen Linwood required a whole trove of lies to account for where had been or had not been. When Wade was twelve, his father abandoned the family entirely, never to be seen again.

Wade studied Grimketil on his sentry patrol. When no animal disturbed the underbrush, he moved his head to scan the forest at a glacial pace, no more noticeable than the trek of the moon across the sky. When he changed positions to cover another corner of the camp, he nudged the bushes to cover his footfalls and travel like a gently moving breeze. Regardless of the circumstances, his vigilance never lessened. Perhaps it wasn't so odd to think of him as Wade did. Pride, protection, and dependability: absent in one man, abundant in another. Grimketil was the sort of father Wade wished he had.

While the adrenaline rush would keep Wade awake for a while longer, the same was true for any of them. Tankred, Odalman, and even Snorri had gone to lie down with their eyes open, listening to the crickets with suspicion. Vigilance burns calories, however, and as there was no eating on guard duty, Wade grew hungry now. He reached into his saddlebag to see what he had, and came upon dried foods he was beginning to recognize, together with an unexpected sheet of parchment. At first he thought it might be a kind of wrapping paper to keep a thinly sliced food fresh. When he unfolded the parchment, he saw ink; a letter in fact, signed Kreindia of Byzantium in an elaborate flourish. His heart leapt. He carried it over to the fire, careful not to get too close.

"Dear Wade, You are ill as I write this. I have complete confidence you will recover soon, and go on to do great deeds. This confidence comes by the strength of knowing you forever from my dreams. Each time you appear to me as a smooth, polished surface made up of Linden wood together with the color of forest green. It is bundled up with a feeling of momentousness, and happiness. I wear the green stole in your honor. Never have you come in person, until now. I know you are not from Aquitaine. You are not from anywhere. You belong to time..."

A thrill of fear, excitement, and revelation shot through him. This fellow synesthete experienced a synesthetic sense impossibly duplicated from dreams to reality. A sense impossibly based on a person. Neither of those things could happen, except that similar things had already happened to him, in his case across a gap of more than a thousand years. Wade reeled, alive to the shock, numb to the implications. *You belong to time.* Kreindia must have placed the note in his saddlebag as the king's men tried to take her to Aachen. The parchment held more, but Wade's heart could not pound any harder. His trembling fingers refolded the letter and placed it deep in the compartment from which it came. He walked stiffly back to his place in the camp. There he sat down, leaned back, and fell insensate into a fog of exhaustion too thick and void of energy to allow the production of a single image or dream.

~ W ~

WADE couldn't remember having fallen asleep when he felt the nudge of Grimketil's boot lifting his elbow, and saw red rays of sunlight in the eastern sky. He would have sworn his unconsciousness lasted no more a second, yet he had the feeling that comes with a few hours of just about slipping into the deepest level of sleep, and being robbed of the rest. He moved like a startled rabbit to reassure himself that the parchment sat where he placed it. He found it deep in the saddlebag, and stroked its textured surface for reassurance. Still, he felt the terrible regret of missing something in Kreindia's message or his situation that he should have understood.

She was blue ice; he was green Linden wood, like his name, Linwood. That was bizarre in itself. They shared things unknown even to other synesthetes. All of that was eerie enough for him, even in the light of day. Yet there was some other major connection between them that he failed to see, something beyond her words in the letter. If only he had more sleep.

They broke camp, obliterating it as well as possible, and mounted up like any previous day, only a shade more wary. Wade felt a growing fondness for Sabine as she responded to him better each day. He took the time to feed her by hand, talk softly, and stroke her nose, which he found as calming for himself as for her.

Wade noted that their road turned nearly due east, into the rising sun. Other than that, the heavy woods continued, unabated, and unbroken but for the signs of a minor village avoided by the group every few hours so as not to be seen. When they no longer had the lake water to draw from, they found meandering streams in the unspoiled forest. Without their mission, Wade would have felt a great sense of peace.

"What's so special about Bavaria?" Wade asked abruptly. While he tried to be careful that his manner of speech would not appear strange, he did not always succeed.

Grimketil stared at Wade through narrowed eyes. "It is a border kingdom, always under near-threat, only now we must add in unrest due to the demise of a king people have known all their lives. What troubles me more is that Raginpert would have guessed that Kreindia would have defenders from The Monk on down."

"He would not dare enter the monastery," Tankred protested, still sure of something.

"Correct, he had to wait until she left its protection to capture her. And then he had to draw the rest of us out. You see, his man Ratpald has proven very thorough thus far. Now we travel past the general direction of Pavia, in Itale, which sits below this narrow strip of Bavaria. We can easily avoid Pavia itself, but Ratpald could have more men coming up from the vicinity. We need a scout of our own."

"I'll do it," said Odalman. "I owe you that much, and I cannot be a great help wielding a sword left-handed or holding it through my bandages."

"Good man," said Tankred, admiring his courage.

Snorri added some noncommittal noise that could have included a warning, while Grimketil just nodded and said, "Very well, then. Backtrack our trail a short way to see if anyone follows, and then return to us to report. Do not go anywhere else yet."

Snorri took charge of the packhorse, and Odalman rode off pleased that he had a job to perform.

Grimketil immediately slowed the party, presumably to give Odalman a chance to catch up easily. When their new scout was cleanly out of sight, Wade asked, "Grimketil, did you give him that task to raise his spirits? There really isn't anything behind us, is there?"

"Odalman should make himself useful, yes. More importantly, I want to make sure our retreat is not blocked."

"Why?"

"Because there is trouble ahead." He drew his sword and pointed with it.

Finally, Wade realized that birds and small animals rushed toward them in greater than average numbers, as if fleeing a disturbance. In a few more strides, the disturbance was upon them.

CHAPTER 18
Sooner To Pannonia

G RIMKETIL BROUGHT THE company to a full stop at the revolting sight of someone clad in fur swinging from a tree, writhing in agony.

No, Wade saw it was a bear, a dead one, and the carcass moved from a hail of stones. He still felt queasy. Tossing the stones were ten laughing men scattered across the road. Beyond them, they had a small clearing set up as a camp. Their horses were left tied up in batches, bumping each other in a dance of restless agitation. The one that stood broadside showed bulging ribs and a poverty line tracing his haunches.

"Longobards," warned Tankred with a sneer of revulsion.

One came toward them and shouted, "We have seen you, and you have seen our sign. I killed that animal in hand-to-hand combat. Now you must understand that nothing gets by us on this road unless it pays the toll."

Judging by their various states of inebriation, this group had waited a long time to say that. The one who spoke staggered closer, causing a medallion to sway loosely at his neck.

"How much is the toll?" Grimketil asked as he eased a hand toward a two-headed axe.

"The toll is everything you have. And you had best be lucky enough to satisfy us."

"And if we don't submit, or don't have enough to satisfy your tastes?"

"Then we make better signs out of *you*." He and his fellows joined in raucous laughter.

"Are you the leader?" asked Tankred, getting the attention of the one who approached.

"I am your lord and master," he replied with a slight bow. "When you have no possessions left, I shall allow you to lick the road from the bottom of my shoe." He glanced over his shoulder to soak up the appreciation of his peers. A couple of them lifted a sloppy mug as though matching him in a toast.

"Then perhaps you would like to begin with ale," said the oblate, drawing a bottle from his pack.

The man smiled and eagerly reached for it. Tankred swung the ceramic bottle cleanly down on his head, shattering the bottle and dropping him to the ground. The body traced half a dirt angel from a convulsive twitch.

His companions expressed outrage, and drew whatever weapons were close at hand. Snorri circled behind them. The Longobard group outnumbered Wade and his companions better than two to one, and worse, with Wade inexperienced in this kind of fight. He knew that even Grimketil and Snorri should not be taking on this many.

The marauders stopped talking, and began to close ranks on foot when Odalman rode up to Grimketil, coming to a hard stop in a dusty cloud. "There is a group coming up behind us," he said. "I know not who."

"Then we go forward. Snorri?" Snorri cut the rope for three encamped horses tied up next to each other and sent them running frantically with the flat of his blade.

"Go!" Grimketil shouted to his people as he charged through a knot of Longobards. His horse—three quarters of a ton on the move—took down the first. One of their own horses claimed a second victim. As he went, the angry Saxon swung his axe from one side to the other, inflicting maximum damage on glancing contact with exposed fingers or necks. His last stroke, straight down, found someone's femoral artery.

A thug without a weapon tried to cling to Wade's leg. Wade was able to kick the drunk down. He suffered a momentary fright when some cloth caught in his stirrup and pulled free with a yank, leaving him with a tattered banner flying from his side. Snorri buried a knife in someone's shoulder, cursing when he couldn't get it back. The rest of the company galloped at high speed through the clearing, regaining the road where it continued into the woods. Wade looked back to see a few men stumbling toward their mounts. One sank to his knees holding his throat. The tortured bear swung high above.

Grimketil caught up with his friends under the shade of the trees. "Our head start may not hold. Their horses are rested, and ours are not. The men, however, are dazzled from too much wine. At a narrow place, we shall turn and fight, and finish them off."

"Wait," said Odalman, holding up a hand to slow them. "It is not necessary. I know that clearing we passed. There is another road coming up if we turn off into the woods right... here."

Odalman brought his horse to a careful trot, picked his way between the trees on a hidden footpath, and proceeded down a gentle slope. The others went single file behind him. Gradually, they descended out of sight of the road while a thundering of hoofs passed by.

After a few thousand yards, they did indeed emerge on another highway, narrower than the first, and less well traveled. They joined it where it bent around the base of a great hill, which brought it close to their original path at a lower altitude before it veered more to the south.

"This road takes us sooner to Pannonia," Grimketil observed.

"Is that good?" asked Wade.

"It is good if you are a Bulgar. For everyone else, the danger increases for every mile passed. Ere long, no road will be safe."

"You call that road we came from safe?"

"A safe road is one you can ride away from," said Grimketil. Wade had no more questions.

They had their midday meal quietly, rested, and moved on, traveling in this way for three more days. Each night, Wade had dreams with hints of Kreindia in human or symbolic form. Somehow he would not or could allow them to fully take shape. And he could not face the truth of the parchment, Kreindia's mystic vision that he was not from anywhere. He wrote it off as poetic.

The unseasonably cold weather moderated, making the going easier. Departing from the road when necessary to avoid the towns, they came upon the occasional farmer's field, and did some trading. The trades were greatly in their favor as information itself had become the most valued commodity. At the same time, they did not meet one marauding soul. Wade reflected that they had gone perhaps sixty miles unmolested. Those who took over the Bavarian highway were more likely common thieves than Ratpald's men. In any event, the road squatters never caught up with them. Wade began to think that Grimketil was wrong about the breakdown of society, and the danger of the borderlands. Aside from a few resentful Longobards, the ninth century countryside appeared to be sleeping. It made sense. The life of a rural peasant probably didn't change no matter who sat on the throne in distant Aachen.

When the forest thinned and the road turned due east again, Grimketil decided it was time to abandon the road entirely. Soon after they went south, the trees gave way to vistas of rolling green hills, great conical blue hills beyond, and rivers everywhere. Sparkling blue rivers, slate gray rivers, amazing emerald green rivers, and swirling beds of white waters moving shallow and fast. Fall had not yet claimed this region of beauty. The warmth felt good to Wade. He longed for the opportunity to fully bathe rather than employ the perfunctory wash Grimketil limited them to for the sake of safety. Of all of them he believed he felt the deprivation most.

The land yielded one astonishing sight after another. Watermills, boats, and timeless stonework of all varieties. Great paved highways, finely carved monuments to gods, and impossibly high walls of stone for mysterious purposes. "Left by Romans," Grimketil said, in the only comment he would utter.

Soon they came upon a pristine lake, fed by an astonishing ninety-foot waterfall, with reeds and ducks nearby. Sight of the far bank proved it much smaller than the Bodensee, but still impressive by Wade's standards.

"We're due for a stop," Wade said to Grimketil. "I'm dying to bathe."

"Unarmed?" said Grimketil skeptically.

"If we don't," said Wade, "it won't matter how well we hide. Our smell will attract attention." Tankred and Odalman expressed similar sentiments.

Grimketil nodded, and surveyed their surroundings. They had a good line of sight to the mountains, unobstructed by trees, with no one in sight. "I know this place. Pliva Fall. It looks fairly safe," he admitted. "Even so, we go one at a time."

Wade went first, shedding his elaborate medieval layers on the bank, and wading in to get a closer look at the waterfall. The aerated water caressed him like the most delicate masseuse. Although it may have been the contrast to days of want, Wade felt sure nothing like this water flowed anywhere. Just a few steps in, he stopped to rub his feet and legs, peeling away layers of road dirt that belonged to two countries and a span of hundreds of miles. He shuddered and went further. The deeper water flowed cool, but not cold. Wade dived all the way in, and went toward the object of his curiosity, stopping before the churning water became too powerful to resist.

Near the base of the waterfall, looking up, the top appeared to vanish in the clouds overhead. The bottom generated a constant wall of mist. The unknown but familiar sight in the strange land stuck Wade with realization. *I've seen this place before in my dreams. There must be something very significant about it.*

Out of the mist, a single rising reed caught Wade's attention. As the reed rose, a face became visible in the water, brown, with almond shaped eyes. The reed fell away, and two strong hands came up to grab Wade about the neck, while something that felt solid as a log swept his legs out from under him. In a moment, the assailant had Wade's head submerged. Wade fought against arms like iron.

~ W ~

THOSE on the bank saw Wade under attack. Before they could move a yard, they witnessed dozens of other hollow breathing reeds rise up and cast off, revealing an army of fantastic brown and olive-skinned warriors to block the path of any rescuers. Lacquered leather rectangles hung from them in rows like shingles. Small shields affixed at the elbow half hid their arms. The one who drowned Wade wore more elaborate attire including a jewel-studded cap. Nearly as large as Grimketil himself, while the others were smaller than average men, this one had to be their leader.

Grimketil came quickest, followed by the others, all dashing into the water. They found themselves blocked by rows of spear points. They could not hope to fight through in time, if ever. Grimketil saw Wade surface briefly, as the leader divided his attention. Then the assailant forced him under again. The army, seeing their advantage, pressed forward.

Grimketil reached into his pouch, and threw two gold coins toward the man that held Wade beneath the churning froth. The large man paused to grab the coins out of the air one-handed, and having caught them, stared at them both with bitter longing.

CHAPTER 19
Avar Encampment

THE DARK SOLDIER suddenly released Wade, allowing him to up sputtering and coughing. When Wade's eyes cleared, he saw his assailant holding a piece of Avar gold, treating it tenderly like a lost child come home. In his other hand, he held a coin with the likeness of Charles The Great clad in his royal cloak and laurel crown. He looked at the second with something more akin to respect.

"Hold," said the warrior to his troops. "We cannot kill them. Their monarch is all that keeps us from falling under the Bulgar swine."

For the first time, Wade saw the eerie heads, shoulders, and ropy arms of armored warriors planted in the water with their weapons like gnarled cypress roots in a swamp. They lowered their spears almost in unison.

To Wade's modern perspective, the one who attacked him had the eyes of an oriental and the skin of an East Indian. His long moustache and jewel-crusted costume distinguished him from the rest. He gestured for Wade to go to shore. Wade saw that Grimketil and the others had waded in waist deep. All emerged fully from the water, and reconvened dripping on the bank.

"I am Abraham Khagan," claimed their leader. Grimketil and Tankred exchanged a look of surprise. Snorri tried to sniff around Abraham until a phalanx of shields and spears brought him up short.

"Your command of the Frankish tongue is excellent," Grimketil replied.

"I speak many languages."

"Are you Huns?"

"No! You are in Pannonia, the Khanate of Avar!"

"I know this land is called Pannonia," Grimketil averred. "I thought all the Avar had been destroyed. Never were they foot soldiers. Rarely were they this far west. If you are an Avar, where is your lance? Where is your horse?"

Abraham's shoulders sagged. "Horses are in short supply. Our lances have been replaced with these crude spears. I am the last of the khagans." He cast his eyes down. "I fear that no kapkhagan will ever follow me."

Grimketil turned to Wade to explain. "What he refers to, used to mean kings and princes among his kind, when they existed."

"I do exist!"

"An Avar called Abraham?"

"Yes, it is true that Abraham is a strange name for an Avar. I was born Arghun-Boke, the name my people call me still. I was a kapkhagan when my father and brothers were killed in the war. When nearly all we had was gone, I went before Charles the Great. I took the name of one of the people of The Book, and accepted baptism to gain protection. Your protection so far has not been worth much. We must shamefully run and hide."

"Are these all of your number?" Grimketil gestured at the assembly that encircled them.

"Except for a couple of women and children, and a few forward scouts, yes, it might be. We think another band separated from us is still alive and we search for them." His voice held little hope of it, as he seemed to forget who was listening. "Capturing you today demonstrates our prowess. Your king of the Franks is a worthy conqueror. It took a force of Franks, Saxons, Frisians, Thuringians, and Bavarians to defeat us. Now the unworthy Bulgars mop us up whenever they think the government in Aachen is not watching."

The last comment again made Grimketil and Tankred exchange a look, this one troubled. "Do you think Aachen is not watching now?" Grimketil asked Abraham.

"I think now we must take all precautions as we are so few."

"We are on a mission to speak with our friends who rule the Greek empire. We need a guide through Bulgar territory who can keep us south of the Danube while staying well away from the coast."

Abraham just stared.

"It will give you a chance to spy on your enemies, and—" he put a hand on Wade's shoulder,"—we can pay."

"You pay in Avar gold?"

"Yes."

"First, I keep the coins you gave me."

"Yes."

"I shall come with you for fifty more of purely Avar gold, provided you meet one added condition."

"What are your terms?"

"That in the field of battle you call me Arghun-Boke." He was absolutely serious.

The Saxon smiled. He admired the way Arghun-Boke thought. He turned to Wade. "You owe me two coins, and while you are about it, pay our new friend as well."

Wade nodded to Grimketil, and boldly stepped up to the Avar leader. He dipped into his pouch, and counted out twenty-five coins. "You get half now, and you earn the other half later," he said to Arghun-Boke, making the Saxon smile again. He liked how Wade thought too.

~ W ~

THAT night they made camp among the Avars in a place where two old Roman walls stood parallel, north and south of them for protection, with rubble strewn openings at either side to the east and west, which afforded them easy access, and escape. They needed no fire in the warm night.

Trees and bushes dotted the surrounding landscape. Sentries stood under cover in the nearby fields, and traveled back within the walls to report, and find relief. Arghun-Boke insisted that only his Avars were stealthy enough for the task. On this, the only occasion where Wade heard Grimketil loudly declare himself a Saxon, he demanded that he and Snorri have a turn at the sentry posts. Grimketil of Lowestoft got his way.

Wade demanded nothing of the kind, looking forward to his first night of unbroken sleep. His companions stayed together, a camp within a camp. Ranged around him were Tankred, Odalman, and Snorri. Grimketil, on first watch, was absent for the time. Wade put his saddlebag beside him, and allowed the pleasant evening to carry him off. Briefly, his old wounds troubled him as the day's other concerns were forgotten. In moments, however, he was breathing steadily. Absorbing the sight of Pliva Falls at the critical moment when Arghun-Boke tried to drown him—the vision from his dreams—unlocked more dreams.

Kreindia, the concept, appeared to him first as an unfurling carpet of fine blue powder racing into the darkness, and consolidating into a smooth, cold plane as it went. Joining her, he experienced the impossible feeling of spreading out with her in every direction. The open plane turned into Kreindia the person, beaming happily at Wade in the only outfit in which he had seen her clad, in her colors of charcoal and forest green.

"What is happening?" he asked.

"I'm well," she said, tenderly taking his hand in hers. In the joining, their hands seemed to melt together, a sensation soaring with joy.

"I'm so glad to see you," said Wade. "What is going on back there? Can you tell me?"

"The Count's first plan was to drag me by horse through the town square. Since your departure and evasion, Raginpert has treated me very carefully for fear of retribution if you should reach help. He knows not if Louis will care what happens to the woman who failed his father, or what reception you will get in the southeast. Beware, for he takes measures to counter you. I have to go now."

Having conveyed her message, Kreindia dissolved away in a trickle of blue dust.

Wade shook himself awake with the first light of sun, and rushed to his saddlebag, not only ready, but eager to learn the contents of Kreindia's letter. He knew the exact location within the bag. There he encountered dried meats and fruits, one half eaten, the way he left it, but he felt nothing resembling paper. In other compartments, he pulled out flasks of wine, ale, and water, as well as rope and a knife. Desperately, he turned the bag upside down and shook it, emptying everything on the ground, including his coins. He looked back into the naked spaces with growing panic.

Kreindia's irreplaceable parchment was gone.

CHAPTER 20
Dissent In The Ranks

WADE'S THRASHING BROUGHT everyone fully awake, including both Grimketil and Snorri, having returned from their watches.

"What stirs you, my friend?" Tankred inquired of Wade.

"My parchment, a letter from Kreindia, it's gone. I checked on it every night, including last night. I secured it in my saddlebag, and now it's gone." He could not help but stare at Snorri as he spoke.

"I have no interest in you." *Snorri could speak!* His voice was an unused rasp. "Ask the Avars what happened to it."

Grimketil said, "No, we must not accuse the Avars of anything, and I vouch for Snorri. He would not do it."

"The Avar have goats with them," Odalman suggested. "They eat anything."

"A goat would have woken me up," Wade replied testily.

"Why is the letter important?" asked Odalman.

"A man can be greatly cheered carrying a woman's letter," said Tankred in Wade's defense. "Was there anything in particular about it?" he asked Wade. "Perfume?"

"No perfume. The problem is, I never read all of it."

"Foolish!" rasped Snorri through his sorely chapped lips.

"Perhaps he was saving it," said Tankred. "Were you saving it, Wade?"

"Something like that."

Tankred sighed, "It's a long road. I can let you look at one of my old letters, if you like."

"No, thank you."

Snorri gave a healthy snort. "I lost my best knife in a Longobard's shoulder. You don't hear *me* crying to the world about it."

Wade didn't want to make too much of it out loud. He couldn't even explain the extent of his distress over the loss, the improbable idea that his very existence could be explained on that parchment. And the possibility that the secret was gone with Kreindia, whom he might never see again. He banished the last thought as quickly as it came. His brief joining with Kreindia felt nearly as real and solid to him in the light of day as it did in the dream.

As he repacked the saddlebag with elaborate care, Wade reflected on who the other suspects could be, if not the suddenly vocal Snorri. He really didn't know Odalman very well. He trusted Grimketil and Tankred. Although, between Saxons and Swabians, and all the new cultures he encountered, he could not be sure of how anyone's motives worked.

In the light of day, Wade could see that the Avar had tens of more warriors then he saw at Pliva. Perhaps Arghun-Boke felt the need to conceal his strength, modest as it was, or perhaps the Avar kaghan was a bit of a liar. The rest of the Avar were a complete mystery. One lingered ominously nearby, and appeared to be gritting his teeth at Wade.

Why would an Avar take the parchment and leave behind the precious coins?

Wade's eyes had passed over Kreindia's words when he looked for the signature at the bottom. As a synesthete, could his brain have absorbed what his eyes only glanced at? He could visualize something. All he could remember from the balance of the page were the words, "By the time you read this…"

"Get ready to travel," barked Grimketil.

~ W ~

INSTEAD of the day warming to the sun, clouds rolled onto the horizon, and winds presaged a change of season. The travelers assembled around the morning cooking fire, and searched their packs for suitable morsels.

The Avar kaghan noticed Wade staring forlornly at the food he had kicked in the dirt while searching for his parchment. The rest were not much better off.

"For a price, you may all share a meal with us," said Arghun-Boke to the group. "We need to earn money to pay your king his tribute."

"What are you having?" asked Grimketil.

"Sheldrake. Caught this morning."

From the smell of it, Wade felt nearly certain sheldrake must have been a kind of duck. From the many bodies of water in the area, he was not surprised.

"We need fresh food, and also supplies," said Grimketil, who had smelled it too. "We'll buy it."

Wade found the duck mouth watering, and the fresh protein invigorating. He saw his companions enjoying it as much as he did. Most of the Avar kept their eyes down, but some appeared to resent the presence of strangers in their midst. For something else to look at, Wade checked the sky again. The clouds had rolled closer, and seemed to push the air ahead as they went. The cooking fire guttered, unattended, and was allowed to go out.

After they breakfasted, the group headed toward the horses, and what looked like a party to send them off. Quickly, they were surrounded. A cocky young Avar led the group that barred their way, leaning into the wind. Although they did not raise their weapons, even the kaghan found himself blocked, face to face with the offender.

Seeing this, Arghun-Boke said, "Step aside, Qorchi-Negan."

Wade recognized the upstart as the same one who lingered near their camp at dawn. The man said, "Hear me, Arghun-Boke Kaghan. Hear me, all. Our leader should not leave us. Guiding the Frankish conquerors through Bulgar territory will only anger the Bulgars if you are caught. They will torture our location out of you, and all will suffer the consequences. Behold, even the skies disagree with you. I say we sell them to Krum. We will get much more than fifty paltry coins. Perhaps we will win his protection."

A second rank of Avars standing further back nodded their assent. Qorchi-Negan seemed to have some support. No one went so far as to cheer.

"Who is Krum?" Wade asked Grimketil.

Grimketil mimed tipping a cup to his lips.

"He's an alcoholic?"

"No! He is the Bulgar khan who beheaded Nicephorus at the battle of Pliska, and turned his skull into a cup." In his ire, Grimketil somehow managed to keep his voice down.

"I guess it doesn't pay to be Nicephorus," Wade muttered.

For the benefit of everyone watching, Arghun-Boke asked, "Qorchi-Negan, suppose I gave you all of the gold for yourself? Would that be fair? Would that satisfy you?"

The rebel thought for a moment, and slowly smiled. "Yes."

Arghun-Boke dealt Qorchi-Negan a blow to his windpipe that made him sink to his knees, unable to breathe. The rebel held his throat with one hand and clawed the ground with the other. As glad as Wade felt not to be sold to Krum Khan, he was shocked at the raw violence the Avar leader was capable of, and awed at his level of skill. He could see why this kaghan survived all the others.

"That was the wrong answer," yelled Arghun-Boke to the upstart, and then to the crowd. "You all live to satisfy me, not I, you. If any oppose me, they may join Qorchi in the kingdom of Erlik-Khagan."

Grimketil informed Wade, "Erlik-Khagan is their god of death."

The group supporting Qorchi-Negan scattered, and quickly found other business to tend to. Some belatedly hid their faces. Two stepped up, and dragged the thrashing man away.

Arghun-Boke turned to Grimketil. "Although our numbers are few, I still must maintain order. Even more so as we dwindle."

Now they reached the horses and began to saddle up. The temperature had dropped several degrees from sunrise to the end of breakfast and their brief dispute.

"I see you have an extra horse," said Arghun-Boke, indicating Sabine, "I will take this one."

"Sabine is not part of the deal," Wade protested.

"Let him have the horse," commanded Grimketil. "He must scout around us. He will need the best horse." Wade felt an irrational pang from the small betrayal. However, after the confrontation between Arghun-Boke and Qorchi-Negan, he knew that the Avar had gone easy on him at Pliva Falls. He was not about to challenge the barbarian.

The Avar hopped on without benefit of stirrups, and executed a stately turn.

Arghun-Boke, part of a breed of legendary horsemen, clearly felt more confident astride a mount. And what's more, Sabine apparently liked him better than Wade. "From here onwards," said Arghun-Boke into the stiffening wind, "life will not be so comfortable as you have come to expect."

CHAPTER 21
Change of Plans

AMERCILESS RAIN came to Pannonia. Despite the prelude of powerful winds, nothing prepared the riders for the sudden downpour, followed by the painful pelting of hailstones. The Avar, with his metal helmet and visor, fared best.

In the first vicious peal of thunder, Wade thought he might fall right off his horse, a mount he knew only as "packhorse." How it burned Wade to see the Avar so comfortable on Sabine! Wade looked for some scrap of leather to protect his face, but found none. He alternated holding his hands above his eyes to form an awning. Neither hand lasted long, especially as he needed one to mind the reins and the other to protect his kidneys. He tried burying his face in the horse's mane, but then his neck got it too. The three stallions and two mares must have wondered why their riders were so crazy as to not seek shelter.

The group stayed together for safety, and rode no more than two abreast. They could barely see each other even at that. Arghun-Boke led the way on Sabine, graceful through adversity, followed by Wade and Grimketil, Tankred with Odalman, and Snorri covering the rear. Although they did not encounter a Bulgar or anyone at all on the morning's journey, Wade knew by now that danger or death had no compunctions about surprising its hapless victims. Were the Bulgar dumb enough to be out in this weather? How would he even know what a Bulgar looked like?

Wade shouted to Grimketil, "Shouldn't we be getting under cover somewhere?"

"And where would that be in this open plain? You see where we are. Arghun-Boke knows where we are going."

Grimketil had slipped lower in the pecking order, and therefore Wade too. Wade wondered about the barbarian they entrusted their lives to. His actions depended on whether he feared Charlemagne or Krum more. Or possibly whether he loved money more. Wasn't "Avar" the root of the word avarice? Were they all being led into a trap, some kind of medieval dark alley? Human nature, whether you measured it a thousand years ago or today, did not change. It's never been truer, thought Wade. On this trip, a thousand years ago *is* today.

After what seemed an eternity, they came to a sturdy wooden structure largely hidden by overgrowth. From a distance, only the Avar knew where to go, like a wolf to its hidden den. You followed the wolf by invitation only, thought Wade.

Seeing the wood rather than stone, Wade did not count the building as part of the Roman's legacy, which made him wonder who to thank, aside from his maker, for the blessed relief. Geographically, the handiwork did not seem likely to come from the kinsmen of anyone in present company.

Once their host lit candles, the interior turned out to be much bigger than anyone could have guessed, including a suite of stables, their first stop. Wade's packhorse refused to slow, finding her own way, and neighing loudly in the comforting shelter as if to say it's about time. If the stalls smelled of recent horses, it was hard to for Wade to discern under the odor of their own wet horses.

"Your Charles the Great built this space to store provisions during the war," Arghun-Boke explained. "The best thing the Franks did for us was to add a few places to hide from our next enemy. Of course, if not for them we would not have needed to hide," he said, his grudge not entirely faded. Again, Wade wondered if it were wise to follow him.

The sun, if it could be seen, would have shown them midday. Wade's stomach confirmed that. Arghun-Boke cooked them sheldrake leftovers, the smell of which made Wade's mouth water, probably the last nearly fresh food they would see in a while. If this turned out to be a trap, Wade would step into it well fed.

Grimketil dug in quickest as though he were accustomed to protecting his food from roving hyenas. Everyone was on notice and didn't look his way again. Snorri entered into the meal most cautiously, and then took it in a few occasional gulps like a frog. Tankred carefully pulled out a set of utensils that Wade envied. Fastidious as he could be, he also ate with gusto. Perhaps they all knew that eating could be a luxury that wouldn't always come around. Odalman happily licked his fingers, although his mood suddenly turned downcast when he arrived at the missing one. Wade did the best he could.

As they ate, Wade hoped to find out what kind of a man Arghun-Boke was. The Avar had an enormous appetite, having eaten as he cooked, and now snapping at everything with crocodile jaws. Not knowing what would be a proper time, Wade simply jumped in. "Arghun-Boke, what happened to Qorchi-Negan?"

"After I killed him? By now, the dogs in camp will have feasted on him."

Wade stopped eating. He felt sick. Grimketil gave Wade

a stare of warning, but he missed it. "Don't you think you already proved your point by killing him?"

The kaghan frowned in contemplation. "We do it that way for safety."

Grimketil waved a futile hand to ward off Wade's next question. Wade asked, "How is that for safety?"

"By custom, we would deposit him on the plain north of camp with all his possessions. All the beasts used to eat our departed there. But placing two corpses at a time attracted too many, and began to give our position away to the Bulgar."

Wade's head swam. "You always leave people above ground for animals to get them?" He thought about it some more. "Two corpses at a time?"

"Certainly. A man's most precious possession is his wife. If you were married, you would know that. People must not be very romantic where you come from."

Wade kept himself from being sick, or at least postponed it, concentrating on the sleet battering their wooden shelter. "Wait, you didn't order Qorchi's wife killed, did you?"

"No, of course not," Arghun-Boke said, pausing to take a mouthful of sheldrake, "Qorchi-Negan did not deserve that honor."

~ W ~

THE rapidly moving storm cleared out, cutting short their rest stop. The Avar kaghan knew all of the back roads, which was no small accomplishment when your foes controlled the highways, and your other choice was carving your own trail through the wilderness. Where there were no trees, he knew how to use hills as cover. Where they had to stop, he knew every abandoned structure that could afford them shelter. With the elements in high gear, shelter could mean the difference between arriving at your destination, and perishing of pneumonia. He obviously enjoyed moving more quickly and less conspicuously than he could with an army. Even so, Wade could not believe how much more expansive the Pannonian plain was than it looked on a map. Although they moved somewhat in the direction of mountains to the south, the peaks never seemed any closer.

As the days grew shorter and colder, it seemed to Wade that the Sun fled the darkness while the party chased toward it at greater and greater speeds. Another blanket of night pulled over their heads while the distant fiery chariot raced to some safe corner they would never reach.

When Wade bedded down for the evening, he took special precautions, pulling everything he valued inside his sleeping roll. Although he now owned nothing that all the others didn't have, the loss of his parchment made him wary. If Qorchi-Negan took Kreindia's letter, Wade would never see it again. He got a nasty image in his head, of the camp's dogs, finished with the Avar traitor, chewing his parchment for sport. He forced himself to believe that someone would have stopped them although he knew it wasn't true.

For Wade, settling in for the night allowed action to give way to reflection, processing that he desperately needed. Nonetheless, it contributed to a feeling of being very much alone. Being cut off by millennia from everything he ever knew made him alone in more ways than any human being should naturally be. What was going on back in the world he came from? Did his disappearance cause a stir, or did time stand still, patiently awaiting his return or demise?

Wade did not so much fall asleep as he did sink into unconsciousness like quicksand. For hours, it seemed, he did nothing but slip and claw and fight against a place he did not want to go. In this kind of sleep, he grew increasingly tired instead of less. When his energy to fight ran out, he found himself in an unfamiliar chamber where he stood before a vaguely familiar prince.

"Tell me about Wade of Aquitaine, witch" said the prince. It was Raginpert, whom he'd only seen from a distance. Close up, his royal finery dazzled the eye.

"I don't know this Wade," he heard himself saying in a high voice. "He was someone in need of care." Wade looked down and saw the charcoal robe and green stole. He saw through Kreindia's eyes. "All that passed his lips was incoherent."

Raginpert drew his dagger to contemplate its bejeweled hilt. "You know more than I do, and probably more than you're saying. I don't like fighting a mystery."

"This trifle would not trouble you," Kreindia retorted, "but for the fact that you are idle, awaiting word from Byzantium, from whence I am protected."

Raginpert flushed red, and loosed the dagger at her feet to strike point down in the floorboards. "You shall not be protected if the fate of you and your friends is never known."

SWIFT movement inside their enclosure woke Wade, cutting off Kreindia's reply. Grimketil favored the last watch, so he could rouse everyone in time to prepare to move before the Avar came back from scouting. All broke camp and mounted up.

When Arghun-Boke returned from patrol, he said, "The Bulgars are on the move. We go north to get around them." The Avar kaghan began to ride away, as he was used to his orders being followed.

"No, wait," Grimketil called after him, extending his arm to the side to reassert his control of the rest of the party. "North is too dangerous."

Arghun-Boke turned Sabine around as easily as the Avar would turn on foot. His face revealed neither irritation nor indulgence. "We are already cut off to our east. The Bulgars are moving into lands they have not claimed previously. They have settled in great numbers on the course we take. Either we go north before moving east again or we must wait several days in hope that they move on."

"We stay below the Danube," Grimketil reminded him.

"Yes, that is our agreement."

Grimketil thought for a long moment. "Very well," he said grudgingly. With this scant acknowledgement, the Avar rode north ahead of them.

"You're troubled," Wade said to Grimketil, as they stared at the dust left behind.

"Yes."

"Can you elaborate?"

"No, nothing has changed to my knowledge since last we laid it out. This more northerly route still troubles me."

"I thought your concerns had to do with people on the far side of the Danube."

Grimketil blinked slowly, the closest he came to a sigh. "Alas, things with legs don't stay where you put them."

"These northerners, don't they fear the wrath of Charles?"

"Oh, they fear Charles the Great as much as the next heathen."

"So what makes the Danes any more dangerous than the Avars or the Bulgars?"

"The Danes act exactly as they please at all times since they have a motherland to retreat to."

From there Grimketil lapsed into a long silence as though he were brooding over the unsettling change in plans.

~ W ~

WADE was not at all certain he could have kept the trail without Grimketil's guidance after Arghun-Boke left their sight. Even without hail to trouble them, they fell into the pattern that served them well the day before with Grimketil beside but slightly ahead of Wade, Tankred paired to Odalman, and Snorri the last. Wade thought of falling back to join the better conversationalists, yet he choose not to. Suddenly the pecking order and his place in it, seemed very important.

They rode into a warmer day than the one before. Watching the night's frost turn to melt water on the trail gave Wade an innocent occupation, almost careless, and less alert than he should have been.

Beyond a stand of trees, a great obstruction blocked their path. Wade stopped and stared. He wondered, not for the first time, whether or not he was sane.

In front of them stood a green pyramid.

CHAPTER 22
The Kingdom of Hell

TO BE EXACT, Wade saw a very distinct pyramid shape rising thousands of feet in the air, and covered by a blanket of soil and vegetation but for one pale corner peeking out. There were actually bushes growing on the sides. More than a hill and not quite a mountain, it was a bizarre hill-pyramid, or possibly a ziggurat, if he could remember precisely what that was. From the position of the sun, Wade saw that the sides faced the four corners of the compass. He would be willing to bet it was a perfect north, east, south, and west. The ancients loved that kind of precision. A second, smaller, or more distant, pyramid was tucked behind. Each had a flat top and symmetrical platforms that could have been stairs running up the center of each face. Together, they framed the entrance to a valley much like Egypt's Valley of Kings. The Aztec style of building made it even stranger.

Had he made another jump in time and space, this time to Africa or South America? He looked around to see if all or any of his companions were still with him. All were present and looked curious save for Arghun-Boke, who had brought them there. Their guide looked not at the spectacle, but at their surroundings, trying to peer through to hidden dangers.

When they got closer, it appeared as though the flat-sided mountain before them bore a grievous wound, baring raw bone just where it turned in a vertical set of knuckles. The cleared portion described a slice as tall as a man. Someone had been excavating the site, dragging out its true man-made nature of cut stone upon stone. From the shallow edges of the dig, and the precarious purchase of existing roots, Wade could see why nothing so large as a tree grew on pyramid hill. Nature hadn't covered it deep enough yet.

"The gateway is as I left it," declared Arghun-Boke. "Welcome to Visocica."

"Do you understand what that is?" Wade asked Arghun-Boke, indicating the pyramid under the hill. He noticed then that the surrounding area was unnaturally clear and flat as though pavement hid beneath the dirt. Perhaps an entire ancient city slept under their feet.

The Avar mistook his incredulity for fear. "Yes, it is well that you hesitate, for this is the private entrance of Yamaharadja, who together with his sister Yamí, rule the Kingdom of Hell. Endless torment and agony await those who trespass."

"Do you believe that?" said Wade, who had seen enough to wonder whether anything called a gateway to another place should be dismissed as myth.

"I believe everything I say. I repeat the rumor as often as possible in order to keep my enemies far away from Visocica. I am the one who peeled it back to show the stone corner."

Arghun-Boke hurried forward, disappearing behind the other side of the artifact he called Visocica.

To Grimketil's surprise, Wade moved more quickly than anyone else to follow. Around the bend, surprises kept coming. The Avar rode up to a gap at the base of the structure, twenty yards of roughly horizontal darkness under a spill of vines. Enormous red stone serpent heads with jaws agape and tongues extended glared wickedly on either side. The space between, with some of the rock collapsed like giant teeth, gave the impression of a hideous crooked maw.

Arghun-Boke said, "For those who doubt the evil nature of these works, any can see that there is no entrance to the building above, only tunnels that lead straight down into the Earth."

If there were ever a candidate for the gates of Hell, Wade thought this place qualified.

Arghun-Boke ducked beneath the vines, then vanished between two of the stone teeth with Wade following close on Sabine's tail. Wade could not see what Arghun-Boke did to light the first torch, but at the second, the Avar pulled a lever that brought two striking surfaces together—what Wade supposed were flint—in a spark like a giant cigarette lighter. In the illumination, he could see a ceiling low enough to foster claustrophobia even though the space was wide. The interior walls were composed of much smaller bricks rather than the stone he saw outside. Alcoves every few feet stood empty. Looted, thought Wade.

"We'll make camp in the safety of the depths," said Arghun-Boke. They dismounted, tied the horses to metal rings as they saw the Avar do, and continued on foot. From there, the narrowing hall led them down and down into more darkness. The sinuous curve of the walls as they lit the flickering lights reminded Wade of natural caverns. Dank air seasoned with limestone pushed up at them, and tiny deposits made stalactite daggers in the ceiling.

"Who really built this temple or whatever it is?" Wade asked Arghun-Boke as he pulled a strike plate lever just visible by the light of the previous torch.

"I believe Visocica was constructed by the Illyrian people, long gone, but not forgotten. They were killed by Slavs before the Avar arrived." He sounded wistful with regret. Wade couldn't tell if the regret was having missed meeting the Illyrians or having missed killing them.

Once again Wade appreciated how little he knew of the past. He wondered if anyone from the twenty first century knew about European pyramids. Arghun-Boke led them down sometimes steep slopes, and sometimes deep steps, further evidence that man had commandeered natural caverns for his own uses. Once Wade's eyes adjusted, he saw that not every treasure was gone. The paintings were never stolen off the walls, because they were painted directly on the walls. Wade was surprised to see images of peacocks and parrots, along with detailed scenes of small figures and obscure symbols, playing out the legends of their time. Aside from Wade, only Odalman was vocal about his delight. The taxman's passion belied his ordinary appearance.

The other's silence could have been awe or disbelief, but by the looks of them, it was not disinterest. It may have been the darkness and torchlight but Arghun-Boke looked more intense than usual, almost grim. He would have seen it all before.

Wade grew concerned as he tried to keep track of their turns through tunnels both natural and man-made, past chambers and shafts reconstructed and repurposed over the years. Wade didn't mind exploring if someone knew the way out, although he did not understand why they had bypassed spaces that seemed perfectly good for stopping. Ahead, Wade saw the largest chamber yet, which he suspected as their destination. If so, it was odd that the Avar should choose a place intersected by several open tunnels. Too many entrances to defend. It couldn't be a desire for ventilation on Arghun-Boke's part; the Illyrians had peppered the pyramid with airshafts, keeping the air only moderately stale. Just as they passed a small side chamber, Grimketil stopped.

"We go no further," said Grimketil, planting his feet in a solid stance. Perhaps, like Wade, he became uneasy about Arghun-Boke leading them. The Avar picking their path through the hills was one thing; being at a disadvantage inside a labyrinth was quite another.

"But we are almost there," said Arghun-Boke.

"Almost where?" said Grimketil, drawing his axe. His voice was loaded with suspicion.

"Damn you. Cooperate," said the Avar kaghan in his imperial command voice. He spoke to Snorri, who answered by advancing with a sword.

Then, as though he addressed the dim path ahead, Arghun-Boke shouted, "Come now."

Wade heard the clanging of armor and pounding of feet before he saw the warriors pour out of the tunnels ahead, charging through the chamber his group was to have entered.

"Vikings!" exclaimed Tankred. "And Slavs!"

"Mercenaries," corrected Grimketil. "Or they would never mix!"

Wade clearly saw two groups dressed differently. No one had horns on their helmet. Wade took the bigger and blonder ones to be the Northmen or Danes, consistent with his own time. From their vantage on the higher end of the tunnel, it was clear that the defenders faced many times their number. Had they gone further down the tunnel, exposing their flanks to the wide space, they would not have stood a chance.

Grimketil plowed into their middle, taking on two at a time, yet others still had room to slowly make their way past him. Wade saw immediately that if he and each of his companions engaged one and held him off, the passage would be too congested for the rest to break through. All would share the disadvantage of flickering torchlight. Wade drew his sword in defense. He heard the echoing ring as it came free and felt a chill at the vibration.

A Slav came through the gap straight at Wade. When the blade came down, Wade's blade came up to meet it. He registered the impact all the way to his shoulder, amazed that he reacted in time. Again and again, Wade instinctively protected himself, his reflexes matching anything that came at him. He had a bit of extra advantage, fighting his shorter opponent on somewhat higher ground. Sometimes the tip of his sword did some damage, while his adversary was thwarted each time. "Maybe I do belong here," Wade said.

In time, the Slav Wade was fighting got caught between the swinging blades of Wade and Odalman, and fell from the accumulated blood loss from many small wounds. Wade stared, shaken up. The man looked so much smaller when the life went out of him.

The next attacker in line, a Viking, was better than the first, immediately thrusting his sword into Odalman's unprotected midsection. He twisted the blade in satisfaction, and allowed the falling weight of his kill to free it up again.

Of all the violence Wade had seen, watching Odalman run through hit him hardest, but he had no time to reflect on that unless he wanted the same fate. Wade now fought the Viking that killed Odalman. An extra burst of angry adrenalin made him even quicker and stronger, strength he needed to turn the heavier Viking blade. With each stroke, however, his arm grew a shade number.

Bodies littered the floor in increasing numbers. Grimketil gained ground and a moment's rest by kicking those he defeated down the tunnel at the others. Even so, the Vikings and Slavs came prepared with shields, and **their fresh** reinforcements stood only one rank behind.

Inevitably, the tiring defenders retreated to the small side chamber that Grimketil had maneuvered to be near. In so doing, he narrowed the front still further, affording him a kind of rest. Several attackers forced themselves inside with them.

Wade concentrated so hard on staying alive that he had difficulty sorting out where his friends and enemies were. As he could not afford to look, he prayed they were seasoned enough to stay out of his way. To stay alive, Wade varied his routine, dodging as well as parrying. That was how the Viking missed Wade and cut down the Avar khagan coming up behind him instead. Wade saw the opportunity. Before that attacker could pull his sword free of Arghun-Boke's body, Wade dealt the killer a desperate, fatal blow.

Meanwhile, Grimketil fought like a demon, the close quarters and a second wind aiding him. He and Snorri beat the hoards back out of the chamber.

Arghun-Boke was not dead yet. Wade had lost track of Tankred, who at any event was not in the room. Wade spied a tall and stout iron stand next to the entrance. Whatever statue it might have held had long been stolen. Wade tipped it at an angle, and rolled it on its edge, using it to block the doorway. Arghun-Boke bled profusely, mortally wounded. "The legend of Visocica must never have reached them in the north."

Wade's accusing stare said he did not believe it. "You're dying," was all he said to the man on the ground. *You're a traitor* could never have fully expressed his anger and resentment over the useless loss of Odalman.

The last of the Avar kaghans looked worried for the first time. "If I tell you the truth, will you please drag me outside... and point me north?"

Wade remembered the Avar belief that the kingdom of the dead was north, probably the North Pole. He nodded, and then realized Arghun-Boke could not see him anymore.

Wade said, "If what you tell me is worth it, I will."

Arghun-Boke gasped for breath. "Theirs was supposed to be an overwhelming force...enough to...take you as slaves.... not kill anyone.... least of all me." He managed a little smile for the last part.

Struggling with what would have been a routine movement, he dug into a pouch, and handed Wade a folded parchment with trembling fingers.

Wade grabbed the familiar sheet, and held on tight. "You took it?"

"I was looking to read your orders from Charles the Great as it concerned the Avar," he managed to sputter out. The rest, down to a whisper, sounded like, "When I removed this parchment, you stirred and I could not put it back without waking you."

Suddenly Wade wanted to know if Kreindia's supernatural observations meant anything to the Avar kaghan." Did you read it?'

"Enough...to see that it was only...a worthless...love letter." His dying words.

Wade opened the letter and stared wide-eyed, trying to read the contents of the page all at the same time as a group of Vikings burst into the chamber.

He felt a sharp pain in the back of his head, and the lights went out.

PART II
Kreindia's Story

"Those things that nature denied to human sight, she
revealed to the eyes of the soul."

—Ovid

CHAPTER 23
Audience With Raginpert

"In the 7ᵗʰ indiction, we are at a critical juncture in the Empire's history. Much has been lost—Palestine, Syria, Africa, and Itale. The die is cast to lose all the rest. The Bulgar are encamped at the Golden Gate. The most disastrous of turning points was said to be when the woman, Irene, was allowed to claim the title basileus— Caesar Imperator, God's Vice-Gerent, the Elect of Christ, Equal of the Apostles—a woman! As a consequence, the Pope has done to us what the Goths, Avars, Huns, Bulgars, and Vandals could not: Handed the imperial crown to the Frank. Thus to armed conflict with the West, and thence to a delicate peace established under Nicephoros the Logothete. The pact destroyed by Michael Rhangabe, we try again."

—From burnt fragments, circa 813 A.D., labeled Scriptor
Incertus *(Writer Unknown)*

"I AM PROTECTED," said Kreindia to the outcast prince, the count of Pavia.

"You shall not be protected if the fate of you and your friends is never known," Raginpert declared, implying that if he rounded up all of Kreindia's friends and killed them, her disappearance could not be traced to him. She did not flinch when he punctuated his words by casting his dagger into the floor by her feet.

The action may have startled her, but for something even more surprising that happened first. Another soul entered the room from a distant place, groggy and dreaming, and merged with her as though the two stood in the same spot. She knew that soul to be her Wade of Aquitaine, who first appeared to her in visions, then in flesh, and now in this form—a unique experience, even for Kreindia the Strange. She felt the comforting presence of Wade like a hug, and knew that he saw as she did, through her very eyes, smelled the anger of the displaced prince, and heard the wooden floor split like a chopping block by sharp metal. While he had no power to assist, through this mingling of souls, he gained knowledge of her plight. She felt, too, Wade's bewilderment at the reality of what must have begun for him as a dream. Was it his power or hers that drew him to her?

She tried harder not to react visibly when Wade left her just as suddenly, awakened from his dream state, and released from their combined consciousness. Without him she felt as half. She was determined to give Raginpert no satisfaction, and reveal no information that he might use against Wade.

Kreindia frowned at the deceptively pretty dagger and replied, "Fair peace becomes men; ferocious anger belongs to beasts."

Raginpert flushed deeper, and shook with rage. "Ever the scholar," he managed to force out. "You quote from the books of The Metamorphoses. You see, I know. Don't be too clever for your own good." But his voice sounded hollow, and she could see his nervousness from the way he turned his back. He was clearly uncertain how to handle this commoner that spoke like royalty, and could not be rattled. His childhood tutors back in Pavia would have been scholarly like Kreindia, but never presumptuous.

Kreindia stared at the back of Raginpert's majestical cloak, thinking of her humble beginnings when royalty owed her nary a glance. She had always been too clever, even as a child. Or so they said of her for knowing things before they happened, envisioned in dreams, nightmares, or feelings. Her parents asked her never to speak of it, nor to speak of her crossed-senses and odd opinions. When they were gone, she remembered their advice, and tried her best to envision nothing at all. Suppressing her dreams was beginning to work. That is, until the otherworldly visions of Wade began. The visions included herself in another mold, and other possible selves in altered circumstances. Then she wanted nothing but to know more.

She closed her eyes as if to block Raginpert from sharing the memories.

"If you cannot tell me anything about Wade—for now— certainly you can tell me about yourself, Kreindia the Greek. What are you doing in the West?"

Where his well-aimed side arm failed to make her flinch, this question succeeded. She only hoped her face did not somehow betray her secrets. She focused on the dagger as she spoke, returning particularly to the largest jewel amid the hilt, an orange amber that gave her the unaccountable feeling of silk. This focus was safer than looking away, or at him. A blade length of two headspans, brass hand guard, and pommel with cross, no doubt from an inherited package of crown jewels.... surely the dagger had been asked to keep a secret or more since first it was forged. Now a flash of something seen in the jewel, Wade in a struggle, battling at a waterfall. Was the vision a remnant of their fleeting connection? Was he safe? She had to keep talking as though nothing happened.

She said, "I'm on loan to the scriptorium at Sintlas Ow to assist with translations between Greek, Latin, and other tongues."

"...And in return you get the details of western history. You're a chronicler."

Kreindia looked surprised. No one was to reveal that she was more than a scribe, one who copies down facts rather than a keen observer of history.

"Oh yes," cooed Raginpert, warming to his subject. "I loosened the tongues of several inhabitants traveling out or back toward Sintlas Ow. I used several different methods, and those who knew, all told the same story."

The revelation drew him one step closer to tearing away her entire façade. Nonetheless, she saw no way to deny it, and could think of no way in which the information he uncovered could hurt Wade. "So you know it to be the absolute truth," she said. "You know I'm here as a chronicler." *Let him settle in on his hard-won fact.*

Raginpert followed her gaze to the dagger, deep into the core of its amber and the unknown particles of life trapped therein. Without the gift of crossed-senses, he saw less than she did there. "Either I have gotten the absolute truth from you and your friends, or you have lied to them all. Look at me."

She looked first at his empty scabbard of black leather with its brass furniture on either end, then to his eyes, equally well dressed and empty. "I'm here to examine source documents that could not be shipped to the east."

"A woman chronicler and scribe with the ability to translate," he summed up. "You've traveled too far for an errand like that, and you have too much respect accorded you by The Monk. If I got my hands on him, he might tell a better story."

"I'm also a healer," she volunteered.

"Yes, summoned to a fool's errand, repairing that ancient king. Why do I get the feeling there is yet more?"

"What you think is your own business. I cannot heal minds."

The jibe set him pacing. She realized it must have occurred to him he should have her flogged, and normally he would have seen to it forthwith. It could only have been fear that stayed his hand for the moment. He had a real chance of finding favor with Byzantium. With his claims to the Longobard throne, he could ride back with a Byzantine army. He would promise to add it to the empire if the expedition succeeded. However, if he worried that she were more important in the east than she let on, then his kidnapping and mistreatment of her would jeopardize his options. Therefore it was critical for her sake that he believe everything she said.

He stopped as though something occurred to him. Then he calmly retrieved the dagger and sheathed it.

"You carried no documents with you for safe passage to Aachen, therefore you are not part of an embassy. I conclude you are a spy."

Her stomach dropped. She could not let her disappointment show. "And I conclude you are a fool. The documents were sent ahead."

"I will give you one last chance. If not a spy, tell me then who you are really are, and what you are doing here."

"I've told you everything. You insist on drawing the wrong conclusions. Perhaps you've forgotten that you arrested me for heresy, not spying. A crude device to get me behind these walls."

Raginpert grinned, a smile that said he knew how to deal with vulgar commoners. "Perhaps you should be treated as a heretic. If you were a man," said Raginpert, "I'd have you castrated. As it stands, there is still much I can do. Antonio!" The servant emerged, jumping quickly to answer. "Antonio, I want you to take this woman to the chamber. There you will remove her right ear. Do not use a knife. I want you to slowly tear it off. If any part remains, you'll tear that off the next day."

With only a nod to his master, Antonio took hold of her. Raginpert held up a finger, indicating that he wanted a final word with the victim.

"You who speak so many tongues can scream in all of them. Start with Greek."

Kreindia had seen some awful things happen to a human being without knowing personally how they felt. She did not doubt that Raginpert was capable of this barbarity or that the loss of her ear would be only the beginning. In a strong, proud voice she said, "No, I think I'll start with Phrygian, the language of my ancestors."

Antonio pulled her away.

"Wait!" the prince commanded. And then more softly, "What is this?"

She continued, "There are times, especially at court, when I consider myself not so much a Greek as an Amorian from Phrygia."

The color drained from Raginpert's face. "You live in the court? Are you saying that you are related to…m-m-Michael of Amorium?"

Kreindia smiled. Michael of Amorium was part of the triumvirate of generals that brought Leo V to power in recent months. "Yes. Also known as Michael the Stammerer. You do an excellent impression of him, whether you mean to or not."

"Release her!" He resumed pacing while he though about what to do in place of his previous instructions. "Place her in a holding cell. Give her a few days or weeks to think about how she got here." He looked at her closely, spewing breath made toxic by his fear. "I will find out the truth. If you are lying, the worst of hell on Earth awaits."

Her bravery was fleeting; the haughty demeanor of a spoiled princess, a mere copy of the manner she observed at the palace. As Antonio dragged Kreindia away to a cell, he could no doubt feel her trembling, and could report the fact to the count's perverse satisfaction. She knew she had won a brief respite, but if in the course of Raginpert's investigations, he discovered the real reason she came to the Frankish kingdom, then no monarch in the known world could save her.

CHAPTER 24
Do You Miss Being a Man?

"In the 6ᵗʰ indiction, General Michael of Amorium did sail the Bosphorus with his retinue out of Hiereia, and beheld the Queen of All Cities, beheld the Column of the Goths on the Acropolis, the incomparable dome and towers of Hagia Sophia, the Augousteion, Zeuxippos, and finally, near the Harbor of Julian, the Great Palace, in which he and his favored would, in due course, dwell."

—*Circa 812 A.D.,* Scriptor Incertus

THE DANGER KREINDIA faced now made her life back in Byzantium seem almost trivial, but for the tragedy of how her final day in the capitol ended. She would never forget how her best friend looked at her that morning, trying to be brave, and turning as sad as she was supportive.

"Are you ready for your big journey to the west?" Verina had asked, causing all the girls to look in Kreindia's direction at once, to see what Kreindia the Strange would say this time.

Kreindia sighed. Another big journey in her life. She honestly thought Constantinople was her last stop, time to settle down in the greatest luxury she'd ever seen. As an army imp, life was uncertain enough, but she never thought she would have to go off to a distant land, and brave all manner of hardships while her uncle, her only guardian, stayed put.

She looked into the polished brass mirror and began to fix her eyeliner. Her eyes were something of a powder blue she supposed. She had never seen them other than through a brass patina that robbed everything of its natural hue. The mind played tricks, trying to correct what it saw, but the inevitable result was nothing but a guess. "No, I'm not ready."

"Well then get one of the eunuchs to help you," said Procopia.

Kreindia looked at Procopia knowing she missed the point. She wanted to tell all, to get the reasons for her journey off her chest, but it was too complicated to explain, and parts of it were state secrets. Instead, she said, "I have. Anthimos is coming."

"Oh, Annnnthimos is coming to help you? Really?" The girls giggled.

"Anthimos," someone repeated in falsetto, and made them laugh harder.

"Why?" asked Kreindia, looking up from the mirror. "Is there something funny about him?"

The girls convulsed in gales of hysterical laughter, and socked each other with pillows.

"Gemma? Kale? Someone tell me what this is about," Kreindia implored.

Procopia cleared her throat. "Anthimos is a most uncommon eunuch," she said, barely able to contain herself. "Deprived as he is, he still likes to have sex with women and girls of all kinds."

"A wild bull with no balls," exclaimed Kale to more laughter.

"I know what a eunuch is!" Kreindia protested, reddening.

"Someone should tell *him*, then!" Kale retorted. Even Verina joined the laughter for that one.

"You're hurting my sides," Gemma complained, "and I'm going to wet the bed."

"Stop it, all of you," said Kreindia catching a bit of an infectious smile.

"They almost caught him in the purple chamber," Gemma whispered. Kreindia gave her an open-mouthed scandalized look. The purple chamber was that of the empress.

"I think that perked her up," said Kale.

"Some recreation would do you good, Kreindia," said Procopia.

"I haven't got patience for such foolishness," said Kreindia.

"Oh, why won't you partake, dear?" Procopia persisted. "It is the most wonderful sex, not for him of course, since there is no ending, but marvelous for us."

"Oh, leave her alone," protested Verina. "Personally, he disgusts me. The worst kind of pervert. Don't you wonder how he maintains an erection? The sheer perverse satisfaction of having another man's woman without any danger or fear of suspicion. He does it right under their noses while pretending the utmost loyalty expected of a eunuch."

Verina could always be counted on to come to Kreindia's defense. "It's probably just gossip," allowed Kreindia. "Anyway, I'm saving myself for Wade."

Procopia picked up her own mirror, to show she had a better one. "Your Wade of Aquitaine, right? There is no such person, dear. You've made him up just as a child makes up her imaginary friends."

"The Heavens have made him up. Not me. It may have been Jesus or Apollo or any of the millions of our deities to choose from."

Procopia said, "You are wicked in your own way, Kreindia. No wonder I like you. Blasphemy is your redeeming quality."

"I'm not blasphemous. I just have my own personal relationship with the Heavens. I pray to the Empress Irene for guidance."

"Yes, Irene was such a strong woman," Procopia snickered. She made 'strong' sound like a dirty word. "Do you also hail from the Isle of Lesbos, perhaps? Kiss me, then."

"Get off me," Kreindia laughed.

"I think we cheered her up," said Gemma.

"Oh, here comes your Anthimos. We'll leave you alone with him, sweet fig," said Procopia with a wink, and she and her cohorts piled out.

"It's time to prepare for your trip, dear," Anthimos smiled as he watched the young ladies go. His age was indeterminate, his dress neutral, yet fashionable and fastidious with a tastefully patterned sleeved tunic cinched at the waist, and over that a straight drape from neck to matching shoes, clasped with a bronze snake insignia at the right shoulder; like Kreindia, he knew some healing arts. He brought traveling bags under each arm, and immediately began assessing what she had available.

"It's good to see you, Anthimos. Those girls were drowning me in gossip."

"You're too smart for them," he winked. "Are you taking any books along?"

"I take a blank codex to write on."

It's a long voyage. Maybe you want to take along something to amuse you."

"Like what?"

"A lyre, or a kithara maybe."

"I can't play them."

"I suppose I could get you an aulos, or some kind of pipes, possibly even round you up a syrinx."

"Ha, I can't play them either."

"This might be a good time to learn. It's sort of expected of you in the palace."

"I'm not musical," she laughed. "I'd probably sink the ship trying."

"You know best," he chuckled. Anthimos proceeded to organize two piles of what should go and stay.

As he helped her pack, Kreindia looked at him curiously, and made as if to speak once or twice.

"I do hope you won't persist in that," said Anthimos over his shoulder.

"Pardon me?"

"Your hesitation. If you don't become more forceful, the ladies around here will eat you alive. I might do the same."

She smiled nervously. Her curiosity had gotten the best of her after all. "Do you mind if I ask you a delicate question?"

"I am at your service," he said, calmly folding her undergarments. "Nothing need embarrass you."

"Do you miss being a man?"

The eunuch laughed. "No, I've been both man and non, and being a man is not all it's cracked up to be. And don't ask me to be a woman, with all their problems. No, being the third sex is the next best thing to being of royal birth, and in many ways better. I'm trusted never to make a grab for the purple. No possibility of children means no dynasty. No dynasty, no emperor: the people would not allow it. Eunuchs are the only ones monarchs can completely trust with high office. And no one is plotting against me...except for other eunuchs. They don't stand a chance."

"What about sex?"

"I thought you'd never ask."

Kreindia laughed at the joke. At least she thought it was a joke. She'd heard it before in Thrace.

When Anthimos laid hands on a long, forest green stole, it quickened her heart. She didn't know why except that it had to be important. When he moved to put it aside, she nearly panicked. Something inside her screamed that she would not be recognized without it.

"Pack that one," she said, forcing a calm she didn't feel.

"I was going to put it away."

"No. I need it. I cannot explain why."

He looked at her and smiled benignly. "Yes, I too have items I keep for luck. There can never be an excess of charms."

With the bags complete, they left the chamber to find her best friend, Verina, and only succeeded a short distance before they ran straight into the woman Kreindia least wanted to see her off—Thamar Argyrina, the spoiled daughter of her uncle's rival.

"Oh, it's you," said Thamar in a voice freighted with disdain.

Anthimos offered rather meekly, "I'll go on ahead, and see that your luggage gets on the ship." Kreindia nodded, and he took the bags with him.

The two women squared off like natural enemies in the wild. Thamar Argyrina had a pigmentation disorder that left her sandy hair streaked in white, and white splotches on her face. She evened it all out with foundation and dye. Kreindia, who was unaware of the problem, once had the misfortune of catching Thamar with a white spot on her eyebrow, and attempted to tell her she had some cotton stuck to her. Thamar returned the favor by trying to scratch Kreindia's face off.

"I have no quarrel with you," said Kreindia.

"You can't afford to have. It's just as well. My father wants to see you. 'Find me Kreindia the Strange,' he said. 'Don't let her dodge me.'"

Kreindia drew in a sharp breath. Thamar's father, Thomas the Slav, stood in competition with Kreindia's uncle, her guardian. After Leo himself, the two of them constituted the balance of power in Constantinople. Whatever the Slav's summons was about, it couldn't be good.

"I'm not dodging anyone. I wasn't set to leave yet."

"I say you flee like a cowardly dog from its just punishment. Where shall I tell him to find you?"

Kreindia shook her head with wonder. "Tell him that whatever he wants of me, he should take it up with my uncle."

"Oh perfect, your uncle, the stammerer. That conversation should take a day and a half to sort through."

"Do whatever you want. I'm not telling you where I'm going."

"Very well. I'll have you followed then." Kreindia believed it, too.

When Thamar was out of sight, Kreindia joined Verina, and they went off together to Hagia Sofia with an offering to ensure the safety of Kreindia's journey. Both of them were looking over their shoulders all the way.

~ W ~

THERE was something slightly menacing about the outside of Hagia Sofia, Kreindia decided, a defect in its ageless beauty. Its worshipper's entrance looked more formidable than the graceful side it showed visitors coming from the sea. It looked almost like a prison, a place you would never leave.

Inside however, the ugly exterior was easily forgotten. With its vast spaces, nothing could have been more awe-inspiring. With each visit, she surreptitiously tried to count all the myriad windows and columns without looking like a foreigner. In the alternating sun glare and gloom it was easy, too, to overlook the many places the walls had been shattered and restored.

She next enjoyed the mosaics depicting the rule of Irene and her near-deification. None of the pictures told the story of her turbulent ouster and reinstatement. Nothing of making her own son a victim of her ambition.

There were vision-sent days when Kreindia believed utterly in the divine protection of Irene, and fog shrouded ones when she did not. On this day, she joined her friend in prayer to Irene, to honor the monarch as the first and only empress of Byzantium to rule as a woman alone. Kreindia needed that kind of inspiration, damn the rest.

Anthimos caught up with them. He stood silently by for instructions, taking a place in the shadows with the servant's knack for blending in harmlessly, Kreindia noticed. Excellent qualities, too, for a sentinel or a spy.

"How long have we known each other, Kreindia?" asked Verina, testing her.

"I don't know. Not very long, I imagine. It must be weeks, but no more than months."

"It's been more than three months, a whole season," said Verina in a gasp of awe. "Kreindia! How could you not know the difference between weeks and months?"

"I have no internal gauge for things that involve time or the order of events. It's why I started keeping journals."

"You've mentioned that before," said Verina, "and I thought you were joking. You are strange. Strange and wonderful."

"I'm sure you're the first to say it in that way. Others say time blindness is a curse, a payment for everything else I enjoy."

"I'll miss you so much," said Verina, with tears in her eyes. "Why do you have to go?"

"It's my job as a chronicler. If no one documents events in the west, history will be lost to oblivion."

"The hell with history as long as we don't lose you." They both sniffled. "In a thousand years, who will care? What possible impact could we have on the lives of people in the future?"

Kreindia could not even tell her best friend the truth about the importance of her mission, although her face must have hinted at the danger. She did, however, secret away a journal in the event that anything untoward happened to her. Based on the European upheaval that unfolded in her visions of the far future, she designed the chamber to withstand the duress of a millennium or more. So far she had tagged them "Scriptor Incertus," author uncertain, in case a woman's world would be doubted.

"Come," said Kreindia, "you can walk me to the ship."

When the trio turned to leave, there across the hall was Thomas the Slav, pale, humorless, and careless of his appearance, with his tunic falling off one shoulder, as it often did.

"Kreindia the Strange, and Verina the...Reckless," said Thomas, his voice carrying. If he wanted to embarrass them in the great hall, shouting his insinuations across the ears of strangers made a great tool for it.

He was not alone. Thomas never went anywhere without his bodyguard Zoticus Macroducas, an uncommonly tall, thin man with sunken, depraved eyes, and stringy black hair. Today he brought another four soldiers for good measure.

"My useful daughter, Thamar, tracked you down," said Thomas, his eyes on Kreindia alone.

"I have no business with Thamar or you, sir," said Kreindia with greater reserve than he.

"No? Then perhaps you can explain why your uncle is trying to spirit you out of the city like one of his Varangian whores?" Thomas said. Other churchgoers stopped to watch them but didn't dare step between the spread out soldiers and the three accused.

"This journey is endorsed by Patriarch Nikephoros," Kreindia countered to shift the focus off her uncle and the general's rivalry.

"Nikephoros doesn't know everything." Thomas' voice had a nasty ring to it.

"Such as what?"

"He doesn't know, for instance, that you venerate icons. He would never guess that General Michael's niece prays to Irene, and he would never endorse your escape from the city if he knew." Thomas shared his hard stare with Verina as though he were marking her down for guilt by association, or perhaps as the instigator.

"It's not against the law, as much as you would like it to be, to worship Irene and follow in her ways," Verina yelled back. Everyone at court knew that Thomas was pushing emperor Leo in the direction of changing the law so that those allied with Thomas could eliminate everyone else.

"It will be, as of this afternoon. I have a feeling we will find icons on your persons." He signaled his men to surround her. "Arrest them."

"I'll slow them down," said Verina to Kreindia. "You run."

Anthimos stood back, as if uncertain of what to do as a neutral employee of the palace.

The Heavens conspired against them. They had warning, albeit a useless one, a shaking, ominous, rumbling, time enough just for your first thought: Balance, or lose your feet. Like a bad dream, Kreindia could not run. Every direction appeared to be uphill. One moment her friend stood next to her, breathless, animated, alive; the next moment a falling stone smashed her head to pulp, and she fell, a lifeless rag doll. More rocks from the ceiling blocked Thomas' men from advancing. One chunk struck Thomas a glancing blow, enough to bring him down.

Everyone else ran pell-mell to whatever spot represented safety in the primitive part of the brain that takes over, right or wrong, in a crisis. Kreindia tried to kneel by poor Verina on the trembling, broken tile. The floor flipped her up and brought her down, pancake style, on top of her friend. Close enough to bring the message home that there was no help for the limp form, its soul fled in an earthquake that was not over. *St. Sophia, why?*

Zoticus Macroducas continued to advance. Kreindia, who had some basic fighting skills taught to her by her uncle, was half his size, and weaponless. She remembered to turn her toes inward for stability as she searched for a weapon and saw none.

Anthimos, who was not entitled to take sides, was nonetheless her only hope. He interposed himself between Kreindia and Zoticus, and bid her away. He tackled Zoticus when the bodyguard tried to follow her. Although in the chaos Anthimos might claim it was an accident, there was a good chance he would pay later with his life.

Kreindia had to push her grief down for the sake of survival, and run. Her bags were already shipboard. Now all that remained was to try to get herself there.

CHAPTER 25
The General's Niece

"All things may corrupt, when minds are prone to evil."

—Ovid

THE EARTHQUAKE OF course was not limited to the Hagia Sophia, although it might have seemed so if she did not exit the building quickly enough to see the last of it. Kreindia turned back, half expecting to see the entire dome cave in, the towers collapse toward each other in a cascading orgy of destruction. Instead, she could not even find the section of roof that was missing.

The first shock ended as quickly as it began. Outside, a large tree branch had fallen like an offering to humanity. All around her, the city wore the mantle of a bad storm. It almost did not seem right that such a terrible tragedy left so little evidence of its wake. She looked up at the sky as many others were doing, only she was thinking surely Verina counted for more than that.

Unlike the rest of the population, Kreindia continued running, her heart pounding, as there was more than just an earthquake after her. There were Zoticus Macroducas, several soldiers, and her conscience as well. She proceeded numbly, one foot swiftly in the front of the other, her thoughts divided from the effort. How can something so terrible happen to the wrong people, especially in a church, she wondered. How could this be meant to happen?

Although Kreindia often had glimpses of a possible future, she was blind to visions for all things fated, something that could not have been changed no matter how much foreknowledge she possessed. That meant Verina could not have been saved by any anticipated action of hers. That at least, was a blessing.

She fled through the palace gate to seek out her uncle, or failing that, to find Procopia. An advisor to the empress, Procopia was a bit older, a kind of senior stateswoman of the girls. Her cynical twist and devious streak notwithstanding, Kreindia and the rest of the flock found comfort in her clever ways.

She found her mentor taking stock of tumbled make-up, scattered clothing, and a wash of broken glass. Procopia was not surprised to find Kreindia distressed. "Don't worry, Kreindia. Everyone at the palace has gotten away with small injuries. If I broke a nail, then you would hear some caterwauling."

At a second shock, much milder than the first, they both braced themselves until it passed. Anything that was not broken before, and not yet secured shattered now. Witnessing the breaking glass reached into her soul as the mere sight of the broken glass had not. She felt the shards go into her in a spray of heat, and then realized it was only a vision flash of some other person in some other time. She shook her head to clear it of the partial and useless vision.

Frantic and breathless, Kreindia sputtered, "Where is Michael?"

"Michael Psellus?" Psellus was the Romanized version of stammerer. Kreindia knew her friend meant nothing hurtful by it.

"Yes, my uncle."

"He is at the baths. You sound odd, Kreindia."

"Verina is dead."

"Oh darling. That's awful. I'm sorry. What happened?"

"We were in Hagia Sophia. Some of the roof fell on her. It just—"

"Oh, Kreindia, don't cry. It will be all right. She's with Irene now," said Procopia, not unkindly.

"I know you don't believe that, but thank you for saying so." The crease on Kreindia's brow deepened again. "I have to warn Michael."

"There, there, child. It's all over."

"No, Thomas the Slav was there too. He tried to seize me for idol worship. He had Zoticus and four soldiers to enforce it."

Procopia frowned in concern. "I doubt they dare follow you here, but it will not be safe outside. It's best you run and board your ship by the secret route. I'll give your uncle the warning. Go!"

She ran, grateful that there was still one person to back her up. The docks were as near the palace on one side as Hagia Sophia was on the other side. She took the underground tunnels, emerging to the breathtaking view of flat-bottomed merchant vessels in the distance, and their sleek dromon escorts up close. The slower ships were already getting a head start in the safety of the well-patrolled waters near home. Kreindia would join a warship.

Kreindia strode up the dock as swiftly as she dared. Knowing it would be a tough job to get the ship's dromarch to cast off in haste, she composed herself to adopt the expected tone of haughty command that she had been taught by example.

The dromarch was working at a leisurely pace, bending over a crate of provisions when she approached abruptly. "Bacchus Briennius?"

"Yes." He stood tall and square in his marine officer's uniform, with skin darkened and roughened by the sea. She drew a tight breath, unable to afford the luxury of liking or disliking him.

"I am Kreindia, niece to Michael of Amorium, sailing under the authority of Patriarch Nikephoros. You have previously been informed of the circumstance. My mission takes priority over defense of the merchant ships. We leave immediately."

"Your ladyship, we're not finished with preparations."

Fighting a powerful urge to look over her shoulder for signs of pursuit, she said, "My luggage is aboard. That's all the preparation you need. Move fast or get left behind."

His face turned a helpless red. Kreindia had never been so rude in her life. It smarted even to say those things. Nonetheless, it was better by far that he thought of her as a spoiled court layabout rather someone running for her life. Any questions raised now would diminish her authority and endanger the mission. When Dromarch Briennius turned away to order raised anchors, she sat heavily on a box of cargo that hadn't been stowed. With the loss of Verina and so much to think about, the voyage would by no means be boring. What would become of her uncle with the threat hanging over him?

Briennius upbraided his first mate to cast off and be quick about it. As Kreindia watched the dock grow smaller, a figure ran across the pier, jumped into a rowboat, and used a blade to cut its line rather than untying it. Before anyone could stop him, he began digging his oars into the water frantically, good enough to gain on them. A man sent by Thomas the Slav? The dromarch had followed the letter of her instructions, having moved the ship away from its pier, but he had slowed to almost a drift to follow a checklist before they were too far away to return.

"Faster, dromarch," Kreindia commanded.

Briennius sneered at her, though he called to the drum master for a faster beat. Before the drum master could repeat the command to his rowers, Kreindia held up a hand to stay him. Rather than the first sign of the trouble she expected, she recognized the man in the small boat, his bald head and nobleman's clothes. She would have known him faster but for the fact that he appeared against her expectations. Her eyes burned with nascent tears of relief, scarcely a step ahead of her embarrassment. She hardly knew the eunuch, hardly traveled five hundred yards from home yet. How difficult would the trip be if she got so emotional now? She had to take command of herself if she were to get any cooperation out of others.

"Dromarch, slow the ship. Pick him up," she pointed.

"Cast off. Go fast. Now stop. Will you be making up your mind soon, madam?" With the Romanized name of Bacchus Briennius, like her adversary Zoticus, he could not have been in the east long. Even as she grew irritated, the historian in her wondered at his country of origin. No, not the historian, she decided, but the Byzantine in her, the instinct for intrigue and self-preservation. She could not ignore the possibility that the two of them were aligned.

"Go whatever speed you wish, Bacchus Briennius. Just see that you pick that man out of the water, and leave the rowboat to wash away." He looked at her like she was mad, yet did not question her further.

The crew hauled Anthimos aboard, wet around the edges and breathing heavily. After thanking the crew that helped him, he said to Kreindia, "You just missed Michael. I told him what happened."

She did not embrace the eunuch, or overtly act in any demonstrative way that might have shown weakness to those watching, but her voice betrayed her. "I was sure that with all the trouble, you wouldn't be able to join me."

"Michael said I should not be around for awhile until things cool off."

When she noticed Briennius examining her closely, she moved near to Anthimos, and whispered, "I need some time to cool off too. I'm really very glad you're here. I just need some time alone for a while."

"I understand," he said.

Anthimos left her as much privacy as she could get on the hard-bitten warship. Had he looked back, he might have discerned her tying to memorize the fading shore.

~ W ~

FROM the Port of Julian, they hugged the coast for a time, and then moved out to where only the keenest eyes could see it. If a land dweller remembers nothing else about an ocean voyage, it is the pervasive salt, creaking, and pitching of the deck that most makes an impression. Even with all her experience at sea, each of these elements worked its magic on Kreindia.

Kreindia watched the direction of the shore as though she could anchor their vessel to it by force of will. She had never taken a sea voyage voluntarily. With isolation came the realization of this very limited environment, one hundred fifty paces stem to stern, cut off from the niceties and resources of home. An odd thing, too, to leave her rooms behind in total disarray. All the small things lost, and one very great one. Even though she did not know Verina very long, a true friend could be very meaningful to a rootless person, and this one certainly was. Her uncle would have said to Kreindia that if she were smart, she wouldn't have grown attached to the girl.

With that thought, she went to the rail, feeling she might vomit aided by the motion and the salt that got right up into the back of her throat, barely covering the stench of hundreds of men at close quarters. Bent forward, and waiting, she watched the chop churning in their wake; the constant flush had an almost hypnotic pull to it, soothing and beckoning. She could well imagine the revolting attraction that the sea exerted on those who plied these treacherous waters as a way of life.

After an interval she couldn't guess, the worst nausea passed, leaving her in unabated limbo and sadness. It might have been better to get it over with. Relieving some bile at the rail would have fit well with everything else that happened. Bad enough to take a trip reluctantly, and alone, and a magnitude worse to flee in chaos. Running away from a place that should have been safe, and plunging headlong into what?

Past the sight of land, Dromarch Briennius approached her with a swagger, unconstrained. Perhaps her weakness at the rail emboldened him. Perhaps he thought the law differed here, a kind of sovereignty of the sea. It seemed he would join her peering over the stern as though the oceans were very much on his mind. Then he turned so that she knew he wanted to face her squarely.

Kreindia said, "Has the water called to you too?"

"You can jump into that water now, for all I care. There'll be no more orders from you out here, you spoiled court bitch. On the sea, I'm in charge. My authority is complete and unchallenged."

Kreindia stared back at him, unblinking. Who had put this poison in his ear while she stood distracted?

Before she could answer him, the edge of a knife appeared at his throat, and for a moment Kreindia thought he held the knife himself, delivering a symbolic message. She did not see the man behind him. The knife moved sideways, and in the unreality of the situation she did not connect the gout of hot red spray with a severed artery. Her confusion was complete when the Dromarch was kicked towards her, so that he appeared to be lunging forward. She went down under the dead weight of the dromarch, pinned until the body was shoved off her. She got up quickly.

Another man stood where Briennius had. "Here, we can't have bodies on you and this filthy, bloodstained clothing." He tore the front of her robes away. She felt the sea air on her breast. "Thamar said to keep you company, and I intend to do that."

He knocked her down again, and leaned over her with fetid alcohol soaked breath.

Kreindia shook her head furiously. Thamar would find no shortage of desperate men. In a land where royalty or peasantry is something you are born into, and fixed for life, murderous violence is one of the few things that can raise your social station. Kreindia understood it intellectually if not emotionally. Emotionally, she was in a rage. With her back on the floorboards, she kicked him to a tenuous upright position.

By this time Anthimos arrived. He acted quickly, and stabbed the intruder in the side, deep within his bowels, skewering his liver. She noticed he wielded an army-issue gladius, short enough to conceal and draw easily, long enough to be deadly. So Michael had not sent him after her empty handed. The man had the strength to turn in surprise and watch a second thrust drive into his throat. At that, the would-be rapist dropped like a sack of cargo.

Kreindia gazed at the eunuch in awe. Having once acted aggressively back in the church, his inhibition seemed much reduced. The sobering reality and need to act may have enforced a pragmatic mindset. Even so, the effect was shocking. He must never have been as mild as he appeared. Earlier, she had been pleased that he never asked why her mission as a chronicler was so important as to put her aboard a warship. Now she remembered that servants always knew more than they let on. Her uncle may have even briefed Anthimos and charged him to look after her. If so, she was grateful for his discretion. She rearranged her robes to cover her reasonably well, and set the clasp to fix it in place just in time to see them surrounded.

The sight of violence and Anthimos' bare bloody sword in front of two hundred marines on the deck of their ship was like raw meat held in taunting range to hungry lions.

The first mate stepped up, stout and young. "I am in charge now." Her remarkable memory of the travel documents told her his name was Kostos Apion. Kostos reached out so that Anthimos could surrender his weapon. Anthimos held on and looked at Kreindia to see her will.

The men around them looked between Kreindia and the presumptive new dromarch, ready to take up arms to enforce a decision. The look toward her was slighting, and only given due to the deference shown by Anthimos, a stranger to them who had proven he could handle a sword. The ship creaked in the quiet of the standoff. She did not know how many more traitors numbered in their midst. If Kreindia had any chance of survival, she knew she had to be uncompromising, an iron will command toward those in a power vacuum who were used to taking commands and might see her as the extended authority of her uncle the general.

"You think to take charge after this, First Mate Apion?" She gestured at the bloody deck.

"Who else?" he asked.

"I sail under the authority of General Michael of Amorium and Patriarch Nikephoros. You have been derelict in your duty of protecting this ship and me. We will take on a new dromarch at Athens where you may face a tribunal to clear your name."

"My name? What of Bacchus Briennius and his name?"

Kreindia looked at the dromarch's immobile form on deck. "Briennius has escaped responsibility. Would you care to do the same?"

He stood open-mouthed in a posture of confusion.

"That's what I thought," said Kreindia. "Anthimos will keep his sword. He answers to me, as do you all."

CHAPTER 26
Petroleum, Quicklime, and Sulfur

"Let your hook be always cast:
in the pool where you least expect it, there will be a fish."

—*Ovid*

O N A SHIP YOU had your choice of aft, where you could see the turbulent wake of where you'd been, the bow, where you could look where you were going and witness the water cleaving to the prow's will, or amidships, where the great murky distance stood still like a thing trapped in time. Kreindia had tried looking back. Now she kept to the forward area. Anthimos stayed by her side, watching the sun slip into the Mediterranean. The orb grew large and bulbous, smearing its color everywhere as it unraveled for the night.

"How long are we at sea?" she asked him.

"Don't you know?"

"No." She kept her explanation to one word with never a glance to the side. She could have explained her time-blindness, admitted everything in a torrent of confession and relief, but this was not the time to emphasize their differences; she worked on a surplus of strangeness as it was. She would reveal only one thing at a time.

He bit his lip with unquenched curiosity. "I make it two

days and a half. If it were not for the port call in Apollonia we would be in Athens now trading metalwork for olive oil."

She looked at her hands so she wouldn't have to look at him. "My uncle Michael is no saint. He's done some awful things to get where he is."

"Why speak of it now? You don't have to apologize for him."

"I feel like I do, especially with what I know."

"What do you know?"

"He's going to be emperor some day."

"Did the oracle at Delphi say that?"

"I am an oracle. I say that."

"You are an oracle?" he said, as if the words made no sense, or perhaps made sense in an entirely unexpected way. "When Leo of Armenia told the story after the fact, of the Delphic oracle predicting his ascension to the throne, I thought it was a myth invented to explain how a soldier outside of the bloodline could take the purple. There was a rumor that the oracle he referred to was actually you."

Kreindia raised a quizzical eyebrow.

"There are no secrets at court," he continued, "but true and false turn on the flip of a solidis. If this is true—."

"All I know is that I have visions. In this vision, Michael is carried in chains to Hagia Sophia where he takes the purple and is blessed by the patriarch."

"Your uncle? In chains like a prisoner?"

"The visions don't explain themselves."

"Is there any more to it?"

She looked at him to see if he were taking her seriously. His brow was shadowed with intensity. Thus assured, she said, "Michael appears to be several years older, and the patriarch is someone other than Nikephoros. So much has passed. I know nothing of what is to happen in between."

"Ah, you worry that because of the plot by Thomas, that Michael will spend all the intervening years locked up."

"Something like that, yes." Neither of them mentioned what his time out of favor might mean for her. In the vision, she was not present and this could have meant she did not survive.

The ship wheeled slowly to port in a minor course correction, avoiding the shoals. The splash could be heard from the rower's oars on starboard. Anthimos sat down with his back to the beam. "There's much you haven't told me about your mission. I know it's important."

"Yes."

"I know it's not all about recording the history of the west. Michael entrusted me with that much. Can't you tell me more?"

She watched the sun relinquishing its wealth, ceding weakened color to the timbers of their ship. "Michael entrusted Bacchus Briennius with slightly more information and he lies dead now."

"Actually the dromarch, and the one who dispatched him, are making their way to the bottom of the sea wrapped in blankets and ballast. If getting more information means protecting you better, I will take my chances."

When the timbers soaked in the color of tarnished copper, Kreindia found she experienced a crossed-sense flavor of marigolds, a new one to add to her catalog of feelings. Then Kreindia jumped a foot off the deck as the sun came back up instantly. No, not the sun, she realized, but something nearly as bright to eyes in the darkness. Anthimos loosed a startled cry. It must have been all the more terrifying for him, since he did not see the threat. His gladius leapt to his hand as he looked all around and saw everything as it was before in the settling gloom.

"A vision, Kreindia?"

"Yes!" With her heart hammering against her ribs, she nearly screeched it. The waking visions of danger were the most intrusive and shocking of all.

"What happened?" cried the commander of the watch from his post on deck.

"Nothing," shouted Anthimos, as he sheathed his weapon, "I won at cards."

"Be quiet about it," the man replied, "or you'll have to share with me."

"We're in danger," said Kreindia softly. "I see a dazzling fire, men killed."

"The way you say it, I believe it." He peered into the dark, covering all sides, though there was naught to see. "This danger comes from where and when? "

"I can't answer either of those questions. There's nothing we can do about it now but stay alert and prepared."

"We'll be in Athens soon, before the next day rises."

"Not soon enough," she said.

"Do we dare sleep?"

"Yes, and the earlier the better. We'll need the strength."

~ W ~

BELOW decks, Kreindia lay nestled in a narrow bunk, another of her recent comforts exchanged for the rigors of travel. She was all too used to it. As much as balancing on a ship always made her queasy, lying down in those tossing waves felt as soothing than a rocking cradle; perhaps because it had been her cradle, and the bed of her traveling youth.

In her mind's eye she could see the close outlines of each rest area. The small rough living spaces gave her nothing to fuss over. She thought how funny it was that she could slip back into life on the road as though she had never left, never taken up residence in that comfortable palace with so much to learn about being a lady at court. The wonder is that she did learn it and retained the skills of both. Yet, if she were so comfortable now, why couldn't she sleep?

Anthimos held down the next bunk, her only buffer zone in the all-male environment. She could feel the weight of the ship above them, could picture the marines going about their night business on deck, their sounds hidden by the groaning of wood reshaped by salt water. Anthimos' breathing told of his wakefulness. She listened instead to the regular breathing patterns of dozens of men sleeping peacefully to inspire her. Her vision state, still powerfully active, helped carry her into the darkness.

If it were a real dream, the intensity would have woken her. Instead, she was held in its grip. The man she had envisioned so many times before, the one she already knew as Wade of Aquitaine, felt white-hot pain, and she shared the pain with him. The sensation radiated from his left wrist and took him over like a malevolent beast. She never felt anything like it before. Only her vision state kept her heart from leaping out of her chest. His world, as always, was hidden from her, appearing as he did, as a light figure in the dark. This time, carrying the pain, he tumbled through a void even lighter than himself. Then she saw something that all her travels told her did not exist in the real world: a wall made of glass. She somehow knew that the glass wall separated his world from hers. She braced herself as Wade fell towards it, and then crashed through it with her. The glass barrier shattered, taking the pain away with it, and disgorging green-edged shards that he carried from his world to hers. He landed to the west.

A man screamed with the grief of the mortally wounded. Kreindia sat up suddenly and struck her head on the bunk above. Her mistake told her she wasn't as acclimated to ship life as she should have been. Everyone was up now, their noise drowning out her groan. Anthimos, who had a lighter sleep, awakened without injury, but looked equally troubled. Both jumped to their feet, fully dressed from the time they laid down.

Someone called out, "All hands on deck," and Kreindia let the flow carry her upward, until many reversed their course in terror, and she had to fight her way through while ducking at the bulkheads. She didn't mind shoving at people with all her strength. This wasn't a crowded day at the forum or the market square. It felt good to be running toward a need rather than away from it as she did at Hagia Sophia. She tried not to think of the reason behind it.

Topside, it was raining flaming arrows into the night. Most went into the water, a few were being put out on deck, and one, so far, resulted in a fatality. Those who ran must have seen the man's suffering as he burned. She saw what caused the panic. He died near the hatch, an arrow in his back, one arm outstretched as though reaching for help. The charred corpse still blazed around its feet. If he had run toward them, and gotten down the hatch at close quarters, everyone might have been lit by his flame. Those who emerged empty handed dare not touch him.

Kreindia surveyed the chaos on deck. Since the ship had not reached Athens, they had no new dromarch to command it. Kreindia had told them they all answer to her. At this point, then, responsibility rested in her hands. She fought a rising panic with a deep, slow breath. Remember, she told herself, Irene once ruled the whole of Byzantium alone.

She and Anthimos joined the first mate, Kostos Apion, in the relative safety afforded by the lee of the xylokastron. Kostos looked to the distance through a long, conical tube to focus on one point at a time. Kreindia made her first assessment from the arrow pattern.

Kreindia said, "They are barely in range, a lucky shot."

Kostos lowered his viewer slowly and stared at her, trying to decide how much trouble she would be. Then he looked at Anthimos, whose arms were crossed where he could easily draw his sword. Kostos licked his dry lips and pointed at the nearest raiders. "Look."

Two ships closed on them, splitting off to both sides. On each, they saw a black hawk outlined by white in a green field. "They fly the Aghlabid flag of Benghazi, Tripolitania," Kostos continued. "They want us to know. They want us to fear."

"What kind of military man are you?" demanded Kreindia.

"The kind that knows the odds. We have only three dromons, and there are six of THEM out there—war galleys just as good as ours. The Aghlabid pirates have never raided in such numbers."

"They are getting bolder," she said.

"Is it an invasion?" asked Anthimos.

"If it were an invasion, their ships would number in the thousands," she replied. "Still, there may be more behind them."

"It won't take thousands to defeat us tonight," said the first mate.

With her uncle missing from her side, she found herself filling in for him, taking on his unflinching characteristics for the sake of those who would fight under her. "They are testing us," she said. "We need to meet the challenge. We will teach them the fear they seek for us."

"What can we do but fight a delaying action and hope for some relief from Athens," said Kostos, his face etched in desperation.

She watched a small flame guttering on the water. "No. Athens will never reach us in time. We will contrive to fight poorly, and let them try to board."

"That's suicide."

"It isn't. When they come near, we'll use Greek Fire."

"We don't possess it."

"This is not my first battle, Kostos Apion. You will find it in the xylokastron, and you will use it."

"Your ladyship, it is a secret, only to be used in large scale conflict."

"Do not try my resolve. We are outnumbered, they may be preparing an invasion, and we have to stop them here."

Another rain of arrows swept them, this time more accurately, and too close to where the leadership stood.

"They're killing us," protested Kostos. "Let us feign to surrender."

"No, if we do that, the Aghlabid may sense a trap. Light the cauldron." Kostos repeated the command and saw that it was done. Other men answered the attack with arrows of their own. Lacking organization, they were not greatly effective. Only the artillery crew and water brigades were brought to the fore. Kreindia kept them busy putting out any flames on deck or in the rigging, and raising personal shields to ward off the next attack.

Seeing the Byzantines in disarray, the two closest of the enemy ships closed on them from both sides, preparing to box them in and board.

"Load the onager," she called, using their private name for the catapults. It was named after the wild ass for the way it bucked. . Anthimos joined in, hauling up casks, and handing them off. The next man fitted each cask with a dowel, dipped it in a viscous black paste, and loaded it into the catapult, where it waited to be lit.

The black hawk flags were six hundred yards distant, then five hundred. The defenders withstood another hail of arrows. Half a dozen men went down. Kreindia shuddered, finding it no easier to bear their deaths for having seen them first in a vision. The preview repeated in real life somehow made it even harder.

"We are in range to fire now," pleaded Kostos.

"Hold fire," she said in her uncle's command voice.

"But they are on top of us. We're taking casualties."

"Hold fire," she repeated in a crisp and steady tone. "I need them well under it no matter where they run." Kreindia watched and waited, holding in cold abeyance any emotion that threatened to rear its head.

"Your ladyship, in case this does not work, we have to prepare to scuttle to protect the Greek Fire secret."

"There will be no scuttling."

"But even if we defeat these, we are so outnumbered, the others will board us, and they will be more careful."

"Not much chance of that. Look again. Three of them are floating trim by the stern. We can run circles around them at eleven knots. With the booty they've taken on, they will scarcely hit eight." Kostos peered into the dark, probably wondering why he did not see the situation on his own. They were not as effectively overpowered as he feared.

At four hundred yards, she ordered, "Fire," loud enough that all could hear she was in charge. Some of the men moved even before Kostos could convey the order.

The onagers bucked in two directions, launching their payloads like fiery dragons roaring with the thunder of heaven. The dromon shook under them as if it could shake apart. The night lit up from both sides as though it were day, matching her vision exactly.

The enemy proceeded to do what anyone would. They used their firemen and water supplies to try to smother the flames. In so doing, they sealed their fate, as the water only spread the Greek Fire. Their screams were deafening, and horrible to hear, but to Kreindia it meant her people, her charges would live.

Still, the threat did not cease as some of their tormentors were able to continue to loose arrows, and the remaining enemy ships drew nearer. Even in this near-victory, a possible disaster loomed.

"Prime the pumps," she ordered. "Fire at will."

Kostos repeated the order to the appropriate crews. Instead of individual rockets, plumes of liquid fire poured from the Byzantine's pumps in continuous stream, devastating the remains of the two enemy ships under their thumb. No sail and no oar survived to be raised for escape. Anyone who didn't burn were taking their chances swimming to reach the safety of the untouched vessels. Even as they tried, the other four ships changed course to run. Crews on all three dromons cheered.

Kreindia stood on the wooden mid-castle and absorbed the dazzling light, while Kostos ordered cease-fire, and Anthimos watched for treachery. From what she'd heard, the waters from Athens to the top of the boot were infested with these pirates. She only hoped they got the message.

CHAPTER 27
Where Are The Horses?

THE SEABIRDS WHEELED overhead and cried incessantly, wishing they could get at the plethora of tasty goods being unloaded at the docks of Piraeus for Athens. The Mediterranean Gulls had a body the color of a pale rainy sky, and black head like a mask befitting a bandit. Once in a while, their sharp eyes discerned a relaxation of vigilance, and they swooped in to steal a fish as the lot changed hands. More often they flew in for close reconnaissance and got swatted away. Some contented themselves with investigating the smell of a carelessly dropped morsel. Fresh meat or rotting, they were just as happy.

Kreindia walked blank-eyed through the wheeling and dashing birds end to end along the pier, and back again, reluctant to venture into the city even with time on her hands. Anthimos had taken the rare opportunity to visit his Greek relatives and friends. Kreindia could not do the same. With her time-blindness always ready to undo her, idle hours were never her friend. She had enough to occupy her mind as she unscrolled a cartographer's rendering of the empire, and forced herself to think like a general. Her escape from Constantinople led to escape from a personal attack, and then a pirate attack. Three attacks in a short space meant that either you were taking a highly vulnerable route or your enemy was impatient. As they were failed attacks, it might have been a little of both.

One of the dock's broad piles made a fine table for her work. She glanced at the position of the sun, and settled in. A map's view of the journey from the capitol of Byzantium to the heart of the Frankish Kingdom looked like a trip down a steep hill to Athens, followed by a torturous climb up an even higher hill. If so, Kreindia was now at the bottom, gazing up at the daunting heights to which she must go.

The convoy's furthest destination was Venezia at the very top of Itale's boot. From there she could easily slip away a few miles east to the port of Aquileia by any means necessary. With surprise generally on the enemy's side, she hoped to recapture some of that element by keeping the last segment of her route off the planning chart. She had to put more thought into scheming than her opponents did—wake up earlier in the morning, so to speak. What else was she missing? She memorized every town's name in the corridor formed by the boot and the Balkan's Dalmatian coast. No matter how hard she stared at the map, however, it would not reveal what dangers could lay in wait.

Placing the map back in its tube, Kreindia inspected preparations for the next leg of their voyage. The wharf was a hive of activity all around her. Each dromon had to be raised and exchanged at Athens, just as First Mate Kostos Apion was to be exchanged for a fit dromarch. Not only did the one vessel suffer damage to be repaired, but all needed to have their hulls dried and patched before their next journey.

Out of curiosity, she watched the ship that protected them so well being taken out of service. A junior officer guided it to a flooded basin, had it fitted with an enormous set of support straps, and at his signal the basin partially drained. A team of men hauled the dromon the rest of the way out of the water. Only when the ship was suspended high on giant winches did

Kreindia notice its name painted on the side: The Delias, a woman's name. Remarkable that she hadn't noticed how badly battered it looked when they were aboard and fighting for their lives. Now that she knew Wade coexisted with her in her world, somewhere to the north and west, she shuddered to think how close they came to never reaching those shores. Traversing the remaining distance to actually meet Wade against the efforts of those who opposed her mission would yet be a formidable challenge.

Here she was on her own, surviving for the unimpressive span of three days. Without the sheltering military successes of her guardian uncle, would she have come into her own by the strength of her talents or would she have floundered in a weakness of spirit? Without her uncle's strong example would she have known how to take charge?

One or two familiar faces drifted back from leave, looking grim. Not all of the crew were changed. Kreindia would have felt better if they had been. On the other hand, how would she know if a traitor were not put in at Athens? Just how far did the personal networks of Thomas, Zoticus, or Thamar extend? When this trip was planned, their treachery was not taken into consideration. She decided she had to consider hiring some soldiers of her own to see her safely to her destination.

She didn't notice the man come up on her. "Ho, my lady, do not be alarmed. I am Maro Sgouros, dromarch of the Pellene. Would you be Kreindia, niece of Michael? I was once attached to his command." Maro stood no more than average height, but with his overdeveloped upper body, and easy, fearless manner, gave a sense of being larger than life.

"Yes, Maro Sgouros, I am told you are many leagues superior to our former dromarch."

His demeanor switched to mock seriousness. "Flattery is a balm for the landward. I can only say I am many leagues more alive. I place that virtue at the top of my career choices."

"Then I can expect a greater concern for security on this trip." By not condescending to make it a question she began to win him over. His bearded, sea worn face creased in an ebullient smile. If not for her attachment to Wade and the age difference, she might have been attracted to the new dromarch.

"Yes, and in return you will not be forced to take over my ship," he winked. "Bring some bodyguards with you this time."

Sgouros had been well briefed on the first leg of her journey. They understood each other perfectly.

"Come see the flagship," said Maro with pride.

The Pellene looked beautiful as they approached, and appeared from a distance to be seaworthy. Kreindia once knew a girl of that name, vacuous in the extreme, capricious to cover her inadequacies. That Pellene was beautiful too. Kreindia hoped the ship did not take after her.

"I've doubled the dromons as a deterrent force," Maro said, as if in answer to her troubled thoughts. "The number of merchant vessels we protect are about the same, so we will have many hands free."

"The Arabs may be preparing for all out war."

He shook his head in disagreement. "You've said so in your report. The cost of fielding our full navy on a daily basis would be staggering. Until we know more, six dromons are all I can do. With these we can easily handle twelve attackers."

She nodded thoughtfully, and noticed that Maro looked past her at something.

Anthimos joined them at the head of a sizable entourage, all of them big and solid. She was glad to see him return.

"Anthimos, did you bring us back all of your relatives?" Kreindia asked.

The eunuch laughed. "No, I've hired you a team of bodyguards." To the dromarch he said, "Don't worry, all of them are marines that know their way equally around a merchant ship or a battle."

"Imperial requisition?" asked Kreindia.

"That's not the best idea for personal services of this, ah, nature. I'm afraid I've promised much of your gold."

"That's all right. All of us today seem to be thinking the same thing."

~ W ~

WITH remarkable swiftness and efficiency, the assemblage of merchant and warrior ships made ready as they did every fair weather day. The cargo-loving flat bottoms pushed off just after a dromon took point, while the rest put their additional time to good use. At last Kreindia sailed, cloaked by commerce and the fleet that protected it. She minded not at all. What seemed a slow trip on the featureless sea actually was many times faster than the shorter distance by land, particularly if you wanted to transport provisions rather than foraging.

Kreindia walked the deck with Anthimos and her new staff, and met the eyes of the rowers when they chose to look up at her. In addition to her bodyguards, every tenth marine on the flagship was in her employ as a lookout, half of them below decks. By that account she was now safer than she ever would be in her life. Anthimos, for his part, looked very much at ease with the arrangements. Still, a ship at sea was an easy place to go missing, and each port of call brought its own uncertainty, not to mention the pirates who made their own ports in the open waters.

"What are you thinking, Kreindia?" asked Anthimos as he bestowed a faint smile of admiration on the xylokastron stowage, something he did for every well-organized corner of the ship.

"I'm thinking that whatever measures we take, our weaknesses will prove to be elsewhere. At the same time, the irrational girl in me says that every mile we pass is a mile more secure. I fear I will fall victim to my own false confidence."

"I know that your visions don't reveal every twist and turn of life, some of which are fit to change. Do your visions ever tell you what ultimately comes of our empire?"

She stopped and looked at him, her eyes flashing prescient blue powder. "You don't want to know."

~ W ~

THE Pelopennese proved quiet with only brief stops at the island of Cythera where they took on goat cheese, flax and small statues of Aphrodite in return for other staples. They next made landfall at Methoni and Pylos where hardened Spartans would retrieve their goods and drag them inland across seventy-five miles to their homes. Between the two places, and for the next several hundred miles, their greatest exposure was the wide-open Ionian Sea to their west flank where a large force could cross less easily detected than in the busy crowd of islands filling the mouth of the Aegean.

In the largest stretch of non-costal water the journey presented, they had to cross the Adriatic Sea from Corfu to Brundisium, exposed on both flanks. That would be the last, best opportunity for pirates to attack them if indeed such an outcome were to be their fate. All she could do was wait.

Late into the night, or what seemed a long time to her, she drifted off to sleep by degrees, flashes of troubled lightning behind her eyelids. Her vision state continued to hold sway, powerful forces at work through the dark hours.

Kreindia stood high on a platform in a prisoner's dock facing a very old priest and a landed noble, the weight of her chains draining strength from her shoulders. She found herself being admonished or instructed, but could not hear the words. Guards on each side tore her shirt away, exposing her bare flesh to a blast of heat. Looking down, she realized it was not her shirt and flesh, but Wade's. In her strangest vision ever, she stood not on a high platform, but inside Wade's tall body, stretched to fill his shape, looking out of his eyes while their shared feet touched the damp stone floor. She lived a portion of his sensations, while he, overwhelmed, did not even notice her presence, or was unattuned to it.

When he turned to the gallery, she turned with him, and saw the handful of odd spectators with their puerile fascination. One cast a look of particular bile. When Wade turned back toward his inquisitors, they were angrier for having lost his attention. Whatever Kreindia had failed to hear, the boiling cauldron in front of Wade spoke volumes. The flames looked like they could get out of control, and indeed someone encouraged them even higher. At a signal, the chains dropped away, making her feel light enough to float. Recoiling from the madness, she did slowly rise up out of his body-space to watch the scene from above. Leaving him, she regained sound, heard every fiery pop, every cough in the chamber, every breath of anticipation. She heard clearly the words, "Do as you're bid, or die where you stand."

After a brief scuffle, Wade plunged his left arm into the boiling froth. Kreindia, in her physical detachment, didn't feel it directly, but his screams roiled her blood. She knew his task was the nearly impossible stone-in-the-slot test. Her beloved Wade drew back and began the agonizing process anew.

Kreindia, aghast, floated still higher, and could not control herself, leaving the chamber, leaving the vicinity, and finally departing from the world itself. Wade's screams followed her, reaching out into space, her only continuous thread. As he screamed, her vision refocused, and she found she could still view his plight, though removed to a great distance, a split view from another world.

As much as she wished she could help Wade, the new situation demanded her attention most immediately. She found herself in the body of an unknown girl, seated in a small chariot, fashioned dangerously close to the ground, and missing its horses. The stranger sat awkwardly and very still, trapped in an invisible cage with bonds that prevented all but the tiniest twitch.

Then something new happened to her vision state. The chariot girl sensed Kreindia's presence. Before Kreindia could decide what it meant, the girl somehow withdrew, and allowed or caused Kreindia to take over her every thought and whim, to take over her very life.

Kreindia, in shock, first tried to stand up, and could not command her arms to push on the armrests. Likewise, she could not lean forward to shift her center of gravity to her legs, which also proved to be useless. I'm crippled, she realized; a creature that, in her world, would typically not live to maturity. Yet to her it felt more like being bound up than crippled. She could feel the pressure of her thighs against the seat, feel the pressure of each foot on its footrest, and still she had no command. Her eyes worked. She tried the lesser muscles, failing with the toes, but finding a finger free. In her random experiments, she nudged a flexible stick, less than one tenth of a foot in size, and her little chariot heaved forward alarmingly. Astonished, she tried again with the same result. A sideways nudge of the stick made the wheeled seat turn and move in the indicated direction. Where were the horses? There was not even a small mule to explain the movement. Were they invisible like the cage that settled over her limbs? She pushed the stick forward and held it there a beat longer than before. The chariot responded in kind. Nothing drove her conveyance. It must be a tiny magic wand she possessed. The wand controlled the horseless chariot with an eldritch willpower that could not command her limbs.

All the while, Wade screamed, desperate and raw. He needed her and she was cut off from him. No, Kreindia thought, this chariot girl was not her, and she was not truly there in the distant world. And yet she played the bizarre role given to her. Was she forced to watch, helpless, while Wade's ordeal played out, or could she assert her will, exert a kind of control in the real world, if only she tried hard enough? She stopped moving the chariot, and focused her mind on the split off view of Wade. She allowed it to fill her thoughts and view until there was no other.

Again she experienced the sensation of floating in the chamber above Wade. She thought of chains and their weight as a device to lower herself back into him. The burning nearly sent her fleeing. Waves of merciless heat racked her with the pain felt by Wade. He had endured it far longer than she had. She wondered, How little time remains before Wade's body and soul are spent?

She broke away from the uppermost part of his form, and peered down deep into the cauldron to a darkness where she brought her own light. Kreindia found the proper slot cut into the side of the vessel. Yet she could not get his attention! She had to take over. She concentrated fiercely; she needed to control only his left hand. The situation was far different than that of chariot girl where control was relinquished to Kreindia. Wade was unaware of her trying to help, and he too focused everything he had on the purposeful movement of his left arm. The advantage to her was that Wade's might waned. With all of her strength, she locked on, guiding Wade's hand to the proper slot, holding fast until the task was declared complete, watching the aftermath in a fading withdrawal, and then blacking out along with him.

Kreindia awoke with a start, and clambered up, almost to prove that she still could. She could not. Kreindia collapsed to the filthy wooden planking. Two of her bodyguards ran over and put her back in her bunk.

Kreindia groaned a thank you, explained that she was unwell, and would need rest for some time. In her weakened state she took stock. Her upper eyelids felt hot against her lower, and the whole bunk stank of her sweat. That was not sleep she had experienced, and the sights and feelings it produced were not the harmless passions of a mind surrendering its earthly and orderly control. Hers was not a body freed of daily tension. Vision sleep was nothing remotely like rest, and this experience proved unique. She had never before managed to change a vision while it was in progress. Her exertions left her drained and feverish. Inside her battered and muted strength, propping it up, came a shared pride. The aid came from Kreindia; the endurance belonged mostly to Wade. Before she passed out, she smiled.

~ W ~

MARO Sgouros checked the position of his fleet in the first morning light. He saw with satisfaction that none had gone astray from their formation in the dark hours despite the rolling fog and the fact that they had left Corfu, their last landmark, well behind. The Pellene now led the way to Brundisium in the heel of Itale's boot across the open Adriatic, exactly on schedule. As Maro inspected the rigging, he spotted a familiar face on deck.

"Ho, Anthimos," said Maro. "I've not seen Kreindia this morning. It's unlike her to miss a sunrise. Did the overcast sky disappoint her?"

"Kreindia is below decks, unwell. She is, however, fully protected."

"You say that so that I either don't worry or don't take advantage. I could play injured at your lack of faith, but it is admirable that you do not let down your guard, even with me."

Anthimos gave him a measuring look. "Especially with you. You would make a most formidable opponent."

"Like Kreindia, you flatter me." But Anthimos could tell he liked it.

Both men were startled by an incoherent cry from above. "Black hawks!" the lookout shouted. "The Aghlabid flag!"

"How many?" the mate demanded, scrambling halfway up the rigging.

The dromarch extended his scope to see for himself. Sure enough, on the port side, they faced a small armada of vessels from Arabian Africa.

"The lookout counts thirteen vessels," his first mate announced.

"The Arabs would never do thirteen," the dromarch said quietly, shaking his head. "There must be at least seven of them out of sight to make twenty."

"Or eighty-seven out of sight to make a hundred," Anthimos averred gravely.

Sgouros paled at the thought. "Let us hope they have a bureaucracy like ours that tells them to first test the number that gets the job done."

"Still," Anthimos muttered, "even twenty ships are bold. But when were these Arab raiders ever less than bold?"

A feint flash enveloped them, almost beyond perception. "Lightning storm," called the lookout, "deep to starboard."

"As though we hadn't enough trouble," Anthimos raged.

While the lookout scanned to starboard, Maro saw the next threat before anyone else—dark shapes in a bank of fog. His great chest heaved up as he gulped the air.

"Seven more Aghlabid to port," shouted the lookout, confirming the dromarch's suspicions. These were even closer, having sneaked in under cover.

"There's your twenty," said Anthimos. "There is still time to send a ship to warn Corfu. Else we may all be killed by the Aghlabid with none to say why."

"I promise you none of us will die today from the Aghlabid," said Maro. Then he barked out, "All ships. Hard to starboard, full ahead, merchant speed. Make for the storm."

"We don't want to fight in a lightning storm!" Anthimos protested. "Your signals will be obscured."

Maro looked to the port side, at the Arab colors picking up the stiffening wind. "Neither do they. That storm is beyond the horizon for the Arab ships. I'm betting that if they knew about it, they never would have attacked."

The Pellene turned first, which alerted the others to look for a string of signal flags that bore their instructions. A light spray came over the bow. Anthimos, in charge of supervising Kreindia's protection agonized over whether to wake her, and questions of where and how she would be most safe. He could see that the storm was coming up on them even as they moved toward it. The gap would close quickly. He headed for the hatch, deciding that it would be best to keep her informed.

Below, he saw Timocrates of the security detail just returning from her bedside.

"How is she?" asked Anthimos.

"Her fever is reduced, but it is unaccountable for sleep to cause exhaustion. The ship's doctor has not seen anything like it."

"Can we rouse her?"

"You can but she knows not what we say."

"I have to try. Kreindia," said Anthimos to her gently. "Kreindia, can you awaken?" he said more loudly, taking her by the shoulder.

She stirred and murmured.

"Kreindia, we're traveling into a storm, and the ship may come under attack. You need to be prepared for the worst."

As though to underscore Anthimos' fears, a high swell lifted and dropped the ship. Somewhere a timber cracked. She opened her eyes and said, "Your arm will heal, Wade."

Anthimos and Timocrates looked at each other. "Delirious," they agreed.

The mate came down and called, "All available hands on deck!"

"Stay with her," said Anthimos. "I'm going up to help. Let me know if she comes around."

"Wait," called Timocrates. "Can you pay us what we were owed if she does not survive?'

"Absolutely not. You had better see to it that she does survive." Anthimos turned to the others. "That goes for all of you dogs."

Emerging into the frenzy of activity on deck, Anthimos could see a series of large waves headed toward them, and he felt grateful at least that the water would not hit them broadside. As the last one out, they made him seal the hatch against the storm.

CHAPTER 28
Brenii Pass

LIGHTNING FLOWED ACROSS the sky like sparkling wine. In the open sea, some of it was bound to strike whatever stuck up out of the water without regard for wood, iron, or flesh, and without reference to Greek or Aghlabid flags. Maro hoped conditions would stave off battle and do his charges more good than harm. The worst of the bargain was that his ships had to surrender to the mercy of the storm first. He succored himself with the thought that they would have had to enter the tempest sooner or later.

Maro cut down the speed of the Pellene so that it would stay closer to the action if any action ensued. Another dromon led the merchant ships under the dark clouds, as the seas grew heavy. He ordered the remaining four dromons to spread out so that the fate of one would not be the fate of another.

Four Aghlabid ships, from the pack of seven, followed them into the gnashing seas as the others executed a retreat. Next, the more distant group of thirteen saw the danger, and also turned to run as the errant group sailed on. Why would four break formation? Maro wondered. It could be the fog, or mixed signals. Yet they would soon have to notice their fellows gone away.

Thunder exploded all around in angry warning as a wooly darkness pulled overhead. Every robust ripple of the ocean rolled his fleet like splinters of driftwood. Still their oblivious pursuers gave chase. What was this insanity? Did they not see that they would be taking on six well-equipped dromons without the support of their fleet? Maro recalled that Kreindia's report said four Aghlabid ships had escaped the last battle. Could this group be them? Were they unaware that Greek Fire was unaffected by water? Did they not notice what happened to their fellows? Did they think a storm forced him to revert to conventional warfare? Perhaps they did not seek battle, but were assigned to mark where the Byzantine fleet went. Or perhaps they were too angry to think at all.

The leader of the four ships ran up red flags that looked much like the storm warning flags used by the Greeks. So they did realize their situation. They struck sails, and beat their drums double-time, leaving no doubt of their intentions.

Maro was not the type to expend any sweat worrying over errors, or denying the current situation. He ordered all hands to battle stations.

As Maro ordered Greek Fire prepared, the enemy wasted no time. The lead ship fired a load of stones on a catapult, scattering them in a vertical pattern. The Arabs were no strangers to the catapult, as Maro knew; they might even have invented it first. The initial shot was fired for effect, to see how a chosen angle corresponded to where they landed. All went into the water. The second shot found its mark as well as any could. Many hit the water; a few landed on deck; and some, disastrously, struck the Pellene in its hull at the waterline.

~ W ~

THUNDER rattled every timber below decks. Kreindia stirred and opened her eyes halfway. Her security detail approached for a closer look. Timocrates said to them, "All the marines and rowers are topside. There is no one to threaten Kreindia here. Go up and help fight. I will stay with her." The men cleared out on his command, leaving a low rumbling echo in the empty spaces. Lamps swayed in their cages, sowing a confusion of light and shadow.

Kreindia struggled up instinctively. "My fever passed. I want to join the fight as well."

"I can see you are no condition to do that," said her remaining guard.

"I'll be all right in a day or two. Just let me—"

Timocrates drew a knife. "I'm sorry. We don't have a day or two. I don't think you're going to make it."

Every sailor carried his own knife. Kreindia found her scabbard empty. Hoping not to reveal her alarm, she said, "No, look, I'm fine. I can get up."

"Come now," he said as he approached. "Cooperate. I did my share of work. I only want what's fair. I'm not going to hurt you."

Michael taught her never to trust the words of a man with a knife. She wondered about her options. Timocrates had the sailor's build, shaped by the sort of labor he did: relatively scrawny legs supporting a large upper body. Even on her best day, any move that led to a contest of strength would doom her. In her depleted condition, her surest bet would have been a sword to keep him at bay. Anything short of that had to be very subtle.

"Anthimos minds the gold," she said.

"No, I've kept my eye on it. You have it under your robe."

"You're wrong," she insisted calmly.

Timocrates moved to cut her purse. The ship lurched, she put up her hands defensively, and he slit her from palm to elbow. The cut did not reach deep. She felt a rush of energy that shuddered through every muscle and nerve in her body, and forced her eyes open wide. If not an exaggerated strength, she was at least relived of her weariness. But by then he had his knee pinning her left arm to her chest while he gripped her bloody right wrist and prepared to stab her unprotected head. His weight made it impossible for her to move.

"Don't you want to know what my visions revealed about you?" she asked. "You have to know before I die."

In Timocrates' uncertainty, he relaxed his grip enough for her to slip her hand downward just a few inches. With the ball of her thumb, she pressed the tip of his, drove it in hard, and twisted his hand past the length of his tendons. When he reeled back in pain, she kicked down and across to shatter his ankle. The knife disappeared somewhere to her left in the uncertain light. Had she not bent to retrieve it, the stone that came through the hull would have crashed into her back. The sea rushed in immediately. She looked up, hoping the stone finished off Timocrates. It had not, although the water had moved him some distance. Through the chaotic eddies, he made his way back toward her, swimming with a loose hull plank under his arms, a creature of raw anger. With the ship filling up with water, and the exit blocked, her only way to go was out through the hole. When she looked back, a surge lifted Timocrates up and smashed his head into the beams. He sank into the water dead or unconscious.

Kreindia grabbed a plank of her own, and washed out into the middle of a war zone. The listing ship above her was painted with splashes of lightning and fire. Engines of destruction rivaled the thunder while tiny flaming embers fell in competition with the rain. All she could do was hope a stray arrow didn't find her before her companions did.

She gulped at air leaden with sulfur. Already, she felt her newfound energy waning. Her one-piece raft was turned barnacle side up, giving the underside of her arms a rough ride. Kreindia didn't have the strength to turn it over. She couldn't focus past the shells of the sticky little animals and the brine that washed over them. Thoughts of The Delia and her last sea battle blurred together with the current conflict in unbidden fragments, and she wondered if that meant that despite all the madness she might sleep.

Something blunt nudged her hard, bringing her wide-awake once more. She saw the distinctive six-gilled shark sliding past, bigger than the length of her body and many times as heavy. It moved with a sense of hubris and entitlement common to its kind. The pale shapes near the surface promised an entire menacing school of them. After swimming a length understood only by him, the first shark came back and hit her harder than the first time. Her fist on its broad snout availed her nothing. She thought she saw her reflection in its pitiless unblinking eyes. Kreindia's freely flowing blood no doubt attracted them. So far only the one great monster was determined to get at her directly while the rest of the school circled patiently. Humans were not often on their menu.

In the next round she had a feeling there would be no more bumping. This shark was certain of her frailty. For the final run it came at her with open jaws. She wedged the plank in its mouth as it bit down. Although it snapped the wood in a single bite, it shoved past her and gave her the opportunity she needed. She carved into its many gills with Timocrates' knife, first down, then across so that a flap peeled away and bled profusely. The other sharks went after their companion instead of her. The sight of their mindless frenzy made her shiver.

Kreindia, more drained than ever, turned back to the Pellene. It looked so very odd from her point of reference. Then too, it looked odd so low in the water and sinking. Soon she would have lots of company.

~ W ~

FROM the listing deck of his crippled Pellene, Maro ordered, "Fire at will." The chaos of trying to fight in a storm was so complete that their shots were more likely to hit by accident than design. In a level playing field, the Byzantines could be expected to win easily. Bad luck meant the early loss of their flagship, a second ship and a merchant vessel. It seemed their tormentors were counting on luck, and wanted to inflict as much damage as possible.

But the repeated flip of a gold piece tends to produce a fair result in the long run. Lightning evened the score, taking out half the enemies' number. Maro now commanded four seaworthy fighters to two of the Arabs'. Once again, the pirates turned and fled. Believing this remnant were the same force that attacked The Delia when Kreindia ran her, he could not allow them to get away. As his last act aboard the Pellene, he ran flags to signal pursuit.

~ W ~

Kreindia awakened to the sight of Anthimos alone putting a compress on her head. She saw her right arm well bandaged.

"Welcome to the Phaedre. Are you awake for real this time?'

"I think so. I was so worn out, my mind did not conjure a single image."

"Maro has been to see you several times. I think he wanted to tell you personally that none of the Aghlabid ships escaped total destruction. No vanity there, hmm?"

Kreindia discovered some bruises when she laughed. They sailed calm seas on an identical ship. It was hard to believe that the Pellene was gone. She thought again of Wade and her vision about the girl in the chariot. A ship, too, is a conveyance without horses. Could the dream have been a foretelling of her helplessness in the squall? With a ship, the wind is the invisible force that moves it. There are sails to control the ship in place of magic wands. If this were a vision, then it mixed dream symbolism with prediction, more like the dreams of ordinary people. But no, in her vision she was certain she was in the other world—Wade's world—where magic wands and horseless chariots could well be possible.

Kreindia believed that all serious danger of further sea battles had passed. There remained one last threat. For an assassin, the open water presented nearly unique opportunities, and by the end of her trip they would be desperate to strike.

"Casualty report on the security detail?" she asked.

Anthimos soaked her compress in a basin before pressing it to her head again. "Everyone in your employ were rescued with the exception of Timocrates. He's missing."

She withheld comment. "So it's nearly a full payroll. Is the gold safe?"

"Of course. It's stowed on a merchant ship with the rest of the luggage."

"Timocrates had some crazy idea that you had given it to me."

"Did he trouble you about it?"

"Not very much. In fact, he was nice enough to lend me his knife. Oh, and that reminds me, I saved this lovely shark's tooth for you. Did you know that when they bite something, they lose a few?"

~ W ~

THE Adriatic corridor from Brundisium northward passed without further incident, confirming that the Longobards of this region were well and truly defeated by the Franks. The fleet made its final landing at Ri'Alto, Venezia, one of only two Byzantine-allied places north of Sicily. Her prior travels never took her to this unique locale, the floating city. It was the opportunity of a lifetime to visit Palazzo Ducale, the Doges' Palace, and offer the hand of friendship to Doge Angelo Participazio, which was exactly why she must not go.

She entered Palazzo Ducale by the main entrance, and ducked out the back way immediately, just ahead of danger, as she would find out later. To pull off the deception, she had to part ways with Anthimos who covered her at the palace, feigning disappointment to Participazio that she failed to appear. By boat, it was a short trip to Aquileia, a rebuilt Roman town. From there she wanted the road to Monte Brenii, one of the mountain passages known to her court in the east. It offered a reasonably direct line to Aachen via the abbey at Sintlas Ow.

~ W ~

THE route to Aachen through Sintlas Ow was a natural and sensible path, both for tactical and political reasons. Although there was only time for a single letter to go to The Monk, and a single reply back, it was sufficient for planning. Tankred, the oblate met her at Aquileia, having waited only one day, but prepared to wait for a week or more. It was he who told her that the mountains at Monte Brenii had ears. He repeated the local superstition that those who spoke classic Latin or Greek were guaranteed free passage. Those who spoke the barbaric Frankish, Gaulish or Gothic tongues could sometimes vanish without a trace. It had been so for hundreds of years. Since Kreindia fell into a safe category, she diplomatically refrained from disputing the mythology.

Certainly the thin air and tall rock walls of Monte Brenii produced some unusual acoustics at night. The general's niece in her also found it peculiar that birds of different species seemed to communicate with each other so readily. If she didn't know better, she might have thought a hidden army lay in wait, but the sounds were too perfect for human throats, and every time she thought she heard something suspicious it blended back into natural sounds. In any case, what unknown army could it be? No war raged between the boundary of Itale and Swabia. Who would it belong to? How would it stay provisioned and invisible? Distant parts of the world held wonders, she concluded. She would concern herself about it only when she had more time.

Kreindia arrived at the monastery Sintlas Ow, met the Monk and Pepin the Hunchback. Pepin seemed perversely ready to welcome someone stranger than he. To cover her high-level mission to the Franks, she had to establish herself both at the monastery and a nearby convent where women were allowed to stay. The few days' rest would be helpful too. Deep in her heart, the selfish reason was that it gave her a better chance to cross paths with Wade.

She sent Tankred on a shopping excursion that she sensed would locate Wade, and it did. She understood that when The Monk sent for her at the convent, Wade had been wide-awake, yet when she first saw him, he was insensate and thrashing about. How astonishing to see him in the flesh without being able to speak to him.

In his presence, she found it relatively easy to communicate with his mind, to heal him with their bond as well as her potions. Much as his battered condition worried her, being with him gave her the false impression that everything would be all right. No sooner was Wade well then she heard the bad news of Charlemagne's illness and the probable failure of her mission after she had come so far.

Riding out to assist the mortally ill Charlemagne, Raginpert had captured her, and her failure was complete.

CHAPTER 29
The Protection of Ravenna

*"It is not unusual for Armenians to be prominent in the army, with
their eager tradition of military service. One might even expect to see
an Armenian rise as far as Stratêgos in an important themata. With
no blood ties to the throne however, it was highly unusual to see Leo
the Armenian take the purple. Failing the combined support of fellow
generals Thomas the Slav, and Michael of Amorium in particular,
no such ascension would have been possible."*

—*Circa 813 A.D.*, Scriptor Incertus

ORGET TIME. It served no purpose here. Only the
occasional tray visited the inescapable box that held
Kreindia. The tray held meals that declared themselves
as neither breakfast nor dinner, consisting as they did of some
sort of lumpy paste with water. The meals came at irregular
intervals so that she could not count them to mark passage of
days. Leaves did not grow; mirrors were absent; day did not
follow night. Kreindia may have been growing younger for all
she knew. Time had lost its role, banished along with flowing
silk, chatty summer breezes, and thoughtful tenderness. All
she could hear was the squealing of mice. She hoped there
would not come a day when she would have to decide whether
to befriend them or eat them.

She touched the skin around her eyes and neck. They felt as tight as ever, if not better. Of course this notion of allowing that one might grow younger was something only Kreindia would think of to amuse herself. She had no reason to think so; nothing but an open mind and the confusion of having no time sense.

Kreindia had become a chronicler to combat her time weakness. The entries served to fix a date to key events. The writing helped her memorize so that any current event she had written about she knew with precision that no one else could claim. Her cell contained no pen and no paper. Away from those, she didn't know five days from a month, just as without the sun, she didn't know a quarter hour from four hours. If someone asserted that she had spent years in confinement, she could not disagree. If they said it were a few weeks she would find the statement equally plausible. It was said that she was given the gift of shapes at the cost of time.

If you are lying..., Raginpert had said about her revelation that she was Michael the Amorian's niece. The threat hung over her. But she wasn't lying. Her choice in telling the one truth brought risks of its own. If Raginpert confirmed that her relationship to the throne's right hand man were true, he would be even more determined to learn what she was really doing in the west. If he did learn, she could be dead, or worse. Therefore she found it hard to wish that her detention would come to an end.

Most people would be broken by the sensory deprivation, ready to confess to anything to get their accustomed rhythms back. Kreindia had no normal rhythms. Furthermore, while her physical body could be confined, her etheric body—that which sometimes joined Wade—could not. Her short period of nervousness gave way to a kind of hibernation in which her thoughts turned inward. After reviewing all the steps or missteps that brought her from the finest palace to the most ordinary dungeon, and then lacking all opportunities to feed her senses, a curious thing happened. Her mental abilities began to sharpen. Her inward thoughts looped back upon themselves, probing deeper and deeper into her mind.

She started out a powerful oracle with a prodigious memory, and crossed senses. Although the ability to taste shapes appeared useless in itself, she believed that all of her other powers drew from that original source—her ability to dip into another dimension known as the astral plane. Now her memory improved to a further degree. Without anything new to think about, she could recall events from whence she was barely conscious or greatly distracted. For instance, she could recall that the six-gilled shark she fought had four kinds of teeth, distinct from all other sharks. In its upper palate, it had spikes and hooks, and in its lower it had what she thought of as short and long combs. Embedded in her plank were two hook-type teeth, one of which she gifted to Anthimos, and one comb-type with eight points. She missed out on making a souvenir of the spike teeth and the three-point combs. Unbidden, she also recalled some words quietly spoken while she lay in torpor. One sailor bragged that he might "have at her" before she woke up.

Perhaps, she wondered, these changes to her mind wrought through deprivation were the most natural thing in the world. If she were left alone long enough, where would it lead?

~ *W* ~

WHEN the door opened, Kreindia gasped. Raginpert stood in the antechamber and beckoned her out. She grew slightly dizzy as she emerged into the light, and the better-circulated air. She saw prepared food and drink but did not move to touch it even though it looked and smelled far better than any in recent memory. He let her wait at length before he spoke.

"I have good information from someone who just returned from the east. He is not a spy, you understand, just someone I talk to."

"Good information. That means you confirmed my honesty. You know you've made a mistake detaining me."

"I know you are Michael the Amorian's niece, and that he is still favored at the court of the Greeks." Calling the palace at Constantinople the court of the Greeks was the western way of diminishing Byzantium and denying its successor status as Imperium Romanum. The Frankish Kingdom now called itself The Holy Roman Empire in some sort of symbolic or moral competition with the eastern capitol.

Kreindia didn't let it bother her. "So I'm free to go now?"

He laughed nervously, "You were never a captive."

"My uncle will be so pleased to hear that." She strode past him unceremoniously and began to walk out.

Over his shoulder, he said, "Do not pass through that door. You won't get far."

"And why not?" she asked.

"It is dangerous outside in the chaos following Charlemagne's demise."

"If not there, then where?"

"You shall remain as an honored guest within these walls under the protection of Ravenna."

"Ravenna? What treachery is this? We're no where near Ravenna."

He turned and addressed her in a strained voice. "In the absence of law and an orderly society, I consider any building I reside in to be the Exarchate-In-Exile. Hence this is Ravenna's sovereign soil, and all inside its bounds are my subjects whether they be Longobard or Greek, normal…or strange."

"How long must I remain?"

"As long as I say it is necessary for your safety."

"Your hospitality and noble works shall become legend."

The prince allowed the hint of a sardonic smile. "Your uncle still does not know you are in my care. If your sovereign lord and master sees fit, that legend may remain forever in your heart."

Kreindia found a chair and sat heavily. She knew what was coming.

"Of course," Raginpert continued as he poured himself a drink, "my confidence in the safety of the streets would greatly increase if I understood which levers of power were being pulled. That would tell me how soon the unrest would end. For example, it would help if I knew why the niece of such a well-favored general would make a great trip across the seas only to live in a convent. Do they not have convents where you come from?"

She took a deep breath to answer and he stopped her savagely, "Do not tell me again that your study of history demands it."

Kreindia flinched as he intended. She knew because he smiled at it. In that moment she confirmed Raginpert's essential nature: whenever his control was reduced, as it was by her confirmed status in the eastern court, he got angrier. As long as Wade and any of The Monk's allies were free, they might expose him to Byzantium's wrath.

Any increase in his ability to manipulate made him calmer. Did she want him to be angrier or less angry? It depended on whether it worked in the other direction. Would more anger further reduce his control, turning his fury into an Achilles Heel? Or would he snap like a vicious dog too often goaded?

Kreindia nodded in apparent acquiescence. This time when she opened her mouth she said, "Let's see what people who are not captives eat in your household."

He eyed her warily as she crossed to the table and sat down. She casually selected and helped herself to some cheese and wine. "What is the name of this person from the east that knew so much about me?'

"It's not important," he answered carefully.

"It is important to both of us. Let's call your great messenger from the east, Hermes."

"Why?" Her growing confidence seemed to alarm and intrigue him all in one stroke.

She carefully selected some bread as though she weren't hungry and had all the time in the world. She buttered and tasted a tiny bite before speaking again. "Do you trust Hermes?"

"Well enough."

"Delicious."

"What?"

"The bread. 'Well enough' doesn't sound like someone who can keep a secret."

"What secret?"

"Can Hermes do a simple tally, and guess why you were asking about me?"

"If he gets curious, I'll skewer him."

"It's too late for that. You don't know who he has told. For that matter you don't know who any of The Monk's people have told. My point is that you will have to treat me carefully no matter how well you like or dislike what I have to say."

"I'll decide that for myself. Tell me."

"Perhaps tomorrow after I've slept in a real bed."

Raginpert swept all the dishes off the table in a fury. "I will get what I want," he screamed. "Even you will not stop me."

She noticed he did not hit her or disturb her plate. How moderate of him. She stopped eating. "Very well. I will tell you."

His eyes were bulging from the effort of restraint. She glared at him until he slowly sat down.

"I was on a mission from Constantinople," she said.

"I knew it. What do you mean you *were* on a mission? Before I stopped you?"

"Circumstances stopped me. There is no more point to my mission if Charlemagne is dead."

"I knew it."

"You knew nothing," she said calmly. "My mission was never to save the king, but to slay him."

CHAPTER 30
Missi Dominici

RAGINPERT'S EYEBROWS AND the skin of his forehead rose so quickly in response to her remark, his wig could not follow. We are not so different to the east and west, Kreindia reflected. Where she came from, wigs were also required to maintain regulation hair length for a man's station in life. The longer the hair, the purer the pedigree. Raginpert's hair was not the longest.

Kreindia went back to eating the healthy food while she had the chance, seeking out delicacies such as fruit. Her revelation would stand up better if she feigned a haughty indifference. From the corner of her eye, she could see he was thinking of something to reply.

"If your instructions from Constantinople were to assassinate the king, why not say so before?" the prince demanded. "Why wait until now to claim common cause with your captor?"

Kreindia cleared her throat. "You knew nothing of my background before, My Lord. If I were to admit of a taste for royal blood, you might have slain me for treason. Even now I take the chance only because I must."

"That is actually plausible. It is very clever." Raginpert paced the length of the antechamber twice before turning back to her. He lifted his chin. "If your new tale be true, then I wonder why the Greeks did not seek out my support, or other support, in advance. Why did not my informant, Hermes, as you call him, know about this? No, do not bother to answer. I do not believe you. There are too many holes in it." He watched her.

"You can scoff at anything. It no longer matters what you believe. Charlemagne is beyond our reach."

"It does matter in my eyes. As long as you are here, strange one, I will see that it matters to you as well. The Carolingian line is not finished. That son of his will never hold the kingdom together. Nonetheless, he is still a threat to me. I see I have your attention now. You may prove your assertions, and win back your freedom, by traveling to Aquitaine and killing Louis."

Kreindia stood up. "The plan was to kill Charlemagne while tending to him. Louis is not ill. I wouldn't get near him."

"Use your witchery, and that clever mind of yours. I will turn you loose to do it."

"I remember what happened the last time I tried to walk out that door."

"You have my word that you will be free to leave your confinement to do as you are bid. I am willing to give you horses, money, and a safe passage escort. But do not think you can go west after your friend The Monk, ensconce yourself in the court of Louis the Pious, and thereby escape my reach. No, your Wade of Aquitaine is well within my grasp. If you do not wipe out Louis, I shall put out Wade's eyes and have hungry wolves chew his entrails for as long as he might live. Now what say you?"

Kreindia noticed the absence of all sharp objects on the table. Being from Byzantium, she understood how complicated politics could get. If Raginpert were to learn that her real mission was entirely at odds with his interests—that the east wanted to preserve peace with the Franks rather than ride against them on behalf of the Longobards as they had done once before—then she would suffer a gruesome fate. If, however, she accepted Raginpert's deal, and fled without assassinating Louis, Wade would never be safe. Although they might never be together, she could not let anything happen to him.

"I say be damned."

Raginpert laughed loud and long. "That was an excellent bluff, my dear, and wise of you not to carry it any further. I like you more now than I did before. It is a shame you are no more use to me, and must die at my hand. We can probably skip the farce of a trial if you like. I can envision far better uses of that time."

Raginpert leered at her as he approached. Kreindia prepared to defend herself against the well-trained scion of Pavia with nothing more than bread.

He unfastened his cloak and tossed it aside.

"What about my witchery? Aren't you afraid of it?" She spent so much energy downplaying her abilities she didn't know what it would take to convince him otherwise. In some distracted corner of her mind she wondered why Fate thought she deserved to be plagued by both Thamar and her father, Thomas, in the east, and Raginpert in the west.

"Your visions and shapes will not help you now," he said.

"Are you certain of that? Do you know everything about how it works?"

"I will take my chances." He lunged at her.

She stepped aside and kicked, striking him in the hip. She had hoped to get him in the gut. Perhaps her extended stay in a cell had taken its toll.

He got up, dusted himself off, and adjusted his wig. "I underestimated you. Let us see what you do against a dagger."

The door burst open, guttering every lamp. One flame doused. The others sputtered back. Three dark figures swept into the room flanked by armor-clad soldiers of the Holy Roman Empire. In the center stood the oldest man either of them had ever seen, judging by his uncountable wrinkles and veins. A shaft of daylight behind him lit tatters of white hair. Yet he stood straight and powerful as though he would never need a cane.

"Who are you?" said Raginpert, too startled to be insolent.

"I am Manentius," the other said in a booming voice. "Patriarch of Aquileia. To my right is Bassinus, Patriarch of Grado. To my left is Petrus of Pisa. Have we interrupted a liaison? Get dressed, Raginpert!"

Kreindia recognized the names of some of the leading men of the age. All had once lived at the court of Aachen from whence they grew landed, titled, and wealthy. Their combined power must have survived that of Charlemagne himself.

"How dare you come into my sovereign land, my embassy, my sanctuary? You violate the Exarchate-In-Exile." Raginpert shouted. "Antonio!"

"We are the missi dominici. A higher authority, the voice of the new king." The soldiers spread out.

Antonio appeared, bending, and clutching his hands to his gut as if in supplication to beg his master's pardon.

"Antonio, why did you not—"

Antonio fell forward to the floor without using his hands to break the fall. His blood pooled under him. Raginpert sneered at him in disgust. "Useless lump of dung. If Ratpald were here, he would dispense both you and these intruders."

"Do not underestimate me," said Manentius. "I fought the Avars at Pepin's side. From those monsters, I learned things about the human scalp that I would be pleased to demonstrate on you if you do not cooperate. My men are also boarded at your castle in Pavia. Everyone in those walls will be held responsible for your actions. If that does not matter to you, your treasury is also in our hands."

"You must recognize my birthright," the prince yelled.

"No Longobard is above the law," said Petrus of Pisa, whose family went back to days long before any Longobard conqueror stepped foot in Itale. "We are not impressed by your claims on Ravenna. I would sooner put you before the dock than anyone else."

Not once in the conversation so far did any eyes turn toward Kreindia. She had stout soldiers on either side of her.

Chastised, Raginpert protested, "She travels here in secret, at the behest of a foreign government." He pointed stiffly at Kreindia like a child telling on a sibling.

"This woman," Manentius continued, "passed through the Aquileian port, and met with my administration's approval. I assure you there was no oversight on our part. We are kept informed of Byzantine intentions through their ambassador at Grado." He nodded and smiled approvingly at Bassinus.

"The Greeks didn't tell you everything," cried Raginpert. Though Bassinus stared a hole through him, he want on, oblivious. "This is a witch you defend. Kreindia the Strange. It was my right, and my duty, to arrest her. As proof I offer the fact that her time locked in the dark cell changed her not at all."

"If heresy be the charge, we are well qualified to test for it," said Manentius with equanimity.

"But Bassinus stands with the Greeks. He will side with her."

"Careful now," said Bassinus. "An attack on a missus is the same as an attack on a king."

Again, Manentius was unperturbed. "We judge by majority, and two of us represent King Louis."

"I have an appointment with the Frankish king," offered Kreindia to anyone who would listen.

The Patriarch of Aquileia stepped under a lamp, showing skin transparent as vellum. He turned his powerful gaze on the prisoner. "Worry not. There will be a fair trial."

For Kreindia, this news of a fair trial brought scant comfort. She knew what that meant.

PART III
United

"Love will enter, cloaked in friendship's name."

—Ovid

CHAPTER 31
On To Elsewhere

WADE AWOKE DIZZY, WITH Grimketil Forkbeard sharing the ground beside him.

Wade sat up, held his aching head and looked around. They were under an open sky in a modified animal pen with sharpened wooden spikes at close intervals along the topmost bar. The door featured three chains at different heights, each with its own padlock. Other miserable prisoners shared the enclosure, nursing their injuries with people helping each other to tie off bleeders in what passed for medical attention. Grimketil was long decorated with the scars of battles past. If he suffered any serious wound this time around he didn't show it.

Through his pain-blurred eyes, Wade could see the Vikings and Slavs going about their business beyond. The Vikings seemed clearly in charge, giving the orders. Slavs patrolled the immediate enclosure while their betters saw to the perimeter. It didn't resemble the last time Wade was in detention in school, but rather a more permanent arrangement. He wanted to yank his head off to stop the pain.

"Now there is the mark of a good skull," laughed Grimketil. "Every man should be struck in the head as you were, just to see what he's made of. If you ever wake up, you're deserving of respect. I saw that Northman deliver the mighty blow. I couldn't help you since I took one of those a moment later myself."

Wade felt the sore lump on his head, and wondered how a golf ball had somehow gotten under there. "How can you welcome a cracked skull?" he asked.

"It's much more dignified than dropping from loss of blood, and far preferable to being killed."

"My parchment?" Wade started.

"The Vikings have taken everything of value."

Wade began to search his pockets anyway. "How is a personal letter of mine any use to Vikings?"

"They can scrape off the surface of the parchment and write something new."

"They can?"

"Besides, you gave them the impression it was of greater value by reading it when you should have been fighting."

"It is of great value."

"Then you should have been more careful with it."

Wade lowered his head in solemnity. He couldn't avoid the bigger questions. "I saw Odalman fall. What happened to Snorri and Tankred?"

"Separated from us. If you look over to yon enclosure, you can see Snorri sniffing about. The last I saw our faithful oblate was at Visocica"

Wade looked where Grimketil pointed and saw Snorri haughtily inspecting every beam. "I hope Tankred is all right." Arghun-Boke's other name for the pyramids of Visocica, The Kingdom of Hell, echoed in his mind as did the bloody fight, and the loss of his friend.

Wade got to his feet and took inventory, from most obvious to least. He had all of his fingers and toes—unlike some unlucky people he could see—his clothes, two empty scabbards, two gold pieces, and his viper's tooth. No parchment, he confirmed. He saw a flash of its shape in his mind, too quick to hold onto. It had a surface of blinding white on which dark strokes appeared as though it were currently being written upon. His head grew even more painful before the sight vanished.

Grimketil studied him carefully. "I too have secreted some Avar gold that our captors did not find, although with just your two bits, they may have allowed your keeping it to cover your demise."

"That's funny," said Wade with dry resignation. "I get it."

"Now that you're up, take these twigs and put them in place of your swords."

"Why?" said Wade even as he obeyed. Wade held two saplings of different lengths. He saw that Grimketil had taken the trouble to trim them as straight as possible, but, thin as they were, they couldn't possibly be used as pikes or anything else he could think of.

"Just do as I say. I want to show you a few things. Stand ready for defense. Good. Now draw your spatha left handed."

"Which is the spatha?"

"Your long sword. It's on your right. Raise it up, use it to block. That's correct. Then draw your gladius to your right hand, and make a quick underhand stab to the belly upward. Get your kill quick and move on."

Wade learned these moves quickly as he had done when he used to take martial arts classes. He tried the maneuvers, and peeked over at the guards. They seemed to take a passing interest, evincing his suspicion with some talk among themselves.

After learning a few more essential tactics, Wade handed the sticks back. "My head hurts when I move that fast. Why are you giving me all this instruction now?"

"True, you seem to endure, so far. Yet, I am the one who outfitted you. I can't stand to see weapons used wrong."

The remark didn't sting. Although Wade learned his karate well, when it came to blades, he had only just play fought like any other kid. If he survived a sword fight it was sheer luck and reflex. "So you think they're not going to execute us, that we will get our hands on our belongings again some day?"

"No, I think they intend a fate worse than death. We are to be sold as slaves."

"To whom?

"To those who can pay the most, and make the slavers travel the shortest distance. The buyers might be traders headed for Constantinople or Persia. They already know I am Christian by the cross I wear. Christians don't buy Christian slaves. That means I am probably bound for the Arab lands. Without a cross around your neck, you may be luckier, if you consider the permanent loss of your freedom lucky. I suggest we find weapons, and then kill these Northmen until we ourselves are dispatched. Die honorably."

Wade actually came from a Protestant background. There was no way he could explain that distinction to Grimketil, the split having occurred eight centuries in the Saxon's future. If he remembered his history correctly, every theological divergence was a form of heresy that meant it might be more dangerous to be Christian with different ideas than to be another religion subject to conversion. Oddly enough, Grimketil's descendants would become major adherents to Protestantism one day. He wouldn't appreciate being told that.

If it suited Wade, he could use what he knew to claim his Christian status, or allow himself to be taken for a pagan.

"And here I thought you were happy just to be alive," said Wade.

"I am happy to get another chance at killing more of these swine."

Wade said, "What's the worst that can happen? I want to go to Constantinople anyway. When I'm transported there, I'll just tell them I'm not a slave."

"But you will be a slave."

"I wasn't born a slave."

"Then you shall be a slave who was not born a slave."

"Look, I confess I don't know how this works, but I find it hard to believe that a citizen of the empire can become a slave."

"How do you think anyone becomes a slave? As far as Byzantium is concerned you are not a citizen of Imperium Romanum, you are Carolingian."

"Well, yes, but we're on a diplomatic mission."

"Where is your letter to prove it?"

"They can just call up the monastery."

"Call up?"

"Contact."

"Ah, then. Let us examine the scope of your plan as it takes shape. A slave with no proof convinces his slaver, or the person he is sold to, to forego his cost, and send a courier at his own expense back to the west, presumably for a reward?"

"Yes, a reward."

"The courier takes, say four weeks under the current conditions, and if he lives, presents your situation to the monastery. If any who know you at the monastery yet live, they decide to send a new letter and more money after you lost what you gave them. If the return trip works, the honest slaver now frees you after two months of captivity in exchange for the price. Have I got this right so far?"

"You have a talent for humiliation."

"Not nearly as much as you will shortly experience if you leave yourself at Viking mercy. My plan is better."

Wade didn't answer. He stared at the spikes around their pen. They had been tipped with fresh animal dung by the color and smell of it. Their captors wanted the prisoners to know that they would be both wounded and brought down by illness if they tried to climb over. "Why did I bother paying so much for health insurance?" he said under his breath.

One of the Slavs who had been watching them ran off, possibly to fetch a superior, or possibly for reasons of his own.

"Wade, Grimketil continued, "we may fight and die here today, but there is always the possibility of waiting for the opportunity to escape. You managed to flee from Gerardus and Egidio. It is every man for himself. Do what you did then, your Aquitainian tricks."

Sometimes Wade had to remind himself that Grimketil was not his father or his uncle. Being bereft of a father surely played a role in his wishful thinking. He couldn't expect the Saxon to be as fond of him in return.

"I won't leave you behind," Wade insisted.

Grimketil smiled knowingly. "I might be able to use the occasion of your disappearance as an opportunity for my own escape."

Wade did want to leave before Stockholm Syndrome set in. Human beings so abhorred captivity, that many were more willing to create a fiction in their minds that they were willing victims. Even the notorious Roman emperor Nero had slaves that loved him.

"If I don't hear from you, I'll be back," said Wade.

"Trust to my skills as I trust yours. I will have Snorri to help me."

"How will I know where you've gone?"

"You forget. I am a bounty hunter. I will find you."

"All right. I'll try."

Activity around their enclosure increased. The Slav who ran off before had returned with several Vikings.

"There is no time to lose," said the Saxon. "Whatever conjurer's method you would do to make yourself invisible, by smoke or misdirection, do it now."

"Turn your back," Wade implored.

To his minor surprise, Grimketil complied. He said, "See that you get another gladius and spatha, and practice with them."

"I will."

It seemed absurd to actually say goodbye since his trick was highly unreliable, so Wade said nothing. As he drew out his viper's tooth, he realized the act had only worked twice before, and each time it brought him to Olich's house. The second time, as now, he was only trying to escape. After all the weeks of hard riding and fighting spent getting him to Pannonia and beyond, it would be a disaster if his own foolish actions landed him directly back in Swabia where he would be no help whatsoever to Kreindia. If he had any control of his ability at all, he had to concentrate on getting to the Byzantine capitol. It worried him that he had been moved while unconscious and so did not know his starting point. He could not know which factors mattered and which did not.

He glanced at Grimketil's mighty back for strength. When Vikings began to remove the series of padlocks on their pen, Wade used the viper's tooth as before, crouching down and applying it to his ankle, and began to experience the color countdown. He tried to picture the old maps of Eurasia's political boundaries as waves of purple, honey, and rust, each in their turn, blanked out his vision. The rust lingered as it carried off some pain he hadn't noticed. He imagined soaring off to the east as he pressed the sharp point deeper to be certain that something would happen.

Then black. Total blackness. The weed-strewn dirt beneath him turned cold. He reached out blindly to find a wall, solid as granite, even colder. Was he sealed in a mausoleum?

Wade screamed. His lungs emptied, he filled them, and let out another burst of madness. During the third time, he began to breathe more slowly. All the air he took in and the breezes he felt reassured him. He might have been in a shallow cave rather than buried alive. In the granite, he felt a carving like an inscription. He couldn't make it out. Groping along, he found that the stone ended in open air. The empty space looked somehow darker. His eyes were beginning to adjust. Directly above him shone stars.

CHAPTER 32
Back To Civilization

GROPING FURTHER, WADE found another stone, this one much smaller, and highly skewed. He could make out a great cross, and others jumbled behind it. He realized that his jump had taken him to a cemetery at night. He shouldn't have been surprised at the darkness; twelve hours, if that's what it was, was nothing compared to twelve hundred years. But where was he, and exactly when?

Wade was ashamed of having vocalized his terror. The circumstances had tapped into some inchoate fear of his. Now that he grew increasingly quiet, the night sounds came back. Crickets, rodents, and something bigger? He shook his head at the night. In his travels with Grimketil and company he had learned better than to give away his position. If pursuers were hunting for him, they now knew where Wade was, even while he himself did not. He was on his own. No Monk, Grimketil, Tankred, Odalman, or even Snorri. He had only the persistent pain in his head to keep him company.

To remedy his mistake, he stumbled to another place, and waited as though he were made of stone himself. For his new location, he had chosen to move about ten yards distant, and settle on the opposite side of a monument large enough to provide complete cover. It didn't take long for him to find a sharp rock for hand-to-hand combat if it came to that.

After what he judged to be a safe interval of long, unbroken quiet, he decided to trace his finger inside of the inscription he found there. He thought it might give him a clue as to his location. While it turned out to be surprisingly difficult to teach himself to read in this way, the grooves were outsized, and he settled in like he had all the time in the world. It would help keep him calm and quiet. The dirt piling under his fingernails no longer bothered him. He made out the name "Linneus of Samothrace." The rest of the words were strange to him, but the dates were in Roman numerals, allowing him to calculate. He stifled a gasp, and started over, finding the same odd result.

Astonishingly, if Wade were right, the man in this grave had lived to be one hundred five years old.

He almost laughed aloud. It had to be a mistake. Anyone from the twenty-first century would not even last as long as a natural resident of the ninth century. He would probably be dead by thirty from war or injury, or just plain poor sanitation. Had there been others like him, displaced in time and doomed to a ninth century existence? Wade couldn't make sense of it so he eventually stopped trying.

Wade focused on what he could glean from the rest of the inscription. He knew his maps from his days at Sintlas Ow. Samothrace was a Balkan island in the Aegean Sea, well east, but hundreds of miles to the south of where Wade's progress had taken him before his group was captured. So what might that tell him about his present location? How far did people travel and resettle in their lifetimes? This centenarian had time to go to the ends of the Earth even at the speed of local transportation.

On the other hand, Wade might have projected himself more precisely than he thought. He supposed that if

Constantinople were as important as everyone said, there might be people there from everywhere. If he were in fact in a Greek locale, however, it would still be easier for Wade to get to the capitol from that friendly territory as opposed to wherever the Vikings had taken him.

When he felt comfortable that no living human other than himself stirred in the graveyard, hunger and thirst became an issue. All of his food was in his saddlebag, long gone. Seeing the first rays of the new day, he picked up his directions. Where the light came in the east, it silhouetted a massive city wall.

Against his grumbling stomach, he forced himself to be patient. Seeing that he had no company, he found a road and began walking on a ground patched with frost. He shivered. Up until now, he had been too heavily dressed, but the cold quickly overtook his wardrobe. The holes in them didn't help either.

From higher ground, he found the city hidden behind three successive walls with an elaborate system of stone towers and gates unlike anything he had ever seen or imagined. It resembled pictures of the finest castles, except that it stretched for miles in either direction. The flags, with their crescent moon, looked Turkish to him. If so, that would mean he had jumped forward by hundreds of years. With each step, he grew increasingly uneasy that he might have left the Dark Ages behind.

Sixty feet before the first wall, he nearly stumbled into a dry moat, a drop straight down nearly four times his height. His heart pounded and he wondered how he would cross. All of the maintenance ladders were on the far side. He looked down into the moat and saw that it contained pipes, and from the mouth of each pipe a pattern of stirred up sediment. At the bottom were bones with birds picking at rotting flesh. He didn't know what they filled the moat with to cause that result, and didn't want to find out.

Only a single guard appeared to patrol the archer's wall beyond. Wade called out several times to no avail. With each effort, he attempted to get louder, wondering if the acoustics prevented his voice from carrying. The patrolman studiously ignored him. Wade thought of walking to another entrance, but he saw that the giant machinery to extend the path across the moat must have required several men to operate, so the patrolman could take no action in his favor even if he wanted to. It was very early in the morning yet. Wade knew some traveler would come along, and others had to come on duty at the gate to meet the day's traffic. He lay down heavily in the dust to rest, and fell asleep.

~ W ~

The coach wheels almost ran over him. The drawbridge had already opened for it. Seeing the opportunity, Wade trotted alongside. No one attempted to stop Wade from crossing with the vehicle, but neither did they fail to notice him.

A soldier-guardsman brought him at sword point to the nearest tower. He shouted to an unseen compatriot, "Have that wagon stand by while I question this one."

The guard in charge stared at the grooves in Wade's wrists and ankles where he had been tightly bound to a hog pole. Wade had no recollection of how they got that way, but it had to be from when the Vikings had him unconscious.

"You are lucky that a coach came along, giving us cause to open the gates," said the guard. "But how you crossed hostile territory is a mystery. The Bulgars let very few long distance travelers through these days, only the merchants they trust. You are not a merchant, a Bulgar, a Viking, or a Slav. Frankish, I imagine. How do you come and what is your business here?"

"You have a keen eye. I am not one of your enemies. I am Frankish, and unarmed." Wade held his hands open in front of him.

"Yes, I see. That is suspicious, too. How do you come to travel unarmed? Are you an escaped slave?"

"No! I am here to see the king."

The guard laughed. "What a fortunate coincidence. There is a message sitting here for the king. When you see him, will you pass along that his wife asked him to bring some goat's milk home?"

"I can't prove my identity because I was kidnapped by Vikings, and they took my letter of introduction."

"Ah, that makes a difference. You defeated the marauding Northmen, then? Will it be the Golden Gate for you and a hero's welcome?" He laughed even harder. "We will ready the Triumphal Way."

The guard called to a subordinate, "This one is an escaped slave. Chain him and toss him on the wagon. Use the Gate of Rhegium, and hold him at Arcadius."

Chained in the wagon, Wade left the tower, and passed into the city, eager to be passed along to more competent hands. In any case, he counted his blessings. Being processed as an immigrant, even a suspicious one, was a far superior fate than staying at the whim of those that derailed his mission and devastated his party. He tried not to think about Grimketil's fate.

The countryside rolled by. He marveled at the densely packed buildings and trees far in the distance, and a large gap of wilderness in between. Game animals grazed undisturbed. In places, the plots were being prepared for construction, but for the most part, the Byzantines still had a great reserve of unspoiled property in the town's outer reaches to build on. When they went deeper, he learned the reason. Hidden in the vegetation was yet another city boundary wall, this one clearly older with many of its stones cut away. The section near the road had been cannibalized the most. It had to be from days when the city limits were smaller. Just before they passed in, he noticed tombstones again. Some of the graves had been disturbed. In a flash of insight he realized there must be a rule to keep the graveyards outside of the city. The bodies would gradually be reburied in the area where he first arrived. Wade took the half-developed city as a good sign that he may not have moved too far into the future, if at all.

He traveled with the merchant to whom the wagon belonged and a single guard. "Is this indeed Constantinople?" he asked of either of them.

"Yes," said the guard.

The merchant, who was busy steering his horses, and had to make a living, was content to pretend Wade did not exist.

"Is it The Year of Our Lord 814?" Wade persisted. "Early in the year?"

Again the guard answered. "Yes to both. Do you have any more stupid questions?"

Wade wanted to ask if the guard knew any good places to eat around here, but he looked at the heavy baton the man carried, and decided against it. "No," he smiled.

"Then sit still."

They took a right turn onto another road that soon led to Arcadius, which turned out to be a magnificent forum with a great square and a statue of a god on a high pedestal. The columned building stretched all around. The guard took Wade off the wagon and sent it on its way.

Once inside, the guard pushed Wade down into a chair before an officious looking gentleman. Overweight, robe-clad, and topped with a small fringe of brown hair, he waved a fan at Wade to ward off the stench.

"Your name?" he poised to write.

"Wade."

The man stared at him crossly.

"Of Aquitaine," Wade amended.

"Thank you."

"Purpose?"

"Business," said Wade.

The man raised an eyebrow, and snorted, "I doubt that." He wrote it down nonetheless. "Status?"

"Citizen of the Holy Roman Empire."

The official cleared his throat. "Whatever you say. It will be tested later."

"That's right. My situation will be sorted out very soon. You'll put it down just as I say if you wish to keep your job."

The man across the desk sat unflustered. His voice never rose above the routine. "I am in the civil service. I cannot lose my employment."

"Wow, nothing ever changes."

"If you should live a thousand years, Wade of Aquitaine, that will not change, no. Religion?"

Wade paused, thinking about what Grimketil said about religion and slave distribution.

The big man cleared his throat again. "Come, sir, this is not a hard question. Do you know your religion or not?"

"Christian," said Wade quickly. "Do you have something to eat?"

The official fished around under his desk, found an old biscuit and slapped it on the table with a resounding thud.

Wade didn't so much as chew it, as he did scrape at it with his teeth.

The official stood to leave. "The patriarch is too busy to see you." His excuse sounded perfunctory. "He will delegate another functionary from the palace."

Wade looked at the humorless guard that remained, and prepared himself for a long wait.

~ W ~

"Remove his chains," said the soldier who entered. "The Lady comes."

Although Wade was used to chains by now, he welcomed the relief, and the promise of better treatment. When the metal links dropped away, the younger one gathered it up, and they both cleared the room, bowing to the lady as she passed in.

If Wade was surprised his savior turned out to be a woman, he was exceedingly surprised to see anyone so clean and perfectly made up, with jewels studding her dark hair. For the first time in his travels, he saw earrings, and bracelets as well as a necklace. They all looked well on her. Her confidence belied her petite size. She moved as though she had never spent a day in her life doubting herself or her important place in society.

"So, Wade of Aquitaine does exist. How marvelous." She walked around, inspecting him.

He jumped to hear that kind of familiarity. "No, you must be thinking of someone else. I'm sure there's more than one person in Aquitaine named Wade. I don't have a monopoly on it."

The little woman wrinkled her nose. "You smell horrible, and speak oddly, but so very handsome just as she said. And tall as she said."

"Just as who said?"

"Kreindia of Amorium, niece of Michael. You are Kreindia's Wade. I have no doubt."

"Yes," said Wade with wide eyes. "That's right! News travels more quickly than I can." He couldn't believe his good fortune that he would not have to convince anyone of his identity.

"No, she spoke of you coming to her in her dreams for years. Kreindia the Oracle, is another name for her. She always said you would end up here. Where are my manners? I am a daughter of General Thomas the Slav." She offered her hand as if to solicit a kiss, but then must have thought better of it as she drew it back.

When it registered on her that the name of Thomas did not alarm Wade, she brightened considerably, her imperious manner put aside. "My name is Thamar Argyrina. Did Kreindia speak of me at all?"

"No, Kreindia and I barely met. I only very briefly saw her in person when she nursed me back from an illness. Then we were immediately...separated."

Thamar smiled wickedly, and clapped her hands together. "I am Kreindia's best friend and confidant. You and I are going to have so much fun."

CHAPTER 33
Thamar's Revenge

WHEN THAMAR INTRODUCED herself, she triggered another flash of Kreindia's parchment hovering in front of Wade's face like a textured wedge of reality. The words splashed across. He tried to make out the parts he hadn't read before, but his head injury blocked it out. Concentrating brought pain and the smell of ink.

It didn't surprise him that there was a synesthetic-type connection between Kreindia and Thamar. The same thing had essentially happened when he touched the box Kreindia gifted to the monastery. He wished he could somehow stop and read immediately from the memory of the parchment locked in his mind, but he looked forward to learning whatever Thamar, and his visit to Kreindia's adopted hometown could tell him.

Thinking of all that Constantinople had to offer, Wade said, "I'm stunned by the opulence of your city, and the goods you produce, like the jewelry you wear."

Thamar smiled wider. "You have not seen the tenth part of it yet. But you may be slightly disappointed. You will not find others as well turned out as I am." She twirled a loose lock of hair girlishly.

Just like that, he walked free from the detention area, emerging with Thamar for another glimpse of the magnificent sunlit courtyard of Arcadius. Birds flew off the central statue, made a wheeling circuit, and returned. *My easiest escape ever,*

Wade thought, if I don't soon starve to death. "One thing, before we leave, Thamar, I'll need food. Maybe I'll feel better."

"I keep some in here." Thamar snapped her fingers, and a brilliantly decorated white and gold carriage drawn by two pairs of mules drove up. It was exquisitely crafted and trimmed like something Marie Antoinette would own some day. Antoinette, of course, would employ horses.

Thamar ducked in and Wade joined her. Like the official, she also produced a fan to protect her sensitivities, this one stunningly fashioned. "Ah," said Thamar, waving the fan vigorously, "my winter carriage has no ventilation. Maybe you had best sit up with the driver, outside the coach. You can eat out there too. Hurry." She slammed the door after him.

Wade happily climbed up to the bench with the driver, who looked pained to suffer his odor.

"What do they call you?" Wade prompted.

"I am Diokles of Hierapolis."

"Seems like everyone is from somewhere else. I'm Wade of Aquitaine."

"Pleased to meet you. Perhaps if I hasten, the wind will carry off some of Aquitaine in the direction from whence it came."

Wade understood how they all felt. The way he smelled now to civilized people was the way everyone smelled to him when he came to Swabia, only worse.

Diokles got his mules moving toward the heart of the city on a remarkably smooth road, making Wade wonder if the coach had shock absorbers. With a statue carved into the brake line, and bells on the mule's tails, its builders probably didn't miss anything.

The day was clear. Wade counted seven distinct hills in the distance, causing him to reflect that he recalled some of his history after all. When Constantine built his eastern capitol, he ensured that the contours roughly matched the Seven Hills of Rome.

Unlike the fabled Romulus and Remus, Constantinople's founding fathers were not nursed by wolves. This part of the Roman Empire was already called Byzantium, after King Byzas, who settled, on the advice of an oracle, opposite "the land of the blind." The king was amazed to find that this highly defensible and fertile horn of land lay vacant. If those across the river had not claimed this territory for themselves, they must have indeed been blind.

Already the most Christianized of Roman territories, Byzantium rose to greatness some centuries later as Rome declined, acquiring many of its treasures in the process. Its emperors would build on the Roman legacy for a thousand years. Wade could already see its gilded domes and spires, its palaces, churches, and finer homes. The rise and fall of the road brought one wonder after another into sight. Other than his encounters with Kreindia, Wade was as happy as he had been since his passage into the past began, and confident that here he would find the help they both needed.

At the next forum, they ran into traffic in the form of people and every other kind of wheeled conveyance. The entire square smelled of fish. Like cab drivers everywhere, Diokles couldn't help but talk to fill the time. Technically, he was more of a limo driver, but his only chance to socialize came when Thamar entertained her less desirable guests. "Busy here...Still the best way into town from all the southern gates. This is Forum Bovi, first stop for everything that comes out of Eleutherius Harbor. That's our largest harbor of the seven. You know we also have seven hills, don't you?"

"Yes."

"The emperor plans to build two more forums so we can have seven of those."

"Seven's a good number," Wade offered in a neutral tone. Diokles couldn't be blamed for waxing enthusiastic.

"The other side of town has got two of the seven harbors on the waters of the Golden Horn. The mouth is protected by the largest chain in the world. I would take a wager that you could wrap it around the Hippodrome. We're not going to get over there to see it. I just thought I would tell you. You should try to see it before you leave."

"I'll do that. Thanks."

After they had passed through several forums and tourist venues well described by Diokles on the long road, Wade assessed that the driver had softened enough to answer the question he'd been sitting on. He said, "Tell me something. Why am I getting the royal treatment?"

Diokles glanced over. "Privileges at court come with responsibilities. The Patriarch delegates his duty to inspect new arrivals to the city."

"But like this?"

"By tradition, it is not done in high style. I know that the Lady likes to be seen well, but when your name was announced at court, that made all the difference. She thought you were important somehow. I would never guess it to look at you."

The end of the line was something Diokles called The Baths of Zeuxippus, a confusing maze of buildings that seemed to delve into every luxury imaginable.

When they stopped, Thamar emerged quickly and said, "Come."

A line of two young men and two young women stood by. They turned out to be Thamar's servants awaiting her return. The first building offered food and drink. Wade found himself still hungry and thirsty. Thamar went straight to the table that held the wine. Wade went for meats, fruit, and also wine since there was nothing else to drink. The place teemed with people coming and going. None of them seemed to mind bumping into Wade even though Thamar's men cuffed them afterward. Thamar showed herself to be expert at navigating the masses without spilling a drop until they claimed a rare set of open seats. It seemed as though the whole city had turned out to bathe in the middle of the day. Wade thought they would be going down into a cavern and a natural spring. Thamar assured him it was all man-made.

"You have running water and central heating for baths?" asked Wade.

"Yes."

"Civilization, I'm home." He didn't realize how much he missed that much of the world as he knew it. When it came down to it, creature comforts beat television and compact discs.

"Oh, you may have seen baths at Aquileia, a forum at Pisa, or some tacky carpeting in a monastery, but not quality like this altogether in one place. I assure you there is nothing else like our city in the world. That's why everyone visits."

"I believe it."

"If you require a doctor in here, find a man in blue. Philosophers are in gray, ascetics are in the scarlet with the hair nets. They have to bathe too." Wade looked at her to see if she were serious about the color-coding.

"Oh yes," she said over her cup of wine, "it's my system. Come, we can watch people exercise."

"I have to speak to King Leo immediately."

"In good time. He is unavailable now, and in any case, he will never see you like this. If I cannot make you presentable it will not matter what you say."

She towed him to the exercise courtyard where men and women mixed. The men were running, boxing, wrestling, and fencing. Some women were curling small weights, wearing only briefs and what looked like sports bras. Others were expertly rolling a metal hoop to each other with a hooked stick. He watched them retrieve and fling the hoops as though the entire arrangement were an extension of themselves. He wished he could learn it.

"The game that so interests you is called Trochus." Thamar said in his ear. "It is only for women."

Wade reddened at the implication. He felt better when she said, "You look like you've had your share of exercise for now. Mind my servants. They will know what to do with you."

The two men escorted him to the baths. What they did with him was to cover every sweaty inch of bare skin in oil, scrape it off, and yank every hair off his body before putting him through warm, hot, and cold baths. Most of it felt terrible while it was happening and great afterward. He was afraid to ask them if they were paid or unpaid servants. For now he was all about minding his own business.

After they emerged in towels from the men's and women's sides of the baths, Thamar got him fresh new clothes comparable to the style he had been wearing. Wade noticed that the fabrics were winter weight and irritatingly coarse on his freshly scrubbed skin.

"Don't be disappointed," she explained. "As much as I would like to dress you as a suitable consort for me, you have your station in life, and I have mine."

The streets teemed with as much activity as the baths. Wade saw men loaded up like pack animals to carry shopper's goods through narrow alleys and to upper-flight apartments. When they got to their destination, they unloaded, took a fee, and immediately took on another customer. He saw women doing this too. They all obviously had stronger backs than he did. Had he ended up in the lowest rung of society as a slave, it might have been a very short career.

Next they passed the Hippodrome, a stadium draped in giant crescent moon flags.

Thamar clapped a few short times in delight. "There's a show coming up tomorrow."

"How do you know?" said Wade.

"The flags tell us."

"How do they tell us?"

She looked at him like he was a dolt. "The flags are THERE."

Wade genuinely wanted to stop asking stupid questions about ninth century customs. He just didn't know how.

At last they arrived at the massive palace gates, where the guards smiled at her and sneered at him. Wade was convinced he looked every bit the awestruck bumpkin they usually saw in their visitors.

~ W ~

In her palace rooms Thamar handed Wade a drink. He took a small sip to be polite. Quickly, he found himself tipsy, and a little confused. Although not a drinker, he knew from the occasional blowout at college that he could hold an enormous amount of liquor.

"I guess I didn't realize how tired I am from the journey."

She took his cup and him into her bedchamber.

When he saw all the pink he said, "I can't sleep here."

"That's right," she said, "you can't." She pushed him down into the pillows, and nestled next to him. "Are you comfortable? Are you happy?"

"I would be if Kreindia were here."

She leaned in and kissed his lips, the pressure of her body light against him like a kitten. His reaction time was delayed before he pushed her away.

"We can't."

"We can. No one will interrupt us here." She pushed back at him, relishing the fight, and then pinched him on the inside of his thigh.

"Ow, that hurts."

"No, it doesn't," Thamar insisted. She climbed on top of him and bit his neck.

"Now we really have to stop," he said.

"Do you only like men?" she asked sincerely.

"No."

"What is it then?"

"I'm just not comfortable with this."

"Ah, then we shall get you some pillows. All that you need."

"No, I mean, I don't think it's right."

"Not right? I have plenty of experience. Ask anyone. There's a reason I didn't buy you a massage at Zeuxippus. I give much better ones."

She put her tongue in his ear. Wade gasped. "I like it, but you have to stop." He got out from under her, forcing her petite frame to tumble away.

"If this is a Frankish game you play, I don't know it."

Wade sighed. "I guess this is what my people used to call a generation gap."

Thamar shrieked. "I know what that means. But I'm only a few years older than you. It is perfectly natural for people of all ages to have sex."

"But where I come from we don't have sex with our girlfriend's best friend and live to tell about it, especially if your girlfriend is an oracle."

"I thought you said you barely met the woman," Thamar said coldly.

Wade hesitated to answer. He could not explain the time Kreindia spent in his head and heart, repairing him, and guiding him back to life. "We bonded. I don't have to explain it to you."

"I'm sorry." She backed off and fixed her hair. "I miss Kreindia too. Sharing her man is just my way of getting closer to her. You do not understand eastern culture."

"Probably not."

"But if you give me a chance, I can provide both Greek and Persian favors."

Wade flushed a heated red. "I have to go."

"No! I'm sorry. Maybe it is just me. My friend Kreindia would not approve. I got too enthusiastic. Stay. I will not attack you again. Who else do you know in Constantinople but me?"

Wade laughed nervously. "All right. You make a good point."

"It's just that I miss Kreindia."

"So do I. That's why I need to speak to the emperor now. Sleep can wait."

"You have to go over your story with me before speaking to Leo."

"Why?"

"I'll help you decide what to tell him. Go on."

Wade shifted on the bed, reluctant to tell her about his origin, regardless of how much Kreindia might have already told her. Instead he described himself as Grimketil saw him, a rich man's houseboy that ran off for adventure. Thamar seemed to like that explanation better than whatever she had heard before. He told her a little about his journey and how Kreindia treated his illness at the monastery at Sintlas Ow before they both found out that Charlemagne was critically ill. He explained how Kreindia intended to treat him.

"And what happened next?"

"Prince Raginpert the Longobard captured her."

"Why?" Her interest sharpened.

"Apparently, he wanted to prevent her from curing Charlemagne. He wanted to seize territory, and maybe the Carolingian throne itself for all I know."

"And your mission here at the capitol?"

"To warn of the unrest in the Frankish Kingdom and get support for Kreindia."

"And you know nothing else?"

"What do you mean?"

"Is that everything you can possibly tell me about Kreindia and what is currently happening in the west?" She sounded unexpectedly hard and urgent.

"I know nothing else."

"Very good then." Thamar snapped her fingers. Her ubiquitous servants overheard, and went running.

Wade asked, "What's happening?" but she ignored him.

In a brief interval, a large group of people wandered into her bedchamber as though they had been walking in the hall and took a wrong turn.

Thamar got Wade to his feet with a shove. "Wade, I want

you to meet someone—my father, General Thomas, and his men."

If Thamar wanted drama, it had gotten lost somewhere. Her father seemed oblivious, engaged in flirting with his retinue. "—and mind that you remember to scrub my horse. Scrub whatever else you like while you're at it," Thomas said in a droning nasal voice, ignoring both his daughter and her guest. He conversed with four soldiers and one who dressed differently.

"Father?"

Thomas was pale, waxy, and sloppy, with his robe falling off one shoulder. He laughed like a playful idiot with a joke only he understood. Wade wondered what kind of general traveled with soldiers he treated like ordinary servants. Why did this whole crowd stroll into the bedroom like they had nothing better to do? Only the odd man out noticed Wade, peering at him menacingly through stringy black hair. Wade waited patiently for an audience. He didn't have much time for an assessment but he sensed something deceptive in the general, a false affectation of carelessness that troubled him.

"—so the maiden said, 'I've wanted to do that for years!'" His men laughed dutifully.

"Father, listen to me, it is time. I'm done with him." Thamar tugged at his robe.

Thomas looked directly at Wade with a sense of purpose that belied his former act. From that cue, Kreindia's parchment came to Wade's mind in full force. It contained an admonition. He saw letters three feet tall that said, "Beware Thomas the Slav and his daughter, Thamar." The wine cleared out of his head immediately.

Wade tried to run. He got caught up by spear points thrust in the shoulder pads of his new tunic. The soldiers brought him face to face with Thomas, whose cheek twitched as he stared.

"Father, finally!" Thamar said, pointing straight at Wade, "I want this loathsome creature torn apart."

CHAPTER 34
Hippodrome

G ENERAL THOMAS THE Slav regarded Wade with great bulging eyes. "I've heard enough. As head of the Barbarian Office, I say there is a case to be made against you as a Bulgar spy."

"You know I'm no Bulgar," Wade came back.

"You may be right," he allowed easily. "I'm told that Avar gold was found on you, and you admit to being in the company of Varangians. Who knows? Perhaps you are a Vandal from Africa. Perhaps you are a Khazar from beyond the Caspian Sea. Fear not, young man, whatever gets the job done. We'll figure out something for you." Thomas gave him a wink.

Thamar smiled and nodded in vindication. She commanded, "Carry him off."

No one moved.

Thomas looked at her with amusement for a long moment, and then said to his men, "Take him away."

They took Wade outside to an elegant courtyard with a fountain, and then turned and dragged him in the direction of the stadium.

"Where am I going?" he wanted to know.

"We're taking you someplace more entertaining."

They transferred Wade to a common area under the Hippodrome, and locked him in with a mass of filthy, lice ridden humanity. He fought the urge to pinch his nose shut, and looked around for an emptier area. No one got out of his way.

No sooner had the jailer left when one of the condemned yanked at his new, if slightly damaged tunic like he wanted it for himself. The man said, "You are soft. You will soon—"

On instinct, Wade laid him out with one punch. In a place where no one was armed, Wade had no fear but that of being put at a disadvantage. In his Tai Chi Kempo classes he had learned that peculiar high torque punch that led with the first two knuckles and targeted a place behind his opponent's head via the base of his nose as if planning to punch through it. It made for an uncompromising shot and knocked the assailant a distance before he hit the ground.

Something in the dim chamber stirred. "You broke my nose," the man murmured from his place on the floor. He made no attempt to get up. The rest cleared a large space for Wade who went to sit by himself in a corner. Years of unswept dirt made a soft seat for him.

In captivity once again, Wade laughed bitterly. "Linneus of Samothrace. A life span of one hundred five years old. Yeah, right." Spies were probably subject to summary execution. He had found the dark side of this wondrous civilization. There's a show coming up tomorrow, Thamar had said. The show was him.

He looked around, making several others look away. The viper's tooth had been easy to secret in his mouth at Zeuxippus. Wade's standards of hygiene had changed considerably. Even if anyone found it, they wouldn't take it for valuable. He didn't want to spend one moment longer in the arena holding area than he had to. But where to go? For this occasion, he needed to move a short distance, somewhere outside of his confines, somewhere safe in the palace. Where was that? He thought of Kreindia's uncle, Michael of Amorium, the only person he "knew" in Constantinople, the only one who would naturally want to help him in order to help his niece. Although he didn't know what the man looked like, he focused on Michael's bond with Kreindia as he traced his finger to the tender spot. Wade found a scab on his ankle, a very bad sign. He would have to try anyway. Wade glanced around one more time, and pressed the spot.

Nothing happened. He couldn't even find the first layer of purple. Maybe it was because unlike visualizing a target on a map, he chose to visualize a person. Maybe that method just didn't work. This time he tried thinking about the space outside the Hippodrome. If he got free, he would decide what to do then. He pressed, and again nothing happened. With the games coming up tomorrow, he had no time to allow the scab to heal. He held a deep breath and yanked the scab off. It bled.

He tried the pressure point again. Aside from pain, the spot was completely inert.

Wade laid back into the corner, his escaping breath turning into a deep sigh. He allowed his ankle to bleed freely. It would not be surprising if he had damaged the nerve he needed by his repeated violent misuse of the area, and in doing so eliminated his one means of getting home.

~ W ~

THE next day, Wade and several others were selectively taken out. Wade found himself alone in a small enclosure behind a door of iron bars at the entrance to the arena stage. From there he could watch everything that would happen until it was his turn. He saw a long thin stadium designed for racing. The seating area under the cold blue sky was immense, with capacity that must have seated one hundred thousand. The actual turn out was not nearly so high. The far half the stadium had been closed off, the near half less than full. VIP seating consisted of an elaborate box that must have been intended for the emperor and his guests. He recognized the best-dressed lady as Thamar. He didn't know any of the other dignitaries, although one stood out for being unusually tall and reminded him vaguely of someone. In the surrounding boxes, one solid section consisted of people in blue robes, and another packed section held green robes.

A figure in white took the podium. "Ladies and gentlemen, allow me, Praetor Scopos Symmachus, to dedicate this day's show to the Greens of the Chariot, representing Demeter, Goddess of the Earth." He gestured elaborately and paused for the leader of the Greens to take a bow amid cheers from his faction and half the crowd.

"And to equally honor the Blues of the Chariot, here to represent Demeter's brother, Poseidon, God of the Sea, and father of Byzas, our city founder." The leader of the Blues took his bow, equally admired. "The Reds for Mars, and Whites for the Zephyr are here in spirit. They each have led their chariot teams—" The crowd booed him, loudly complaining that they had heard that story.

Praetor Symmachus continued, "Well, we have a special treat for you today. It's a shame I see more than half the seats empty. I suppose not everyone approves of our entertainment, but you do, don't you?" Thirty thousand voices responded enthusiastically. "Today we will tell exciting stories about Goddess Athena, who built the first chariot,"—here he nodded to the Blues and Greens of the Chariot—"and the God Apollo, known for his many love affairs with mortals. I carry in my hand an urn of lots—" The crowd cheered wildly.

"Get on with it," was heard very clearly.

"The first lot...names a group of three brothers from a little town called Amphipolos—I think we've all heard of it—convicted for...Adoptionism. According to my notes, they believe that Christ was born human and became divine at his baptism. Oooo." The crowd booed the three. "But that view was recognized as heresy at the Council of Frankfurt in 794. Ten years. You would think they would learn by now!" The crowd laughed.

The three were dragged out of the enclosure opposite to Wade's position.

Symmachus explained, "Athena and her uncle Poseidon were both very fond of a certain city in Greece. Both of them contentiously claimed the city, and would not give it up. So they agreed to a contest: The one that could provide the finest gift to the city would then own that city. Leading a procession of citizens, the two gods mounted the Acropolis. Poseidon struck the side of the cliff with his trident and a spring welled up. The people marveled, but the water was as salty as Poseidon's sea, and none could drink it. Athena touched the Earth and produced an olive tree, which was a far better gift because the many olive trees that grew from it gave the people food, oil, and wood. Athena was awarded the prize, so of course she named her city Athens, after herself. Poseidon in his great anger, flooded the entire Attic Plain to people Athena's conquest with the dead. Today, our three brothers from Amphipolos—Vitus, Mark, and Cyril—will play visitors to Athens who drowned in that flood." He raised his hands to encourage the cheers.

Jailers bound each of their wrists to thin ropes and stretched them against a wall.

The Praetor called, "Let us have our sea water, please." The brothers immediately began struggling with the ropes in fear of what was to come.

A team dragged out three great hoses, and pointed each at a brother. When the water surged through, they struggled mightily to hold the hoses steady at each head. Each of the condemned tried to turn with nowhere to go, drowning where they stood. The water poured at them until one by one they sagged and lay still to thunderous applause from stadium.

The Praetor cried, "Wait! Hold your approval. We may not be done yet. There goes little Mercury with his hot iron!"

A small naked man with large comic wings on his hat ran around in circles with a brightly glowing poker. The crowd loved it. After his introduction, he commenced sticking the victims with the iron. He got no reaction from the first two. The third one, named Vitus, flinched.

"Mercury has found a faker," called the Praetor. "He is not dead!"

The victim jumped up, slipped his thin bonds, and ran. Mercury gave chase, poked at him until he fell, and then stuck him in the back with the still-glowing point. The crowd roared with laughter.

Wade watched in horror and helplessness. He turned away and emptied the contents of his stomach.

The Praetor reached into his urn a second time, pulled out a slip of paper, and held it up to read. "The next lot bears the name of Wade of Aquitaine, and he is a...suspected Bulgar spy!" The crowd cheered louder. "Wade will play the role of Linos. For those of you not familiar with the story, Linos was the Son of Apollo and Psamathe, whose father was the King of Argos. Psamathe feared her father and therefore gave the infant Linos to shepherds to raise. While still young, Linos was torn apart by dogs as he was left unattended by his shepherd foster-parents." More cheers. "As a shepherd's boy, he had a stick, so let's give our actor a stick and see how he does." The jailer handed Wade a club half of his arm length and shaped like a bone. Some of the crowd booed, and others chuckled. "Oh, but I almost forgot to mention—he will be chained to stakes. We want to make it fair for the dogs, don't we?" The crowd came alive again as they chained Wade securely.

Wade swung his arms to test the chains. He had freedom to fight and move around, if not to run away.

The Praetor said, "We shall provide him one dog to start, and see how it goes from there." Some delighted laughs came back.

Wade's neck was smeared with animal fat. The jailer released a large dog at the far end. The dog came bounding across the field, a slavering beast of the kind bred for violence, and probably long starved.

From his karate classes, Wade knew the principle of dealing with a single attack dog, although he never had occasion to try it out in practice. He had one chance only. His timing had to be perfect.

The dog came toward him. He saw saliva splash out.

He took the top of the club in his left hand, aligned its length with his forearm. As the dog leaped for his throat, he raised his arm to block. The dog bit into the wood and sank some of his forward teeth into Wade's arm. At the same time, Wade reached around behind its head with his right arm so that both his arms were parallel. In one continuous motion of desperate strength, Wade pushed his left arm forward against the teeth as he pulled his right arm toward himself. The dog's head flew back dramatically. In the wonderful acoustics of the

Hippodrome, all could hear a resounding crack. He freed his club from its teeth and let it drop to the ground.

The stadium fell quiet.

The silence was broken by boos led by Thamar, but quickly followed by even louder applause. The carcass was hauled away.

"Excellent!" the Praetor decided. "Quiet down, quiet down. Now let us see what happens when the Bulgar spy, I mean our shepherd boy, must face three dogs all at once!"

A barred door drew up to release the animals.

The dogs charged side by side. All three cut more menacing figures than the first. Their fur had large gaps as though they had been tortured. Wade could not afford to have one of these dogs bite him in the neck.

Wade brought the serpent's tooth to his hand.

The doctor. What did he do so far in the future in that world so far away? There were two places Nesky accessed to stop the pain. They had to be connected or related. One was the ankle that had served Wade until it gave out, and the other was his wrist where his carpal tunnel pain originated. The wrist.

All three dogs leapt for his throat.

As they left the ground, he pressed the spot he remembered on his wrist with the serpent's tooth and witnessed the stadium shift around him. It was as though he had one eye squeezed shut and then rapidly opened it as he switched to the other eye shut, a tiny perspective change. He had moved several feet from where he stood before as though he moved the Hippodrome itself with a mighty shrug.

Wade didn't trouble himself about how it looked. Persistence of memory fooled the eye. Looking from one image of Wade to the other would have made the audience fill in the blank with a similar image. A rapid move made more sense to the observer than his disappearance and reappearance would have.

As the closest dog bit the air, Wade swung his club, cracking its skull and bouncing its head nearly as hard off that of the next dog. The crowd gasped. The third and furthest dog whined at the mystery, and scrambled to find him again. Wade tried to gather up the chain in the hopes of choking the last dog, but found he had come free of it. Making it his best bet, he still went for the chain. The animal charged him before he was ready to use it, so he pressed his wrist again, moving behind the hound. Once there, he wrapped the chain around its neck as many times as it would go, and still give him something to hold onto. The beast bit into the meaty part of his hand between his forefinger and thumb. The shock only hardened Wade's resolve to hold fast and kick solidly until the dog passed out from some combination of the chain's pressure on its neck, and losing wind.

Wade worked the teeth loose from his hand while he watched the dazed one go after the dead one.

The stadium erupted in savage approval.

A man in a rich, dark robe of blue stood quickly. "The Blues hereby request an audience with the hero."

Another man, clad in a bright robe of green, jumped up. "The Greens hereby declare unconditional sponsorship."

A fight broke out, first between the leaders, and rapidly spread to their followers.

The tall man stood, and halted them with his words. "I, Alcuin of York, claim my Right of Privilege as the Carolinian Representative. I would speak with this man, and take first refusal on any and all sponsorship opportunities."

Thamar's objections got drowned by the cheers.

The guards hustled Wade to a well-decorated empty room where he had to wait. There he had fresh food, wine, carpeting, mosaics playing out scenes from mythology, and gold and marble trim everywhere. He even found running water and first aid to dress his wounds. Remarkable how he went from the filthiest hole to the VIP suite in the same day. With the club to protect his left forearm, the dog's teeth had not gone deep. In his right hand, nothing vital was struck. He was accustomed to being stabbed with a tooth.

After about a quarter hour, during which he satisfied his appetite, and used the facilities, the Praetor came to make an announcement. He brought the tall man and the Blues and Greens leaders. He said, "My apologies for the time it took to sort things out. Now you may meet your benefactor, Alcuin of York from the court of Charlemagne, and now Louis." Wade could see he was expected to bow and scrape, but he was too transfixed to move.

The white haired man was almost as tall as Wade, with a face nearly as familiar but for the thin white beard tracing his jaw. Wade felt the blood drain from his face, and the hair rise up all over his scalp. This had to be the strangest occurrence yet; it could get no stranger.

"He's not Alcuin," said Wade. "He's Allen. Allen Linwood, my father."

CHAPTER 35
The Truth

THE LEADERS OF the Blues and Greens looked at each other in bafflement.

"I'm afraid you are mistaken, young warrior," said Alcuin of York. "The name you mention is mysterious to me." To his company, he said, "Excuse us, please. I need a word with this misguided young man."

"We wish to be present at all negotiations," said Blue, standing fast.

"That goes for both of us," retorted Green in a voice that said theirs was a familiar argument.

"And you will be present when we get to that part in a little while," replied Alcuin, gently pushing them out.

"You may be an honored guest in these walls, but I have the right of second refusal," said Blue in rising ire. "The hero's speed is amazing."

"I disagree," said Green to Blue. "I have noted that both his speed and his strength are unparalleled. My declaration of unconditional sponsorship supersedes your tentative claims. Your uncertainty has you legally boxed in."

Wade shouted, "Both of you shut up and get out. I want to talk to him."

Nonplussed, Green said to Alcuin, "If the champion refuses your sponsorship offer, you are bound to tell us."

"And we want a proper introduction in any case," added Blue.

"I give you my word on both," Alcuin assured them.

When they were alone, Wade said, "Dad? Aren't you my father?" If it was not him, then he shared a remarkable ancestral resemblance.

Alcuin rubbed his bearded chin. "Maybe."

"How can the answer be 'maybe'?" Wade demanded. "Are you Allen Linwood or not?"

"Ages ago, or from now, I was once Allen Linwood, one of the fathers of one of the Wade Linwoods. It's not likely that you and I match up. Almost impossible, in fact."

"One of the Wade Linwoods?"

"I had hoped that you would figure that out before I ran into you, if ever I did. Once either you or I have been through a break in space-time, we can't ever expect to end up in the same part of the multiverse again."

Wade realized he had his mouth open. "Whatever Wade Linwood you fathered must have been a great deal smarter than me because I don't know what the hell you're talking about."

Allen sighed. "I'll start from the beginning. By now you believe that you've gone back in space and time."

"Haven't I? Haven't WE?"

Allen held up a hand. "It's much more than that. It's probably more exact to say that you're in another reality as well."

"What other reality is there?"

"The parallel ones. You've heard of multiverse theory, the infinity of worlds?"

"Yes," he said slowly, "I've always been interested in the oddest areas of science."

"With your synesthesia, I thought you might be."

"Infinity of worlds theory has been around since the ancient Greeks. No one really accepts it because they can't test it."

"Or maybe they test it so often they don't even realize." He smiled at Wade's bewilderment. "Every person on Earth faces a decision point from moment to moment. Should I have orange juice or grapefruit juice for breakfast? Do I have time for coffee? Who knows what will happen or who you run into at the store when you go to replace one or the other? At one place in time or another you could find a robbery in progress, or a dear old friend. The robbery has a tragic ending, but the friend recommends you for a job. Different small choices leading to different large outcomes. According to one version of the theory, therein lies the information pool for the infinity of worlds—every choice from every moment of life for every person who ever lived: They all get their own parallel world to live out the consequences."

Wade looked at him with narrowed eyes. "You believe that?"

"Not quite. I like to say time looks both ways before it crosses the street."

"Meaning what?"

"Meaning that only those decisions that can potentially lead to a sufficient diversion of events cause the bud of possibility to break off into a new universe. Crossroad periods in history have a high probability of its people, individually or collectively, taking decisions that shear off into new sets of realities. The early ninth century, with all of its danger and opportunity, is one such time."

"Who decides what would be important enough to start a new universe?"

"Decisions that have the most ripples, the big decisions, cause a split in reality when their quantum parts diverge too far—the Quantum Divergence Threshold. The ripples are communicated backwards to the point of origin. So you have one possible universe in which, say, Napoleon was defeated, and another in which he was not, a very large difference that then forces the alternate reality to come into being. Therefore, the word 'universe,' signifying 'one,' is a misnomer, since there are many more than one. I call each variant 'verses.' Look, I don't know if all this technical information is any practical use to you."

"If nothing else, it helps convince me that I haven't lost my mind."

"I could have told you that much."

"But you're right. This is all academic. None of it proves you're not my father."

"Back to that, huh? Okay, try this: When you were four years old, did I let you have that pet monkey you wanted?"

"No, you gave me a picture of one instead."

"That's as I remember it so far. When you were nine years old, did I put on white makeup and a red nose to get you over your fear of clowns?"

"Yes, and it scared the crap out of me. I don't count that as a good deed if that's what you're getting at."

"No, no, bear with me. That part of my timeline checks out too. But when you were seventeen, did I insist you follow in my footsteps and go to Brown University?"

"You left home when I was twelve, and never came back."

"There you go. We're from two divergent verses."

Wade stood up straighter. "Notwithstanding that the Allen Linwood I know would not have been above making up that last fact, genetically, you're my father. If I were under eighteen, you'd be legally responsible for my welfare. At the very least we are some kind of relatives."

"There are no paternity tests in the ninth century, and no laws about alternate realities in the twenty first. Go home, Wade." He sounded weary. "I don't know why you followed me here in the first place."

"I wish I knew how to go home, but I haven't even thought about it since I met Kreindia."

"Kreindia of Amorium? She's the one who we expected at Aachen to cure Charlemagne. It's a pity she never arrived. Kreindia the Strange," he mused.

"Don't call her that. She was kidnapped."

Allen said, "That's not so uncommon here as you may think."

"Oh, I know it. And I didn't follow you. I think I followed her somehow. What are you doing here anyway?"

"The way I see it, I'm here to safeguard history."

"Safeguard?"

"Well, I don't know how to do things any better than the way they came out. For all I know, my natural inclinations could make the world turn out worse. This Kreindia, as far as I can tell, provided the advice that allowed, or will one day allow, Michael Psellus to ascend to the throne. If that happened before I want it to happen now."

"So you don't know why you're here either."

"I have a better idea of it than you do."

Wade had a lot to think about. He sat down hard, his brow furrowed. Even before he was twelve his father had disappeared a lot. "How is it that I come here and end up chased across Europe, dragged through all kinds of hell, and you come in as the king's advisor?"

Allen smiled "You're paying attention after all."

Wade's eyes widened. "Wait a second. Alcuin of York was a real person with a whole history behind him. I read about him in school. You couldn't have replaced him from birth. What did you do with the real Alcuin?" In a very soft voice, Wade said, "You didn't kill him, did you?"

Allen stiffened. "No…I mean, not on purpose."

"Oh God."

"Wade, this is a barbaric world by our standards, but I would never do that. In the verse that you and I occupy now, Alcuin never met Charlemagne at Parma in 781. He died mysteriously on the Via Francigena, coming back from Rome. Only two other people in the world know that. Three, if you include me."

Wade felt cold. "You materialized in his space!"

"I'm sorry, two things simply cannot occupy the same space at the same time. Look at this, you have me apologizing for physics now. The original Alcuin was violently shoved aside like a man dashed to the ground by lightning, only worse. He died instantly, and I'm sure, painlessly."

"Then what?"

"Alcuin was on a mission for Northumbria's King Elfwald. The people who were supposed to protect him didn't dare try to explain how they lost him. I did some fast talking. They soon discovered that I too was a very learned man, and they had to believe I was a powerful conjurer."

"You couldn't possibly have gone back to Northumbria as Alcuin. Elfwald would have known."

"You're getting ahead of the story. I predicted, among other things, that Charlemagne would intercept us in Parma to try to convince Alcuin to join his court. I recalled that the Carolingian was making a collection of the best advisors in the world. Sure enough Charlemagne showed up wanting to see Alcuin. Alcuin's men had to take a chance that I could impersonate him. The Frankish king was ready to pay Elfwald handsomely for Alcuin's services. So now Alcuin's handlers had two sovereigns to worry about. That is, unless I didn't go back to England at all, a concession to which I readily agreed."

"And that helped convince them that you could successfully replace Alcuin. If Elfwald never got a look at you, they would be off the hook."

"Exactly. The only difference is that the original Alcuin ultimately died in 804. I lived on."

"Changing history," Wade completed for him.

"No, simply making history. This verse was already separated from the one that you and I read about in history books from the moment Alcuin died in 781."

"Because of you," Wade reminded him.

"The point is once that happened you couldn't keep things the same if you wanted to. Now, I like to think that as Alcuin was going to do, I too helped make Charlemagne's reign as civilized as possible."

"781 to 814. You're here twenty-three years!"

"That's why I look so much older."

"I thought it was a disguise. I still need your help. Why does none of this feel right? In this world, my synesthesia goes in and out."

"I'll tell you as much as I think I know. Two objects cannot occupy the same place at the same time. But can a single object occupy two different places at the same time? Quantum physics says yes."

"So I'm both here and still living my life in the twenty first century?"

"No, you're mostly here. The portion of you left there is insignificant. Nonetheless, the limitations you no doubt experience result from straddling two time periods."

"How do you know these things?"

"Let's just say that ninth century Europe isn't the only place I've been. I was one of the many who ran hypotheticals past the old father of relativity."

"You told Einstein about your time travel?"

"I didn't have to. He doesn't mind working from a set of assumptions. He helps lots of people play around with their theories. I have to admit, he is the one who came up with the Quantum Divergence Threshold even though he can't stand quantum theory at all."

"You say all that like he's still alive."

"He is to me. I can go and visit him at any time. When you have the level of ability that I have there is no such thing as dead. Everyone you want to meet is alive within the boundaries of a period of years."

"When you say there is no such thing as dead, you're not talking about yourself, are you?"

"From my perspective I don't know what happens, but you will always find some version of me somewhere."

"Tell me how I get back to my time."

"I don't suppose I can."

"Is that your way of being cruel?"

"It's my kind way of telling you that what you want is impossible. Everyone's synesthesia is different, even within the same family. The way I travel would not be the way you travel."

Wade knew enough about his condition to believe Allen wasn't lying. "Then get me in to see Michael of Amorium."

"For what purpose?"

"To raise an army to settle the unrest in the Frankish kingdom and rescue his niece for starters. That shouldn't be a difficult thing to ask."

"I'm afraid it will be. He's presently preparing for the largest battle of all time, one that could mean the end of civilization. Emperor Leo seems to have pissed off Krum the Bulgar by trying to ambush and kill him under a flag of truce. Now Krum is going all out to break down the walls. He's already burned the suburbs to the ground. So I don't know how Leo or General Michael can spare anyone, even to rescue a niece."

"You can try to help me for once in your life." Wade's voice was raw.

"I'll try," Allen said softly. "I can't promise anything. If worse comes to worse, I can at least buy your freedom and turn you loose in a safe direction. But I can't do it if you're going to fight me."

Wade studied the mosaic on the wall, small chunks of colored glass set into some kind of mortar built up to form a picture. Poseidon did battle with a demi-god, bringing mayhem and destruction all around them in a world where magic transcended science. For Wade and Allen science came full circle and ended up magic. Neither brought peace.

"Wade?"

"Yes?"

"I'm sorry I'm not your father."

Wade had to take that for an answer.

CHAPTER 36
Psellus

WADE'S CURRENT ESCORTS wore no armor. Instead of being pushed, he was shown into what must have been one of the most exclusive parts of the palace, one of the better places he had been asked to wait. The realization that he survived the arena alone after being condemned by Thamar rushed in on him. He walked about the airy atrium taking in the sumptuous visual feast with new appreciation.

He didn't know marble came in so many colors, yet there it was: the center rectangle held a shallow pool of water backed by a stormy sea of azure stone; the bordering marble rose around it like a forest. The walls held marbles the color of sails; of chocolate; of cherries; of early sunset; and of dusky smoke. The last was a fragile alabaster shielding numerous lamps. Since Constantinople was a seaport, their designers naturally had scalloped shell designs adorning the corners of various furnishings. Buried in the leafy detail of elaborate scrollwork Wade found a sea monster, sailing ships, fruit, shields, and mother and child under a shining star. Statues and busts came in all shapes and sizes, and they were marble as well. A centaur battled with a man; a musician strummed his lyre; some kind of muse exposed one delicate breast.

"Admiring the calcium carbonate?" His near-father had joined him.

Wade looked at him, trying to absorb what he was seeing. "Is that all it is to you, Alcuin of York?"

Allen tentatively traced the thin line of his beard. "It might have been once. I'm actually developing a great appreciation for the precious stones. Part of the reason Aachen authorizes my trips here is to learn how to copy high civilization. Charlemagne was a great secret admirer of this Byzantium. That marble fireplace consists of Travertino Silver, and Travertino Rosso Persiano. The dark columns in this room are Nero Marquina. I know half the varieties of Bianco, Verde and Arabescato. My assistant has a sketchbook full of this room."

"It sounds like there is a lot of Persian influence here."

"Oh yes. When Islam comes to conquer this city in six hundred years, it's all going to look very familiar to them. Of course the influence runs the other direction too. Arab lands are peppered with Roman columns, arches, architraves, amphitheaters and aqueducts. That sunken area you're looking at in the middle of the atrium is called an impluvium. They have those little touches too."

Wade looked at him, unfamiliar with this version of his father. "Is there something you don't want to tell me?"

Allen ran a finger along the mantle. "No, not at all. Have you seen the gardens? They do a different type of sculpture in there."

"It's bad news, isn't it?"

"Bad news is relative. I got you an audience with the general."

"What's wrong with that?"

"There are some, er, conditions that you have to fulfill." Allen coughed.

"Conditions?"

"You have to meet Michael Psellus under special circumstances. Come, I'll let the doctor explain."

"The doctor? That doesn't sound good."

They took shortcuts through courtyards, dodged projectiles in game rooms, and tramped through long hallways tinged with must. Whenever they ran into a seasoned denizen of the palace, that person inspected Alcuin's clasps and jewelry before nodding in respect. All ignored Wade as though he were a servant, except for actual servants who passed with a wink. Allen kept a guilty silence while Wade worried about how much depended on the general's good will.

Eventually they came into another room, this one done entirely in white marble with screened off areas and shelves holding a bewildering array of incomprehensible silver instruments. Here the air was fresh, and the illumination brighter.

Allen said, "Wade of Aquitaine, I'd like you to meet Doctor Zerro Andreas of Athens." The doctor was small and thin with a large head and unusual auburn hair piled high on top of a face filled mostly by a smile. From Wade's gift of languages, when he heard "Andreas" he also heard its Greek origin "manly," just as he knew Psellus meant stammerer. The doctor wore a robe of sky blue, as Thamar had predicted. Wade still doubted her boast that she invented the system.

Andreas took him in and said, "So good to meet you. You are perfect. Perfect." His soft voice, almost a whisper, belied the manly surname.

"I'm perfect for what?"

"For the general's treatment."

"I'm not a therapist."

"Of course not. That's my job. You have heard of the four humours?"

"My sense of humor's not what it used to be."

"What does that mean?" Andreas passed a quizzical look to Allen.

Wade said, "It means: not that I can recall."

Andreas sighed. "Aquitaine. What has happened to the educational system in your empire? The greater part of our medical wisdom comes down to us from Hippocrates and Galen. The four humours are blood from the liver, black bile from the gall bladder, yellow bile from the spleen, and phlegm from the brain and lungs."

"The brain and lungs," repeated Wade. "I'll take your word for it."

Andreas continued, "They govern your temperament, making you sanguine, melancholic, choleric, or phlegmatic. The general's humours are out of balance. He is a choleric temperament by nature, and therefore has an abundance of yellow bile, sometimes leading to his stammer. With your help we are going to attempt to balance him."

Behind the doctor, Wade saw the back of someone he presumed to be Michael, curly black hair shot through with gray, robes trimmed in dazzling embroidery.

"Excuse me for looking away, my visitor" said Michael to the far wall. "For now, I am pretending you are someone I know."

"I need to ask you—" Wade started.

"No, no, quiet! Pretending, pretendiiiiiiing. To me, you are Phocus Mellitus. Phocus! Can you kindly act as such?"

"I wouldn't know how."

"The worst of it begins when I look at you. It happens more around peop-ule I don't know very well. Therefore the doctor says meeting new peop-ule is the best opportunity. That is when my treatment mu-uust take place. Now I don't want to know who you are until I turn around."

Wade scratched his head.

"I have tried herbal remedies and talking into a well with some success," Michael continued. "But this particular therapy wor-urrks best with an unimportant person. I don't have to wor-rrry about decorum."

"What do I do?" asked Wade.

"Starting from when I first turn to you, whenever you speak, I shall vomit before I respond."

"Did you say vomit?"

"He will eliminate an excess of yellow bile and thereby re-balance his humours," Zerro Andreas said with pride. Doctor Andreas, all head, hair piled to the sky, must have seemed infallibly cerebral to the average person.

"I have a tickler stick to induce it," Psellus told Wade, "but I hope that with practice, I can vomit spontaneously every time you open your mouth."

"This is good. You are improving already," Andreas said softly beaming. "Now turn around."

Somewhere Wade recalled that the condition could be exacerbated by other people's impatience when the stammerer would repeat parts of words, prolong sounds, and take long pauses. Wade needed to be careful not to react badly to whatever might happen. He still felt nauseous from what he witnessed and did in the arena.

Michael turned to reveal a seasoned warrior, somewhat round in the middle from recent inactivity. He kept his eyes on the silver bucket in his hands; brass would not do for a man of his status.

Wade didn't like the looks of it. "I never agreed—" he began.

Michael used his stick and started to gag.

"No wait," Wade spoke quickly. "You can't do this because I'm not perfect. I'm entirely the wrong person for this."

Michael stopped, and quickly retreated to the wall again.

"Explain," Zerro Andreas demanded, his smile lost for the first time.

"General, I'm important. I am bonded with Kreindia, your niece."

"En-en-en-gaged?" Michael vomited into a bucket without the aid of the stick. Wade made a face and looked away.

"No, no, general," the doctor became vocal, shaking his big head. You're supposed to vomit before you reply."

"He startled me," said Michael into his bucket. "So you say you are en-engaged t-t-to my neice?"

Wade said, "Not exactly. We share a strong bond."

Wade knew that neurological disorder, and not bile, should likely have been the real cause of Michael's stammering. Michael's was probably a complex of motor and vocal tics involving words, phrases and sentences. Altering the sounds was a modern treatment.

"Look," offered Wade, "do you stutter in Latin? I can speak Latin if you start." Allen looked duly impressed.

"Ah, that's what I do with my niece," said Michael. "I never stammer with her."

"That's who I want to talk to you about. My connection to Kreindia makes me very much like someone you know. That's why your therapy won't work properly with me." He did not presume to mention that the connection lent him status as well.

"Very well. I will turn to you then, Wade of Aquitaine. Do not make any sudden moves."

The general carefully rotated, as though he expected to land in a pit of snakes. The sight of Wade seemed to reassure him. He studied his visitor with great curiosity, looking past the garb he wore to Wade's bandages and highly visible scars. In Latin, he said, "You've seen many great battles, young soldier."

"That he has," said Allen, unaccustomed pride prompting him to speak for the first time, his Latin a bit rusty.

Michael turned his curious gaze on Alcuin of York. "You are his mentor?"

Allen, in turn, looked at Wade for reassurance. "I hope to take on that role, yes."

"That's news to me," said Wade. He thought it sounded rather opportunistic following a compliment by the general. Again, he wondered whether he really knew who this father figure was, or if the time away had really changed him.

"Say your piece," Michael said to Wade.

Wade filled his chest. He had used his many weeks' journey to rehearse well. "General, you know that Charlemagne is no more, replaced now by his son, Louis. A Longobard in the line of princes, named Raginpert, has chosen to test the strength and resolve of Louis. One of the reasons Charlemagne is dead is that Raginpert intercepted Kreindia when the Abbas Palatinus called upon her to heal the king. Raginpert now holds her in a dungeon, claiming she is a witch."

The old soldier's face turned hard, no more readable than the marble statues in the atrium. Wade couldn't tell if it was a good sign or a bad one. "What is it you have come to ask of me?" said Michael.

"I ask you for an army," said Wade.

Michael laughed from his belly. "Is that all?"

"If not an army, then some dignitaries and soldiers. A force large enough to convince Raginpert and any other dissatisfied princelings that the east will not tolerate petty uprisings to tear apart the west, and will certainly not tolerate harm to its finest citizens."

Even though Kreindia was indisputably his niece, Michael said, "You must do something for me." Michael, all business now, thrust his silver bucket at Andreas. "In return, you can have your fighting force."

Wade tensed, wondering if he could pay the price. "Tell me."

"I have heard that your skills are unparalleled in the arena. Do not be so surprised. I know everything that goes on, big and small. While you dallied at the Hippodrome, Byzantium plunged into a state of war with the Bulgars dangerous enough to topple the empire. One man stands between disaster and us, and I don't mean Leo. With your natural abilities of strength and speed, I want you on the team—no, on second thought I want you to lead the team—to assassinate Khan Krum."

Wade shot an accusing and wounded look at Allen, who only shrugged.

Michael said, "Any on that team who survive the attempt are yours to command in the west. I suggest you don't waste them."

He turned back to Michael. "May I have a word with my...mentor?"

"You may."

In the hallway, Allen started, "Now look, Wade, I didn't know anything about this but it only makes sense."

"To you it makes sense? To Allen or Alcuin? You're supposed to be representing King Louis. You should be the one appealing for aid from the east."

"I'm representing humanity first. This, the highest civilization on Earth is on the brink. The west, and your individual needs, and my needs for that matter, have to wait."

"What about changing history? You don't think killing Krum is big enough to start a new universe?"

Allen grew quiet. "That sort of thing is likely to lead to starting a new verse, yes. But the Kreindia you know will be in it."

"How do I come to have the responsibility of bringing a whole new verse into existence? Where's the morality of my killing someone to do it?"

"Assassination is a routine part of ninth century politics," Allen explained to Wade. "Don't tell me you never of heard of Byzantium before you got here."

"Really? How many people have you assassinated in twenty-three years? I guess I don't want to know. You're forgetting a little something, dad. Michael thinks I have amazing strength only because the chains came off when I jumped two feet in space-time. I've had one sword fight—exactly one—and two minutes of sword fighting instruction, if that. I would be going up against the greatest Bulgar warrior of all time, the same one who threatens the empire's very existence."

"With your team, yes."

"That's a comfort, this team I haven't met."

"But you do have the speed. You have abilities no one else has, and you'll have the element of surprise."

"And no one will be more surprised than me," said Wade.

"You'll be going in behind enemy lines."

"Which is another way of saying I'll be surrounded."

Allen frowned. "Take my advice and don't rely on the team. Be mentally prepared to kill Krum personally."

"In cold blood?"

"You said you've been in a sword fight, right?'

"Yes."

"Who lived and who died in that one?"

Wade stared back at the room that held a general so coldly different from his niece, so ready to leave Wade with all the hard choices. "Maybe I'll stand a ghost of a chance of killing Krum by sheer accident, and maybe I'll be able to do it if he attacks me. That at least will be self defense."

"That's childish," said Allen, "but on that plan you are sure to do it. Khan Krum is as bloodthirsty as they get. He will not fail to attack you if he gets the chance. There's your self-defense, and there's your precious morality. But I wouldn't recommend you leave the initiative to him. Then again, according to the calendar, it's possible you won't have to."

"Why? Does he go on vacation at this time of year?"

"Not exactly. I suspect Krum won't give you too much trouble because I know my history, son. Maybe that's why I've done so well in this world and you've done so poorly."

"Is that what you call it?"

Wade looked around at the treasures of Byzantium that his fight was supposed to preserve. He meant to prove his alternate verse father wrong and do what was necessary to rescue Kreindia without compromising his principles.

His other task was to live.

CHAPTER 37
Preparations

*W*ADE SAW A DUNGEON *antechamber and the back of a moderately longhaired man in a belted satin print. The man in the princely garb shot back the bolts and put his back into wresting open the forbidding door. Feint light scattered on the slight-built prisoner inside. Even that was too much for the pitiful figure who put up an arm to block whatever came.*

"Step out," came the strangled snarl of Raginpert. He added an impatient beckoning.

Kreindia came into the light, her face a mask of confusion and hunger. She nearly fell, and the Longobard did not move to catch her.

Wade's heart quickened. He struggled to come closer. A wall of green-tinged glass arose to block his way. He couldn't hear what they were saying, and Kreindia seemed entirely unaware of him. They sat down to a long discussion or negotiation, sometimes quiet and tense, sometimes openly combative. At times like the latter, Wade punched at the glass until his knuckles left red streaks.

They drank and ate, and when Raginpert shouted, Wade could sometimes read his lips. Frustratingly, he saw phrases like, "I knew it," and "your witchery." At one point he even saw Raginpert sneer out, "Wade." Kreindia very clearly said, "be damned."

When Raginpert dived at her, Wade threw his whole body against the glass barrier. He slammed it again and again to no effect but an aching shoulder. A spectral shadow of Thamar stood next to him, laughing. He charged it, making it dissolve to smoke. Behind the glass, Wade saw that Kreindia had won the first round, but Raginpert came at her again, this time drawing his dagger.

Three aristocrats and a complement of armed Frankish soldiers burst into the room. The lamps nearly went out, making Wade panic about what accidents might happen in the dark. He willed the embers back to life, or he felt like he did. The aristocrats, led by an ancient and hard looking gentleman, took charge. They were the missi dominici that Grimketil had predicted! They had to be.

Then the vision went dark.

Still in a cold sweat, Wade ran to his father's chamber, demanding more details on what kind of assistance he could expect if he agreed to go up against Krum. Allen handled him calmly, remarkably lucid in the first light of day. His was not a chamber, but a self-contained apartment with all the amenities. The servants had brought in a basin with a hot towel, which he gave over to Wade, while he got dressed.

Wade was relieved to learn that the Byzantines didn't do anything half-assed. There would be one month's training for the mission, during which time Wade and his team would get weapons, evasion and survival training, as well as assassination training, whatever that was. Krum would easily be occupied that long terrorizing the countryside and preparing his war, and Raginpert, with his more modest means, could do no less. Of course that plan assumed Wade had basic military training, which he didn't.

Wade's main concern was Kreindia.

Allen told him, "This is the ninth century, Wade. Primitive communications and travel slow everyone else down as much as us."

"I don't know how much spare time Kreindia has." While

he tried to load sarcasm into his voice, it only reeked of his longing.

"I'll send a message to Swabia to tie their hands legally. I'm the only one authorized to do it. A month's delay for a trial is nothing in the legal system of this or any century. If you like, we'll tie it up longer."

"That's not the point," Wade blurted. "You're talking another month in captivity for her."

Allen smiled condescendingly. "The missi dominici will treat her just fine. In the next four weeks of your training, she'll have regular meals while you eat bugs."

"The missi—How did you know?"

"Aside from you screaming in your sleep down the hall? I have excellent contacts, ones that don't get themselves captured by Vikings."

Wade returned to the basin for another swipe of the towel. It had turned cold already. He shook his head. "You're a synesthete very much like me, father or whoever you are. Are they visions I'm having, or only dreams?"

Allen wrinkled his nose. "Visions or nightmares, you mean. The way you were yelling, it seemed like you suffer plenty of both."

~ W ~

LYDAS the Slug distinguished himself with a head that grew wider until it met his neck, and an annoying habit of sucking spit-filled air through his teeth. Since Allen had called him a brilliant tactician, and he was the briefing officer, Wade could do nothing about it but stand with the rest and listen. Joining them late, taking extra sleep to make up for what he had lost, further compromised his standing. Allen reminded him that he couldn't do that in the field.

"Our advantage over the Bulgar is our control of the sea," said Lydas, snapping his wooden pointer to the table. They stood over a marvelous three-dimensional model of Constantinople and the surrounding area. The capitol lay at the point of a long peninsula, choking off the Black Sea from the smaller Sea of Marmara on its way to the Mediterranean, and controlling passage to all at the mouth of the Bosporus Strait that connected them. The land opposite, the gateway to Asia Minor, and indeed every city ringing Marmara, was also theirs. Selymbria, a westward suburb was marked off, a smoking memory now under the Bulgar's thumb, but famous cities like Chalcedon, Nicomedia, and Abydos left commanding access for any sea-to-land attacks Byzantium wished to wage. They could open a front at any time and retreat with impunity. That kept the Bulgars off the immediate coast. What's more, the leadership could never be cut off from their Asian provinces to the east, their Balkan provinces to the west, or the sympathetic Frankish empire in the same direction beyond.

Wade oriented himself from the most familiar features. He could immediately see the moat and triple wall system he passed through on his way into the city. He could even see the graveyard he started out in. Defenses continued, as sea walls, all around the city. The level of detail was high wherever it mattered militarily. Within the city, that meant the inclusion of every road that led to a gate or a harbor; every factory for munitions or supplies and the path from them; every stable; every training and testing field; command and control centers at each palace; and every soldier mustering point. Optimistically, no other part of the city was illustrated, as the leadership expected no fighting inside.

Places beyond the city in every direction were fully detailed, showing terrain, important buildings, and the distribution of all forces, friendly and enemy, land and sea. Even though the Bulgars laid siege from land, giving them one direction only, invaders had been known to enlist other forces by means of the purse or common cause, and in any case, the diorama was sure to be used in other wars. Lydas gave them the last fact with a slurp, relishing the idea of future wars entirely too much.

The Slug maneuvered unevenly around the large model, on the gimpy leg that kept him out of the fight. He jabbed his wooden pointer in the middle of Thrace. Without outside help, he explained, the Bulgars were land bound; no major waters ran through the territory they controlled. They had learned early in their series of conflicts with Constantinople that any ships they could build or buy would be a wasted investment up against one of the world's finest navies in a concentrated defense posture. More than once the Bulgars had tried only to discover that Byzantium could make splinters of anything afloat near their capitol.

The essence of General Michael's plan was simple. Wade's team would sail west on the Marmara beyond the city walls. Just before the first light of dawn, Constantinople would light the night with Greek fire and ride out to engage the enemy. When Wade's group saw the fire from their position, they were to wait for forces to be drawn off or otherwise oriented toward the city. They would slip ashore and find Krum, kill him and anyone that stood between them, and then return to the ships before the distraction ended. If the initial plan failed they were to hide in the countryside and live off the land for days or weeks and await their opportunity to strike. There was a chance that Krum would be located for them by spies inside the camp, but they couldn't count on it. They couldn't count on anything. Lydas dismissed them with a wet whistle.

Wade was anxious about joining up with his unit. Up until now his work with a fighting team could best be characterized as tagging along; he never led one. Grimketil had led his group, and later, Arghun-Boke. If either of them fell prior to the debacle at the pyramids, it might have been Tankred who took over, or Snorri. Wade was certain it wouldn't have been him.

Lydas took Wade to meet the team, which included some who had been at the briefing. Counting Wade, there were twenty of them. Too few for an army; too many to get to know well in the short time remaining. In a way he didn't want to get to know them in case the worst happened. He also figured the more he knew, the better.

"It's not enough men," Wade complained to Lydas. "What about the ship?"

"The ship's crew are not included here. They don't go ashore so they shouldn't know the plans. As for the landing party, any more would be sure to attract attention no matter how stealthy they were." The Slug punctuated his statement by drawing in a sharp hiss, as though contemplating the fatal consequences of attracting attention.

"Wade, although you are in charge administratively, I'd like you to listen to Neon Ferro for his military advice."

Neon smiled modestly, and nodded in greeting.

Wade said, "I'll take all the advice I can get."

~ W ~

THE assault team sparred together every chance they got. Wade tried out Grimketil's advice, outfitting himself with a gladius and spatha in the late Roman style even though

Byzantines generally used other combinations. When he got his first sparring "kill" with the moves Grimketil taught him, some of the soldiers reconsidered their choice of weaponry. Still unsure of himself, Wade was a little worried about anyone he could defeat so easily. He kept asking if the man threw the match. He didn't.

Neon Ferro, spare and wiry, served as their training officer for survival and evasion. Because he had so much ground to cover, his sessions began immediately and ran concurrent with all other training.

"You need to be able to evade, carry out your mission, return to friendly control and, at the same time, not be detected by the enemy. You are at a high risk of capture. Whatever happens, turn your situation positive. Always analyze how a setback can be turned to your advantage by taking stock of the merits of your position. I hope you brought your appetite today. For the purposes of this first exercise we are to assume you are starving. I command you to find something to eat right now where you stand."

The group cast around awkwardly. Some turned to saplings, others chased after birds. Wade had been forewarned. In preparation for this day, he actually was starving. He knew nothing about which plants were poisonous and knew he would never catch a bird, so he dug up a worm. Closing his eyes, Wade ate it with the absolute minimum of chewing. It tasted something like a fish covered in dirt. He wondered if Lydas the Slug could do that or would consider it cannibalism. He decided it was too close to call.

The next lesson was how to make a bow and arrow, another thing Wade was never interested in doing.

Throughout the training, only one person gave him trouble. Vitus of Carthage looked like an advertisement for a

Byzantine health club. He balanced his muscular development as though he were in contention for the title of Mr. Universe. When he wasn't showing his physique, his clothes had to be better than everyone else's as well. When they sparred, Vitus would say, "Where is your amazing strength? Where is your breathtaking speed? You must pardon me since I don't see them." Sometimes he invited others to look for those attributes in Wade too.

Wade, answered him only once, "I won't waste my talents on you." And that of course was a fact. Wade didn't want anyone idly studying what he did. He was tempted to drop the swords and see how his tormentor took a punch to the head.

~ W ~

NEON and the other trainers brought Wade a buffet of knowledge: building animal traps and smoking the parts to get your scent off it; making a signal without setting yourself on fire; building a shelter with escape routes; and the most lethal way to use each weapon. He found out an unlucky arrow could deflect off a rib. If he could not hit Krum squarely in the neck, he was not to use an arrow at all. The more Wade's proficiency grew, the more he realized how much more there was to learn than he could ever have learned in a month. The fact that he would never kill anyone in cold blood was a question he constantly had to put aside if he was to learn anything at all. He asked Neon if they really needed Vitus of Carthage. It turned out he was their best marksman and most likely to take the first shot. That was all Wade needed to hear to keep him on. After the mission, he could send him home and never see the man again.

On the eve of his mission, before the light was gone, Lydas the Slug took him to a tower at the city walls to see what the empire was up against. Beyond the safety of the walls, the Bulgars labored to build the largest and most formidable siege engines the world had ever seen. It took five thousand carts to bring them in.

"Because of our moat, the Bulgars cannot dig under us to weaken our walls, nor can they get close enough to use a battering ram on the gates."

"I take it they found some solutions," said Wade.

"There you can see they use a sheltered conveyance to dump rocks in the moat. They will follow up with prodigious amounts of earth. Then they will drive a sheltered battering ram across."

"And you can't stop them because they have that traveling roof over their heads. What are they doing with all those mechanical devices?" Wade pointed at a complicated rig that might have been used to drill for oil.

"That is a kind of catapult called a trebuchet. They will load those trebuchets with stones to break the masonry of our walls."

"Will that work?"

"With enough of them, it eventually will."

Wade could see that not everything went the Bulgar's way. Several bloated bodies floated in the water with no obvious wound even before the fighting began. "What happened to them?"

"The water in the moat contains a gaseous poison that overcomes the swimmer."

"You let them rot in there?'

"Go fish them out if you like." He sucked his teeth at the thought.

"I understand this is actually the second assassination attempt on Khan Krum. If you know anything about that, I want to know exactly what happened in the first."

"After a number of successful attacks, Krum demanded concessions of land, gold, and ten thousand of the finest young maidens of Byzantium. Leo sent a message to the Khan that he was willing to discuss a peace treaty. Krum agreed to meet face to face. Krum was told to wait by the Golden Gate right over there at the coastline. By then our archers lay hidden for an ambush. Leo sailed out under a flag of truce to meet Krum on a barge to show that he concealed nothing. While everyone watched Leo disembark, we sprung the trap. Our archers wounded Krum, but not sufficient to bring him down."

"So that's why I got all those admonitions about the use of arrows."

"The bodyguards formed a human shield to cover his retreat, and sacrificed themselves for Krum's escape."

How do we know that won't happen again?"

"This time, you'll have cloak of darkness added to the element of surprise."

"What if they see us coming anyway?'

"Then you won't have the element of surprise. They will still be distracted by the full frontal assault. Just see that your timing isn't off. You have to be done before the assault is over."

"There's a lot that can go wrong."

Lydas sucked judiciously on his teeth. "All battles are like that."

CHAPTER 38
Enemy Lines

WADE AND HIS assault team moved to Boucoleon, the main palace's private harbor, for maximum secrecy. The area had been cleared of all other traffic. Wade boarded their ship, The Clymere, with some trepidation, prompting Vitus to ask Wade if he had ever been on a battleship before. Wade gave a bare smile, inured to the petty taunting. Vitus only wanted to confirm that he was better than other people, and Wade didn't care whether his underling got that affirmation or not. Wade had been on rowboats, rafts, canoes, ferries, tour ships of every size, and old wooden ships like the one they would use for the mission. The only vessels that gave him pause to think about the fragility of floating on the open water were the ones where the movement of one hysterical person could cause tipping. It wasn't the battleship he was worried about.

The Clymere had been painted and rigged dark to blend with the night and run quiet. If they ran the risk of another ship ramming them unwittingly, it was just one more risk they would have to take. Wade's head was spinning from trying to think through all the eventualities. Learning what he did from Allen Linwood about how you could never get back to your own verse after passing through a break in space-time, made him feel more isolated than ever. Kreindia was the only constant, and the only one he could count on. At the same time he wanted to get back to some semblance of his old life whatever verse it might be. Not the part where he sold insurance, but the part where he wasn't constantly hunting or being hunted. He wanted it all, which was easy to fantasize when he didn't have anything. Grimketil gave him a sense of the father he never had. Allen-Alcuin reminded him of the father he did have. Memories and feelings he was not ready to deal with battered at his consciousness to make themselves known. He had too much else to deal with.

One thought that kept returning to him was the image of Thamar laughing while he tried to get through the glass wall to save Kreindia. He knew that part wasn't real, but it reminded him that she might not be finished with him. Did she have spies or saboteurs on his team, and if so who were they? If anyone, he suspected it might be those he had the most contact with. Vitus of Carthage, in his belligerence, was too obvious, and not very smart. No good spy would give away his animosity like that. On that basis, anyone who associated with him might be ruled out too. Neon Ferro seemed unlikely for all that he taught Wade. Why give away survival secrets when you were trying to kill somebody? The Slug, of course, wasn't coming along at all. There were others he suspected. Wade shook his head. This line of inquiry would only cripple him from doing his task. That would give Thamar exactly what she wanted with scarcely an effort on her part.

~ W ~

THEY cast off on a moonless night, struggling against a heavy chop. A cold wind out of the south seemed to want to return them to their point of origin. Wade refastened his tunic and watched the shore. His rowers strained against the elements, past the manmade walls that shielded the harbor, deep into the watery night until the lighthouse grew small and the majesty of Constantinople unfolded. At once they could see the harbors and grand entrance gates of Contoscalion, Julian, and Boucoleon from whence they came. The Hippodrome and the Forum of Constantine rose behind them, marked by soaring monuments that competed for attention. From a distance it seemed a Dark Ages paradise twinkling from the hills where no one could be seen in irons or torn apart in the arena. Far more than a bulwark against erosion, the sea walls were heavily fortified, notched for archers and densely populated with towers to protect what citizens had. Wade struggled to believe that any part of it belonged to him.

They passed the largest of the harbors Wade had seen from the other side, and several gates that lacked a harbor entirely. After what must have been another mile of solid crenellated walls and towers, the mission burst onto the countryside and the incongruous enemy camp on the city's doorstep.

Wade convinced Neon to hold their vessel back slightly so they could sail alongside the front lines and see the Bulgar's reaction to the attack. Somewhere in the growing powder keg, as they drifted silently and anonymously, Wade remembered to breathe.

Right on schedule, the pyrotechnics began. The initial enemy reaction was disarray, with those in the front falling back, and those in the back coming up. Officers emerged to push those in retreat forward again. When the wooden trebuchets caught fire, large numbers were sent to drag the remaining heavy machines out of range. They attempted to douse the fires that began, and as usual, that only made the Greek Fire worse. Satisfied with the attack and ineffectual reply, Wade ordered

The Clymere onward to where their scouts spotted the officer's tents in the distance.

In three quarters of a mile, they dropped anchor in position for rowboats to make landfall.

As Wade had been told, the Bulgars stayed at least one thousand yards from the beach in fear of the Byzantine navy, which would allow for a safe landing. That was where the reliable information ended. If the phrase "hornet's nest" came to mind, Wade knew that was a bad sign. The rear area was only slightly less turbulent than the people running to the front. In fact, he estimated that only six out of ten vacated the area.

That's when Wade realized they sailed a suicide mission. The Bulgar rear lines contained so much support that they could mop up any covert force even while fighting on their main front. Michael must have known they had little chance of success. Had Wade been a military man, he would have known too. If they knew exactly which tent belonged to Khan Krum, things might have been different.

Neon must have read his expression. "I have instructions to order summary judgment and execution for anyone reluctant to join us," he said softly. Wade nodded as though it either made sense or he wasn't going to argue. "Time to go," said Neon. "This is the only chance we have."

Something flashed on the shore. "Wait," said Wade. "A quarter mile down. What do you see?"

"It looks like a mirror signal," Neon agreed.

From training, Wade knew that you could shine it on your hand to discover where it would go. He said, "We control the sea so it has to be for us. Whoever we have inside has identified Krum's tent."

Neon ordered the crew to weigh anchor and take them

further up the coast. Wade breathed a small sigh of relief. At least they would commit suicide in the right spot.

~ W ~

FORTUNATELY, whoever stood by Krum's tent continued flashing his mirror for the raiding party to home in. The spy must have reflected the light from a fire, thought Wade. By the time they got to shore and moved in five hundred yards toward the source of the signal, they knew the defense arrangement was denser than any they planned for. Neon, with his quick military mind, said to Wade, "Rho Psi Formation?"

Wade had night training in blind scenarios. Rho Psi in their code meant they would pair off and charge in a spearhead formation with the third pair and those behind them peeling away after penetration to secure a perimeter around the operation for as long as they could hold security forces back. It afforded them the cleanest surprise, and the quickest strike, allowing them precious moments to sort through the confusion. It also offered the highest casualty rate. With the number of people around, no other option stood a chance, and his team would be highly vulnerable no matter what. All of these factors raced through Wade's mind in the time it took for his skin to go hot. "Agreed."

"Amyntas and I will take point and clear the way. You and Vitus go next. Vitus will make the first attempt to strike the target. The rest pair up behind, and fall in."

Neon and Amyntas jumped off immediately. Vitus looked at Wade like he couldn't be trusted. Beyond the fact that he was going in, Wade honestly didn't know what he would do.

The camp had so much to worry about that the first two perimeter guards did not hear or see their attackers in time.

Neon's pair, the spearhead, punched a hole in the defense and moved to deepen it. That was the cue for Wade's pair. They surged forward together, Vitus soon gaining more ground, but keeping track of Wade's location with the instincts of a third eye.

With the rest of the team running interference, Vitus and Wade faced light opposition, striking to disable their opponents, and rushing onward to the target. Wade became confused about their direction, but Vitus moved with certainty. Then Wade caught sight of Neon and Amyntas just as Amyntas got cut down in the clearing by Krum's tent. Neon turned to see if there was anything he could do for his partner, and Krum himself stepped into the fray. His almond shaped eyes promised a terrifying revenge for their unexpected incursion. Wade had been warned that the Khan's anger was already on constant boil from the first assassination attempt. Weathered and battle scarred, he looked not much different than Arghun-Boke, only larger and dressed in more wealth. He wielded a pole with blades on both ends. When he swung his waist and dipped the right side of his pole, Neon's head came cleanly off from the blade on the other side. A spray of blood doused Krum's fur before Neon fell and emptied his artery in another direction. In the moment Krum's left arm was raised high, his heart was undefended, and Vitus stood in the perfect position to strike.

Instead of striking at Krum, Vitus turned the weapon on Wade. Fortunately, the dim witted killer stopped to say, "This is a message from Thamar and Ratpald." Someone took Vitus out with an axe to the back of his head. A gore splattered Wade looked up to find Grimketil and Snorri close behind. Snorri had just dispatched an assailant Wade hadn't even noticed. It was Evaristus, one of Vitus' friends. The man who fought back to back with them had to be Tankred. When you traveled with someone long enough you knew them from all sides.

Had the momentum not been lost, they might have killed Krum and stood a chance to negotiate. As it happened, the clearing filled with a large number of troops, some of them bearing ghastly Bulgarian spoils of war. One by one, they made a pile of sixteen heads in the center of the clearing. Together with Neon, Amyntas, Evaristus, and excepting Wade, that accounted for everyone he went in with. All of Wade's strike team had been killed, leaving no one from Constantinople to help them. Surrounded by large numbers, surrender was the only option. Their wrists were tied together, and they were made to stand in a line.

"I am gravely disappointed," Krum said to Grimketil, Snorri, and Tankred. "You three were very expensive slaves."

From the briefings, Wade had expected an effort to capture him alive. More than a body count, the Bulgars needed to gather intelligence. Covert operatives could be expected to know much more than the average soldier, and they would know everything about the assassination attempt.

From the briefing descriptions, Wade recognized Krum's rivals, Chok, Dukum, Ditzeng, and Krum's son, Omurtag who looked to be in shock.

Chok said, "You came to kill our Khan." He held up Grimketil's signal mirror as evidence. "Now we have you and we shall have all the details of your plan from your very lips. The one who speaks first will be spared." Krum nodded his approval.

No one spoke.

"I will enjoy making you talk," said Krum. "I will blind all of you, one eye at a time." Wasting no time, Krum took a spear from Dukum and came to within a short distance of

Wade. Wade recalled his lessons. You don't throw a spear. You jab with it. To hoots of enthusiasm, Krum prepared to jab it in Wade's eye. Wade readied his wrist. It wasn't much of an escape. He would be like a rabbit that could hop only two feet. It might work against dumb dogs, but not a crowd of warriors. What's more it would do nothing to help his friends, but he couldn't just stand there and get blinded. Wade made a decision. If he lived through this, he would get Kreindia and take her home with him to whatever twenty first century verse he could reach.

Khan Krum stiffened and dropped the spear. " I cannot see," he cried. He put his palms to his temples and screamed in agony. Omurtag, the son, came close to him and asked, "What is happening?"

"I feel as though my head is tearing in half." He spit blood onto his son, and toppled to the ground. He twisted to one unnatural pose after another, kicking up dirt, and ending perfectly still.

Wade blinked in sudden comprehension. The irony that Krum would go blind and die instead of his intended victims was not lost on him. This had to be what Allen meant when he said that he knew his history and that according to the calendar they might not have to kill Krum. The Khan must have had a stroke or an aneurism.

Omurtag felt for a heartbeat. Dukum, a rival to Krum, pushed Omurtag roughly aside and also felt for a heartbeat. He stood up.

"I, Dukum, say Krum is no longer Khan. I am now Khan."

Another came forward. "I, Chok, oppose you."

Still another said, "I, Ditzeng, oppose you both!" He

pointed at Omurtag. "Leadership belongs to the House of Dulo. It passes in legitimate succession only."

"He is too young by a year," said Chok. "He cannot possibly lead us in our fight with the Byzantines."

Ditzeng, who hoped to be Omurtag's stand-in, took exception by kicking Chok in his midsection. Krum's Bulgars fought each other in a wild melee for supremacy over his dead body. Each of the factions represented by Omurtag, Dukum, Chok, and Ditzeng, fed into the battle, their prisoners made incidental by the civil war.

Wade and his friends fled to the dark ship moored nearby.

~ W ~

ON the short trip back, Wade saw that each of his friends bore wounds from the battle or weeks that led up to it. Tankred in particular, needed immediate shipboard attention, if he were to survive. For himself, nothing had gone deep below Wade's armor but mental strain. His drive to the capitol, the betrayal from Thamar, the enforced wait during arduous training, the extended separation from Kreindia while she was in danger, and the pile of severed heads combined to a level of stress that took its toll. The moment The Clymere dropped anchor in the safety of Boucoleon Harbor, Wade collapsed.

An impossibly smooth, cold surface identical to what he had seen in the past, stretched its boundaries far into the distance. The icy horizon pushed the darkness, racing out to infinity, behind him, and through him. The healing blue powder danced in the air, scattered, torn, fine enough to be shaped by the sound waves, and reforming to harmonious patterns despite all manner of turbulence. Only after it healed him, it did not reform, not all of it. Some portion remained turbulent, locked out of the harmony of the rest.

She appeared to him in charcoal grey robes with a long stole of deep forest green. Embroidered gold crosses at each end of the stole formed the only ornamentation. A white garment swaddled her neck and forehead, a dark grey cover on top. The first thing he saw was her trembling smile. His heart soared at the sight of Kreindia. That smile of hers was indelibly etched into his memory, represented by powder on ice, blue to match her sparkling eyes. This time something didn't match.

"You're hurt. You have a broken rib." In their joining he knew exactly what ailed her. He did not know why.

"Yes," she admitted. "It will heal."

"How did it happen?"

"Raginpert risked everything by clashing with the missi dominici. He seized me for heresy. He said that if he takes over the kingdom, the missi must answer to him, and his treasury will be restored. When he takes Louis' castle, I'm to be executed as an example, one of many. I need you to reach me in person as soon as possible."

Wade stared in helpless anguish. "I'll have to reach you by ship. My ability to travel long distances instantaneously is gone. I've damaged the spot, my access to the power through my ankle."

Kreindia covered her face. When she lowered her hands, her eyes penetrated the icy horizon. "Find a preparation of mint oil. There is a chance that it will eventually repair the damage."

Wade brightened. "That won't help you right now, but I have an idea I've been wanting to try. Is it possible for you to find a pointed object like a viper's tooth?"

"Will a shark's tooth work?"

"Yes! If I show you the spot on myself, would you be able to find the precise corresponding spot on your ankle and test it even as we dream?"

" *This is not a dream. Yes, I can test it.*"

"*Focus on me. Try to come here.*"

Wade showed her his ankle where a new scab had formed. Kreindia took out the shark's tooth and applied it to her own ankle in the way he demonstrated. Because of the their joining, he knew she had the right spot. As the surface of her skin slowly gave way to her gentle and steady pressure, the blue powder around them turned to fiery sun burnt orange, then the color of a wet sand dune, and finally a clouded watery yellow like the juice of a lemon. She concentrated on Constantinople and Wade specifically as she increased the pressure one last time. The final manifestation held fast against further intrusion, steadily clouding. His mind reached out simultaneously to find... nothing. The watery yellow spread until their linkage and the entire vision dissolved.

Wade awoke, shaking with frustration. He knew he must somehow teach Kreindia how to travel to safety on the astral plane. The ankle did not work for her; it could not, and now he realized why. As Allen had said, No two synesthetes are exactly the same. Where did she get a shark's tooth? he wondered.

~ W ~

WITHIN two days, Allen secured Wade another audience with General Michael. The Bulgar armies were in disarray, and had been driven back in at least a temporary retreat. Somehow it didn't seem to make the general as happy as Wade expected.

"I was very clear, was I not, that you could have every soldier who survived to take back to the west under your command." Psellus spoke in Latin, letting him have it in measured, lecturing tones.

"General, it's true that we were wiped out. The opposition were too numerous. But Krum is dead."

"You did not assassinate Krum, and as a result I have no trophy, nothing to prove me superior to my rivals. Therefore you have done nothing for me, and you get no army."

"What about your niece?" Wade couldn't believe the man could be so callous. "You can't punish her for my failure."

"I taught Kreindia to take care of herself. I pushed that bird out of the nest. Take the ship with my compliments. It will have to do."

Allen took him aside and explained that Michael needed the trophy to justify a take over from Leo. There was always a plot afoot in Byzantium.

"Forget the Byzantines," Grimketil growled. "We'll do this on our own."

"I'm sorry," said Wade. "You can take The Clymere and head west. I have to go back into the city and catch up with you later."

"For what purpose?"

"How well do you know Constantinople?'

"I've been there several times, but you've been here more than a month. Surely you know it better than I."

"I didn't travel freely. Is there a Chinatown? I assume that all big cities have one."

Grimketil wrinkled his brow. "Do you mean a Chinese Quarter?"

"Yes, that would be the same thing."

"I've heard there is a small one, but they keep to themselves. No one knows what goes on there."

"There is one thing that I know goes on there."

"And that would be?"

"Acupuncture."

CHAPTER 39
Acupuncture

IN THE CHINESE Quarter, Wade loomed even larger than the average person in Constantinople. Though they were prone to politeness and averting their eyes, some could not help doing a double take at the white giant in their midst. From what Wade observed, no non-Chinese cared to go among them in their streets of incomprehensible signs unless they were collecting taxes, and they could sense that Wade was not a tax collector. He had learned that if outsiders wanted what this community had to offer, like exotic women or food, residents went out to Zeuxippus to meet the need. If the Chinese wanted something from Mese Street they likewise went out for that purpose. No doubt their insular strategy was the best way to insure their society went unmolested.

Whoever the white giant was looking for, the locals were not prone to cooperate. They only spoke to him when cornered. That is, until they found out he sought medical treatment and came to the flattering realization that he believed in their methods better than western methods, and passionately so. Even the liberals on the royal court had spurned them, seeing acupuncture as a novelty out of fashion. That was how Wade came to be worthy of an introduction to the greatest healer of all, Taoist Lord Du Sian.

One shining admirer went so far as to walk Wade to the house of the healer and make him known in the reception area.

The receptionist bowed and led Wade in without a word. The Chinese style of architecture had a comfortable familiarity, unchanged in its flavor by the last thousand years. Wade passed through rooms with various screens, reminding him of the modest oriental influence he saw in Doctor Andreas' office. In the waiting area, however, Dr. Andreas was far outdone. The sunlight shone on large blocks of elaborately carved wooden dragons as it streamed through sheltered slots in the ceiling. Fountains spilling over irregular rock designs doubled as catch basins for the rain that came in with the light. Well-nourished bamboo shoots stretched toward the sky.

Despite the urgency of his situation, Wade found himself becalmed, almost in the meditative state taught by his martial arts classes. He cursed himself for falling prey to the subtle seduction. He had to get to the west before anything more happened to Kreindia. If she were in Wade's place, she would never leave him to suffer. No matter what happened, Wade was not leaving without some answers.

A little woman walked to the center of the room, and stopped, her eyes at the floor. Wade opened his mouth to speak first, but she quickly said, "May I serve you tea?" She spoke in nearly perfect Greek. The offer reminded Wade that in this culture he had to be patient. Courtesy in service of his goals didn't have to lessen his determination.

"Yes, please. Whatever you have and however you make it is good enough for me."

She bowed low and left.

In a short while, the little woman again walked to the center of the room, and stopped with eyes downcast. She managed not to convey a sense of shame, but of respect. "The Taoist Lord will see you now." Wade took the woman to be the Lord's wife. He followed her into the next room, a simpler place adorned with painted scrolls of landscapes and birds in the Chinese style. After formally introducing him to the master of the house, she retreated to a nearby corner, facing outward, waiting to be of assistance.

Wade bowed deeply to Du Sian. The healer cupped one hand in the other before his chest and gave a slight nod, making Wade wonder if that was what he should have done. He doubted he could duplicate the gesture correctly, and the man seemed pleased enough, so the bow would have to do.

The Taoist Lord Du Sian was an older man, tall for his people, and stocky in his robes. Outside of Thamar's reach, this doctor wore red trimmed in yellow rather than the sky blue of his city counterparts. At Du Sian's gesture, Wade sat on the floor across from him at a low table.

"Glad to meet you," said Wade. "I like what you've done with the place." Wade knew that "Du" would be the family name, and "Sian" the given, but he deferred using either as he wasn't sure how much of the name he was supposed to say.

Du Sian smiled pleasantly. A white Byzantine might have questioned Wade's contention that he had done something with the place. The Taoist simply replied, "Thank you. How can I be of assistance to distinguished guest Wade of Aquitaine?"

From anyone else, Wade would have taken the remark as sarcasm. At the same time the automatic honor didn't warm him. "I need medical treatment and a special lesson in acupuncture."

They paused while the presumptive Mrs. Du silently poured the tea.

The older man said, "While I do not give lessons, I would be pleased to know what is a special lesson."

Wade smiled at the Oriental's sense of humor. He hadn't realized how much of a loss he would be at to explain his circumstances. He tested the tea. Mrs. Du had kindly served it at a temperature ready to drink. The tiny cup made that easier. It also made him drain it at one gulp. "I suppose I made up the term. Let me try another way. Do you believe that there is more to acupuncture than just curing illness?"

"Both the spiritual and physical are subject to illness. Both can be cured."

"Yes, there is that, but I mean to ask whether you believe that some people can go places that others cannot go—a transference of mind and body."

"I have not heard of this." His expression closed down in denial.

"I was told you were the greatest of your profession."

Du Sian hid behind his cup of tea, sipping it slowly. "I cannot help what you were told. My profession does not extend to entertaining fantasy."

Wade looked disappointed. "Maybe local greatness is not the same as greatness."

He managed to irritate Du Sian. To make it worse, he said, "May I?" and reached for the teapot without waiting for an answer.

When his fingers closed around the handle, a twine with hanging threads like a tassel burst into flame six inches in front of Wade's eyes. He called out sharply and dropped the ceramic to smash on the floor. The flaming manifestation vanished, but a scent of burning spice lingered. He stared into the air moments longer and flared his nostrils in reaction. It had been a long time since Wade experienced a synesthetic reaction to an object. The flame combined with the teapot made him think he had been burned.

Du Sian looked horrified. In his native tongue, he said to his wife, "Make an excuse so I can get away from him."

Likewise, his wife answered, "What should I say?"

"Say there is an emergency."

Wade heard the original sounds like the gentle tones of a xylophone, and the related English sounds beneath. He extracted the English and ignored the rest. "Excuse me. There is no emergency. You cannot hide in another language."

Du Sian blinked in alarm. "You speak Hakka?"

"I speak them all, Taoist Lord Du Sian," Wade said in Hakka.

Du Sian cast his eyes down. "I should have known. You are zhí guän lì.'

It was an idiom. "I know the words but not the meaning."

"It means you cross perceptions as one would hop across stones on a stream." He looked aggrieved.

"Where I come from we call people like myself synesthetes. They are very rare. How did you know I was a synesthete, Taoist Lord?"

"I knew from your reaction to the teapot. It belonged to a zhí guän lì. You are only the second I have met in my entire life." He made a slight nod to the broken pot and his wife hastened to clean it up. "Taoist Lord is my honorific title. Du Sian is my personal name. You may use my courtesy name, Du Zongwu."

Wade smiled. "It means Baby Bear."

"My father's idea."

Wade heard the pride in his voice. "Your father was famous."

"Du Fu, the poet. You are intuitive, as can be expected from a zhí guän lì."

"I admit it was a guess, Du Zongwu. Maybe you can meet my expectations too."

"What do you want of me, Wade of Aquitaine?"

"My courtesy name is Wade Linwood. As you said, I can hop across a stream of perceptions. But it's not just perceptions. With acupuncture, I can hop to another place and time as well. That is to say, I used to be able to do that. I injured the spot I use and I need your help to fix it and to find an alternate way for another zhí guän lì to travel."

"I respect you, Wade Linwood, but why should I not fear you? How do I know you have proper moral values?"

While Wade welcomed the breakthrough he did not want to engender fear. "Linneus of Samothrace," he said desperately. "What do you know of him?"

"The oldest man in the cemetery outside of Constantinople. I have seen his headstone. How do you know the name?"

"When I hopped across space and time to travel here, that was the spot I was drawn to." Wade counted on the Chinese veneration of the elderly.

Du Sian nodded his acceptance. "You will find another showing a woman who lived to one hundred fifteen. It is not surprising you were drawn to the man instead."

"How is it possible?"

"There have always been people who lived a long time, Wade Linwood. The rest balance them. My own father died at fifty-nine. I am fifty-eight today. There is no telling what Heavens may demand from me."

Wade chose that opportune moment to change the subject, "I have a gift for you."

He brought out two small carvings of swans. They were Grimketil's idea. A single item or any odd number of items would have been unlucky. An expensive item would have been seen as an offensive bribe. The thought of giving a trivial gift was most meaningful and respectful. Wade also chose that moment to switch back to speaking in Hakka rather than Greek.

"You are most thoughtful," said Du Sian. Wade knew not to expect a gift in return. The host's gift was being the host. Wade did hope for some cooperation.

The healer took a book from his shelf. "This is the Nei Jing, the oldest medical book in China. The Nei Jing is divided into two parts. The first part, Su Wen, Essential Questions, is based on theory, while the second part Ling Shu, Spiritual Pivot, deals with practical application. There is a third part that we do not speak of based on principles of Feng Shui, wind and water, for those special beings who are already highly compatible with nature."

"What would Nei Jing Feng Shui say about me?"

Du Sian took a deep breath. "The text is rarely needed and I do not own a copy. However, I can tell you that qi, the life force, is circulated about one's body on meridians like rivers. The needles in acupuncture are used to clear blockages in the flow of qi. They perform the same function in your case, only the rivers flow differently in you. They double back like an oxbow or cross each other with unexpected consequences."

"Why would they be unexpected? I thought that all of acupuncture is mapped out."

"I regret to say, there have been too few zhí guän lì to come to an understanding."

Wade licked his lips. "That may not be a problem. I already know part of what I need. The place I used on my ankle has stopped working. Are there alternate locations on the body that correspond to the same places?"

"Yes, of course. The ear has a place for every part of the body."

"Please show me."

He located a spot at the top of Wade's ear under the fold and slightly forward of the middle. "This precise spot corresponds to the ankle, left for right."

"It's that simple?"

"I don't know what effect it will have on your friend. It will do nothing for you."

"Why not?"

"It is an alternate treatment for ordinary people. A zhí guän lì is unique."

Wade remembered something Kreindia said in his vision. "Do you have mint oil?"

"Naturally, I have mint oil. It's for the nerves."

"Can you put it on my ankle?" Wade put three gold pieces on the table.

Du Sian's eyebrows went up. "Yes, we accept money." He nodded at his wife, who eagerly collected the gold without comment. Soon Wade had a compress of leaves tied to his foot.

"You must wait three hours to have any effect. However, if you wait less than one week to try it, you may cause permanent damage. I wish you good fortune in your task ahead."

"I may need much more than luck, Du Zongwu."

The Taoist Lord put away his Nei Jing neatly. "You have heard of Confucius, Wade Linwood? He says, 'If I keep a green bough in my heart, the singing bird will come.'"

CHAPTER 40
Pax Nicephori

*"The schism between east and west, left unchecked,
could easily undo the Romaic State."*

—*Circa 813 A.D.*, Scriptor Incertus

WADE DIDN'T HAVE a week to wait. He had a handful of hours to settle his business at the palace and stay out of trouble. Too much time and not enough.

On impulse, Wade tried the docks at Boucoleon. Powerful winds ushered in the new season. He found out that Grimketil and Snorri had already taken their crew and sailed off into the Marmara. Even though he was deprived of their company, the departure pleased him. If Wade's ideas were going to work, his companions certainly needed the head start. Even Tankred, with his injuries, boarded The Clymere on a stretcher.

With a wave of his hand, Allen told Wade, "The oblate said he would rather fight than die standing still."

"A brave man," said Wade. "We came a long way together."

"He was liquored up," Allen complained. "Short, troubled lives breed fatalism."

"Does being a king's advisor breed cynicism?"

Allen gave him an appraising look. "Maybe it does. Tankred left you this flask of ale. Does it mean anything?"

Wade smiled fondly. "Just his calling card."

"I suppose that figures. I also have something for you." He gave Wade a letter to take to the west, and an advance on gold solidis to be reimbursed from the treasury at Sintlas Ow. "It's the king's money either way," Allen commented cheerfully. "Take my advice and leave this time period as soon as you can. Go back to selling insurance."

"It was good seeing you too."

Allen laughed. "Good luck."

In his second order of business, Wade contrived to attach the shark's tooth to a bracelet on his right arm so that he could alternately press the spot on his left wrist, and fight. That was the theory anyway. He went all over the palace looking for a proper cement, and finally found it with a visit to Dr. Andreas. They used it in surgery and dentistry. The doctor suggested he fix the tooth to a long curved animal bone, which could then be snugly sewn into a leather band. The need for Wade's device baffled him, but the smile on his giant head said he liked the challenge.

After he secured the outfit he needed, and filled a pack with provisions, the sundial told Wade that nearly four hours had blown by since he departed the house of the Taoist Lord, putting him past his three hour healing minimum. Time to go to her if he could; he dared not wait any longer. But where was she exactly? Raginpert originally took Kreindia to Konstanz in Swabia, most likely because the town was closest to her original capture, and he didn't want to risk his prize changing hands again too quickly. After wresting her back from the missi dominici, he would likely have headed for someplace where he had more support.

In a palace library Wade found and memorized an old map. In northern Itale, at the time of the Longobard Kingdom so fixed in Raginpert's mind, his safe house could have been any of six major towns from Trento to Genoa. It could also have been one of a half dozen lesser towns, or even in southern Itale, but Wade was guessing he took her as far as Pavia in the northwest, to his own castle. That became Wade's first target destination. What would he do then, he wondered, a house-to-house search? He shook his head at all the things he could worry about. He would have to decide a course of action when he got there.

Wade retired to his private chamber for a place to work in unmolested secrecy. He donned a helmet and the armor parts worn by the Byzantines. Lastly, he removed the leafy mint-oil poultice and examined his ankle. The scab remained on an area of skin that had always been delicate. A ring of angry red stretched all around. Whatever condition it was in would have to do, just as he would have to live with the consequences of poking it again so soon.

I'll risk whatever it takes to save her.

He put the poultice away for another time, and put himself in mind of the last time he spoke to Kreindia, imagining her now in Pavia. He leaned the shark's tooth bracelet into his ankle until he penetrated the scab, ignoring the pain.

~ *W* ~

LATE April snow, and the thin air bitter with cold and darkness. The flakes came heavy and wet in the moonlight, dragging the boughs of forest pine. Wade shivered, startled and distressed. Unlike his graveyard entrance to Constantinople, he saw no markers or clues to his whereabouts, and no lights in any direction.

He began to hike to look for a landmark and generate warmth. Snowflakes lapped his exposed face and hands like a big grateful dog. Wind-tossed trees in every direction made it even darker and his path more treacherous. If he were anywhere near Pavia, everything would be all right. If not, he might have made any number of mistakes he didn't want to think about.

Within minutes of his arrival, the forest grew livelier, with all manner of rustling and chattering from all sides. The animals somehow fell into a pattern of call and answer. He got the odd sensation of being at a dinner table with people rudely holding an extended conversation across him. But for a disturbed bird or stray rodent, everything managed to stay out of sight.

After at least five miles of unchanging wilderness, he saw that walking through the night wouldn't help him. From his survival training, he knew he needed shelter even before food. He looked for places that wouldn't appeal to large animals. If he dispossessed some rabbits for one night he could live with it.

Digging in against the wind, he found evidence of a recent camp, remains of a fire and several well-tailored sleeping areas. Apparently, someone else liked the spot too, someone too fearless to worry about leaving signs of themselves behind. Wade examined some of the lightly buried garbage as best he could in the moonlight, running his fingers over them carefully. Most telling, the items included a broken clasp of an unusual design, and armor links unlike anything he had seen in the east or west. What had he stumbled into?

Wade tucked away the metal fragments to study later. He concentrated on drying himself off. A kind of jet lag set in from the verse shift. His internal clock screamed that the sun should have been high in the sky. He fought against the weariness, willing himself to do everything he could to make a safe camp. The wildlife again became talkative, insistent. When the animal sounds receded, he heard mingled voices that reminded him of his conversations with Michael Psellus. "Who is out there?" he called in Latin.

The night fell silent. In a cloud break, the stars of Cassiopeia told him it was past three in the morning. The howling wind told him he might be imagining things.

As he went about his business, placing branches around to warn him of an approach, the unnatural animal sounds resumed, bringing him alert. He tried shouting again in Greek and in his proto-German Frankish, but those attempts did nothing to interrupt the cacophony. He stared as though his eyes could penetrate the darkness. His training and his senses told him someone was out there, someone that could hurt him but didn't choose to. They didn't care if he knew, because he was powerless against them.

He went ahead and built a fire, cooking the food he brought with him. The sudden cold and the verse lag had sapped his energy. After eating, he made sure the fire was safe in a stone enclosure, and went to sleep, his last thoughts being *What am I doing here and how far do I have to go?*

~ W ~

FIRST light brought him around with no sign of unwanted company. The blizzard had stopped except for drifting snow in the distance. He noticed the weather conditions before he realized the snow blew off rippling blue mountains that rose to meet a hazy sky. The presence of mountains where he had not expected them was a very bad sign.

In breaking camp he suspected it was pointless to try to make it look like he hadn't been there since the whole forest seemed to know. Nonetheless, he didn't want to get into bad habits so he went to scatter the remains of his campfire. On his stone circle, unmistakable in the bright spring light, he found a gold coin. There was no way it could have been there before on one of the stones he brought in. The coin again was different from any that passed through his hands. He told himself it did not mean anything, that his experience with this world was limited. Even so, he squirreled it away outside of his coin sack so he wouldn't spend it before getting some answers.

After a last look around at the desolation, Wade went in search of higher ground. He found a ridge, and at the top of the ridge, a well packed dirt and gravel road. It passed him east to west and wound through the foothills so that he couldn't tell which way it would end up. He chose to follow it downhill, to better weather. After a while, a cart came along, driven by a peasant. Wade put out his thumb in an attempt at hitchhiking. The traveler stopped, astonished to see him. With a wave and a smile, Wade joined the man on the driving bench. His objective, as always, was to get the other person to speak first.

"Did you fall off another cart before you found mine?" the stranger said in a Germanic dialect. He seemed amused.

"No."

"Then how did you get here?"

Wade said, "I really have no idea."

The man held back his mules. "I only stopped to hear your story. If you will not tell me…"

Wade raised a hand in supplication. "I wandered here in confusion. I don't know exactly where I am."

The traveler gazed at him steadily. "This must be an example of God protecting his fools"

"What do you mean?"

"This is the Brenii Pass."

The man seemed smugly satisfied at Wade's alarm. Wade asked, "Are we headed north or south?"

"North, toward Swabia."

Wade's alarm worsened. "That's not what I want."

The man laughed. "Then you'd better show that thumb of yours to a mountain goat because I'm not turning around." He hurried his mules ahead, probably wanting to show off the wandering fool to his friends.

~ W ~

THEY came down into sleepy fields of grazing animals, and wooden dwellings tucked into folds of the hills. The word "chalet" came to mind with their sharply sloping roofs and widely overhanging eaves forming magnificently sheltered porches, the sort of thing he associated with pictures of Switzerland. By mentally superimposing old maps on new, he could see this passage through the Tyrolean Alps was not far from the Swiss border of his time.

His ride took him to the largest of the buildings with a roof that peaked like it wanted to be its own mountain and came down all the way to the ground. The peasant jumped out and ran to a knot of friends. He began by whispering, but couldn't contain himself. Stepping off the cart, Wade heard him say, "He came out of nowhere. I keep looking at him, wondering if he's going to disappear just as easily." He snapped his fingers to illustrate the point. The attention and accuracy of the description was making Wade uncomfortable.

A hefty villager came forward and said to Wade, "I am Abelard. You speak Latin, don't you?" By his appearance, Abelard might have been the innkeeper.

Wade said, "Yes, how did you know?"

The innkeeper rubbed his belly in delight. "Yes, yes, they like you. They let you live."

"Who let me live?"

"The Children of Romulus." Abelard laughed. "That's what I call them anyway. They live in the forest and kill most of the travelers."

"You seem pretty happy about it," said Wade.

"Leave him alone," a woman called out. She pushed through the men, as stout and strong as any. "You don't know anything, Abelard."

"Mind yourself, Dreda."

She ignored him and turned to Wade. "It's all nonsense, and rumors of nonsense. What be your name, honey?"

"Wade."

"Oh, it's a good name, Wade. We have that name here too, but your accent and odd bracelet says you're of elsewhere."

"I'm of Aquitaine."

"Oh, Aquitaine," Abelard cut in, "I mightn't have bothered." He sounded sour. Dreda elbowed him out of the way.

"Come inside," she said, "I'll make you something to eat, and take you away from the crazies." She guided him by his upper arm through her fellows and into the big building. "We don't get to enjoy the company of many strangers around here."

Wade cast a wary look around. "Is that because the Children of Romulus usually kill them?"

"Hmm, as a matter of fact, yes. I just didn't want to give Abelard the satisfaction."

"Who are the Children of Romulus, really?"

"Fierce warriors that hide in the mountains and jealously guard their secrets. They don't like to be seen, and they don't like foreigners to know about them. They're descendants of the Brenii tribe grown hard by the harsh territory they control. No one wants their poor, rocky land, but you can't tell them anything. They used to raid us in the night along with all the other villages north and south of the pass. They harmed none of the locals, and just took a little from each, so we took to leaving food and blankets out for them. Sometimes other things."

Wade nodded in fascination. "If they're the Brenii tribe, then how did they get that other name?"

Dreda's eyes went wide. "I don't know. Don't ask me. Abelard's myths and nonsense."

"I see. I have some gold. I would like to buy a horse."

"We don't have one to spare." She said it fast and crossed her arms resolutely.

Wade caught her gaze. "None to spare, Dreda, or you don't want me to have one?"

Dreda smiled sadly. "You know things that you shouldn't, Wade. If you try to leave town, it's not safe for us. Stay. Our village is as good as any to live in."

"That's a very good point. I like the people here already. Look, I'm wet from the snow. Do you at least have some dry clothes and a room to change in?"

"Of course, dear. Try to keep on that wonderful smell of mint."

"Oh, I will."

Once inside, Wade set about barricading the door with everything he could find. He put on the dry clothes close to his skin and most of his other garments back on top. Between his two activities, it must have taken longer than expected.

"Hey, you've been in there too long," Dreda shouted after him. "What are you up to?" She tried the door, opening it slightly to a hard stop against the jumbled barrier. Wade ignored her. "I'm going to get the men," she warned him.

Wade tried to concentrate. Both Brenii Pass and Pavia were in the crown of Itale, pretty much on opposite sides. After jumping over half the nations of Europe, past the war-addled Bulgars, and the unrest of the middle Frankish Kingdom, that put him a scant hundred and fifty miles away. He could probably go out the window and leave the simple folk behind. Eight days of hard marching would do it, but that might be eight more days than Kreindia had. No, Wade had to take another chance. When he thought of it, his foot ached. Wade removed the poultice again, and pictured himself sweeping across the Alps to the south side, veering west all the way to Pavia and Kreindia's arms.

~ W ~

"NOW then, where were we, little witch?" said Raginpert, shrugging off his robe. "Preparations for war have kept me busy, but I haven't forgotten you. I haven't forgotten what you are, and what you deserve."

Kreindia's bruised face couldn't help but react slightly when she saw Wade crouched down pressing a bracelet to his ankle. Wade had materialized behind the prince and to his left side. Beyond that, he had no time to get his bearings or allow his emotions to overwhelm him. It helped that his opponent was even more surprised. "Where did you come from?" Raginpert said.

Wade wanted to reply "From your own personal hell," yet he remembered how Vitus died talking when he should have been fighting. As Wade came to his feet, he drew out his long-bladed spatha with the most satisfying ring he ever heard. Raginpert came up with a long sword of his own. He also drew the long dagger that never left him.

As he was taught, Wade waited for the strike. He caught Raginpert's sword by sweeping up his own for a high block. They took each other's measure under raised arms. Raginpert said, "I shall kill you and rob the witch of hope."

Wade had no illusions about being able to best a royal with all his leisure time for training. To finish it quickly, Wade thrust his gladius straight at the gut. The prince had prepared for that trick. He struck Wade's weapon aside close to the hilt, almost dislodging it from his hand. Wade took that opportunity to press his viper's tooth bracelet on his right hand against his left wrist, shifting him in space a quarter turn from where Raginpert expected him to be. That prevented Wade's nemesis from slicing him in the chest. Wade swung wildly, whacking the prince on the side of his head with the flat of the blade. The last blow was enough to make him go down.

A slave rushed in and came to Raginpert's aid, kneeling before him. Wade kicked the man in his rump, took Kreindia's hand, and ran.

After a quick scuffle with a surprised guard, Kreindia was armed with a spear. With Raginpert's army out in field training, they had little trouble from his assorted staff on their way out. They followed their noses to the stable, where their luck held. A groom had just saddled a row of horses. Chances were that whoever was on their way rode tired or were not atop horses at all. When Wade and Kreindia took control, they drove off the extra horses, and fled from both castle and city.

Miles away, where they watered their mounts, they desperately came together for a long, crushing hug. Kreindia found his shaking hands, traced her fingertips along his scars, and kissed his fingers. Wade looked into her eyes of powder blue ice from his visions, and kissed her on the lips, melting in and holding her as though he would never let go.

When they separated, her words were, "We haven't much time to rest," but her voice came choked and husky.

Wade let his fingers play along her hair, dark like coffee with none of the sun-washed highlights he recalled from last time he saw her. Would it brighten now that she was out of captivity?

As they stood together every conflict he ever knew diminished. His father abandoning him, the torture meted out by Gerardus and Egidio, the bloody road to Constantinople, and the wild dogs of the arena were all made painless by her presence in front of him. He wanted for nothing outside of her. "We don't have to do any more running and fighting," he said. "Come with me to my world. Let's go right now."

She swallowed hard, and squeezed her eyes against a single tear. "No. The Pax Nicephori. I can't."

CHAPTER 41
The Lost Legion

WADE AND KREINDIA mounted up and moved on. He followed her lead, lost in thought, riding too close to the tips of passing tree branches without noticing their sting. Of all the excuses Wade had heard from women over the years, "Pax Nicephori" was by far the strangest and least satisfying.

Kreindia must have gotten the explanation sorted out in her mind because she began to speak again. "Before the emperor Nicephoros was slain by Khan Krum, he sent emissaries to heal the growing rift between Christianity and Catholicism that fueled the split of east and west. As a result of his negotiations, Imperium Romanum formed a tentative pact with Charlemagne."

"The Peace of Nicephoros," Wade nodded, beginning to understand the first part of it, and wondering where it led. "And the peace may have died with him."

"It began to fall apart without the emperor that began it, yes. I had a vision of a possible future, with west fighting east at the same time as Constantinople faced a Persian attack sweeping through Asia Minor. The combination would be disastrous. I told my uncle, and he told the emperor Leo. They sent me on this mission to finish writing the treaty and make it official."

"So now you have to complete your mission with Louis instead of Charlemagne."

"The Longobards have made it far more difficult than that. Raginpert's army of Longobards cannot win an all out war even with a lesser Carolingian such as Louis. Raginpert told me he planted rumors in Louis' court of Byzantines having designs on western territory. Raginpert intends to attack Louis under a Byzantine flag, do enough damage to destroy the Pax Nicephori, and go to ground. If successful, he would let the two weakened kingdoms fight it out, and then step in to see how many pieces he could pick up."

"And there might not be much left of the Byzantine capitol if attacked from both sides. Raginpert hopes to rule west and east. I see the problem."

"Even if we could go 'home' to your world, the peace here has to be preserved. After we finish the mission, you and I can try to leave together."

"So you understand how timelines work."

My visions tell me both our worlds are bound up with each other. That tells me that even your home will not be safe if the Pax Nicephori isn't safe."

Wade pressed his lips in a line. He didn't want to get into a discussion of the multiverse. Even without grasping the physics, he sensed that Kreindia was right. "Grimketil, Snorri, and Tankred, if he makes it, are on their way."

"They won't be enough to dent Raginpert's latest plan. He gathers a force eight thousand strong." Her eyes looked haunted, her bruises dark.

Wade wanted desperately to help her, but not with a plan formed of desperation and false hope. The warmth of the low country made him sweat in his layers. Did he have something legitimate to tell her or not? Thinking of Brenii Pass, he worried at his lower lip with his teeth. "I may know a place to look for help."

Kreindia brightened in admiration and hope. Committed to telling the full story so he wouldn't sound foolish, Wade had them stop and tie up the horses. Explaining that he had found some clues in his travels, he reached into one of his pockets and brought out the broken bits of metal he had saved. In the daylight, he could see the clasp showed a loosely rendered eagle, dark like a crow, poised to fly with two imperial standards beside it. Another bit was an armor link shaped like a round leaf.

He let Kreindia examine those first, in the order he found them. Then he presented her with the final prize. "They also left me this on a rock as some kind of message." Wade handed Kreindia an undated gold coin, roughly struck without trimming, like a royal seal. The obverse showed a man identified by name, with braided hair covered in jewels, and hefting a spear over his shoulder. The reverse showed a hybrid man-eagle standing upright with wings and talons leaning on a sword that would have been over five feet long.

Kreindia drew close, making his heart beat faster from the smell of her skin and brush of her stole. "Who did these things come from?" she asked.

"From a people the villagers called 'The Children of Romulus.'"

"Where do these villagers live?"

"At the northern foot of the Brenii Pass. They picked me up in the middle of the pass, where the mountains were highest."

She delighted in the news. "Did the night speak to you in Latin?"

He smiled. "It did, or someone did."

"And did you answer back in Latin?"

"Yes. I think that's how I earned the coin."

Her face shined with awe. "The Roman Empire began and ended with an emperor named Romulus. The last one was Romulus Augustulus, just a boy of fourteen. This coin was minted in his era."

"Do you know what it all means?"

"It means that something impossible has come to pass. Is Grimketil docking in Venezia?"

"Yes."

"Then we must risk going into the next town."

"That would be Monza. Why are we going there?"

"We need to send word for Grimketil to meet us in the Brenii Pass."

~ W ~

In the city they traded their horses for fresh ones, and afterwards pushed hard to resume their pace. From the people in Monza, Wade discovered the troublesome truth that he had lost several days in his last jump. He speculated that either a flaw in his method, or the failings of his flesh might have caused it. With Kreindia safe at his side, little could bother him. The good news was that his friends might be able to make it into the fight. He never thought he would be anxious to lead Grimketil and company to danger. Although Wade's reservations remained, the logic differed in the current instance. At this juncture, the battle for civilization was all they lived for. Was it due to their short, savage lives, as Allen had claimed, or because they found a cause to die for rarely encountered by the average person in the modern world, one that would give their lives meaning?

Wade and Kreindia had to be careful, not only of the cities, but also the fields across the country where Raginpert's men were being gathered. Staying a step ahead of the news of their escape saved what would have been several close calls. Traveling mostly at night, they crossed the countryside in several days, arriving at Itale's side of the Alps and the foot of the Brenii Pass. They took in the rocky vista with solemn resolve and began to climb.

Their first sight of snow at their level came washing across the slopes just as their ears popped. At altitude, winter still reigned in the Tyrolean Alps. Wade's throat felt sore. He let out a well-justified sneeze. In short order he had experienced the first warmth of spring in Constantinople, the cold of the Alps, the warmth of Pavia, and a return to the high, cold pass. The horses offered some resistance in the unfamiliar territory, but they were hearty and accustomed to changing riders. Wade wished he knew as little as they did.

When they could climb no higher, they left the trail for the low-lying woods. They dismounted in the narrow confines and led their reluctant horses forward. After several minutes' hike, birdsong came to them subtly altered in patterns that Wade and Kreindia recognized, a kind of Latin syntax.

They looked at each other, and Wade yelled in Latin, "I'm back. You have seen me before. I spent the night in these woods." When they did not reply, he said, "Come out and face us."

More silence followed by a flurry of coded discussion.

"I have the coin you gave me," Wade shouted. "Are you the children of Romulus? If so, the empire needs your help."

Out of the stillness, they heard a sharp whistle. From the snowy slopes arose a man for every tree. Over their armor, they wore cloaks of tie-dyed green, brown, and white. Camouflage.

Three tall men came forward, Roman helmets atop their heads. They had been hiding much closer than Wade would have dreamed possible. The man in the center removed his helmet and said, "I am commander Lucius Sergius Honoratus. This is centurion primus pilus, Flavius Helvetius Pansa, and this is centurion princeps, Gneaus Horatius Armiger." Each came to attention and nodded proudly in his turn.

Wade stood agape, bewildered by the sea of appellations. "Kreindia whispered, "You only have to remember the last name of each."

"I'm not sure I remember any of them," Wade whispered in exasperation. "Did he just give us the names of his entire army?" Out loud, Wade introduced himself and Kreindia, feeling somewhat like he might disappoint his new friends by the lesser names he gave back. Honoratus acknowledged them without prejudice, and bid them to follow.

Wade and Kreindia followed them to a clearing and sat down on carefully arranged logs. They had agreed that Kreindia would ask the questions. She said, "Commander Honoratus, are you all who you appear to be, and if so, how do you come to your present state?"

Honoratus drew himself up. Six others gathered around as though they could not hear their favorite story often enough. He said, "In 476, on the beaches of Cape Misenum from whence Pliny the Elder once suffered to witness the eruption of Mount Vesuvius, a handful of legion deserters from the rule of the barbarian usurper Skyrian Odoacer gathered before the deposed Romulus Augustulus, the last legitimate Roman imperator. There we swore a secret oath to the ages on behalf of ourselves and all who came after, to restore the old empire when the signs were right. Since then we have preserved the traditions and honor of the legions for some three hundred forty years and twelve generations. You are the first non-barbarians to come seeking our help."

Some of the men had come forward to examine Wade's arms. He handed them his gladius and spatha. They compared them to their own with satisfaction and handed the weapons back.

Honoratus asked Pansa to continue. In a higher voice, he said, "We began with the few remaining loyalists, fifty five in total, mixing with the Brenii tribe. We stand now with five thousand five hundred men. We kept in touch with the outside world. We knew that the eastern part of the empire flourished. Some of us awaited the day they spread west once again. Others among us believed that the barbaricum would weaken, play itself out, as did Rome before it. They did continue civilization after a primitive fashion, yet they endured. The Carolingians were the strongest of all, Charlemagne in particular, uniting warlords under him, civilizing, restoring order, and stopping the waves of new threats from all sides. At one time there were as many as thirty Roman legions; we are but one. We have been debating whether Charlemagne's death was the time to expend our forces, for if we break out and fight without success that will be the last of us."

Armiger faced Wade. "How do we know your cause qualifies?"

Wade drew out his letter and handed it to the commander.

Honoratus saw the royal seal and unfolded the document with reverence. He read it aloud to the assemblage, "Order to Render Assistance to Bearer, Wade of Aquitaine. I do Hereby Request and Order Full Cooperation on Behalf of the Emperor of the Holy Roman Empire to Meet the Longobard Threat at This, the Most Grave Time Since the Fall. He Who Meets This Need Will Be Forever Remembered as The Savior of Civilization. Most Gratefully Yours, signed Alcuin of York."

"Raginpert's army numbers eight thousand," Kreindia added.

"And what does he want?"

"He wants what his ancestors once took for themselves and Charlemagne took back—Itale as far as the Papal States. He'll turn the empires of the east and west upside down to do it, and he will take them too if he can." He did not have to explain to the secreted legion how geography favored them; they had chosen it. The Brenii Pass was the invaders' only known option for a reasonable passage to their goal.

The legionnaires all stood. Their commander nodded for Armiger to speak. He raised his shoulders in a deep breath. "The centuries have lent us great patience. We tally the signs in order to know when to reveal ourselves. Fourteen years ago, Charlemagne declared the territories the Holy Roman Empire. This year, as they buried Charlemagne, we came up to full legion strength. Now you bring that letter, and news that a momentous occasion is at hand. If you agree to fight beside us, we will reveal ourselves and go into battle."

"I am at your service," said Wade. "My heart is entirely in this fight."

"I too commit to fight," said Kreindia. "I cannot be kept away from it."

"Then we shall put you in irons to prevent it," said the commander. "No woman fights in my army."

"No, wait!" Wade turned to the commander. "Don't your forces include positions other than fighting troops?"

"Yes. Some soldiers are exempt due to their positions as surveyors, medical orderlies, huntsmen, horse trainers, water engineers, swordcutlers..."

"I get the idea. What about scribes?"

The commander nodded in understanding. "If we are going into battle, we will need more than the one we have, to observe the different points of reference."

"Kreindia is a scribe by profession."

Honoratus called someone forward. A man with the slighter build of a scholar handed her a roll of parchment and a quill. She took them with appreciative reverence. "You do me a great honor which I choose to accept proudly. Very softly, she said, "Still, I will fight if it comes to it."

"Ready the ambush," called centurion Pansa.

At that moment, Grimketil arrived, large in presence and out of breath. Snorri supported Tankred who straggled behind with an armed Roman escort. Grimketil said, "You will have no time to make an ambush. Raginpert's men are less than a tenth of a day behind us."

A scout quickly confirmed to Honoratus that the front of the enemy line had been spotted at a short distance. He squinted at the newcomers as though he were angry at being upstaged.

Wade grasped Grimketil's firm hand, hugged the brave and too-pale oblate, and backed away from Snorri, who had raised his chin high against any potential signs of affection. Wade made quick introductions.

Centurion Armiger said to Grimketil, "You are wrong to think that our options are so limited. We have drilled for this eventuality and prepared this ground for three hundred years." Addressing Wade and his friends as a group, he said, "We have our attacks coordinated. Do not join the fight until we give you the signal."

Wade sneezed three times in a row, and pinched his stuffy nose. Kreindia clutched Wade's arm. He looked at her, worried. Her gaze was elsewhere.

"Wade," she said, "I just saw...something. We need to get out of here when the battle is almost won. Someone else can finish the treaty. Promise me we'll go."

Wade looked deep into her powder blue eyes, wishing they had more time to discuss what she saw, wishing he could see it for himself. He never expected her to worry like this. For her to give over the completion of the treaty to some anonymous third party, their plight had to be serious. All he said was, "I promise."

~ W ~

THE legionnaires enjoyed a perfect view into the valley from their high ground on two sides of an enemy strung thin. They waited until the first of Raginpert's army reached the mid-point of the mountain range. The first wave fell on the long line, sowing perfect surprise and confusion. Behind them, soldiers wielded shovels, finding their predetermined trench lines, and shifting the dirt to form a wall. Another row of builders added pre-positioned stones as the walls accumulated at remarkable speed. Archers stood ready behind the new defensive lines. The trench diggers left gaps so that survivors of the first wave, of which there were many, could fall back to fight from superior positions. Each group of legionnaires remained hidden until they joined the action.

While a few Longobards were petrified, many were enraged at the ambush. They surged forward, probably thinking that they outnumbered the attackers by tens or hundreds to one, and could win if they could only reach their oppressors. Raginpert rode forward, trying to shape the tide. His horse tripped on the many dead bodies in its path, sending him down to a location that Wade marked well.

Honoratus rose out of hiding, and dropped his hand, shouting, "Now."

Wade thought of the bruises on Kreindia's face, and said darkly, "He's mine."

Wade intended to make his declaration clear to Grimketil and Snorri in particular. However, his fellows had slipped forward to position themselves closer to the fighting. At the signal, all three of them got out ahead, running down slope to the fray. From his higher position, Wade could see them as they engaged.

Tankred appeared to make a wise choice of launching two throwing axes. His aim was true. Two targets went down before a single slash of a blade cleaved his chest. His assailant stepped in and hacked at his head a few times to make sure of the kill. Like so many confrontations Wade had witnessed, everything was won or lost in seconds. Despite all that he had seen and done, despite his training under Neon Ferro, despite the stakes he faced and the importance of holding himself together, Wade felt a sting in his eye.

Grimketil skewered Tankred's killer through the neck, picked up Tankred like a bundle of cordwood, and fought his way to the earthen walls one-handed.

In the last Wade saw of any of them, Snorri found himself in a desperate battle with several attackers, including Raginpert. The prince stuck a sword deep in Snorri's shoulder. Then Wade was in the thick of it himself, fighting his way toward Raginpert. When he had passed enough people to come to an open break, Wade saw Snorri's head, its jaw slack, nothing underneath. Raginpert held the head by its hair as a war trophy, the custom of his ancestors. Wade did not expect the jolt of horror that ran through him at that sight.

Raginpert was responsible for everything that had happened, including Tankred's death. Now the prince smiled savagely as though he were happy to see Wade, and said, "At last I will get the satisfaction of killing you." Wade smiled even wider. The man was talking when he should have been fighting.

Wade had no more than the basics of swordsmanship, and his keen reflexes. Raginpert would have known every move Wade had been trained in. On that basis, Wade would surely lose. Wade relied instead on his karate training, and used his fists as though he were not holding swords. In the second it took Raginpert to rid himself of Snorri's head, Wade struck. In the combination he had practiced for years, he hit Raginpert in the face, then the stomach, and then the crotch. Each time, Raginpert reflexively moved to block Wade's sword, which was not the threat. When the prince doubled over, Wade remembered his gladius and spatha, and used both to run the man through.

Seeing their leader fall, the Longobards fought a rear action to cover their retreat. At the last, some fought with rocks.

Wade had done more than his share. He made his way back to Kreindia's side. Before he got there he saw Kreindia take up her parchment and quill, and begin to write. As arduous as it was to fight a retreating action, he smiled.

When Wade still had twenty yards to go, he saw Kreindia struck down by a small rock. The projectile connected with a sickening pop, and bounced off while she took an uncontrolled fall. In abject panic, he ran stumbling to close the distance to her side. Cradling her gently, Wade touched two fingers to her neck. Her pulse came strong and fast.

He glanced back at the fight to see where the rock had come from. The unmistakable hatchet faced Ratpald smirked in satisfaction until he caught Wade's eye, and then ran away. Wade was in no position to follow.

The rock had drawn the copious blood flow of a head wound. He took out Tankred's flask and a cloth to clean the area. Then he bandaged her up. He used another cloth and some water from his canteen to dab her face. She did not wake up. Wade knew that he and Kreindia didn't need to remain at the battle until the final blow. The idea of going home with Kreindia filled his mind. Yet the inaccuracy of his last two jumps scared him. Leaving Kreindia in that condition, hard to defend, and without medical attention, scared him even more. Having defeated Raginpert, and the fighting all but over, he knew her will was to come with him. He could delay no longer.

If his father were right, there was a remnant of Wade left in the twenty first century. With all of him that mattered in the ninth century, how much did that fraction help him? In truth, Wade was unfamiliar with how to cross vast swaths of time. Under his own conscious volition he had managed jumps in space, and inadvertent, tiny shifts in time by focusing on physical locations, spatial coordinates that he could picture on a map. More important than shifting their locations to the United States, he had to move them forward by twelve centuries. How did one visualize the passage of time? When he went from the twenty first century to the ninth, it must have been Kreindia that chose for him, allowing him to zero in on her like a distress beacon buried in the ages.

Worse yet, he had to travel for two, with one of them unable to add their conscious cooperation in a simultaneous feat. True, Kreindia was a synesthete as well, but no two synesthetes were alike.

Wade pictured the world he hailed from, the things it had and his place in it. He visualized being safe in his apartment with Kreindia at his side. His apartment did not exist at all in the ninth century so it was both a location with imaginable coordinates, and a point in time. He counted on space and time being tied together.

With his right hand, he pressed the shark's tooth to her ear at the same time as he employed his viper's fang by bringing his right ankle to his bracelet. In that graceless symphony of motion he had to hit two precise points simultaneously, one of them untested. He had to do it in the middle of a war zone. The physical absurdity would have made him laugh if there were not so much depending on so many tenuous connections. In addition to the physical challenge, success required an absolute belief in the information from Taoist Lord Du Sian Zongwu, the master healer and baby bear, combined with his own leap of intuition about how to use it.

He reminded himself that acupuncture, at least, did not require the patient's belief in the process in order to work. He had no expectations when he went for his carpal tunnel treatment. His movement through the tunnel of space-time likewise required no belief and indeed no knowledge of the process at all. What he possessed was neither belief nor disbelief, a mind opened by a lifetime of being a synesthete where the bizarre happened every day. More than that, he had a mind of crossed wires.

He looked at Kreindia's beautiful face in repose, and said aloud, "Let me be able to do this one last time and do it right." And for the first time he added, "Please God." An honest entreaty and a harmless one. In the complexity of the multiverse and especially in light of all that happened, like

Einstein he believed there had to be a God at the end to make it all comprehensible.

Now he put all his mind on his task and where he had to go.

He made contact.

The purple of royalty came first. Wade didn't see the color; he experienced it in a way that blanked out all other vision and became a feeling. At the same time, Wade focused on his apartment as he remembered it. His imagery was solid, his memory infallible.

The melee continued unmistakably around them, the sounds threatening to disrupt Wade's delicate concentration. Go further.

Honey, fresh in a bee's nest. His ability to picture Kreindia there at his side was also infallible, assuming his method had any validity. Linking her in his mental shift—drawing her along—was the least proven part of his plan, and the part he needed most. A flicker of forest green and charcoal, thin like a sample on a laboratory slide, or did he imagine it? At the last minute of his physical and mental challenge, he didn't care where they ended up, as long as they were together.

Someone fell down next to them and groaned in agony. It sounded like centurion Armiger. Wade fought an urge to respond, and instead pressed deeper.

Blissful rust. He kissed the Frankish Empire and Byzantium goodbye.

One last push to freedom.

~ W ~

"In the Year of Our Lord 814, on the 29th day of the month Pharmouthi, as they called it, the lost legion of Rome took up arms

against the traitor Raginpert The Insolent, Prince of the Longobards. Each force was spent against the other in the mountains that swallowed their secrets."

—*Scriptor Kreindia of Amorium*

CHAPTER 42
Zhí Guän Lì

WADE CROUCHED ON the rug in his apartment in the twenty first century, dressed like a fool. He held Kreindia's shark's tooth and retained his viper tooth bracelet as well.

Not seeing her, he spun around, and groped through the air as though she might be invisible. But she wasn't there, gone from him as though she never existed.

Wade tore through the apartment, finding few places to look, tore outside careless of his armor, and screamed her name raw. He came back in, put his head in his hands, and listened to the emptiness.

He failed her. That was all it came down to. There were so many things that could have gone wrong. He hadn't allowed himself to think about them all before. He had run the risk of the spot on his ankle not working properly since he had not waited a week for it to heal. He ran the additional risk that a corresponding spot could transport her in space-time. In Kreindia's case, Du Sian had said, "I don't know what it will do for your friend. The ear is an alternate treatment for average people. A zhí guän lì is unique."

If it were the right spot for her, did he increase the pressure on his location and hers simultaneously? Was the level of penetration in an ear the same as in an ankle? He had to go on the assumption it was, but he could have been wrong. And he was wrong—about something.

Kreindia didn't have the benefit of a concrete target to visualize; wasn't even conscious. Another reason she never arrived. Mostly, he should have paid attention to the consequences of his debilitated state, his loss of precision landing him in the Brenii Pass when he meant to land in Itale.

Wade straightened up. All was not lost yet. He had to go back for her. Instinctively, he checked his weapons first: one sword lost on the battlefield of the past, one retained. Good enough.

Wade still had the viper's tooth. With the greatest of care, he located the familiar spot and touched the point to it. No colors came, and he got no synesthetic reaction of any kind. He went deeper, finding blankness, more blankness, and then went too deep. He tried it a little over and angled back to get underneath the scab. The method worked no better. He jabbed his ankle hard, and watched the blood flow while saying the word "Needuhl," over and over again as though an incantation would make the difference. Motor oil came in flooding drafts. The pain came in blinding waves so that he had to wait and clear his eyes to see what world he was in.

He had none but the Present.

Finally, he had to admit his nerves in that precious, irreplaceable spot were destroyed. With horror he realized he had forgotten to pack the mint oil poultice the last time he removed it. He didn't know what else the formula contained. He would never travel to Byzantium again. He tried his wrist, and failed, unable to move even two feet. He took off his clothes, stood naked, and jabbed himself all over with the tooth in frustration and a blind germ of stubborn hope he was no longer entitled to. Sluggishly, his mind registered various injuries he sustained in battle. He did nothing to tend to them.

Wade reviewed everything that he did reaching all the way back to the first time his wrist ached. He'd had plenty of time to think about it on the road. He went further and examined his entire life, searching for connections that might be useful. Only Allen Linwood linked his two lives together. Maybe his father didn't abandon him. Maybe he went instead to where Wade would need him the most. If something like that happened with Kreindia...

He went to his computer and looked up the current date: September 9, 2009. Checking further, he found it was Wednesday, and it was five o'clock. An odd coincidence, since that was exactly four weeks since the first appointment he took for acupuncture. He had to get over to the clinic. It was tempting to feel that this was right, but the idea was so irrational that the hope that stirred in him couldn't rise beyond a flicker. A steely resolve to find out moved him towards the door, slowly at first, and then with growing urgency. He dressed to a minimum, sockless, and took off towards the doctor's office.

The transition from running to gridlock made the drive seem endless and futile. With his growing desperation came a numbness, a withdrawal. The life he knew before at the Wheelwright Insurance Group was worthless to him. Wade felt himself on the way to a third place: Not Byzantium, not the Present, but a fugue state, dissociating him from his actions. The only thing that kept him from slipping away was the slim reed of hope that his only remaining theory might be the right one.

Wade entered the third floor office grimy and rank. The receptionist, inhabiting a place familiar to the old Wade, looked up and didn't like what she saw, or smelled by the way her nose wrinkled. Wade's matted hair whipped around as he looked for a friendlier face and did not find one. He hadn't a haircut or a much-needed scrubbing in what? Six weeks? Back in what he thought of as The City, Constantinople, part of that other world, now fading and nonsensical, where casual violence and horror mixed easily with the highest hope of civilization. A world exemplified by Grimketil, that sturdy father figure who, at the stroke of a serpent's tooth, lay twelve hundred years dead. Although little subjective time had passed for Wade, the permanence of his travels gave him ready reason to grieve. He simply wasn't ready to grieve for Kreindia as well.

He asked the receptionist, "The girl, Keindel, is she still in a wheelchair?" Stunned, she reached for a telephone, probably wanting to consult with Dr. Nesky. She looked as though she might retch.

"Answer me," Wade shouted.

"Of course," she said. Wade knew he looked like an idiot, or worse, and he didn't care anymore.

"Is she still here?" he said in a gentler voice.

"Kreindel just went down in the elevator with her family. You missed her," she said with satisfaction.

Wade tore down every flight of stairs, outside and across the parking lot to the van where he spotted Kreindel and her family. He felt like an unstoppable shell with a compulsion, a lemming set to perform his one last act of throwing himself off a cliff. They were not pleased to see a maniac coming towards them, trailing blood. The father hastened to leave.

Wade stopped her father from rolling her onto the lift gate, unconcerned with how his actions seemed to others, completely having lost his mind.

Oddly, though, the numbness was gone, his cold was gone, and he felt a rush of sensory input. He smelled everything carried on the breeze, hot tar, cut grass, and the smell of her skin. He sank to his knees in front of her. He could feel rough pebbles of concrete biting through his pants.

"It's me, sweetheart, it's me. Is it you?" Tears began to flow from his eyes. Whatever happened—a nervous breakdown or institutionalization for him—he would make his stand at this poor girl's feet. If he was wrong, then he had lost everything, and these strangers could witness his final breakdown. Nothing mattered.

"What the hell are you doing to my daughter?" With his heightened senses, the father's words were harsh in Wade's ear. Nothing made him look away from her eyes. The father could have been whacking him in the head with a two by four, and he would not relent.

Wade pleaded, "Sweetheart, can you move?" The trouble was she didn't look at all like Kreindia. Nevertheless, he said, "Please speak to me, please move for me." He said it in a choked voice so complex and loaded with emotion it couldn't help but wrench a reaction out of any thinking being. But would her reaction be visible through her paralysis?

Her face transformed as it did the first time he saw her, that sense of temporarily breaking free from a narcotic, the burgeoning recognition, charging the air between them with sparse synesthetic flakes of blue powder. She moved the fingers of her right hand toward the joystick as the girl Kreindel had always done, then her last strength seemed to fail her, absorbed by the unaccustomed excitement.

Her father exhorted, "She can't move, or even speak, you idiot. She's a total cripple quad nothing. What do you want from her?"

A lick of heat that felt in turns like anger, shame, and despair invaded Wade's chest. He wanted to help whoever this was. He wanted to move her limbs for her as though doing so could snap the bonds of her cage. Instead, he took her ravaged left hand in his own, and kissed her palm, his eyelashes brushing her fingers, the tenderness she never had.

"I'm calling the police," said the lame girl's father, but Wade's eyes were locked into hers. The receptionist had already called the police, and he could hear the sirens.

After her brief rest, Kreindel tried moving her right hand again towards the controls, and then hesitated and changed course. Now, for the first time, she raised her trembling hand and her arm with it. It came one inch off the armrest, then two, then six. Her father dropped his jaw in astonishment. She fully extended her arm, and touched all five fingertips to Wade's cheek. Now she was able to cry too. As the sirens grew louder, she tilted her head and looked deep into his eyes. A teardrop leapt from the tip of her nose.

"Oh, Wade, we made it," she said.

Made in the USA